DANGEROUSLY CLOSE

Robin raised Maxie's chin and kissed her. As soon as their lips touched, his emotional control disintegrated. But what he felt now went beyond passion to a raw need for her blessed warmth and the bewitching mysteries of her body.

Robin blew lightly in her ear, then traced the delicate whorls with his tongue. She hummed with pleasure, stretching her neck like a cat. He tasted the sensual arc of her throat.

"Time to stop, I think," Maxie whispered breathlessly.

"Not yet." Robin sought and found her mouth. He lifted Maxie's skirt and petticoat with both hands and rested his palms on her stocking-clad knees while he deepened the kiss.

Maxie responded with open-mouthed generosity, but she was too clever to be distracted. When he caressed her inner thighs, she turned her head away and instinctively tried to close her legs. She couldn't, and the pressure of her knees against his hips inflamed him still further.

"Robin, we should go back inside now. This is not the right time or place."

Maxie was not afraid—not yet. To frighten her would be unforgivable, but Robin was incapable of moving away. . . .

Angel Rogue

by
Mary Jo Putney

A TOPAZ BOOK

TOPAZ
Published by the Penguin Group
Penguin Books USA Inc., 375 Hudson Street,
New York, New York 10014, U.S.A.
Penguin Books Ltd, 27 Wrights Lane,
London W8 5TZ, England
Penguin Books Australia Ltd, Ringwood,
Victoria, Australia
Penguin Books Canada Ltd, 10 Alcorn Avenue,
Toronto, Ontario, Canada M4V 3B2
Penguin Books (N.Z.) Ltd, 182-190 Wairau Road,
Auckland 10, New Zealand

Penguin Books Ltd, Registered Offices:
Harmondsworth, Middlesex, England

First published by Topaz, an imprint of Dutton Signet,
a division of Penguin Books USA Inc. Previously published in a different form as
The Rogue and the Runaway.

First Printing, April, 1995
10 9 8 7 6 5

To the furry friend who's always there.

*With special thanks to Theresa Jemison,
for letting me use her Mohawk name, Kanawiosta.*

Dear Readers,

For those of you who have been wondering about the fate of Lord Robert Andreville, the handsome, dangerously enigmatic spy in *Petals in the Storm,* the wait is over.

Quick-witted, silver-tongued, and with a core of pure steel, Robin has always been one of my favorite heroes. He needed a very special heroine, and I found her in Maxima Collins, who is as much a maverick as Robin. With laughter and passion, the two of them find each other and a future in the course of a wild chase the length of Great Britain.

I first wrote their story as a long Signet Regency, *The Rogue and the Runaway.* The book was always more historical than Regency, so it was a pleasure to come back and expand it into a full-fledged, simmeringly sensual historical romance.

Though Robin is technically not a member of the Fallen Angels, his life connected with all the men who were, so I considered his story a suburb of the series. The last official Fallen Angel book, *Shattered Rainbows,* will bring Lord Michael Kenyon to a happy ending in December 1995.

I hope you're enjoying my dangerous men as much as I am.

Mary Jo Putney

Prologue

The great estate of Wolverhampton graced the Vale of York like a royal crown, its placid majesty dating from the late days of the seventeenth century. The mansion had been built by the first Marquess of Wolverton, whose grand taste in architecture had been matched by his eye for heiresses; in his long life he had married and buried three of them.

In the century and a half since its completion, Wolverhampton had been visited by the great and notorious of every generation, and had provided a splendorous setting for a succession of worthy lords and ladies. The Andrevilles were the first family of northern England, its members known for unimpeachable honor, conscientious management, and sober behavior.

At least, most of them were.

It would have been more sensible to hire a post chaise, but Robin preferred to ride through the English countryside after so many years away. The weather was dry and relatively warm for early December, though there was a hint of snow in the air, the hushed stillness that heralds a coming storm.

The ancient Wolverhampton gatekeeper recognized him and rushed to open the gates, almost falling over himself with eagerness. Robin gave a brief smile of greeting, but did not linger to say more.

The mansion itself was half a mile farther, at the head of the elm-lined drive. He reined to a halt and scanned the vast granite facade. Wolverhampton was not a homelike place, but nonetheless it had been his home, and it was here his weary spirit had demanded to return when his duties in Paris were done.

A footman spied him and bustled out. Robin dismounted and wordlessly handed over his horse before climbing the steps to the massive, ten-foot-high double doors. He should have notified his brother that he was coming, but he had chosen not to. This way, there was no chance to be told he was unwelcome.

The footman who crossed the marble-paved foyer was young and didn't recognize the newcomer until he looked at Robin's calling card. Eyes widened, he blurted out, "Lord Robert Andreville?"

"In person," Robin said mildly. "The black sheep returns. Is Lord Wolverton receiving?"

"I shall inquire," the footman said, his face properly blank again. "Would you care to wait in the drawing room, my lord?"

"I can find my way there on my own," Robin remarked when the servant started to show the way. "I was born here, after all. I promise I shan't steal the silver."

Coloring, the footman bowed, then disappeared into the depths of the house.

Robin strolled into the drawing room. He was overdoing the nonchalance; anyone who knew him well would realize that he was nervous. But then, he and his elder brother did not know each other well, not anymore.

He wondered how Giles would receive him. Despite their vastly different temperaments, they had been friends once. It was Giles who had taught him to ride and shoot, and who had tried—with little success—to keep peace between formidable father and contrary young brother. Even after Robin left England, he and Giles had maintained a tenuous contact.

But it had been fifteen years since they had lived under the same roof, three years since the last brief meeting in London. The occasion had been bittersweet, the pleasure of reunion undermined by a tension that had ended in a short, furious quarrel just before it was time for Robin to leave.

Giles seldom lost his temper, and had never done so with his brother, which had made the incident all the more upsetting. Though they had managed to patch matters up and part amiably, the painful regret was with Robin still.

He studied the drawing room. It was brighter and more appealing than before: Versailles softened by a touch of English coziness. Probably that was Giles's doing; he had never had much patience with pomp. Or perhaps the redecoration had been done by the woman who had briefly been Giles's wife. Robin had never met her, did not even recall her name.

He considered taking a seat, but it was impossible to relax when he could almost hear the echoes of old rows with his father rebounding from the silk-clad walls. Instead he paced the drawing room, flexing his aching left hand. It had not healed well after the incident several months earlier when an unpleasant gentleman had carefully broken the bones one by one. A pity that Robin was left-handed.

Portraits of stern, upright Andrevilles adorned one wall, their reproachful gazes following their unworthy descendant. They would have respected the goals for which he had worked, but they certainly would not have approved of his methods.

The place of honor above the carved mantel belonged to a portrait of the Andreville brothers, painted two years before Robin had left Wolverhampton for good. He paused to study the painting. A stranger would not know the two youths were brothers without reading the engraved plate. Even their eyes were different shades of blue. Giles was tall and broadly built, with thick brown hair. At twenty-one he had already worn the grave air of someone who carried great responsibilities.

In contrast, Robin was no more than average height, slightly built and brightly blond. The portrait painter had done a good job of catching the mischievous twinkle in his azure eyes.

Superficially, he knew that he had changed very little, though he was now thirty-two instead of sixteen. Ironic that he retained that boyish look when he felt so much older than his years, from having seen and done things better forgotten.

He moved to the window and looked across the rolling, green velvet grounds, immaculate even in late autumn. The first light flakes of snow were starting to fall.

What was he doing here? A scapegrace younger son didn't belong at Wolverhampton. But Lord Robert Andreville didn't belong anywhere else, either.

Behind Robin a door swung open. He turned to find the Marquess of Wolverton poised in the doorway, slate-blue eyes scanning the room as if doubting the footman's announcement.

Robin suppressed a shiver at the sight of his brother, for Giles's stern, handsome face was far too reminiscent of their late and unlamented father. The resemblance had always been there, and years of authority had strengthened it.

Their eyes met and held for a long moment, wary azure to controlled slate. Using his lightest tone, Robin said, "The prodigal returns."

A slow smile spread over the marquess's face and he moved forward, his hand extended. "The wars have been over for months, Robin. What the devil took you so long?"

Robin clasped his brother's hand in both of his, almost dizzy with relief. "The fighting might have ended at Waterloo, but my special brand of deviousness was useful during the treaty negotiations."

"I'm sure," Giles said dryly. "But what will you do now that peace has broken out?"

Robin shrugged. "Damned if I know. That's why I've turned up on your doorstep, like a bad penny."

"It's your doorstep, too. I've been hoping you would come for a visit."

After too many years of deceit, Robin felt a powerful need to be direct. "I wasn't sure I'd be welcome," he said baldly.

Giles's brows rose. "Whyever not?"

"Have you forgotten that the last time we met, we had a rousing argument?"

His brother's gaze shifted. "I haven't forgotten— I've regretted it ever since. I shouldn't have spoken as I did, but I was concerned. You looked as if you were at the breaking point. I was afraid that if you returned to the Continent, you'd make a lethal mistake."

Perceptive of Giles; that had been a difficult time. Robin looked down at his damaged left hand and thought of Maggie. "You were very nearly right."

"I'm glad I wasn't." Giles put his hand on his brother's shoulder for a moment. "You've had a long journey. Would you like to rest and refresh yourself before dinner?"

Robin nodded. Trying to keep his voice casual, he said, "It's good to be back."

They talked through dinner and into the night while silent snowdrifts rose outside. As the level in the brandy decanter declined steadily, the marquess studied his brother. The signs of strain that had concerned him three years earlier had intensified to the point where he suspected that Robin was on the edge of mental and physical collapse.

Giles wished there was something he could do or say, but realized that he did not even know what questions to ask. He settled for saying at the next conversational lull, "I know this is premature, but do you have any plans for the future?"

"Trying to get rid of me already?" Robin said with a faint smile that didn't reach his eyes.

"Not at all, but I think you'll find Yorkshire rather flat after all your adventures."

The younger man tilted his gilt head back into a corner of the wing chair. In the flickering light he seemed fragile, not quite of the mundane world. "I found ad-

ventures to be deucedly tiring. Not to mention dangerous and uncomfortable."

"Are you sorry for what you have done?"

"No, it was needful." Robin's fingers drummed an
irregular tattoo on the arm of his chair. "But I don't
want to spend the second half of my life the same way
I spent the first half."

"You are in a position to do anything you wish—
scholar, sportsman, politician, man-about-town. That's
more freedom than most people ever have."

"Yes." His brother sighed and his eyes closed. "The
problem is not freedom, but desire."

After an uneasy silence, Giles said, "Since you were
occupied on the Continent and communications were
chancy, I didn't notify you at the time, but Father left
you Ruxton."

"What!" Robin's eyes snapped open. "I assumed I
would be lucky to get a shilling for candles. Ruxton is
the best of the family estates after Wolverhampton.
Why on earth would he leave it to me?"

"He admired you because he could never force you
to do anything you didn't want to do."

"That was admiration?" Robin asked, his voice
edged. "He had a damnably strange way of showing it.
We couldn't spend ten minutes in the same room without quarreling, and it wasn't always my fault."

"Nonetheless, it was you who Father boasted about
to his cronies." Giles gave an ironic half smile. "He
used to say that the blood had run thin in me, and that
it was a pity his heir was such a very dull dog."

Robin frowned. "I'll never understand how you
could be so patient with the old curmudgeon."

Giles shrugged. "I was patient because the only
other choice would have been to leave Wolverhampton, and that I would never do, no matter what the
provocation."

Robin swore softly and rose from his chair, crossing
to the fireplace to prod the embers unnecessarily. After
coming down from Oxford, Giles had taken over the
hard work of administering the immense Andreville

holdings. He had always been the reliable one, quietly doing the difficult tasks with little reward or recognition. "Typical of Father to be insulting when you were making his life so much easier."

"It wasn't an insult," Giles said calmly. "I *am* a dull person. I find crops more intriguing than gaming, the country more satisfying than London, books more amusing than gossip. Father must have found some satisfaction in knowing his heir was reliable, but that didn't mean he particularly liked me."

Robin searched Giles's face, wondering if his brother was genuinely detached about such painful insights. Yet he couldn't ask; their friendship had very clearly defined limits. He settled for saying, "People are interesting because of what they are, not what they do. You have never been dull."

Expression unconvinced, Giles changed the subject. "I imagine you'll want to visit Ruxton. I've been looking after the place, and it's doing well."

"Thank you." Robin watched a log break apart and send sparks dancing up the chimney. "Between Ruxton and the inheritance I received from Uncle Rawson, I'll have more money than I know what to do with."

"Get married. Wives are excellent at disposing of excess income." For the first time, there was bitterness in Giles's voice. After a brief pause, he continued more smoothly, "Besides, Wolverton needs an heir."

"Oh, no," Robin said with a flicker of amusement. "Producing an heir is your duty, not mine."

"I tried marriage once, and failed. Now it's your turn. Perhaps you'll be more successful."

The flat comment made Robin wonder what the late marchioness had been like, but his brother's expression did not invite questions. "Sorry, but I've only ever met one woman I thought I could live with, and she had more sense than to accept me."

"You refer to the new Duchess of Candover?"

Robin gave his brother a hard stare. "Apparently I

am not the only one in the family with a talent for spying."

"Hardly spying. Candover is an old friend of mine, and when he returned to England, he knew I would be interested in news of your welfare. It wasn't hard to deduce that there was more to the tale than what he told me." Giles's voice warmed. "I met the new duchess. An extraordinary woman."

"She is indeed," Robin agreed in an unforthcoming tone. Then he sighed and ran his hand through his fair hair. Though they had never been as close as Robin would have liked, he knew he could trust Giles's discretion completely. "If you've met Maggie, surely you understand why the idea of marrying a bland English virgin is so unappealing."

"I take your point. There can't be another like her." His brother smiled slightly. "If neither of us is willing to do our duty by the family, there's always cousin Gerald. He has already sired a whole string of little Andrevilles."

Remembering Gerald, Robin assumed that any children would be dull, but worthy.

If Maggie had children, they would not be dull. He felt the familiar ache, and forced himself to cut it off before it could worsen. The past was a damned unhealthy place to live.

His thoughts were interrupted when Giles asked, "Do you intend to stay at Wolverhampton long?"

"Well," Robin said cautiously, fearing that speaking the words aloud might invite a rebuff, "I had thought through Christmas. Perhaps longer. If you don't mind."

"You can spend the rest of your life here if you choose," Giles said quietly.

Lord Robert Andreville, rebellious younger son, master spy, black sheep, and survivor, shut his eyes for a moment, not wanting to show how affected he was by his brother's welcome. Then he returned to his wing chair and settled in again, the peace of Wolverhampton beginning to dissolve tensions so old that he had thought they were part of him.

Giles was right to say that Robin was unlikely to spend the rest of his days rusticating in Yorkshire. God only knew what he *would* want to do.

But for now, it was good to be home.

Chapter 1

The moors of Durham were very different from the forests and farms of America, but they had their own kind of beauty. Since her father had died two months before, Maxima Collins had walked the hills every day, absorbing the wind and sun and rain with mindless gratitude. She would miss these barren moors more than anything else she had found on this side of the Atlantic.

After two hours of wandering, Maxie settled cross-legged on a hillside, absently nibbling a tender stem of wild grass. The bright spring sunshine seemed to dissipate the haze of grief that had numbed her since her father's death. Quite clearly, she saw that it was time to return to America.

Her uncle, Lord Collingwood, was kind in a distant way, but the rest of the family regarded their guest with feelings that were dubious at best. Maxie could understand their position; she was an oddity that never should have set foot in an English country house. She suspected that the fashionable world would be even less welcoming. No matter; she had no desire to enter that world. In her own country, there was more room to be different.

The major deterrent to returning home was that she had less than five pounds to her name. However, Lord Collingwood would surely lend her the fare to America, plus a little extra to support her until she was established.

His lordship would probably balk at first, worrying whether he was doing his duty by his late brother's only child. Proper English girls would not want to go off on their own; the correct behavior was to live on someone else's charity.

However, Maxie was neither proper nor English, as had been made clear in a hundred subtle and not-so-subtle ways in the four months since she and her father had arrived in Durham. She did not choose to become one of her uncle's dependents.

Even if his lordship was reluctant to see her leave, he couldn't prevent her from doing so. Maxie had just turned twenty-five, and she had been taking care of herself and her father for years. If necessary, she would find work and earn her own passage home.

Her decision crystallized, she rose to her feet with an unladylike athleticism, brushing crushed grass from the skirt of her black dress. The mourning gown was a concession to the sensibilities of her English kinfolk. She herself would have preferred no outward display of her loss. Well, it would not be for much longer.

Half an hour of brisk walking brought her back to the magnificent pile known as Chanleigh Court. Unluckily, as she cut through the gardens, she came upon her two female cousins languidly engaged at the archery butts. Portia, the elder, fired and managed to miss the target entirely from a distance of no more than a dozen paces.

Maxie was about to retreat when Portia glanced up and saw her. "Maxima, how fortunate that you have come by," she said with a note of malice. "Perhaps you can show us how to improve our skills. Or is archery one of the fashionable amusements of which you have been deprived?"

Portia was eighteen, pretty, and petulant. Even at the beginning she had not been friendly to her cousin, but after Maximus Collins's death caused Portia's London debut to be postponed, her attitude had become positively hostile, as if Maxie was personally responsible for the disappointment.

Maxie hesitated, then reluctantly joined her cousins.

"I've done some archery. As with most things, it is practice that refines one's skill."

"Then perhaps you should practice your hairdressing," Portia said with a significant glance.

Maxie had gotten very good at ignoring gibes. "You're right," she said mildly, "my appearance is quite disgraceful. I had hoped to slip into the house unobserved." Even at the best of times her hair was too long, straight, and black for fashion, and at the moment she was windblown and disheveled from her walk.

Portia and Rosalind, by contrast, were as bandbox neat as when they received callers in their mother's parlor. They also towered over the smaller American. Almost everyone did.

Sixteen-year-old Rosalind, who was friendlier than her sister, looked uncomfortable at Portia's rudeness. "Would you like to use my bow, Maxima?" she offered in a timid attempt to warm up the atmosphere.

Maxie accepted the bow and expertly drew it several times to get the feel. Though she had not handled one for some time, her muscles remembered the old skills.

Portia murmured, "I should have remembered that archery was a skill for savages long before it became fashionable."

For some reason, that remark penetrated Maxie's calm as nothing else had. She swung her head toward her cousin with such a flash in her brown eyes that Portia involuntarily stepped backward. Voice dangerously soft, Maxie said, "You're quite right, it is a skill for savages. Move back out of the way."

As her cousins hastily retreated, Maxie scooped up a handful of arrows and stepped back until she was four times as far from the target. She shoved all but one of the arrows point-first into the earth near her right hand, then nocked the remaining shaft.

Drawing the bow, she focused not only on the act of aiming, but also on sensing what it was to be an arrow seeking a target. That had been the first and most important archery lesson that she had ever learned.

Then she released the shaft. An instant later, it buried itself in the exact center of the circle.

While the arrow still quivered in the target, she sent the next shaft on its way. In less than a minute, five arrows were clustered in the bull's-eye so closely that several touched.

Nocking the final arrow, she turned in the direction of her cousins, who watched in paralyzed horror as Maxie let fly. The arrow neatly clipped the lime tree under which the sisters stood. Portia yelped as a severed branchlet fell into her hair, rendering it far less neat than it had been.

Stalking back to her cousins, Maxie returned the bow to Rosalind. To Portia she said, "Since I am a savage, as you are so fond of pointing out, I have a talent for mayhem and violence. You would do well to remember that."

Then Maxie turned on her heel and continued her interrupted path to the house, head high and expression set. It had been foolish to lose her temper with Portia, but there had undeniably been satisfaction in it.

Inside the house, she paused at the end of the hall that passed her uncle's study, wondering if she should visit him now or make herself presentable first. The decision was taken out of her hands when a footman entered the far end of the passage, escorting a burly fellow with a battered face to the door of the master's study. Since neither of the men had seen her, she slipped away to her own bedchamber.

Having an indecently comfortable room all to herself was the single best aspect of life at Chanleigh. Maxie would also miss the luxurious hot baths and the library, which contained over a thousand volumes, most of them sadly unread.

But she would miss little else, particularly not her cousin Portia.

An hour later Maxie sat on her window seat, her dress brushed and her hair arranged in a demure knot at her nape. Less demurely, her knees were pulled up and her arms looped around them as she gazed out.

Her attention was caught by a figure emerging from the side door. It was the crude fellow who had come to see Uncle Cletus earlier. She wondered what business had brought him to Chanleigh. He seemed an unlikely associate for her uncle.

Dismissing the thought, she checked herself in the mirror. She was much neater than when she had returned from her walk, though her appearance was still hopelessly un-English.

Her expression, however, had returned to its normal determination after two months of drifting. Hoping that her uncle would grant her request for a loan, she squared her shoulders and headed downstairs.

As she raised her hand to knock on her uncle's study door, she heard her Aunt Althea speaking within. She halted and thought a moment before deciding that pleading her case in front of Lady Collingwood would be an advantage. While her ladyship had always been civil to her husband's niece, there had never been a trace of real warmth or welcome. Surely she would endorse Maxie's request as a way to be rid of an unwelcome guest.

Maxie's hand was poised to knock on the paneled door when Lady Collingwood's sharp voice said, "Was that horrid man worth what you paid him?"

"He was. Simmons may lack refinement, but he handled the unpleasantness about Max very well." After several unintelligible words, her uncle finished, ". . . certainly can't let it become public knowledge how my brother died."

Maxie froze. Her father had experienced chest spasms in the past, so it had not been a surprise to learn that he had died suddenly in London. His body had been sent back to Durham and he had been buried in the family plot with all due respect. There had been no reason to believe his death was unnatural—until now.

Pulse pounding, she glanced around to ensure that

she was unobserved, then pressed her ear to the oak door.

"Trust your brother to cause as much trouble in death as in life. A pity he didn't stay in America," her aunt complained. "The matter of the inheritance is proving to be a great nuisance, and what if Maxima finds out how her father really died?"

"The legacy question is nearly resolved, and she won't learn the truth about her father. I've made sure of that."

"You'd better be right, because if she does find out, the fat will be in the fire," her ladyship said waspishly. "The little heathen isn't stupid."

Voice edged, her husband said, "Would you be so rude about the girl if our daughters were as pretty as she is?"

After a shocked pause, his wife sputtered, "The idea! As if I would want my daughters to look like Maxima. They are well-bred young English ladies, not dusky little savages."

"Well-bred they may be, but no one will notice them if their cousin is in the same room."

"Of course men notice her, just as stallions notice a mare in heat. No real lady wants to draw that kind of attention," Lady Collingwood said viciously. "I'll never understand how your brother could bring himself to marry a Red Indian. That is, if he did marry the creature. The audacity of him, bringing his half-breed daughter here!"

"Enough, Althea," her husband snapped. "Max might have been a wastrel, but he was a Collins, and Maxima is his daughter. I have seen no deficiencies in either her manners or her understanding. Indeed, she has been far more of a lady to you than you and Portia have been to her."

"Not an hour since, she threatened Portia with a bow and arrow! I live in terror that she will run mad and murder us in our beds. If you won't get rid of her, I will."

"Just be patient. We can present her in London next

spring when she comes out of mourning for her father.
Rosalind will be old enough to bring out then, so
we can fire off all three girls together. With her looks,
Maxima will have no trouble finding a suitable husband."

Maxie's recoil at the thought of a London season
was profound, but it paled next to her aunt's reaction.
Lady Collingwood gasped. "You can't possibly expect
me to present her with our daughters! The idea is unthinkable."

"I can and do expect it. There's nothing unthinkable
about presenting cousins together."

"We can't keep her here for a full year," his wife
said in a voice that could have scratched glass.
"Marcus will return from his Grand Tour soon, and
you know how susceptible he is. Are you prepared to
risk your son becoming infatuated with his cousin?
Would you welcome the little savage as a daughter-in-
law?"

After a long silence, her husband said in a shaken
voice, "It is not the match I would wish for him."

Lady Collingwood made a reply, her voice blurred
as if she were moving away from the door.

It didn't matter, for Maxie had heard more than
enough. Feeling nauseated, she retraced the route to
her room, forcing herself to walk slowly. After locking
her door, she collapsed on her bed and curled into a
tight, shuddering ball while she tried to make sense of
what she had overheard.

First and foremost was the clear implication that her
father's death was not of natural causes. Could he have
been killed in an accident, or at the hands of footpads?
But in that case, there would be no reason for her uncle
to conceal the fact. Could Max have died in a whore's
bed? Not only was that unlikely, but such an occur-
rence was not scandalous enough to require such extraordinary efforts to suppress.

Try as she would, the best interpretation Maxie
could find was that someone had murdered her father.

But why would anyone want to kill charming, feckless Max?

Money and passion were the usual reasons for murder. Since Maximus Collins had scarcely had a penny to bless himself with, no one would have murdered him for gain.

Yet lethal jealousy seemed even less probable. Her father had never been a womanizer, and he had been away from England so long that ancient feuds were unlikely to be still smoldering.

Lady Collingwood had mentioned an inheritance. Maximus had been disinherited by his own father, but perhaps he was heir to some distant relative, and he had been killed to prevent his claiming the legacy. If so, was she herself in danger since she was her father's heir? Maxie shook her head in disbelief. Such things belonged only in melodramatic novels, not real life.

Could Max have made money from some mad scheme, then been murdered for it? The night before leaving for London, he had said cheerfully that their financial problems would soon be at an end. His darling daughter could be a lady and have the life and grand husband she deserved. It was not the first time he had made such statements, so Maxie had only laughed and said that she was quite content as she was.

It was hard to imagine any legitimate way that Max could have made a large amount of money. Unfortunately, it was not inconceivable that he had tried an illegitimate method. She had loved her father dearly, but she was aware of his weaknesses. Perhaps he had scandalous information about some long-ago schoolmate and had threatened to reveal it. If so, his intended victim might have decided that it was easier to eliminate a blackmailer than to pay. It wouldn't have been a great risk, for no one would miss an impecunious reprobate.

Except, of course, his daughter.

If her father had tried blackmail, could it have been aimed at his brother? Family secrets would be the easiest to come by.

Maxie's fists clenched so tightly that the nails gouged her palms. She must consider the possibility that Lord Collingwood might have had his own brother killed. Perhaps the villainous-looking man from London was a hired assassin.

Was her uncle capable of such a monstrous crime? She wished that she could dismiss the idea out of hand, but she couldn't. Though her uncle had seemed fond of Max, filial affection might have vanished in the face of attempted blackmail. One thing that Maxie had learned in the last months was that the English had a passion for appearances. Threatening to reveal a particularly ripe scandal could easily have gotten Max killed. Her uncle would have undertaken extreme measures with regret, but she did not doubt that he would do what he thought necessary.

It was all horribly far-fetched, but then, so was murder. She closed her eyes, wondering if she were going mad. She had always had a vivid imagination—lurid, according to her father—and that imagination was running riot. Perhaps there was a simple, noncriminal explanation of what she had overheard.

If so, she could not guess what it was.

The logical thing would be to ask her uncle what he had meant in that damning conversation, but that did not seem like a prudent course. He was unlikely to reveal what he had gone to such trouble to conceal. Worse, if he were guilty of a crime, he might be a threat to her. She didn't think he would want to harm her, but if he had ordered his own brother's death, he was unlikely to have compunctions about doing the same to his niece.

She bit her lip, her mind churning with grief and confusion. Only two things seemed sure: Her father had not died naturally, and she herself was persona non grata in her ancestral home. She had known that Lady Collingwood did not like her, but even so she was appalled by the depth of hostility revealed in that overheard conversation. *Heathen . . . dusky little savage . . . half-breed.*

She must leave Chanleigh this very night, after the household had retired. But she would not return tamely to Boston—not until she had gone to London and discovered the truth about her father's death.

She sat up, the need to plan steadying her chaotic emotions. She had the address of the inn where Max had been staying, as well as the names of several old friends he had intended to visit. That was enough to begin an investigation.

The only question was how to reach London. While she had a few pounds, it was not enough for a coach ticket, so she would have to walk. The distance was easily two hundred and fifty miles, but that was no great challenge to someone who had spent half her life traveling the back roads of New England.

This time, however, Maxie wouldn't have her father's protection, and traveling alone would be foolish—for a female. She had never deliberately masqueraded as a male, but the rough roads of America had made it advisable to dress as one much of the time. Luckily, she had brought her masculine attire to England. With her breasts bound, her hair under a hat, and a loose shirt, vest, and coat, she would look like a nondescript young boy. And if someone wanted to investigate too closely, she had her knife.

Packing was easy, for she had accumulated very little in a quarter century of living. Besides her male clothing, she would need one female outfit for London and a cloak that could double as a blanket. Her precious packet of American herbs would be useful protection on such a journey. Her mother's silver cross was already around her neck, and her father's watch, her own simple gold earrings, and her harmonica would be safe in an inside coat pocket. Cooking and eating utensils could be purchased from a tinker.

Everything fit easily into her small, battered knapsack. Then it was only a matter of waiting until after the household had gone to bed. Unable to face her aunt and uncle at dinner, she sent down a message that she had a headache and requested a meal in her room.

The hardest task proved to be writing a note. Having been a guest in the Collingwood home for months, it would be very shabby to disappear without a word. Odd how manners remained even when she was deeply suspicious of her host and hostess. More important, she did not want them to realize that she had overheard that cryptic, disquieting conversation.

Maxie gnawed on the quill pen for some time before inspiration struck. All she had to do was say that she had decided to go to London to visit her other aunt.

Desdemona Ross was the much younger sister of Cletus and Maximus, and a widowed bluestocking of ferocious and unbridled opinions. Since she was cordially loathed by Lady Collingwood, she seldom visited the family seat. Maxie had never met Lady Ross, but they had corresponded. In fact, a letter had arrived only the day before, so she would say that Desdemona had invited her niece to London.

Maxie bent to the writing paper with satisfaction. It was rude and eccentric to leave at night with no warning, but no one would pursue her, which was all that mattered. She doubted that anyone would bother to wonder where she had gotten coach fare.

In fact, she really would visit her aunt, whose letters had always been amiable and witty. It would be pleasant to discover some member of her father's family for whom she felt kinship.

Leaving Chanleigh Court was easy. Maxie was delighted to don her boy's clothes again after too many months in skirts. Among her mother's people, women wore leggings, and she was as comfortable in them as in the white man's gowns. Her farewell note was left in her room. With luck, it would not be found until well into the next day.

She stopped by the kitchen for cheese, bread, tea, and a slab of ham, which would spare her limited funds at least until Yorkshire. After some hesitation, she also took an old map of the road to London from her uncle's study.

She let herself out a side door. It seemed a good omen that the skies had cleared after an evening of intermittent rain. The night air was damp and rather chilly, but she drew it into her lungs eagerly, already feeling happier and freer.

Her practiced stride took her swiftly down the drive, but she stopped for a last glance at the great house. Maximus had been glad to return to his family home, and wherever his spirit was now, he must be pleased that his bones rested here.

But while Chanleigh had been her father's home, it was not hers, and it was unlikely that she would ever return. She had been a mere discordant ripple on the surface of a deep pool of Englishness, and like a ripple she would soon be forgotten.

She covered five or six miles before the moon set. Seeing a small building silhouetted against the starlight, she picked her way across a soggy field to a storage shed. Remnants of the previous year's hay crop were stored inside, and it made a fragrant nest. She settled down with her pack for a pillow and her cloak as a blanket.

It was not the first night she had spent in a barn, and it would not be the last. It was, however, the first time Maxie had been entirely alone. In the past her father had always lain an arm's length away.

The thought produced an ache deep inside her, a pain that was both grief for her father and sorrow for her own isolation. On the verge of a sob, she curled her fingers around her mother's silver cross. She was a Mohawk, an American, and a Collins, and she would not feel sorry for herself.

But as she drifted into sleep, her last conscious thought was to wonder bleakly if her father's death meant that she would spend the rest of her life alone.

Chapter 2

The brothers shared breakfast in a silence broken only by the occasional flutter of a newspaper page. However, the news was uninspiring as well as several days old, so the Marquess of Wolverton began studying his brother over the top of his *Times*.

When they were boys, the five-year difference in their ages had been significant and Giles had been very much the elder brother. He had hoped that over the winter, they would finally have a chance to become friends as adults and equals.

That hadn't happened. Robin had revealed some of himself his first evening at Wolverhampton, but after that night, he had withdrawn. He had been the perfect guest, always ready to talk, be silent, or participate in the neighborhood social rounds when required. Yet his thoughts and feelings were concealed behind the formidable barrier of his humor and charm.

It wouldn't have mattered, except that Giles knew that something was gravely wrong. The zest for life that had been Robin's most vivid characteristic had vanished. Too often Giles had found his brother sitting silently, staring at nothing. The marquess wondered if the blame should be laid on the woman who was now the Duchess of Candover, or if the reasons were deeper and less easily defined.

Whatever the cause, he felt that something in his brother had been broken, perhaps past mending. He grieved for that, for his own sake as well as for Robin's, but he had no idea what he might do to help. With a sigh, he laid his *Times* aside. "Do you have any plans for the day?"

Robin hesitated. "Perhaps I'll take a stroll through the west woods. I haven't visited that part of the estate yet."

Knowing he sounded overhearty, Giles said, "I can't believe what a tame life you're living. I keep expecting you to vanish."

His brother smiled. "If that happens, don't worry. It would just mean that I found something amusing like a band of Gypsies and couldn't resist going off with them."

Giles would be delighted if Robin did find something interesting enough to lure him to unpredictability. Rising, he said, "I have a magistrate's session that will occupy me all day. I'll see you at dinner, unless you find some Gypsies."

After Giles left, Robin made his way to the kitchen to request food for his expedition. The cook gave him four times as much as he could possibly eat; she was determined to fatten him up. A pity his appetite wasn't better.

Then he headed across the hills to the west woods. Too dense for easy riding, the area was best explored on foot, and walking suited his mood.

He had hoped that the peace and familiarity of Wolverhampton would heal whatever ailed him. Up to a point, it had. He was physically stronger, and he had fewer nightmares. There was nowhere he would rather be—and that in itself hinted at what was wrong. In the past, Robin's usual problem had been deciding what fascinating activity should be tried next.

Now he was submerged in a gray melancholy unlike anything he had ever experienced, a weariness of the soul rather than the body. Apart from a brief duty visit to Ruxton, he had spent the last six months sleeping, riding, tramping the countryside, and catching up on his reading and correspondence.

His most energetic activity had been avoiding the lures of wellborn local maidens. The two eligible

Andrevilles had been much in demand at winter social gatherings. While Giles had the title and the superior fortune, it was generally assumed that he was unlikely to remarry, so more feminine wiles had been exercised on Lord Robert. Besides his blond good looks, mysterious past, and more than adequate assets, the chance that he would inherit the title had added to his appeal.

He sighed and hitched his bag of provisions over his right shoulder. He would not have objected to falling madly in love, but it was impossible to imagine marrying one of the vapid innocents he had met in the great houses of Yorkshire. He had not known Maggie when she was a proper young lady, but even at seventeen she would not have been so bland.

The day was warm, and it was pleasant to reach the shady forest. Robin had worn old clothing, so he was unconcerned about the snagging undergrowth as he explored the winding paths made by deer and other wildlife.

The sun was high when he reached a little clearing by the stream that wandered through the heart of the forest. He smiled at the sight of the fairy ring of mushrooms. The gardener had said that a ring this large must be centuries old. As a child, Robin had thought of the spot as magical. He would lie under the tree, dream of the world beyond Wolverhampton, and hope that a fairy might call. Perhaps he would find magic here again.

He set down his bag and stretched out on the grass in the shade between a tree and a bush. Arms crossed beneath his head, he gazed idly at the branches above.

It was a mistake to let his mind become empty, for soon a dark thread of despair began winding through. Grimly he fought it off. It was possible to chase the demons away in the daylight, though he knew from experience that they would return as nightmares. Each spell was worse than the one before, and sometimes he feared that it was only a matter of time before he fell over the edge of sanity.

But he wasn't there yet. He forced himself to think

about his future. Despite Giles's generosity, Robin could hardly spend the rest of his life at Wolverhampton.

He could travel. Though he knew Europe like a mother knows her child's face, he'd never seen the Orient or the New World.

But he was weary of traveling.

Giles had suggested Parliament; one of the Andreville-controlled seats would be vacant soon, and it would give Robin a forum for his opinions on public affairs. Another possibility, more in keeping with his temperament, was political journalism. Journalists were a rowdy and irreverent lot. He would fit in well, if he recovered his rowdiness and irreverence.

Apparently the clearing was no longer magical, for his thoughts circled in the same vague paths as they had for months, striking no sparks of enthusiasm. Since the sun was warm and the grass scents sweet, it was easier to slide into sleep, and hope that the nightmares would wait for night.

Maxie enjoyed the coolness of the forest road after the heat of the midday sun. The farmer who had given her a wagon ride in the morning had done well to recommend this route. She had been avoiding the main highways in favor of quieter roads where a lone boy would attract little attention. This track was so quiet that she hadn't seen a person or dwelling for hours.

The only drawback was that she had run out of food the day before and her stomach was complaining. From what the farmer had said, she wouldn't find a place to procure food until late in the day. In America she could have lived off the land, but England's ferocious game and property laws made her wary of doing the same here. Though if she got hungry enough, that would change.

The sound of hoofbeats and wheels made Maxie stop and cock her head. A heavy vehicle was coming along the track behind her, and she would rather not meet anyone in such a remote spot.

She scrambled up the bank into the underbrush, then swung away from the track into the forest. Skirting tollgates in order to save money had given her plenty of practice at such detours. In three days of travel, she had experienced no difficulties at all. Indeed, except for rides with two taciturn farmers, she had not so much as spoken with another person.

Harness jangled and hooves clumped as a wagon rumbled by. She was about to return to the track when a bird trilled a liquid *hu-eet, hu-eet.*

She paused, a smile spreading across her face. Discovering new creatures and plants was one of the pleasures of traveling. This birdsong sounded like one of Britain's famous nightingales. She thought she had heard one the month before, but her cousins had been unable to confirm it. The only birds they recognized were roasted and served in sauce.

Silently she made her way through the underbrush. Her search was rewarded by a brief glimpse of brown feathers in a thicket ahead. She pressed forward through the shrubbery, her gaze on the leafy canopy above.

Her carelessness caught up with her when she tripped over an unexpected obstacle. Swearing, she tried to regain her footing, but the weight of her pack wrecked her balance.

She crashed with humiliating clumsiness, falling sideways so that her shoulder struck first. In the next instant, she realized that instead of hitting the cool forest floor, she was sprawled full-length on a warmer, more yielding object.

Warm, yielding, and *clothed.*

As gasped for breath, she realized that she was lying on top of a man. Apparently he had been dozing, but he awoke with a start, his hands reflexively jerking upward, skimming her body before locking on her upper arms.

The two of them were chest to chest and eye to eye. Startled alertness showed in the vividly blue depths, followed an instant later by amusement. For a long moment they stayed pressed together, strangers as close as lovers.

The fellow's mouth curved into a smile. "I apologize for getting in your way."

"Sorry," Maxie said gruffly. She broke away, giving thanks that her hat was still in place, shadowing her face. "I wasn't watching where I was going."

She scrambled to her feet, ready to vanish into the forest. Then, like Lot's wife, she made the mistake of looking back.

Her first impressions of the man had been fragmentary. Compelling eyes, fair coloring, a well-shaped, mobile mouth. It wasn't until she stepped away that she realized he was the handsomest man she had ever seen. His longish hair shimmered with every blond shade from gilt to dark gold, and the bone structure of his face would make angels weep with envy.

A fairy ring in the center of the circle gave her the wild thought that she had stumbled over Oberon, legendary King of Faerie. No, he was too young, and surely a fairy would not be wearing such mundane clothing.

The blond man sat up and leaned back against the tree trunk. "Females have thrown themselves into my arms a time or two before, but not usually quite so hard," he said, the skin at the corners of his eyes crinkling humorously. "However, I'm sure we can work something out if you make a polite request."

Maxie tensed. Lowering her naturally low voice still further, she said brusquely, "You haven't woken up yet. My name is Jack, and I'm not a female, much less one interested in hurling myself into your arms."

He raised his brows. "You can pass as a lad at a distance, but you landed with considerable force, and I was awake enough to know what hit me." A sapient gaze surveyed her from head to toe. "A word of advice—if you want to be convincing, make sure your coat and vest stay in place, or else find looser trousers. I've never seen a boy shaped quite like you."

Maxie colored and tugged her rucked coat down-

ward. She was on the verge of bolting when he raised
a disarming hand.

"No need to run off. I'm a harmless fellow. Remember, you assaulted me, not vice versa." He reached toward a lumpy bag that lay a few feet away. "It's time
for a midday meal, and I have far more food than one
person needs. Care to join me?"

She really should put some distance between herself
and this too-handsome fellow. But he was friendly and
unmenacing, and some conversation would be pleasant.

Her decision was made when he pulled out one of
the odd-shaped meat pies called Cornish pasties. A
fresh, delectable scent wafted toward her.

Her stomach would never forgive her if she refused.
"If you are sure you have enough, I would be pleased
to join you." She lowered her knapsack to the ground,
then settled on crossed legs beyond pouncing distance,
in case young Apollo proved more dangerous than he
appeared.

The blond man handed over the pasty. Then he rummaged in his bag again, producing another pasty, cold
roast chicken, several rolls, and a small jug. Uncorking
the jug, he set it midway between them. "We'll have to
share the ale."

"I do not drink ale." She did, however, eat pasties. It
was an effort not to wolf hers down. The crumbly crust
and well-flavored shreds of beef and vegetables were
delicious.

He chewed and swallowed a bite of his own pasty
before saying pensively, "In most circles, it is considered rude to eat with one's hat on."

Maxie was reluctant to expose herself to the other's
gaze, but she could not ignore the appeal to manners.
The acceptance of hospitality imposed obligations.
Raising her hand, she removed the shapeless hat, keeping a wary eye on her companion.

For a moment he stared, face tightening. She had
seen such reactions before, and her hand shifted so that
she could reach her knife quickly if necessary.

Luckily, he refrained from foolish or vulgar comments. After swallowing hard, he asked, "Care for some chicken?"

Maxie relaxed and accepted a drumstick. "Yes, please."

He took a piece for himself. "How do you come to be trespassing in the Marquess of Wolverton's forest?"

"I was walking along a track when I heard someone coming. I decided that being unobserved was the better part of wisdom, then got distracted by a nightingale. What is your excuse—poaching?"

He gave her a wounded look. "Do I look like a poacher?"

"No. Or at least, not a successful one." She finished the chicken leg and daintily licked her fingers. "On the other hand, you don't look like the Marquess of Whatever, either."

"Would you believe me if I said that I was he?"

"No." She cast a disrespectful eye over his garments, which were well tailored but far from new.

"A young woman of excellent judgment," he said with approval. "As it happens, you are right. I am not the Marquess of Wolverton any more than you are British."

"What makes you say that?" she asked, thinking her host was altogether too perceptive.

"Accents are something of a specialty of mine. Yours is almost that of the English gentry, but not quite." His eyes narrowed thoughtfully. "My guess is that you are American, probably from New England."

He was good. "A reasonable guess," she said noncommittally.

"Is your name still Jack?"

Her eyes narrowed. "You certainly ask a lot of questions."

"Asking is the easiest method I know for satisfying curiosity," he said with perfect logic. "And it often works."

"An irrefutable point." She hesitated a moment longer, but could see no reason not to tell him. "I'm usually called Maxie, but my name is actually Max-ima."

"You looked more like a Minima to me," he said promptly, examining her scant inches.

She laughed. "You're not precisely Hercules your-self."

"Yes, but I'm not named Hercules, so I'm not trying to deceive anyone."

"My father was named Maximus and I was called after him. No one thought to wonder if I would grow up to fit the name until it was too late." She finished eating her roll. "If your name isn't Hercules, what is it?"

"It isn't a lot of things." He took a swig of ale as he weighed what to say. He was obviously a wayfaring rogue who had had so many names and identities that he didn't remember himself what he had been chris-tened.

Eventually he said, "Lately I've been using Lord Robert Andreville."

Startled, she asked, "Are you really a nobleman?" Despite his old clothing, he did have an air about him. Then she frowned. "You're hoaxing me, aren't you? My father explained titles to me once. A real peer does not use Lord with his Christian name. I reckon that Lord Robert is a pretend title that you invented to impress people."

"And here I thought I could fool someone from the colonies." An impish light showed in his eyes. "You're quite right, I'm a commoner, not the least bit noble. My friends call me Robin."

Whatever his name, the man had a marvelously ex-pressive face. Perhaps he was an actor rather than a swindler. Of course, he could be both, but still Maxie found herself smiling back. "In that case, you should give something to your namesake for luck." She ges-tured at the bright-eyed English robin that had landed in the middle of the fairy ring and been hopping closer and closer as they ate. Smaller and more lively than the American robin, it did rather resemble her companion.

"A good idea." He tossed a fragment to the bird, which grabbed the morsel and flew away. "One should always offer to the gods of luck." Delving into his pouch again, he asked, "Care for some shortbread?"

"That would be very nice." She accepted a wedge, trying not to look too greedy.

He had a marvelously engaging smile, with the charm of a man who could sell you a dozen things you didn't need. Maxie and her father had met many likable wastrels on their travels, and the self-proclaimed Lord Robert was another of that breed. Actually, Max could have been considered one as well. Perhaps that was why his daughter had a weakness for beguiling rogues.

She ate the butter-rich shortbread with pleasure, thinking that this was the best meal she'd had in a very long time. After finishing, she went to the stream to wash her hands and drink some of the cool water.

Robin watched his improbable guest thoughtfully. Though she had done her best to disguise herself with shapeless clothing, his palms remembered the shapes of concealed curves. When she returned, he asked, "Do you live near here?"

"No, I'm on my way to London." She picked up her hat and knapsack. "Thank you for sharing your meal."

"London!" he said, startled. "Good God, do you seriously intend to walk that whole way alone?"

"It's only about two hundred miles. I'll be there within a fortnight. Good day to you." She settled the hat back on her head, tugging it down so that it shadowed her clear brown eyes.

He bit back the impulse to tell her not to put the hat on, that it was a crime to obscure that exquisite face. When she had first crashed down on him, he had thought her a mischievous young tomboy in a brother's clothing. Then she had doffed her absurd hat, and he had briefly forgotten how to speak or breathe.

Maxima—Maxie—had the exotic beauty sometimes found in those of mixed race. While her delicate features were almost English, the smooth dark complexion, glossy black hair, and subtle modeling of the bones were definitely not.

It was a face one would not forget.

Yet beauty was the least of it. What drew him like a magnet was a quality of focused directness as strong and true as a blade, a still strength that showed in every word and gesture she made. Seeing her had triggered a flood of long-suppressed emotions, and they battered inside him like ice breaking up in the spring rains. The effect was far from comfortable.

In the midst of tumult, one fact was blazingly clear: He must not let this extraordinary creature walk out of his life.

Robin swept up the remnants of the meal, then got to his feet, slung his bag over his shoulder, and fell into step beside Maxie. "The distance to London is not insurmountable," he admitted, "but the roads are not safe for a young woman alone."

"I have had no trouble so far," she replied. "No one except you has realized that I am female, and I will not be so careless as to trip over anyone else."

"A young boy could be equally in danger." Looking down at Maxie, Robin realized how small she was, scarcely over five feet tall, but so perfectly proportioned that it was hard to judge her height unless standing next to her. "In fact, some of the gentlemen of the highway would probably prefer a lad."

The brown eyes looked at him askance. A proper young lady would not have understood the remark, but Maxie did. Perhaps she wasn't entirely naive.

"Here in the north the roads are fairly safe, but the closer you get to London, the greater the hazard," Robin continued as they emerged back on the grassy track and turned south.

"I am quite capable of defending myself." Her patience was beginning to erode and her voice was snappish.

"With that knife you carry?"

That gained him a hard stare. He explained, "You did land on me rather hard, and the haft of a knife feels quite different from a human body." Especially from a soft, rounded female body.

"Yes, I have a knife, and I know how to use it," she said with a definite note of warning.

"It won't be enough if several highwaymen attack you."

"I don't intend to get involved in any pitched battles."

"One doesn't always have a choice," he said dryly.

They continued in chilly silence, Maxie studiously ignoring his presence and Robin thinking hard. Even though he had only known her for an hour, he knew better than to try to change her mind. This was not someone easily swayed from her course.

She might reach London without incident, but the odds were that she would meet trouble along the way. Even if he weren't fascinated by her, he would be very reluctant to permit a female—and an undersized one at that—to make such a journey.

The conclusion was inescapable.

As the woods began to thin at the edge of Wolverhampton, he remarked, "There is really no help for it. As a gentleman, I shall have to escort you to London."

"What!" Maxie sputtered, coming to a stop in the middle of the track to stare at him. "Have you run mad?"

"Not in the least. You are a young woman alone in a foreign country. It would be quite dishonorable to let you continue alone." He stopped also and gave her his most trustworthy smile. "Besides, I have nothing better to do."

Her expression equal parts of outrage and amusement, she said, "What qualifies you as a gentleman of honor?"

"Gentlemen do not work. Since I do not work, therefore I must be a gentleman."

Maxie laughed. "You are the most absurd creature— that logic wouldn't convince a babe in arms. Besides, even if you don't work, surely you can't just take to the road on impulse."

"But I can. In fact, I have already done so."

She surveyed her companion. He was no more than average height, and while that made him almost a head taller than she, his elegant frame did not look designed for brawling.

"You appear not only harmless, but downright ineffectual," she said as she resumed walking. "I am more likely to have to protect you than vice versa. I have spent much of my life on the road and know how to take care of myself. I do not need or want an escort, no matter how honorable your intentions."

When he smiled, she said tartly, "For all I know, I would be in more danger from you than from any hypothetical highwaymen."

An offended expression crossed his mobile face. "The lady doesn't trust me."

"I can't think of any good reason why I should." She cocked her head to one side. "Are you an actor? You are constantly performing, and actors are often without work."

"I've played many roles," he admitted, "but never on a stage."

She should have realized that; if he had tried the theater, he would have been wildly successful if only because of the females who would pay for the privilege of gazing at him. "Have you ever done any kind of useful work? Or are you purely a lily of the field?"

"Work fascinates me," he protested. "I can sit and watch it for hours."

She struggled, with little success, to keep a straight face. "I see there is no getting any sense out of you." Deciding to try another tack, she added, "I might reconsider if you have enough money to buy us coach tickets to London, but I can't afford to feed two people. I may not have enough for myself."

That gave Robin pause for a moment. Then he brightened. "I am not in funds at the moment and my banker, alas, is in London. However, I can conjure money from the air when necessary."

Before she could retreat, he reached under her hat.

His fingertips grazed her ear. Though his touch was light, her skin prickled with awareness. As she caught her breath, unnerved, he moved his hand in front of her face to show the shilling that had materialized in his grasp.

"Not bad," she allowed, "but sleight of hand is not in the same class as turning lead into gold."

"Sleight of hand!" He looked offended. "We are speaking of magic, not mere trickery. Give me your hand."

Amused, she stopped walking and did as he requested. He placed the shilling on her right palm and folded her fingers around it, his clasp warm and strong. "Make two fists and I will magically move the shilling to your left hand."

Obediently she did as he asked. He made several graceful passes in the air, murmuring unintelligibly as he did. After a final flourish, he said, "There, the shilling has moved."

"You need practice, Lord Robert, because the shilling is still in my hand." She opened her fingers as proof, then gasped. Lying on her palm was not the single coin he had given her, but two. "How did you do that?"

"Very well." He grinned, dropping his showman's manner. "True, it's only sleight of hand, but I'm fairly good at such things. I've often done conjuring to earn food and lodging when my pockets were empty."

Her companion was definitely a shiftless vagrant, albeit an entertaining one. Maxie handed back his two shillings. "This has been very pleasant, Lord Robert, but why don't you return to your nap in the forest and leave me alone?"

"The roads are public." He pocketed the coins. "Since I have decided to go to London, you can't stop me."

She opened her mouth, then closed it again. What he said was quite true. Unless her unwanted escort actually assaulted her, which didn't seem imminent, he had as much right to the highway as she did. And if he chose to walk the same road at the same pace, what could she do about it?

She thought of the dogs that had sometimes followed her and her father. Like a dog, Robin would soon get bored and fall away, since charming wastrels had a span of attention somewhat shorter than that of the average mongrel. All she needed was patience.

Chapter 3

The Chanleigh Court morning room was full of choice little objets d'art, but having come nearly three hundred miles, Desdemona Ross wasted no time in admiration. "What do you mean, Maxima has gone to London to visit me?" she inquired, her thick auburn brows rising. "I am not in London, I am here in Durham. Against my better judgment, I might add."

Lady Collingwood gave her sister-in-law a frosty glance. "Read her note for yourself." She took a folded sheet of paper from her desk and handed it over. "The ungrateful chit decamped in the middle of the night three days ago."

Desdemona frowned as she read. "Maxima says I invited her for an extended visit, which simply isn't true. I came north to meet her, with the idea that she could return with me if we got on well, but I had not suggested that in writing."

"Maxima is a most unaccountable creature, not at all civilized or gently bred." Lady Collingwood gave a bored shrug while she evaluated her sister-in-law's clothing. Desdemona had a talent for dowdiness that amounted to genius. Looking attractive must be against her bluestocking principles.

Then again, perhaps Desdemona was wise to go about swaddled in dark concealing cloaks and bonnets. Her flaming red hair was hopelessly ungenteel, and deserved to be pulled back ruthlessly. And her figure . . . there was no way that figure would ever be fashionable, either.

With a smug thought for her own undeniable elegance, Lady Collingwood continued, "Bolting off at midnight to catch a mail coach is exactly the sort of thing one would expect of her. For that matter, so is lying." She yawned delicately behind her hand. "Really, Desdemona, you're fortunate to have missed her. It amazes me that Maximus dared bring her to Chanleigh. She belongs back in the forest with her savage Red Indian relations."

"As opposed to staying with her savage English relations?" Desdemona said with lethal sweetness. "Her mother may have been a Red Indian, but at least her family wasn't in trade."

Althea Collins flushed at the gibe, for she had spent years attempting to forget where her father had made his money. Her furious retort was forestalled by the entrance of her husband.

"Dizzy!" Lord Collingwood said, his long face showing pleased surprise. "You should have written that you were coming. It's been too long since you visited."

In spite of the twenty-year difference in age and no physical resemblance whatsoever, Desdemona and her brother were fond of one another. She rose to give him a quick hug, feeling him flinch at the demonstrativeness. She had known that he would flinch, just as he had known that she would hug him anyway. It was long-established family tradition. "Apparently I should have arrived three days ago, Clete."

His lordship looked pained. He didn't like the nickname any more than Desdemona liked being called Dizzy.

Formalities completed, she favored her brother with a scowl. "I came to see how my niece was faring, only to be told that she has run off with some story about visiting me."

He frowned as he realized the implications of his sister's presence. "Why aren't you in London waiting for Maxima?"

"Because I didn't invite her," Desdemona snapped. "Apparently the poor girl was so miserable here that she ran away in the hope that I would treat her better. What kind of care have you been giving your brother's only child?"

"Maxima is not a child—she's a woman grown, only a few years younger than you," her brother said defensively. "She did not consult my wishes before vanishing."

"I'm surprised she had money for the coach fare," Desdemona said. "I thought that Max was virtually penniless when he died."

There was sudden silence while the Collingwoods exchanged glances. "You're right, she had little money," her ladyship said, a line appearing between her brows. "I had to pay for her mourning clothes when Maximus died. We *have* been taking care of her, though she's shown precious little gratitude."

"If she was expected to be grateful, no wonder she left." Desdemona swung around to her brother again. "She may be a woman grown, but she is a stranger to England. Anything might happen to her, particularly if she is walking to London."

"Good God, surely she would never consider such a thing." Lord Collingwood halted, his face reflecting uneasiness. "This morning I noticed that my old map of the London road was not in my desk. I assumed that someone must have borrowed it."

"Apparently that is exactly what happened. Since she and Max spent much of the year roaming the wilds of New England, a journey to London must have seemed quite tame." Desdemona gave up trying to hold her temper. "You two should be ashamed of yourselves! Surely Max had a right to believe that his daughter would be safe here at Chanleigh. Instead, you drove her away."

Collingwood flushed. "I thought Maxima was happy here. I was planning to present her in London with the girls, but never pressed the issue. It didn't seem appropriate to talk about her future until she had recovered more from the loss of her father."

Desdemona fixed her sister-in-law with a gimlet eye.

"Did you make her welcome, too, Althea? No snide little comments about her background? Did you order a proper wardrobe for her, introduce her to the young men of the neighborhood?"

"If you were so concerned about the little savage, why didn't you do something yourself?" Lady Collingwood said with the anger of the guilty. "You could have visited anytime these last four months, but all you did was write a few letters."

"We've been working for a Parliamentary bill that would protect apprentices, and since we were finally making progress I was unable to leave London," Desdemona said uncomfortably. "But you're right, I should have done more. I thought she would be safe here until I had time to come north."

"There's no point in recriminations," Collingwood said, hoping to head off a major altercation. "The important thing is to get Maxima back here safely."

"How do you intend to accomplish that?"

After a moment's thought, her brother gave a relieved nod. "I know just the man to send after her. Simmons is in Newcastle now. I'll send for him and explain what needs to be done. With luck, Maxima will be home in no time."

"Send for your man if you wish, but I'm going after her myself," Desdemona said tightly. "Someone in the family should care enough to try. What does she look like?"

Lord Collingwood started to say that his sister was being absurd, that such matters should be left to those with experience. A glance at Desdemona's set face made him decide that it was easier to let her go. After all, his sister was an independent and worldly widow, attended by her servants. How much trouble could she get into?

The miles and the afternoon rolled by, and Maxie's unwanted companion showed no signs of boredom. He didn't flag from the brisk pace she set, either. Occasionally Robin made an entertaining comment on the passing scene and they would converse a bit. Sometimes he whistled, very musically. Maxie had to admit that his presence made the miles go more quickly.

They left the forest and joined a wider road with more traffic. It was coming on to dinnertime when they entered a quiet, gray stone village. Robin gestured at an inn called the King Richard. "Shall I buy you dinner? Anything you like as long as it costs less than two shillings."

Maxie gave him a cold stare. "You may stop if you wish, but I intend to continue. Have a pleasant journey, Mr. Anderson."

"Andreville," he said, impervious to the snub. "Anderson is too common to impress anyone. Are you sure you don't want to stop? While I have enough food for another day, a warm meal would help us make it through a cool night."

"There is no *us,* Mr. Andreville," Maxie said in a doomed attempt to maintain formality. "We are two individuals who have chanced to travel the same road for a few hours."

"You still don't take me seriously, do you?" Her companion seemed unfazed by the observation. "People seldom do, so you're in good company. Very well, cold food it is."

"For pity's sake," Maxie muttered as she walked past the inn and Robin stayed at her side. The man was becoming a blessed nuisance.

An idea occurred to her. If she agreed to stop for dinner, she could surely find an opportunity to slip away from him. With a few minutes' lead, she could vanish into one of the small side lanes. The next day she would cut across to another southbound road and he would never find her. "You're right, a hot meal would be welcome, but I will pay for my own."

His blue eyes danced, and she had the uneasy feeling that he had guessed her intentions. She would have to relax and behave as if she had resigned herself to his escort.

They entered the inn and found seats in a high-

backed booth in a corner of the smoky taproom. It was
so dark that no one would notice that Maxie didn't remove her hat. There was no choice of meals. They ordered the specialty of the day and were served plates
of food described as griskin and potatoes.

At Maxie's questioning glance, Robin explained,
"Griskin is from the loin of a bacon pig. It's not bad."

Maxie took a bite and chewed it thoughtfully.
"You're right. It's not bad. On the other hand, it isn't
good, either."

"True, but it's hot, and it tastes better than one
would expect anything named griskin to taste."

She hid her smile with a forkful of food. "I've had
worse. Porcupine, for example, is good only if you're
starving."

As they ate, she exerted herself to be friendly. It
wasn't hard, but success proved treacherous. There was
too much intimacy in laughing and sharing a table with
an attractive man who gave her all of his attention. The
darkness of the taproom made it seem as if she and
Robin were quite alone. Even eating humble griskin
couldn't destroy the romantic effect.

The thought strengthened her resolve. The last thing
she needed was to take up with an alluring wastrel. She
bent her attention to her plate and waited for a chance
to slip away.

Robin finished before she did. His idle gaze went to
the back wall of the booth, where devices made of
hammered, interlocked iron pieces were hanging from
nails.

"Do you have this sort of puzzle in America? The
object is to take them apart, then remember how to put
them together again." He took one of the devices
down. "They're hard enough to solve when sober—
frustrated drunkards have been known to use crowbars
to rip the pieces apart."

"I'm familiar with tavern puzzles. They probably
exist wherever there are blacksmiths to forge them, and
taverns where people like to amuse themselves." She

swallowed her last bite of potato. "I suspect you're rather good at solving them."

"On the grounds that I would excel at all useless skills?"

She had to smile. "Precisely."

He frowned at the puzzle. The outline was vaguely bell-shaped, with several interlocking circles and triangles attached to it. "I guess I haven't spent enough time in taverns lately. I'm not even sure which pieces are removable."

As she gazed at the device, she noticed that his left wrist and fingers were subtly misshapen from what must have been numerous broken bones. He had elegant hands that he used expressively, more like a European than an Englishman. A pity that one had been so badly damaged, especially since he was left-handed.

She studied the irregular contours more closely. The pattern of breaks was unusual, so regular that it seemed the result of a deliberate effort. Torture? A shiver ran down her spine. Perhaps an angry husband had chosen this way to wreak revenge for injured honor.

She reached across the table and took the puzzle from him. "This reminds me of a specimen called the devil's stirrup, only this version is more complicated. I think these pieces should come apart." After a minute of study, she made several quick twists and the puzzle separated into three sections.

He chuckled. "Which of us has the useless skills?"

"Taking it apart is only half the battle. Reassembling it is just as hard." She pushed the pieces across the table to him. "I'll wager sixpence that you can't get it back together by the time I return from the necessary."

"You're on." He lifted a triangle and a ring and tried to link them together.

The moment had come. No man would admit that a woman could best him at something like this. He would be so intent on solving the silly puzzle that he wouldn't miss her for the next hour.

Maxie slid out of the booth, holding her knapsack unobtrusively at her side. The food had been paid for when ordered, so she could leave with a clear conscience. She headed across the taproom to the door that led into the back courtyard. Once she was outside, she cut quickly through to the lane that ran parallel with the high street, behind the buildings.

Her sense of satisfaction was short-lived. The lane was only a dozen buildings long, and when she returned to the high street she almost collided with Robin, who was lounging against a garden wall, his arms crossed on his chest as he waited for her.

"Your opinion of my intelligence really is low if you thought I could be eluded so easily," he said with undiminished good nature.

She glared at him, for the first time believing that the imbecile man truly meant to accompany her all the way to London. "The issue is not your intelligence, but your presumption. I do not want your escort, your company, or your free meals. Now, leave me alone!"

She turned and started stalking down the street. Robin stayed at her elbow. Whirling angrily, she snapped, "I have warned you. Believe me, I am quite capable of defending myself."

She was about to say more when he cut her off with a sharp warning gesture. "People are coming. If you want to maintain your masquerade, don't make a scene here."

Several approaching locals were watching them curiously, but even so, Maxie would have exploded with fury if she hadn't been caught by Robin's gaze. His blue eyes had measureless depths, the eyes of a man who had seen more of shadows than sunshine.

He was also older than she had thought. She had assumed he was near her own age, but she revised that upward, past thirty. She stared at him, feeling that she was in the presence of a dangerous stranger.

Before she could react, Robin took a firm grip on her arm and started walking toward open country. As they passed the interested group of villagers, an elderly woman said in a broad Yorkshire accent, "Eh, Daisy, isn't that gent—"

"No, it isn't." Robin's clear tones cut across the woman's sentence. His interruption was accompanied by a dazzling smile that made her mouth go slack with admiration. Leaving a murmur of voices behind them, he marched Maxie down the road before anything more could be said.

Fuming, she considered calling to the villagers for help, but that would require endless explanations, and she was sure that Robin could talk his way out of any accusation she made.

Besides, she did not feel threatened by him. On the contrary, he was in far more danger from her than vice versa.

She waited until they rounded a bend and were out of sight of the village. Then she stopped and jerked free. "If I had any doubts about traveling with you, they are resolved," she said furiously. "You arrogant, egotistical—"

"You're quite right, I am presumptuous," he said in a steely voice. "But you had better accept that I intend to see that you reach your destination safely."

She reached for her knife, but he grabbed her wrist. Though his hold was light, it was impossible to wrench free.

"Don't do it, Maxie," he said, his gaze holding hers as implacably as his hand. "You are one of the two most formidable women I have ever known, but you are a foreigner crossing a country rife with unrest. Besides the usual bandits, there are starving soldiers released from the army and unable to find work, angry radicals who want to destroy the government, and God knows what else. You might be lucky all the way to London, but it's not likely. I guarantee you will be safer with me than alone."

She could have fought him, but the last few minutes had changed her views on his ineffectuality. His desire to protect her seemed genuine. Probably he had other, less honorable motives as well, but she was experienced at resisting seduction and didn't think it likely that he would force her. If his fraudulent lordship

wanted a woman, all he had to do was give out one of
those melting smiles in a village and females would
follow him down the street like mice after cheese.

Reserving judgment on whether she might choose to
escape him in the future, she said coolly, "Very well,
Mr. Andreville, I accept the inevitability of your company, at least for the moment. Just remember to keep
your hands to yourself, or you will find them taken off
at the wrist."

"I'd sooner tease a tiger." All traces of shadow vanished, and again he was the easygoing charmer she had
met in the forest. But she would not forget what he had
revealed of himself.

As he released her wrist, she found herself asking,
"Who is the other of the two most formidable women?"

He grinned. "An old friend of mine. You'd like her."

"I doubt it." She turned and resumed walking down
the road. It would be light for another hour, so they
might as well cover more ground. "I hope that your
pseudoaristocratic self can survive sleeping under a
hedge when there isn't a barn."

"There are worse places to sleep than a hedge," he
said as he fell in beside her. "Almost any jail, for example."

"Have you been in many jails?" She suspected that
he had, and hoped it had been for no more than va-
grancy, though doubtless he was guilty of much worse.

"A few," he admitted. "The best was a castle in
France with very tolerable food and wine, and a duke
for company."

From the glint in his eye, she guessed that he had invented this particular tale, and that he was aware that
she knew it. "Sounds pleasant. If that was the best,
what was the worst?"

He pondered. "That would probably be the prison in
Constantinople. I didn't speak much Turkish, and I
didn't even know the local gambling games. A sad situation. But I met the most interesting Chinese chap
there . . ."

They headed into a stretch of barren moor, Robin's flexible tenor weaving an outrageously improbable and amusing tale of subversion and escape. He was undeniably a rogue. But while he spoke, Maxie could temporarily forget her grief for her father.

Chapter 4

Shortly before the sun set, they encountered a family of Gypsy tinkers heading north. As the two parties approached each other, Robin waved and called out something in a language Maxie had never heard before.

She said with surprise, "You speak Gypsy?"

"The language is called Romany, and I only speak a little." The corners of his eyes crinkled humorously. "But I need to buy a few tinkerish things, and if you address people in their own tongue, they won't try as hard to cheat you."

The wagon stopped and the driver climbed from the box. Though Robin deprecated his linguistic skill, he seemed fairly fluent. He and the man of the household began talking energetically, both with their hands flying. Despite his blondness, her companion looked very un-English.

Several children emerged from the wagon, followed by a handsome, brightly dressed woman with a baby on her hip. She sauntered up to Maxie and said something in Romany.

Maxie shook her head, "Sorry, I don't know your language."

"No?" The woman cocked her head to one side. In English, she said, "I thought you might be *didikois,* a half-blood Rom, and that you'd taught the Gorgio to speak our tongue."

"No, I'm from America."

The woman's eyes widened. "Did you ever see any of those bloodthirsty Indians?"

Maxie had been hearing equally silly statements ever since she had arrived in England. "Madam, I *am* one of those bloodthirsty Indians," she said dryly. "Just as you are a thieving Gypsy."

The woman's dark eyes flashed with fury and a child who had been circling ducked behind its mother's skirts. Then, understanding, the woman laughed. "People often have stupid ideas about those who are different, yes?"

"Yes," Maxie agreed. Though glad to have made her point, she regretted having spoken in front of Robin. She was not ready to share her past with a man who was such an enigma.

Luckily, he was still deep in his negotiations and hadn't heard her. She watched him in admiration; his haggling skills would do credit to a horse trader.

At a critical point, he produced a shiny sixpence from the ear of the nearest child, reducing the little girl to helpless giggles. Her doting father threw up his hands and concluded the deal, giving Robin a razor, some battered cooking and eating utensils, and a small, ragged blanket in exchange for the princely sum of two shillings. Robin also traded his well-made pouch for a shabby knapsack large enough to contain his new possessions.

They set off again after a round of friendly farewells. When they were out of earshot of the wagon, Maxie said, "Where did you learn Romany?"

He shrugged. "I've traveled with the Rom on occasion. Once they accept you, they are the most hospitable of people."

Before she could probe further, he continued, "The Rom, Gregor, said there was a good campsite about a mile from here."

She glanced around at the empty moors. "I hope he's right. We haven't seen a barn or shed for the last hour."

They continued until Robin pointed out a small pyramid of stones to the right of the road. "That's a Gypsy trail sign. The campsite is this way."

Ten minutes of walking along a faintly marked trail led them to a dip in the ground that was invisible from the road. Small trees gave protection from the wind, a stream provided drinking water, and there was a fire pit circled with stones. Maxie never would have found the spot on her own.

The air was already cooling, so as the light faded from the sky, they gathered firewood. Maxie used her flint and steel to start the fire, then rigged a crossbar to suspend a pot of water over it. As the water started to boil, Robin emerged from the dusk with an armful of large, springy ferns.

"Bracken," he explained as he laid down his load. "It makes quite a decent bed."

"I assume you mean it will make *two* quite decent beds?" she asked frostily as she poured steaming water over some tea leaves.

"Of course." Robin's voice was serious, but his eyes laughed at her suspicions. He made three more trips, shaping the bracken into pallets on opposite sides of the fire. All very proper, and surprisingly comfortable when she tested hers.

By the time the beds were made up, the tea had steeped. Maxie handed Robin a mugful as he settled cross-legged on the far side of the fire. "You're quite mad, you know. Surely wherever you slept last night was more comfortable than this."

"Correct but irrelevant," Robin replied. "I haven't enjoyed myself this much in a long time."

"Quite, quite mad." But harmlessly so. They sipped their tea in friendly silence. Though she had been wary about this strange partnership, Robin's matter-of-fact attitude made everything easy. Now that she was resigned to his presence, she felt remarkably at ease with him. It was hard to believe that they had met only a few hours earlier.

She put more water on to boil, and when her China tea was finished, she prepared a cup of her special herbal blend.

Robin wrinkled his nose at the odor of the steeping herbs. "What are you making now?"

"It's a tea for women," she explained.

"What makes it particularly female?"

With a mischievous desire to disconcert, she said, "It prevents conception. When I set out on this trip, I knew I couldn't necessarily avoid assault, but at least I can protect myself from the worst consequences."

His face went blank. After a long silence, he said, "What a remarkably cold-blooded young female you are."

She took a sip of hot, bitter fluid. "I have never had the luxury of being able to avoid unpleasant realities."

Very quietly, he asked, "Have you ever been raped?"

"No."

He stared down at his mug. "I'm glad. I've seen the results. That is not something I would wish on any woman." His face and voice were shadowed with the darkness she had glimpsed earlier.

She shifted uncomfortably. She had wanted to disconcert him, not trigger bad memories. Still, his few words made her utterly sure that whatever else might happen, she need never fear that he would force her.

Wanting to change the mood, she reached inside her coat for her harmonica and began to play. Robin's expression eased and he lay back in the bracken, his arms crossed behind his head.

As she played the plangent notes of a frontier ballad, Maxie studied her companion. His speech and obvious education marked him as a child of privilege. Why had he been banished to the world of ordinary mortals who must struggle for existence? Her father's sins had been the obvious ones of youth, gaming, and women, but there was something about Robin that made her doubt that the conventional vices had been his downfall.

The flickering firelight gilded the blond hair, and his profile was as remote as it was flawless. Perhaps he had not been cast out for his sins, but had come from a family that had fallen on hard times. Or perhaps he was illegitimate, raised with some advantages, then thrown into the world to make his own way. She would probably never know the truth about him.

Her music drifted between traditional ballads and themes from famous European composers. Finally, as the fire crumbled to embers, she began to play the music of the Iroquois. The first songs she had ever heard were her mother's lullabies. Later she had learned many of the ceremonial and work tunes of the Mohawks. Though there were no Indian instruments like the harmonica, with practice she had learned to approximate the plaintive intervals and strange, ever-shifting rhythms.

She had thought that Robin was asleep, but when the music changed, his head turned in her direction, his eyes shadowed and unreadable. She played a little longer, then tucked her harmonica away and pulled her cloak from her pack.

"Good night." Robin's voice was scarcely louder than the wind over the moor grasses. "Thank you for the concert."

"You're welcome." As she rolled into her cloak and settled into the bracken, she silently admitted that she would sleep better for having him near.

A strange sound brought Maxie instantly awake, her hand reaching for her knife. At first she thought the soft choking noise had been made by an animal. When it was repeated, she realized that it came from the other pallet.

Wondering if Robin was having some kind of breathing attack, she rose and crossed to kneel by his side. His face was a pale blur in the starlight, and his breath came in shallow gasps, the bracken rustling as he shifted restlessly.

She laid a hand on his shoulder. "Robin?"

His muscles spasmed under her fingers. The choking sounds stopped and his eyes opened, though it was too dark to see any expression. He said huskily, "I was having a nightmare?"

"I think so. Do you remember what it was?"

"Not really. Could have been any of a number of things." He drew in a ragged breath. "The price of an uneasy conscience."

"Do you have nightmares often?"

"Regularly, if not precisely often." He rubbed his hand over his face. "Sorry I disturbed your rest."

She was about to say more when she saw a faint glimmer of moisture on his cheeks. No wonder he was trying so hard to be nonchalant. She laid her hand on his, where it rested near her knee. "No great matter. I'm a light sleeper." His fingers were cold, and she did not think that was because of the chilly night air. "Better to be woken by you than by a hungry wolf."

"Around here, sheep are far more common than wolves." He squeezed her hand briefly. "Not that I don't have faith in your ability to protect my ineffectual self from the perils of the wild."

"If any wolves attack, I'm sure that you can talk them to death," she said lightly. "Good night."

She returned to her pallet to take advantage of what remained of the night. Yet sleep eluded her, even though Robin's breathing was soon quiet and regular.

The Iroquois took dreams seriously, regarding them as wishes of the soul that must be satisfied. Maxie's mother had gone further, saying that nightmares were injuries of the soul that must be healed.

As she drifted back to sleep, Maxie wondered what haunted Robin's nights.

If Desdemona Ross had known how difficult it would be to find a runaway, she would have left the task to the fellow her brother was going to hire. Having begun, however, she was not about to admit that she wasn't equal to the challenge.

The search had seemed a simple exercise in logic. Knowing her niece's background, Desdemona had calculated how much distance a vigorous walker could travel in the time Maxima had been gone. Then she had targeted the three most likely routes and started making inquiries at taverns and posting houses along the way. She asked for a boy, sure that her niece had too much sense to travel in female garb.

Her inquiries produced either too many sightings of young boys or none at all, but never anything useful. After three days of futile searching, Desdemona was thoroughly sick of the business. Only her considerable stubbornness kept her going.

She was all the way to Yorkshire when her luck changed at an inn named the King Richard. It was midday, and a scattering of locals nursed their ale in the taproom when Desdemona entered. She marched over to the woman behind the bar. "Excuse me, madam. I am looking for my young nephew. The lad has run away from school, and it's possible that he came this way."

"Aye?" the landlady said with profound disinterest.

"About this tall," Desdemona gestured with her hand, "dark coloring, but probably wearing a hat to hide his face. Dressed so that he wouldn't be easily noticed."

"There was a lad like that in here t'other day." The answer came not from the landlady, but a toothless beldam in a group across the room. The old woman clambered to her feet and made her way to Desdemona. "But he's found hisself a friend."

"Oh?" Desdemona asked in an encouraging tone.

Another woman joined them, a sturdy female smoking a clay pipe. "Aye, if 'twas your nephew, he's all right. Lord Robert Andreville was with him. Happen you might know his lordship, all the Quality being related-like. Lord Robert must've recognized the lad and taken him home to send him back to you."

The beldam disagreed. "Gent said he wasn't Lord Robert."

"Nothing wrong with my eyes, Granny. That was Lord Robert, no matter what he said," the pipe smoker insisted. "I saw him in York right before Christmas. That yaller head couldn't've belonged to anyone else."

Before the beldam could disagree again, Desdemona asked, "What happened?"

"The lad and his lordship had a bite of dinner here," the landlady contributed, showing more interest in the debate. "Sat in that corner, which is why no one recognized Lord Robert. After they ate, the lad slipped out the back."

"Aye, tried to run away again," the pipe smoker said. "That's why I think it must be the lad you want. His lordship caught up with him outside, then made your nevvy go with him."

Desdemona frowned. "You mean he forced the boy?"

The other woman nodded. "Took the lad by the arm and marched him out of town. Must have had a carriage waiting. Shouldn't think a lord'd walk very far."

Desdemona had heard of the Andrevilles, of course, and knew that their principal seat was nearby. But none of that family should know Maxima, who had only been in England for a few months. At least, no one should have recognized the girl as a runaway of good family. "Tell me about this Lord Robert."

An enthusiastic chorus explained that Lord Robert was the younger brother of the Marquess of Wolverton, that he had done dire and dangerous things during the wars, that he was as handsome as a fallen angel and a devil with the ladies. The zeal with which the villagers described his exploits showed how proud they were of their neighborhood black sheep.

If even half the tales were true, the portrait that emerged was alarming. Lord and Lady Collingwood had said that Maxima was strikingly attractive, exactly the sort to draw unwelcome attentions from a rake. It seemed likely that the dissolute Lord Robert had seen through the girl's disguise and forced her to accompany him for no good purpose.

Face grim, Desdemona asked, "How do I get to Wolverhampton?" After receiving directions, she dipped into her reticule and laid a gold guinea on the bar. "Thank you for your help, ladies. This afternoon's ale is on me."

Desdemona stalked outside to her waiting coach, ignoring the toasts to her continued good health. She was too busy planning what she would do to a depraved aristocrat who would ruin an innocent young girl.

Chapter 5

The Marquess of Wolverton had set the afternoon aside to answer his correspondence. His secretary, Charles, would read a letter, Giles would dictate a reply, and they would move on to the next. All perfectly, boringly normal.

Normality was shattered, however, when an angry Amazon burst into the library. "I don't care how busy Lord Wolverton is," she barked as she stalked in. "He will see me *now*!"

Floundering behind her came a red-faced footman. "I'm sorry, your lordship, Lady Ross insisted on seeing you," he said apologetically. "She's here about Lord Robert."

Giles looked up quickly. Robin had vanished three days earlier. Though he had said not to worry if he wandered off someday, it was proving difficult not to feel concern.

He blinked at the newcomer. Lady Ross was sweeping toward him like a ship in full sail, her full cloak and bonnet billowing around her and a parasol gripped like a weapon in one hand. Tall and Junoesque, she might have been handsome in a happier mood, but her present fury was not a sight for the faint of heart.

Wondering what on earth she had to do with Robin, Giles rose politely. "I am Wolverton. You have news of my brother?"

Lady Ross scowled. "So you don't know where he is, either."

"He has been away for several days. I am unsure when he will be returning," Giles said, trying to remember what he had heard about Lady Ross. Though her name was familiar, he couldn't recall the context. "What business do you have with him?"

"The question is not my business with him, but what he has done with my niece." Her ladyship glowered at the marquess. "The evidence suggests that your brother has abducted her."

"The devil you say!" Giles's jaw hardened. "Who is spreading such preposterous slander?"

The tip of her parasol quivered like the tail of an angry cat. "Some of your tenants saw Lord Robert forcing a young person to come away with him. From the description, it was my niece, Maxima Collins, an American girl."

The marquess fixed his visitor with a steely gaze. "How and when did the girl come to be abducted? I cannot believe that my brother kidnapped an innocent young girl away from her family."

Lady Ross's eyes shifted uneasily. "I'm not sure exactly what happened. Maxima has been living with my brother, Lord Collingwood. Her father died soon after they arrived in England, and the girl was distraught. About a week ago she impulsively left Collingwood's house, leaving a note that she was on her way to me in London. In fact, I was coming to visit her in Durham. I have been looking for her since we realized that she had disappeared." Her gray eyes narrowed. "It was three days ago that the villagers saw Lord Robert with his unwilling companion."

Giles kept his expression blank, but inwardly he groaned. Robin would not abduct an innocent, but might he have taken off on a lark with a young and willing runaway? That would depend on how young and how willing she was. "How old is your niece?"

Lady Ross hesitated before admitting, "Twenty-five."

"Twenty-five! The way you were carrying on, I assumed she was fifteen or sixteen. Your niece is hardly a green girl—at her age, most females are wives and mothers. If she went with my brother, it must have been voluntarily."

"Maxima has only been in England for four months, and she was orphaned almost immediately," Lady Ross said with a glower. "She is an innocent, alone in a foreign country. A man who would take advantage of that is beneath contempt."

Giles took a firm grip on his temper. "We have not established what, if anything, has happened."

"If Lord Robert hasn't run off with her, then where is he?" she demanded. "From what you said when I arrived, you don't know where he is. According to the villagers, he has the reputation of a rake—exactly the sort of man to kidnap a young girl."

"That's utter nonsense," Giles retorted. "Robin has been out of England for years. In the six months since his return, he has been living here quietly, not cutting a swath through English womanhood."

"Your tenants didn't seem to think so."

"People enjoy spinning lurid tales about the local gentry. I don't provide them with much fodder for gossip, but Lord Robert is an attractive and romantic figure. If he so much as smiles at a local girl, I'm sure the tenants fancy him an incurable womanizer." Giles considered a moment. "Even if my brother had a female companion, are you sure she was your niece? As a runaway, she could be almost anywhere."

"I am sure that Maxima must be in this area, and the description the villagers gave sounded exactly like her," Lady Ross said, refusing to give way. "I fear the worst."

The marquess took a deep breath. "You have provided no proof that Robin has behaved badly, or even that he and your niece are acquainted. While I will make allowances for your concern, I advise you not to make baseless charges against my brother. Good day, Lady Ross. My footman will show you out." He sat down again and made a show of studying his correspondence.

His visitor should have accepted her dismissal and

left. Instead, the footman yelped with dismay and the marquess caught a glimpse of swift movement from the corner of his eye. He raised his head just in time to see Lady Ross's parasol slicing through the air. Before he could move, it smashed down on the desk in front of him, missing his face by inches and scattering papers across the carpet.

As he gaped in stunned disbelief, she snapped, "Don't think you can dismiss me like one of your servants, Wolverton. I know your reputation. Instead of attending Parliament, you sit out here in Yorkshire like a toad, ignoring your responsibilities. With you as an example, it's hardly surprising that your brother became a wastrel." Her full lips curled into a sneer. "Though perhaps it's just as well that you don't take advantage of your seat in the House of Lords. No doubt your views would make Attila the Hun look compassionate."

Giles had never been rude to a female in his life, but a few minutes with Lady Ross had changed that. He leaped to his feet and leaned toward her, bracing his fists on the desk. "I attend the Lords whenever a vital issue is being debated, but most of my responsibilities are here. There is no better fertilizer for the land than the weight of the owner's foot, and managing my property is a better use of my time than playing faro and assassinating reputations in London."

Realizing belatedly how immature his behavior was, he said in a more moderate tone, "Not that it's any of your business."

The parasol jerked, and for an instant he thought she was going to swing it like a cricket bat.

Instead, she said through gritted teeth, "I'm sorry. Your properties are known as models of progressive land management. I should not have spoken so." Looking as if the apology had half killed her, she went on, "No doubt your brother developed his beastly vices without any help from you."

Unmollified, Giles said, "I suggest that you leave before your unfounded charges make me forget that I am a gentleman. I'm sorry your niece is missing, but I can do nothing to help you."

"I was a fool to expect any cooperation," Lady Ross said with disgust. "Men of our order will ruin a girl as casually as they will discard a cravat. I came here hoping that Lord Robert had found my niece in need of protection and behaved as a gentleman by restoring her to her family. Instead he has taken her away against her will, and you are covering for his crime. However, Maxima is not without family, and I swear that if Lord Robert has injured her or her reputation, he will pay for it."

Appalled realization dawned on the marquess. "So *that* is what this is about! Your niece set out to seduce Lord Robert. Then you came here crying that she is an injured innocent and justice must be done, hoping that I will force my brother to marry her. Well, it won't work, madam, not on my brother and not on me. If he went off with her, it was because she was willing."

He leaned forward, his broad shoulders taut with anger. "Mark me well, Lady Ross. I personally guarantee that my brother will never marry a round-heeled wench who is trying to entrap him."

If Lady Ross's parasol has been a sword, there would have been murder done. Gray eyes flashing, she said furiously, "Believe me, I have no intention of forcing the girl into marriage with a degenerate wastrel, and I will stand up to the head of my family or anyone else who might try to coerce her. What I *do* intend is to see your brother in Newgate. Remember, Wolverton, kidnapping is a capital offense. Don't think you can buy his freedom with your influence. I am not without influence of my own. If a crime has been committed, I intend to see Lord Robert prosecuted to the fullest extent of the law."

She spun on her heel and marched toward the door, her parasol clenched in her fist like a club. "If your benighted brother returns here, you would be wise to advise him to leave England, instantly and forever."

As Lady Ross reached the door, the marquess belatedly remembered who she was: a bluestocking reformer who had the ear of some of the most prominent politicians of both parties. Giles had heard of her for years and vaguely assumed that she was much older. Instead, the celebrated firebrand reformer was several years younger than himself, probably not much past thirty.

Bloody hell, she might indeed have the influence to cause the Andreville family considerable grief even if Robin had done nothing illegal. After swearing under his breath, Giles said, "Lady Ross, please hold a moment."

She turned and said ominously, "Yes?"

Giles crossed the room to his visitor, saying in his most conciliatory tone, "We should not have let our tempers run away with us. Naturally you are concerned for your niece, but truly, I think you are making a mistake. What matters is locating the girl, and I doubt you will find her with my brother. While there are certainly men whose behavior toward females is unconscionable, Robin is not one of them."

Her auburn brows arched. "Are you absolutely sure of that?"

Giles started to say that he was, but hesitated. "How much in life can one be absolutely sure of?"

"That is not a convincing endorsement for Lord Robert's honor," she said dryly.

"I have no doubts at all about my brother's honor." Incurably honest, Giles found himself adding, "However, some of his actions might be unconventional."

Her lip curled. "The more you speak of his honor, the more I want to count my spoons."

"I would trust him as I trust myself."

For a moment Lady Ross's face softened and Giles thought he might be persuading her. Then the stubborn set came back to her jaw. "You have the reputation of a just man, and your loyalty to your brother is commendable. Unfortunately, men can be honorable with each other, yet think nothing of mistreating women. If

Lord Robert has been away from England for so many years, do you really know what he is capable of?"

The blasted woman was right. Emotionally Giles believed in his brother, yet he was uneasily aware that Robin could not have survived a dozen years of spying in the heart of Napoleon's empire without a capacity for ruthlessness. "Robin has been shaped by forces different than the English beau monde, but I am sure he would never injure an innocent."

Lady Ross shrugged and turned away. "We shall see. I will not stop searching until I find my niece. And if your brother has harmed her, may God help him."

Then she was gone. Giles stared at the closed door for a long moment, feeling as if the church steeple had fallen on him. No one had ever made him so angry in his life, but even so, he was not proud of the way he had spoken to Lady Ross.

He turned back to the room, shaking his head. To his secretary, who had been watching in horrified fascination, he said, "What did you think of all that, Charles?"

The other man hesitated, then said tactfully, "I think that I would not like to have Lady Ross angry with me."

"And that if Robin is dallying with the lady's niece, he may find himself up to his chin in boiling water?"

Charles smiled ruefully. "I'm afraid so, my lord."

The marquess settled deep in his leather-upholstered chair and considered. Preposterous though the idea seemed, the missing Maxima must be traveling to London by foot. Otherwise, Lady Ross wouldn't be so sure that her niece was in southern Yorkshire a week after leaving Durham.

It was hard to imagine a gently bred female undertaking such a journey; the chit must be desperate, depraved, or mad. Or perhaps it was merely that she was an American.

On the day he disappeared, Robin had planned to visit the west woods. The road that cut through the area might have been chosen by someone heading south from Durham. Robin had been emotionally drifting; if he had encountered an attractive, madcap girl, he might have decided on impulse to go with her. While Robin was no rake, he was also no saint, and he couldn't know the potential for scandal in taking up with this particular female.

Robin would have had little or no money on him. Maxima Collins must not have any funds, either, or she would have taken a coach to London. Giles thought that a romantic interlude without a feather to fly with sounded deucedly uncomfortable, but of course he was boringly conservative.

Could Robin have decided to escort the girl to London? Giles seized on the thought with relief; it was exactly the sort of quixotic thing his brother might do. However, if the wench was twenty-five and willing, they might soon be on terms far more intimate than the girl's aunt would approve of.

Lady Ross seemed more agitated than the situation warranted. Perhaps there was more to the story than she was admitting. Then again, maybe she was merely a termagant who enjoyed thundering about like a March storm.

Remembering the woman's rage at the suggestion, he acquitted her of conspiring with her niece to entrap Robin, but that didn't mean the girl herself was innocent of such intentions. Between his fortune and his personal attractions, Robin was a very good catch indeed. Possibly the wench had recognized that fact and decided to take advantage of the situation.

The marquess frowned as he reviewed his thoughts. The facts were that Robin had gone missing, and so had Miss Collins, and they had tentatively been identified as being together. The assumption was that they were traveling south toward London. If trouble befell them on the road, Robin would be handicapped by lack of money and identification.

Lady Ross was pursuing the fugitives, breathing fire and brimstone. If she found them, the results would be damned unpleasant. A scandal would injure the girl far more than Robin, but a vengeful Lady Ross might be too angry to care.

Robin might be indifferent to the prospect of scandal; the marquess, however, was not. Though he would face down the gossips if necessary, it would be far better to keep the affair private if at all possible. Which meant that he must go after the runaways himself. With luck, he would find them before Lady Ross, in time to head off disaster.

If the Sheltered Innocent insisted that only marriage would save her from ruin—well, the marquess would have something to say about that. Quite apart from Robin's personal happiness, his brother's wife would likely be the mother of a future Marquess of Wolverton, and Giles would not permit the line to become tainted with the blood of a vulgar, scheming hussy.

Gloomily he thought about how much he hated travel. Long hours in a jolting carriage, damp sheets, barely edible meals. And he didn't even have a proper valet at the moment since his previous one had just left and not yet been replaced.

In addition to the routine discomforts, he was going to feel like a damned fool chasing across the countryside after an American doxy, a retired spy, and a fire-breathing reformer.

As he considered the prospect, the Marquess of Wolverton realized that he was smiling.

Chapter 6

Maxie adjusted her hat against the sun, using the gesture as an excuse to slant a covert glance at her companion. Once again she was caught in one of those strange, breathless moments that occurred frequently when she looked at Robin. He was too beautiful, too enigmatic, to be real.

Not that he was hard to talk to. On the contrary, he was the only man she had ever met who was as easy to converse with as her father had been. When Robin tired of silence, witty words flowed from him like a burbling brook. He had drawn her into conversations about the passing scene, the fine weather, the late regrettable war between their countries.

Yet he never said a single blessed thing about himself that Maxie felt sure she could believe. Lord, she still didn't know what his real name was. Never again would she assume that mysterious meant silent.

Stranger yet was the fact that he was behaving as a perfect gentleman—so perfect that she was beginning to wonder what was wrong with her. Not that she wanted to be assaulted, but at least that was behavior she could understand.

Instead, she had a charming companion who was utterly incomprehensible. It was all quite unsettling, and far too easy to forget that in spite of his charm, Robin was basically an unreliable rogue.

As the road wound into a small grove of trees, Robin broke the silence by asking, "Did I tell you about the time I worked in a circus in Austria?"

She smiled, wondering what he would come up with

this time. "Not yet. Your repertory of entertaining and wholly unbelievable tales seems to be limitless. Tell me about the circus. No doubt you were the star of the high wire act."

"Not at all," he said affably. "Horses are much easier, so I confined myself to daredevil riding tricks. My Cossack routine was much admired."

"Robin, do you ever tell the truth?"

He gave her an offended glance. "Any fool can tell the truth. It takes real talent to be a good liar."

She was laughing when two horsemen burst from the underbrush in a clamor of shouts and thundering hooves. The riders separated, one jolting to a halt in front of them and the other behind, the horses kicking up clouds of gritty dust. Both wore half masks and held pistols in their hands.

The leader bellowed, "Stand and deliver!" He was wiry and blond, with ferretlike eyes gleaming behind the mask.

Maxie's heart spasmed with fear. Though she was willing to face the perils of the road, she had not truly expected armed highwaymen. These two looked nervous and very, very dangerous.

Beside her, Robin raised his hands in the air. "You must be right hard up to rob folks like us," he said calmly, his accent that of a laborer. "We've got naught worth stealing. You'd do better over on the Great North Road, with the fancy carriages."

"Too damned much traffic there," the man behind grumbled. Dark-haired and beefy in build, he kept his pistol trained on Robin's chest. "Easy to get killed."

"Times are hard," the blond man said. "You might not have much, but a couple of shillings are better than nothing. Jem, see what they got."

Jem dismounted and searched Robin's pockets, where he found a handful of coins. After pawing through the knapsack, he said irritably, "He weren't lyin' about not having much."

The blond man gestured with his pistol. "Do the lad.

He might be carrying valuables because he seems less likely."

Maxie stood rigid while Jem searched her, praying that he would not feel the unboyish curves concealed by her loose clothing. Though she had mentally accepted the possibility of rape, such detachment was impossible when a criminal was running rough hands over her body and breathing boozy breath into her face.

Luckily, the binding on her breasts prevented him from realizing the sex of his victim. He didn't find the knife in her boot, either. However, he quickly located her inner coat pockets. He pulled out her harmonica. "What's this, Ned?"

"Some kind of mouth organ," Ned replied. "Probably good for a shilling or two."

Maxie bit her tongue against her automatic protest. At least he hadn't found the earrings that were in the same pocket.

It was harder when Jem found her father's watch. He whistled when he pulled it out. "You was right, the lad has the valuables. This is gold, and worth a pretty penny."

"Give it to me." After inspecting it, Ned gave a nod of satisfaction and tucked it inside his coat. "Now check the boy's neck. He's wearing a silver chain."

As Maxie cringed back, Jem stuck a dirty finger under the chain and fished out her cross. "Well, I'll be damned, this is our lucky day." He flicked open the latch and pulled the chain from her neck, then dropped the cross into his pocket.

"No!" she pleaded. "Don't take that. It was my mother's—the only thing I have of hers."

"Too bad," Jem said with a nasty laugh as he started to dig through her knapsack.

Blind with rage, she was about to go for her knife when Robin grabbed her elbow. Under his breath, he said sharply, "It's not worth your life."

When she gave him a wild glance, he said, "Think,

dammit! Would your mother want you to die for a piece of metal?"

His words cleared her mind. She glanced up and saw that the barrel of Ned's gun was trained on her.

He grinned wolfishly. "Take one step toward Jem and you're dead, boyo." He thumbed the hammer of his pistol. "Maybe I'll shoot you both anyhow, before you can report us to a magistrate."

Maxie felt the tensing of Robin's hand on her arm, but his voice was easy when he said, "Leave two corpses on the road, and they'll look for you right hard. Easier to leave us alive. We won't be able to get to a town fast enough to cause you trouble."

With a hint of regret, Ned said, "I s'pose you're right."

Maxie let out a sigh of relief. Seeing that she was in control of herself, Robin released her elbow.

Jem patted his pocket. "This is a damned good haul. We'll have to rob walkers more regular-like."

Ned asked, "Jem, have you got everything worth getting?"

"What about this bloke's coat? It'd fit you pretty good."

Ned inspected Robin's worn but well-cut blue coat. "You're right. he must've bought it used, 'cause no village tailor made that. That fellow Brummel wouldn't be ashamed of one like it." He gestured with his pistol. "Take it off."

Robin looked stubborn. "Stealing clothes off a man's back is pretty low. If you want my coat, you'll have to take it."

Maxie gasped. "Show some sense, Robin!"

"If they shoot me, the holes and blood will ruin it," he said calmly.

Conceding the point, Ned ordered, "Take it off him."

Jem grinned and rubbed his right fist against his left palm while he savored the prospect. Then, with sudden savagery, he slammed a massive fist into Robin's belly, following it with another blow to the chest. Robin gasped with pain and bent forward, falling against his assailant.

With a disgusted sound, Jem shoved him away, then wrenched off the coat. Robin submitted meekly, his face white and his shoulders heaving as he fought for breath. Maxie wanted to hit him herself for his stupid obstinacy.

Jem tossed the coat up to his partner. Ned nodded with pleasure and waved his gun toward the road. "You two get moving while I'm feeling merciful."

Maxie grabbed the knapsacks from the dusty road, then took Robin's shirt-sleeved arm and towed him down the road. He was still bent over and gulping for air.

She hissed, "Idiot! How could you cause trouble over a coat? At least my mother's cross meant something."

They were almost around the next curve when a shot cracked through the air and dust spurted two feet away from Robin. From the roar of laughter that came from the highwaymen, she guessed that the shot was intended to harass rather kill, but she wasted no time in hauling her companion out of view.

As soon as they rounded the bend, Robin straightened up, all traces of injury gone. "Down this lane. We have to disappear before they realize what happened," he said in a clipped voice as he took his knapsack from Maxie.

She glared at him. "What the devil are you babbling about?"

He grinned and opened his hands. In the left was her mother's cross and a wad of money, in the right her harmonica.

She gaped at the objects. "How did you get these back?"

"Picked his pockets, of course." He gave her the cross and harmonica and dumped the money into his knapsack. "Come on, there's no time to waste." He entered the lane at a fast jog.

"Picked his pockets?" After a moment of astonishment, she stashed her possessions inside her coat and darted after him. "Robin, you're disgraceful!"

He gave her a laughing glance. "God will forgive me—that's his business." His expression sobered. "Sorry I didn't get the watch, but I couldn't think of a good way to get close to Ned."

Good heavens, he had deliberately taken those blows in order to retrieve her cross. And she had thought him stupid! As a pickpocket, he was first-class. She had been standing right there and seen nothing.

Shoving aside thoughts of where he had learned such appalling skill, she said, "Never mind. Letting yourself get beaten goes well beyond the call of duty."

As Robin climbed onto a stile that crossed over a fence, he said, "Jem didn't hit me as hard as he thought he did."

Maxie followed him over the stile and dropped lightly to the ground. "What do you mean?"

"Just as there are ways of hitting, there are ways of being hit," he said vaguely.

"It still must have hurt. Thank you for taking the risk. The cross means a great deal to me." She made a sound halfway between amusement and exasperation. "You have the instincts of a gentleman—one who is seriously warped."

His mouth twisted. "There are many who would agree with you."

She regretted the remark, but before she could apologize, Robin went on, "A good thing this area is a maze of fields and woods—it should be easy to disappear. I think we should swing north. If they come after us, they'll probably assume that we continued south, since that was the way we were heading."

A shout of fury sounded from the direction of the road. Maxie made a face. "Time to stop talking and start running."

For the next two hours, they snaked their way through the quiet countryside at a punishing pace, alternately jogging and walking. The sun was dipping toward the western horizon when they crested a hill and found themselves looking down on a substantial road. Two carts, a man on a donkey, and a dozen ambling cows were within view, which meant this route was busier and safer than the quiet tracks they had been following.

They both halted. Every muscle in Maxie's body was trembling with exhaustion. She lowered her knapsack to the ground and wrapped her left arm around Robin's waist for support. When his arm circled her shoulders, it occurred to her that her gesture had been rather forward. Yet it felt natural, for sharing danger had created camaraderie.

After a few blissful moments of relaxation, she panted, "Do you think we're safe now?"

"I doubt they could have tracked us this far," Robin replied, his chest heaving. "They probably decided to save their efforts for the next travelers."

She frowned. "We should tell the authorities."

"Tell them what? They have to know that there are highwaymen in the district. By the time we could lay information, Jem and Ned will be long gone." He chuckled. "I think we came away with almost ten pounds. If not for the watch, I'd say that we got the best of the encounter."

Maxie began to laugh, letting her head fall against Robin's shoulder. "Can you imagine the expression on Jem's face when he found his pockets empty? You made such a fool of him!"

"The Creator beat me to it."

She laughed even harder. He joined her, his arm tightening around her shoulders as they surrendered to the uninhibited hilarity of relief.

She raised her head to speak at the same moment Robin looked down. His shirt had fallen open at the throat to expose several inches of naked chest, and his hair clung to his forehead in damp glittering tendrils. He was vital and beautiful, and she wanted him as she had never wanted a man before.

Trying to distance herself, she said feebly, "Your sense of humor is blasphemous."

"Blasphemy is one of my specialties." He raised his free hand and brushed her lips with feather-light fingers. She touched them with the tip of her tongue. The salty taste made him seem sharply real, no longer enigmatic.

He exhaled roughly and curved his hand around the back of her head, tilting it up for his kiss. His lips were warm, his tongue a delicate tease. As naturally as breathing, she opened her mouth. The kiss deepened and desire coiled deep within, drawing the strength from her limbs. Her eyes drifted shut and she stroked the back of his neck, the silky strands of hair twining around her fingertips.

He murmured her name, the sound coming from deep in his throat. His right hand slid down her back, warming her spine and pressing her close. Her hands opened and closed on his ribs, mussing his linen shirt. She had thought him cool, but there was nothing cool about his mouth, or his hard, demanding body.

She stood on her toes and locked both arms around his neck. Her head tilted back, her hat falling to the ground. The air was chilly on her unprotected scalp and her heated skin, which seemed scarcely able to contain the thunder of her blood. His hand slid up under her coat, kneading the curve of her hip.

A whickering horse brought her back to her senses. With a rush of disbelief, she realized that she was kissing a *pickpocket*—a rogue who probably didn't even remember what his real name was. And she wasn't simply kissing him, but eating him up like the first piece of spring maple sugar after a long, cold winter.

Her eyes snapped open, and she took a step backward, pushing against his upper arms as she gasped for breath. Their gazes met, and in his eyes she saw the shadows she had glimpsed once or twice before.

Sensing danger, she instinctively retreated to safer ground. "You'll look conspicuous without a coat. How far do you think it will be to a town where you can find another?"

He took a deep breath, and his expression smoothed

out. "I think this road must lead to Rotherham," he said in his usual voice. "There will be a used clothing shop there, if not before."

She bent over for her knapsack and hat, giving the latter a hard tug so that her eyes were in shadow. "Being robbed and having to go north again has cost us easily half a day."

Robin lifted his pack. "It could have cost us a lot more."

She thought of that kiss, and knew that it had. No matter how energetically they both pretended that it hadn't occurred, matters had changed between them, and not for the better.

As they descended the hill toward the road, she wondered if she dared to continue their journey together.

Desdemona gazed out the carriage window without enthusiasm. She was becoming heartily sick of scenery, but her pursuit should soon be over. At the last village, she had been given exact descriptions of Maxima and her disreputable companion. They couldn't be more than a couple of hours ahead. If they stayed on this road, she would overtake them by the end of the afternoon. A good thing they didn't know that they were being pursued.

She hoped Lord Robert wouldn't turn ugly when Desdemona removed Maxima from his clutches. Not that it mattered; her driver and guard were former soldiers, and they could deal with a wastrel who had never done a bit of honest work in his life.

Desdemona tried not to consider the possibility that Maxima might *want* to stay in the fellow's clutches. She really couldn't kidnap her niece, even for her own good. But at least if Desdemona had to abandon Maxima to her fate, she would have the satisfaction of knowing the girl was acting of her own free will.

Her musings were interrupted by a drumming of hooves and a hoarse shout of "Stand and deliver!"

Her maid, Sally, who had been dozing in a corner, awoke with a shriek. Desdemona barked, "Get down!"

Then she dived for one of the pistols that were essential equipment in a traveling carriage. A shot was fired and the coach jolted to a stop, the horses neighing frantically.

Her fingers trembled as she loaded and cocked the gun. But whatever happened, she would be ready.

The Marquess of Wolverton lounged drowsily against the comfortable seat of his coach. At least this ridiculous pursuit was taking place during good weather and the roads were in tolerable shape. He yawned, automatically covering his mouth even though he was alone, Charles having been left at Wolverhampton to attend to routine business.

Giles wasn't sure if he was tracing the runaways accurately, but he was definitely close behind Lady Ross. Her yellow-trimmed carriage was much easier to follow than a couple of dusty pedestrians. He wondered how she would react if and when she discovered that he had joined the chase. He hoped there wouldn't be any sharp objects near to hand when that happened.

He was on the verge of falling asleep when a ragged volley of gunshots shattered the silence. Instantly alert, he opened a window and called to his driver, "Can you see what is happening?"

"There appears to be an attempted robbery ahead, my lord," his driver called. "I assume you do not wish to turn around and avoid the fray?"

"You assume rightly. Prepare to intervene if necessary." Giles drew a carriage pistol from its holster. As he loaded it, he suddenly wondered if the victim might be Lady Ross. Surely not. Yet she was not far ahead of him, and a carriage such as hers was a prime target. Good God, she would probably start scolding the highwaymen and get shot for her pains.

His carriage swung around a bend, then lurched to a wild halt to avoid crashing into a vehicle angled across the road. Giles threw open his door and leaped to the ground. A moment later he was joined by his guard, who carried a carbine in his hands. Ahead of them, a riderless horse bolted into the woods.

It was indeed the yellow-trimmed coach, but their assistance was not required. Lady Ross stood staring at a sprawling body while her guard examined another body farther away. The metallic scent of blood was in the air, and both coachmen had to struggle to keep the nervous horses under control.

Giles was relieved to find Lady Ross safe. It would be a great waste for such a splendid virago to die so pointlessly.

She looked up and recognized him. Despite the hostility of their first encounter, she seemed glad to see a familiar face.

He lowered his pistol and walked toward her, saying, "Are you and your people all right?"

She nodded and tried to reply, but no words emerged. After swallowing hard, she said, "The highwaymen must not have been expecting much resistance. A pair of amateurs." She raised her hand to brush at her bonnet, then stopped and stared at the pistol in her hand.

"Good God," Giles exclaimed. "Did you shoot them yourself?"

"Luckily it didn't come to that. My men are veterans of the Peninsula." Her smile was a little crooked. "They were having trouble finding work after being invalided out of the army. I thought I was doing them a favor by hiring them. I didn't expect my good deed to be rewarded so dramatically."

"It's a good argument for charity." He looked over at the man who lay by the carriage. "Are both robbers dead?"

"I believe so."

As Giles studied the fallen highwayman, his heart gave an odd lurch. The hair was very blond, a little longer than average. No, it couldn't possibly be . . . He stared, pulse pounding. "That coat—" he said tightly. "It's like the one Robin was wearing the day he disap-

peared. And the hair is rather like his." He began strid-
ing toward the body.

Desdemona sucked her breath in. Surely the dead
man couldn't be Lord Robert. Yet it was not unknown
for wild young gentlemen to play at being highwaymen, and the robbers hadn't seemed very skilled at
their trade. She gave a horrified glance to the other
corpse, but it could not possibly be Maxima.

That didn't mean the blond man wasn't Lord Robert.
The idea that the rogue might have committed such a
vicious, irresponsible act enraged her. He couldn't be
anything like his brother.

The marquess knelt beside the dead highwayman
and turned the body for closer examination. Then he
exhaled and dropped his head, covering his face with
one hand.

Desdemona's anger vanished, replaced by compassion. She had also looked into that shattered, bloody
face herself, and knew it would figure in future nightmares.

She joined the marquess and put a gentle hand on
his shoulder. "I'm sorry, Wolverton. It's your brother?"

"No." He raised his head, visibly struggling for
composure. "But for a moment I thought it might be. I
was . . . relieved to learn I was wrong."

So the marquess defended his brother not only out of
family loyalty, but love. She wondered what the wayward Lord Robert had done to deserve it. "You believed your brother capable of highway robbery?"

Wolverton made an impatient gesture. "Of course
not. The idea was absurd." He touched the highwayman's sleeve. "But I'm willing to wager that this coat
is Robin's. You can see from the cut that it's French,
not British. I wonder how the devil this fellow came to
be wearing it."

"Perhaps your brother sold it and this villain bought
it?"

"I'm not sure I believe in that much coincidence."
Expression grim, the marquess began searching the
dead man's pockets. He found several coins, a folding

pocketknife, and a gold watch, but nothing that could identify the highwayman.

Desdemona frowned. "Let me see that watch." When the marquess passed it to her, she snapped open the case with a fingernail. Inside the lid was engraved "Maximus Benedict Collins." Silently she showed it to the marquess.

He whistled softly. "That belonged to your brother?"

She nodded. "It was a gift on his eighteenth birthday. I believe. When he died, it must have gone to Maxima." She gave her companion a worried look. "Obviously the highwaymen encountered your brother and my niece. You don't suppose that that . . . they might have robbed and killed them?"

The marquess's slate-blue eyes darkened to near-black as he got to his feet. "I doubt it. There would have been no need to kill two unarmed people. Also, Robin and your niece were seen alive and well in the last village. Any murderous assault would have had to have taken place within the last few miles, and I saw no signs of that. There was probably a robbery, and the coat and watch were part of the loot."

Her hand curled over her late brother's watch. "Vicious men don't need a reason, and shooting two people and hiding the bodies wouldn't leave many traces."

The marquess scowled. He knew that as well as she, and would rather the words hadn't been spoken aloud. "Possible, but unlikely. Robin is good at getting out of trouble. I can't believe that he would be so easily murdered, or that he would fail to protect a young woman in his charge."

"So Lord Robert has had vast experience at getting out of trouble. Honorable men don't need such skills," Desdemona said acerbically. "Money and influence have saved many a loose fish from hot water, but they won't save your brother this time."

The marquess must have been equally on edge, because he retorted, "If your trollop of a niece makes it safely to London, it will be because of my brother's protection, since she is apparently as deficient in sense as she is in morals. What kind of gently bred girl would even consider walking the length of England? Though at least she had the sense to take up with a man who could help her get there."

"She didn't 'take up' with him; she's being forced!" Desdemona snapped back. "You must be concerned about Lord Robert's behavior, or you wouldn't be following me."

"It's you who concern me, not my brother," the marquess said, his voice rising. "After you stormed out of Wolverhampton, I decided that I must try to protect him from the most pigheaded, vindictive female I've ever met in my life. It's obvious that you've already decided what happened, without a shred of real evidence."

"Who are you calling a pigheaded, vindictive female?" Desdemona's hand jerked upward as she fought an instinctive desire to box Wolverton's ears.

She had forgotten the pistol. As her fingers clenched, the gun discharged with shattering loudness, the bullet blazing past Wolverton. One of the drivers shouted, and both guards dropped what they were doing and hastened toward her.

"Jesus Christ!" Ashen-faced, the marquess instinctively dodged to one side. "Are you *insane*?"

She dropped the pistol and her reticule and pressed her hands to her temples, her whole body shaking violently. "I d-didn't mean to do that," she gasped, feeling on the verge of fainting. "I forgot I was holding a gun." She looked down to where the pistol lay in the dust, acrid smoke curling from the barrel. "I swear before God, it was an accident."

Wolverton waved off the guards, then took her arm and helped her to her carriage. She thought he was going to thrash her, but instead he sat her on the top step of the carriage and pushed her head between her knees. Speaking past her, he asked, "Does Lady Ross carry any brandy?"

Her maid answered in the affirmative. A minute

later, Wolverton pressed the flask into her hand. "Drink this."

She raised her head, took a gulp, and choked, but her head cleared. Looking directly into his face, she said painfully, "I have a beastly temper, and too often I say things I regret, but I would never, ever try to hurt someone."

"I believe you," he said soothingly. "If you'd actually intended to shoot me, I'd be lying bleeding in the dust."

She shuddered at the image. "Please don't say that."

"Sorry." He took the flask and downed a goodly swig before handing it back. "We're both upset, and understandably so. But truly, I'm sure that our runaways are all right."

She smiled wanly. "I hope you're right. I suppose I must carry the bodies of the robbers to the next town and report the incident to a magistrate. With luck, I'll find Maxima and Lord Robert between here and there. They may have had enough of adventures if they've just been robbed of everything of value."

"Perhaps." Wolverton straightened. "It's also possible that they might have cut across country to a busier road, so I'm going to look for them on a parallel route."

She nodded, knowing that she and the marquess were not allies, even if they were being civil for the moment. "If you locate them, could you send a messenger to find me? So that I'll know that Maxima is all right."

"Very well. I'd appreciate it if you did the same."

"Of course." She got to her feet. "And ... thank you, Wolverton. For being willing to help another traveler who might be in trouble, and for being so tolerant of what could have been a fatal mistake on my part."

He smiled, and she realized that he was really very handsome when she wasn't driving him berserk.

"Lady Ross, my life has become infinitely more ex-

citing since meeting you." He turned and walked back
to his carriage, collecting his servants with a glance.

She watched him leave with mixed feelings. His
search complicated her own. Yet she didn't mind the
thought that she might see him again.

Chapter 7

Half an hour after Robin and Maxie started walking south on Rotherham road, a taciturn farmer offered them a ride in his wagon. Robin accepted for both of them, since they had agreed that the less Maxie spoke, the better. Ignoring Robin's hand, she scrambled into the wagon and burrowed into the crevice between two sacks of seed corn. Then she pulled her hat over her face and gave an excellent imitation of sleep.

Robin frowned as he settled back, pillowing his head on his knapsack. Maxie hadn't looked him in the eye since they had kissed. He didn't blame her for being unnerved; he was, too. What had started as an impulsive, affectionate embrace had turned out to be searing. Emotions that had been numb so long that he had forgotten their names were smoldering into life, and it felt damned uncomfortable.

How long had it been since he had truly desired anything or anyone? Too long.

He glanced over at his companion. Poor Maxie; no female so determined and practical would approve of becoming involved with a vagabond. Nonetheless, she had certainly participated enthusiastically in that kiss. Now she was regretting it. He doubted that she was the sort to waste time feeling guilty. More likely she was afraid that he would press his attentions on her. He would have to convince her of the nobility of his nature.

He smiled wryly at the thought. Noble he was not, but his self-interest forbade any attempts to seduce his companion. Trying to bed her would surely destroy the companionship that was making him happier than he had felt in a long, long time.

Not that he wasn't lusting after her. She had fascinated him from the start, and that kiss had made him obsessively aware of everything about her. The rhythm of her breathing, the shapely legs that looked so good in trousers, her small brown hands, as strong as they were graceful. He was so conscious of her as an alluring female that it was hard to remember that the world saw her as a boy.

But it was her spirit that drew him. Her bright clarity made him feel younger. Less tarnished. He tried not to think what would happen when their journey ended. Maxie obviously had some goal in mind, and it didn't include him. But he was going to be very reluctant to see the last of her.

Yet what could he offer her? She thought him a worthless vagabond, and he preferred to leave it at that since his real past was far uglier than what she believed. As an American, she would not be overimpressed with the aristocratic birth and fortune that meant so much to English girls. Rather the contrary, he suspected.

It was better that she think him hopelessly ineligible. Her low opinion would prevent her from doing anything foolish if his willpower weakened and he tried to kiss her again.

He found himself watching the slow rise and fall of her chest. What would she look like if her breasts weren't bound?

Damnation! He forced himself to look away when he realized how his body was responding to his speculations. While it was a pleasure to feel desire again, if he weren't careful it would increase to the point of pain.

With a sigh, he settled back on the seed sacks and started considering ways to mend bridges with his wary companion.

The next village had a shop where they were able to buy a decent coat and hat for Robin. After treating themselves to a hot meal in the village tavern, they headed south again.

Shortly before sunset, Robin pointed toward a small barn across a field. "Shall we shelter there for the night? It looks suitably isolated."

"Fine." Maxie turned and headed across the field, wondering uncomfortably what would come next. Though Robin had been his usual easygoing self, she could not forget that unnerving kiss, nor the shameless way she had responded.

The barn proved to be quite comfortable, with few drafts and a stack of sweet-scented hay. As they examined the place, Robin said, "I'm considering writing a guide for impoverished travelers, rating the relative merits of various barns and hedges. Do you think there would be a market for it?"

She set her knapsack down by the far wall, as far as possible from where Robin had placed his possessions. "Those who would need such a guide could not afford it."

"Mmm, I knew there would be a catch. There goes another plan to make my fortune."

She almost smiled before she remembered that she was trying to look forbidding so he wouldn't take her earlier weakness as an invitation. Moving past him, she said, "I'll gather the wood."

Robin went to bring water from a nearby stream while she collected an armload of dry kindling that would burn with a minimum of smoke. Then she built a small fire in a gravelly, protected spot not far from the barn.

As dusk darkened to night. Robin sat by the fire a few fee from her and began to peel the bark from a short stick he had found. In a conversational tone, he said, "You needn't think I'm going to try to ravish you, Maxima."

Her head shot up, and she stared at him.

"It won't do to pretend that we didn't kiss," he continued. "It happened. I enjoyed it. You seemed to also. That doesn't mean that I regard you as prey."

"You're very blunt," she said uncomfortably.

"Directness is not my specialty, as it is yours, but I am not incapable of it." With his pocketknife, he began to whittle a rounded end on the stick. "I decided to speak up since I don't want to walk the rest of the way to London with you acting like a stunned rabbit."

Outraged, she said, "A *rabbit*?"

He grinned. "I knew that would engage your attention. You're worrying too much about that kiss. It was an accident that occurred because we were relieved and happy."

She sat back on her heels, knowing that she must be as honest as he. "Perhaps it was an accident, but ever since we met, I've sensed that ... that you find me attractive."

His brows rose expressively. "Of course I do. What man wouldn't? You are very beautiful."

"I wasn't fishing for compliments," she said, embarrassed.

"I know. You've probably had them hurled at you so often that you find the whole subject tedious."

"What I've usually heard is that I look beddable, which is not the same thing as beautiful," she said dryly.

"No, it isn't," he agreed. "But you are both. Small wonder that you've learned to mistrust male attentions." With the edge of his blade, he began to smooth the surface of the knob he had carved. "Perhap it's my imagination, but I've had the feeling that you find me somewhat attractive also."

Her face colored. She had been trying to conceal that fact. Deciding to toss his words back at him, she said lightly, "What woman wouldn't? You are very beautiful."

Instead of being disconcerted, he chuckled, "I heard that often as a child, and hated it. I longed for black hair, saber scars, and a pirate eye patch."

"Be grateful that you looked angelic," she advised. "It probably saved you from any number of well-deserved beatings."

"Not enough." He blew some wood chips away. "To return to the main subject, attraction is perfectly normal between healthy adults." He glanced up, his eyes piercingly blue. "But not all attraction is meant to be acted upon. Think of our mutual awareness as merely a bit of spice to enrich our companionship."

She studied his face. He was so reasonable. Yet she kept thinking of how little she knew about him.

"You still look doubtful. Let me conduct a small demonstration." He set down his knife and stick and slid sideways around the fire until he was sitting next to her.

She was about to retreat when she made the mistake of looking up and seeing the lazy sensuality in his eyes. She froze, as wide-eyed and helpless as the rabbit he had called her.

He drew her into his arms and bent his head. She shivered from sheer nerves when his lips touched hers, but the kiss was light and sweet. His mouth moved tenderly against hers, warm and firm, while his hands slowly stroked her back.

Her tension began melting away. Before it melted too far, she turned her head and released a soft sigh against his throat. "That was nice, but what were you demonstrating?"

"That a kiss needn't be alarming." He traced the curve of her ear with his tongue, and bright sensations spiraled through her veins.

"Then you're successful," she said a little breathlessly. "I'm not alarmed—yet."

He chuckled and sat back a little. "You look very fine in breeches"—he brushed her knee with his fingertips—"but someday I would like to see you in silk."

She spread her palms on his chest, feeling the taut muscles beneath the linen. "Speaking of clothing, did you know that you manage to make the nondescript coat you bought today look almost as damn-your-eyes elegant as the one that was stolen?"

"It's a gift," he said modestly. "A friend once said that I was every other inch a gentleman."

As she laughed, he pulled a pin from her hair. A heavy coil dropped to her shoulder and tumbled down her back. She looked into his eyes, and her laughter died. His gaze was pure flame, yet controlled, not menacing.

Pin by pin, he released her hair, the falling locks caressing her breasts and shoulders. Then he drew her head against his shoulder and combed the thick tresses with his fingertips, spreading her hair in a mantle over her shoulders. "Black silk," he murmured. "The most obvious of metaphors, yet I can think of none better."

He felt warm. Strong. Even safe, though her common sense knew that was an illusion. She closed her eyes, enjoying the yearning that curled through her body. Clever of him to make this demonstration. He was revealing his desire and evoking hers, while at the same time proving that passion need not blaze out of control. They were adults; they could be together without mating like mink.

She should move away, but was reluctant to do so. It was seductively pleasant not to be alone.

As soon as the words formed in her mind, she remembered why she should be wary of Robin. They were merely traveling companions on a journey that would soon end. She must not become too fond of him.

"You've made your point." She straightened and moved away. "I shall stop behaving like a stunned bunny."

Robin moved back to his side of the fire. His chest was rising and falling more quickly than usual, but his tone was teasing. "If you become alarmed in the future, another demonstration could be arranged."

A lock of fire-lit golden hair had tumbled over his brow. She swallowed and glanced away. "Once was enough. This sort of demonstration could promote the behavior it is supposed to prevent, particularly when provided by a slippery character like you."

He grinned. "Nonsense. Surely you've noticed that I

am far too indolent to plan a serious campaign of seduction."

"You've never had to seduce a woman in your life.
All you need do is smile and wait for them to melt at
your feet."

His smile faded. "Not really." He picked up his
knife and stick again and started to sharpen the end opposite the knob.

Thinking there had been enough seriousness, she
asked, "What are you doing with that piece of wood?"

"Just a fidget stick." He held it out for her inspec-
tion.

The stick was perhaps six inches long and half an
inch thick, with a natural curve that nestled comfortably in her hand. As she gave it back, she said, "Some
sort of toy for adults?"

"Exactly. I'll carry it in my pocket and play with it
when the scenery palls." He rubbed his thumb over the
knobbed end. "It's convenient to be so simple that such
things amuse."

She put more wood on the fire and hung a pot of water above. "You are many things, Robin, but simple is
not one of them."

He grimaced. "Perhaps not, but I'm working on it."

"That's your problem. One doesn't work at simplicity." On impulse, she sat cross-legged next to him and
took his misshapen left hand in a loose clasp. "Close
your eyes, Robin. Don't talk. Don't think. Just be."

He allowed her to rest their joined hands on the
grass between them, but she felt tension in his fingers.
Softly she said, "Listen to the wind. Hear the stones,
taste the moonlight. Feel the spirits of the trees and
flowers and creatures that share the night with us."
They were the same words that her mother had used
when teaching her to appreciate the world when she
was a small child.

At first he resisted. His energy was restless, full of
jagged angles. She tried to send him peace, but she
could not, for she was not at peace herself.

She was startled to realize that she had not sat and

meditated like this since she had heard of her father's death. Though she had spent endless hours riding and walking on the Durham moors, her knotted grief had prevented her from reaching for the one source of solace that had never failed her.

Deliberately she opened her physical and inner senses to the night. An owl gave a lonely call as it hunted the woods, its wings swift and silent. Beneath her was the living earth, its deep thrum exactly the same as it was in her homeland. Fertile soil and ancient stones and small, determined growing things. The wind that rippled the leaves was familiar, though it had blown through skies she would never know.

Earth calm entered her, flowing through limbs and veins until it filled her heart. If not for Robin's gentle lesson, which had smoothed the grief-roughened edges of her spirit with sensuality, she would not have been able to find such peace.

Wanting to return the gift, she reached out emotionally, letting stillness flow from her hand into his. He was like a nervous colt, strained and ready to bolt.

Soft as shadow, she whispered, "Know that you are part of nature, not separate."

Gradually he calmed, the tautness disappearing from his fingers. His breathing became slow and regular, and for the space of a dozen heartbeats they were in harmony.

Though she was trying to teach simplicity, she recognized that he was innately a being of great complexity. His spirit was a tangled mass of contradictions, with glittering wit and cool acceptance. Sparks of laughter and curiosity, and a deep pulse of kindness. And darkness—darkness beyond her imagining. With an instinctive desire to comfort, she reached toward one of the pools of tortured regret.

In the space of a heartbeat, harmony shattered. She felt Robin jerk away from her emotionally an instant before he released her hand. He drew a shuddering breath, then said coolly, "How very interesting. I never

knew that one could hear stones. Are you a witch,
young lady?"

Ruefully she recognized that she had startled him as
much as he had alarmed her that afternoon. It would be
better for them to keep their relationship safe and superficial. Matching his lightness, she said, "Not a
witch. Not even a lady."

"Nonsense." He scanned her from tangled hair to
dusty boot tips. "At the very least, you're every other
inch a lady."

She smiled as she made two cups of tea, regular for
him and herbal for herself. Robin might be a pickpocket, a vagabond, and heaven only knew what else,
but for as long as their paths lay together, he would
stand her friend.

That would have to be enough.

Chapter 8

As a token of reconciliation, Maxie moved her pallet from the corner of the barn so that she was nearer Robin. All they had to do was avoid kisses and joint meditations for the balance of the journey, and they would have no problems.

After a night of pleasant dreams, she awoke with a jolt when the barn door creaked. Sunshine flooded into the dim interior, followed instantly by furious barking. Her eyes flew open to find two huge mastiffs looming less than two yards away, all red mouths, white fangs, and deafening racket.

She froze, knowing that any movement might precipitate a lethal attack. Her knife was in her knapsack, and the dogs would be on her before she could cover the two-foot distance. Without moving her head, she shifted her gaze to Robin. He was as still as she, his eyes coldly calculating as he studied the hysterical mastiffs.

A voice bellowed, "Hold!"

The dogs stopped barking, but glittering eyes and hot, panting canine breath demonstrated their eagerness to tear the intruders into bloody shreds. An angry farmer appeared behind them, silhouetted against the morning light. "Filthy vagrants," he growled. "I should turn you over to the magistrate."

"You could, o' course, but we've done no harm," Robin said meekly. To Maxie's foreigner's ear, he seemed to have acquired a perfect Yorkshire accent.

Cautiously he sat upright in the hay. "Beg your pardon for the trespass, sir. We meant to leave early so's not to upset anyone, but we walked a long way yesterday and my wife is in a, um, delicate condition."

Maxie sat up also, giving her companion an indignant glare. With her hair down she couldn't pass as a boy, but did she have to become a pregnant wife? Robin returned a suspiciously cherubic glance as he stood and assisted her up with tender care.

Unimpressed, the farmer, a portly middle-aged chap, scowled at them. "That's none o' my concern, but tramps on my property are. Come out here 'fore I turn the dogs loose."

"If you have some chores, sir, we'd be happy to do them to pay for our night's lodging," Robin offered.

While her companion acted the earnest innocent, Maxie began talking to the mastiffs, murmuring in Iroquoian that they were fine brave fellows and she was pleased to make their acquaintance. At first they growled, but she had always gotten on well with dogs. Soon the larger beast's tail began to wag and the ears unflattened.

She extended a hand, introducing herself by her Mohawk name, Kanawiosta. The mastiff stepped closer and gave a tentative sniff, followed by a rasping lick.

She smiled and began scratching behind his ears. He rewarded her with a lolling, imbecilic doggy grin. The other mastiff gave a jealous whimper and pressed forward, demanding equal attention.

The farmer was in the middle of another tirade about worthless thieving vagabonds, but he broke off as his mastiffs began twining around Maxie, almost knocking her from her feet. "What the devil . . . ?"

"My wife has a way with animals," Robin said, rather unnecessarily.

"Ain't that the bloomin' truth," the farmer muttered, impressed in spite of himself. "Either one of 'em weighs more 'n she does. Your wife, you say? Where's her wedding ring?"

Maxie glanced up and was amazed to see the transformation Robin had undergone. Usually he looked like a wayward aristocrat, but his casual elegance had vanished. Now his demeanor was that of a man of modest birth and fortune who had fallen on hard times.

She stared at him, thinking that she would be a damned fool if she ever believed a word he said. With his acting talents, it would be impossible ever to know if he were telling the truth.

"Had to sell her ring," Robin said sadly. "Times are hard now the war is over. We're on our way to London, where I've hopes of a job."

"Were you a soldier?" the farmer said, ignoring the last sentence. "My youngest boy was with the Fifty-second Foot."

Robin gave a nod of grave recognition. "One of the army's finest regiments. I was in the Peninsula myself. Was lucky enough to meet Sir John Moore once, a few months before he was killed at Corunna."

The farmer's thin mouth worked for a moment. "My boy died at Vittoria. He used to say that Moore was the best, bar none." His hostility had disappeared. Unlike Maxie, he didn't notice that Robin had not actually said he'd been in the army.

"The general's death was a terrible loss," Robin agreed.

The farmer took off his hat and ran his fingers through his thinning hair. "My name's Harrison," he said gruffly. "You folks have a long journey ahead. If you're hungry, you can have a bite 'fore you move on."

A fifteen-minute walk brought them to the house, and a single smile from Robin charmed the farmer's wife to blind adoration. Over a massive breakfast of eggs, sausage, hot muffins, strawberry preserves, and tea, he talked about the Peninsular campaign and the life of a soldier. He was utterly convincing; if Maxie hadn't known better, she would have believed him herself. He sealed his popularity by repairing Mrs. Harrison's cherished mantel clock, which hadn't run in years.

Maxie was fluttered over, told gruesome stories

about the trials of childbearing, especially for "a little bit of a thing" like her, and sent off with extra food and an admonition to take care of herself for the baby's sake. Mrs. Harrison waved good-bye to the travelers, and the two mastiffs trotted in escort to the edge of their master's land, halting with obvious reluctance.

Maxie waited until she and Robin were well out of earshot before saying icily, "Aren't you ever ashamed of yourself, Lord Robert?"

"Why should I be ashamed?" he said innocently.

She gave him an exasperated glance. "You have no respect for the truth."

"On the contrary, I value truth enormously. That's why I use it with great care."

"*Robin,*" she said in a dangerous tone.

"Our hosts have the satisfaction of having done a good deed, we had an excellent meal, the dogs made a friend, and Mrs. Harrison's clock now works. Where's the harm in that?"

"But so many lies!" she said helplessly.

"Only a few. I did spend time on the Peninsula, and I did meet Sir John Moore once. I never claimed to have been one of his soldiers or to be an intimate friend." He assumed an anxious expression. "I know why you're out of sorts. It's because you're breeding."

"You, you . . . impossible man!" she exclaimed, torn between irritation and laughter. "How dare you tell him that I'm your pregnant wife!"

He regarded her pensively. "If you object to the falsehood, we could correct it easily enough, or at least part of it."

She gave a disgusted sniff as she moved to the edge of the road to let a pony cart pass. "I have received many dishonorable offers in my time, but that has to be the least flattering. Even if I were interested, which I'm not, it would be a nuisance to be breeding while traipsing the length of Great Britain."

"I was thinking of the other part. We would have to head north to Gretna Green, since we're too far from Doctors' Commons to get a special license."

Even an American knew that meant marriage. "Your jests are getting worse and worse, Lord Robert," she said tartly. "It would serve you right if I accepted that idiotic offer and shackled you for life."

"I can think of worse fates."

She stopped stock-still to stare at him. The previous night's illusory sense of closeness was long gone, and this was the glittering, enigmatic Robin that baffled her. Yet there was something serious and unreadable at the back of his blue eyes. She was startled by the realization that if she agreed, he would turn, escort her north to Gretna Green, and marry her.

Quietly she asked, "Why did you suggest such a thing, Robin?"

"I have no idea," he said with rueful honesty. "Except that it seemed like a good idea."

The last thing Maxie needed was a charming rogue. What shocked her was that the idea was not without appeal. Robin might be temperamentally unsuited for gainful employment and unreliable in word and deed. Yet he was also kind, amusing, and so attractive that if she allowed herself to think about it, she would be wrapped around him like a mustard plaster.

But he was still a rogue. If she ever married, she would choose a man who could keep a roof over her head. She broke away from his unnerving gaze and resumed walking. "I expect you have three or four wives scattered around Europe already, so that acquiring another would be the merest trifle. Unfortunately I detest crowds, so I will decline the honor."

"No other wives. As you observed, I'm not skilled at making offers. The only time I did—" He stopped abruptly.

When he remained silent, she prodded, "What happened?"

"The lady declined, of course. A woman of great good sense. Not unlike you." He smiled. "I'm not sure I would want to marry a woman who had the bad judgment to accept me."

He was back in the realm of impenetrable whimsy

again, though she guessed that some painful truth was buried in his words. Shaking her head, she continued on. They might be friends, but she would never really understand him.

Tracking Lord Collingwood's niece was no great chore for a man of Simmons's skills. Since the chit didn't know she was being followed, she had walked along one road like a goose waiting to be plucked.

Dressed as she was, at first the wench was easy to overlook, for not many folk recalled seeing a little lad with a big hat. It got easier after she took up with a blond gent. All the females along the route remembered him quick enough.

With a touch of malicious amusement, Simmons wondered what Collingwood would say to the news that his niece was no better than she should be. Maybe his lordship wouldn't care; his main concern had been to prevent her from reaching London, where she might find out about her pa. Not that Simmons blamed Collingwood for wanting to conceal that nasty bit of business.

Though he lost his quarry for a time when they decided to skip across country from one road to another, south of Sheffield he picked up their tracks again. They weren't more than a couple of hours ahead of him. Likely the girl and her fancy man were dossed down in a barn or a camp within the next mile or two. With luck, he would find them this very night.

He gave a rusty chuckle. The chit might not want to leave her man to return to Durham, but no matter. Simmons was a match for both of them.

Chapter 9

Grateful that they had found a suitable campsite, Maxie swung her pack to the ground, then went to gather wood. By the time she returned with a load, Robin had laid a fire and was striking flint and steel together.

He glanced up. "Once I get this going, you can keep an eye on it while I bring water for tea."

She laid down the wood and rolled her tired shoulders. "I'll get the water."

"Will you take it as a mortal insult if I suggest that you sit and rest for a while? You look tired, and the stream is a bit of a distance."

The thought of sitting down was enormously tempting. Still . . . "I didn't ask for special consideration."

"I know you didn't." The tinder blazed up. After blowing on it until the flames were crackling merrily, he stood, his blue eyes teasing. "However, considering the difference in the length of our strides, you've done about a third more walking than I. Since I had an easier day, I should haul the water."

She laughed, and felt less tired. "An ingenious argument. You could sell rope to a man on the gallows." She subsided onto the grass and tugged off her boots. "Or if honest labor wasn't against your philosophy, you could have become a lawyer, arguing either side of any case."

She pulled off her hat and unpinned her hair, sighing with relief as it spilled over her shoulders. She was getting very tired of boots, pinned hair, and bound breasts. The thought of a hot bath was enough to make her whimper with longing. "Actually, did you once read law? Sometimes you talk like a barrister."

Robin shot her a horrified glance. "Good Lord, no. I may have done a number of reprehensible things in my life, but I do have some standards."

Chuckling, she lay back on the grass, her hands tucked under her head. "Are you never serious?"

There was a long pause, and she glanced up to find him watching her, an unreadable expression in his eyes. When he caught her looking, he smiled and said in his usual light tone, "As seldom as possible."

He picked up the cooking pots, then went into the woods toward the stream.

Maxie closed her eyes, half dozing. After the robbery, they had fallen into a safe, superficial routine. Robin had demonstrated no more kisses, and she had not suggested that he listen to the wind. It had worked well; there had been no more real closeness, but there had also been no conflicts.

She turned her senses to the woods around her. Liquid bird calls. The sliding rustle of leaf on leaf. The sweetness of honeysuckle. Wholeness. Contentment.

Listening to the wind, she drifted into sleep.

When Robin reached the stream, he decided to have a thorough wash. He thought about his companion as he splashed cold water over himself. He had known from the beginning that she had an exotically lovely face and a razor-sharp mind. It had been a surprise, however, to learn that she had a dash of witch in her.

Or perhaps she was something of a saint. Nothing else could explain that strange episode when she had tried to teach him simplicity. He had willingly followed her lead, and been intrigued to discover that it was possible to sense the world around him in a way he had never experienced before.

It had been very restful, and he had felt very close to Maxie. He had even considered kissing her again, in an entirely staid fashion, of course.

Then something had jarred him from his relaxed

state into an instant of flat panic that was like a waking nightmare. Perhaps he was not made for simplicity. It had been an interesting episode, but not one he cared to repeat. It was easier to drift from hour to hour, enjoying Maxie's company and living in the moment as he had not done for more than a decade.

He dried himself, then filled the water pots and headed back toward the camp. At the edge of the clearing, he paused behind a screen of shrubbery. His dozing companion was an enchanting sight. She lay on her back by the fire, her head pillowed on one arm and her glossy ebony hair partially veiling her face. Her petite, curving form inspired an unsettling mixture of tenderness and desire. He wanted to protect her from the whole world. Except for himself, of course.

Her worldly knowledge and contraceptive herbal tea strongly implied that she was a woman of experience, yet at the same time there was a kind of innocence about her. Probably that was a result of her natural directness. Whatever her past, it was safest to think of her as a virgin. That reinforced his restraint, which needed all the help it could get.

His thoughts were interrupted by the sound of twigs cracking under heavy footsteps. He glanced across the clearing and saw a tall, burly man approaching from the other side.

A broad smile of satisfaction crossed the man's face at the sight of Maxie. "There you are, Miss Collins. Time to go 'ome now." The intruder had a thick London accent, and his superficial cheer did not disguise an air of menace.

Maxie jerked awake and pushed herself to a sitting position. Her eyes narrowed. "I saw you at my uncle's," she said with admirable coolness. "Who are you?"

"The name's Ned Simmons, and your uncle sent me to bring you back," he said, advancing toward his quarry.

Mouth tight, Robin set down his water and silently began to work his way around the edge of the clearing so that he would be behind the Londoner if action proved necessary. Keeping a sharp eye on the scene in the clearing, he pulled his wooden "fidget stick" from his pocket and locked it in his left hand, half an inch of wooden knob showing above his fist.

Maxie scrambled to her feet and watched Simmons warily, looking like a terrier facing a bull. "You have no right to force me to return to my uncle," she said, backing away across the grass in her stocking feet. "He is not my guardian, and I have committed no crimes."

Still with that eerie geniality, Simmons said, "Come, now, miss, don't be difficult, or I'll have to take you to a magistrate and explain how you stole a map, and some food as well. In England, folks can be 'anged for crimes like that. Not that yer uncle will be difficult if you come along like a good girl." He reached out to grasp her shoulder. "Where's yer fancy man? 'E run off and leave you already?"

Laying a hand on Maxie proved to be a mistake. She twisted away from his grip, at the same time kicking out with wicked intent. Robin winced; Simmons was lucky she was not wearing boots, for her aim and quickness were dead on.

The man dodged, but could not entirely avoid the blow. He doubled over with a howl. "You little . . . !"

The curse that followed was so filthy that Robin was glad it was spoken in thief's cant, which Maxie was unlikely to understand. Still swearing, the Londoner reached under his coat and pulled out a pistol.

Before he could aim it, Maxie had dived at him and grabbed the weapon, using her weight to wrest it free. Her momentum carried her into a rolling, controlled tumble across the grass.

She leaped to her feet while Simmons was still gaping with astonishment. The ugly click of hammers being cocked filled the clearing. "I would prefer not to use this, Mr. Simmons," she said in a low, dangerous tone, "but I will do so rather than go with you. Now turn around and *leave*."

Simmons stared at her in stunned disbelief. "Put that

down, you little bitch, or I'll make you sorry you was ever born."

He was making the potentially fatal mistake of underestimating Maxie. Knowing that if he didn't intervene she might kill the man, Robin sprinted across the clearing as she raised her pistol and took aim.

Since he was directly behind the large Londoner, Robin didn't know if she was aware of his approach. Hoping she would shoot high, he launched himself in a long, flat dive and caught Simmons around the legs. As they fell together to the turf, a shot blazed by too close for comfort.

"You slimy, cowardly bastard! I'll teach you not to jump a man from behind," Simmons bellowed as he began grappling with this new threat.

The cockney fought with skill and brute strength, but Robin had the advantage of surprise. He also had the knobbed stick in one fist, and it added ferocious power to his blows.

Simmons staggered back from a hard hit to his jaw, then slammed his fist into Robin's shoulder. With the cunning of a street fighter, he grabbed the neck of Robin's shirt and tried to drag the smaller man close enough for a fight-ending blow.

Robin yanked away at the cost of a tear that ripped his shirt to the waist. He feinted a right to Simmons's face, then used the other man's instinctive attempt to block as an opportunity for a numbing punch to the solar plexus.

Eyes wide but muscles helpless, Simmons folded to the ground. Robin swiftly rolled him facedown in the leaf mold, then twisted the other man's right arm behind his back and held it at the excruciating point just short of breaking a joint. "The fancy man is still around," he panted. "You should have been more careful."

Simmons had plenty of bullheaded courage and a high tolerance for pain. He began thrashing with such furious power that he threatened to break free. Robin leaned forward and applied intense pressure to precisely chosen points below the Londoner's jaw. The blood supply to his brain cut off, Simmons made a strangled noise and one last convulsive heave before slumping into unconsciousness.

Maxie lowered the pistol. "That's an impressive trick," she said unevenly. "Will you show it to me?"

"Definitely not. It's dangerous to use because it can cause death or permanent damage if held too long." Robin rolled Simmons onto his back, then used the man's own handkerchief to tie his wrists together. "Not to mention the fact that you might try it on me the next time I did something to irritate you."

"Probably wise of you not to teach me," she agreed. For all the insouciance of her words, her dark complexion had a gray tinge. "When I lose my temper, anything might happen."

"So I noticed," Robin said dryly. "Were you shooting to kill?"

"No, though I was tempted." She retrieved her boots and pulled them on. "I was aiming to graze his arm, hoping that would stop him. I still had another barrel if it didn't." She tossed earth on the fire with trembling hands. "I'm sure we agree about leaving as soon as possible."

"We do." Robin deftly searched Simmons's pockets. "He'll wake soon. I didn't tie the handkerchief very tightly, so it's not going to take him long to free himself."

He removed the Londoner's concealed ammunition pouch and tucked it inside his coat. Continuing his search, he found that Simmons had little in the way of identification, but he carried a well-filled wallet.

Robin considered the money thoughtfully. There was more than enough to buy two coach tickets to London, but, if the truth be known, he was in no hurry to deliver Maxie to her destination.

"Are you going to rob him?" she asked disapprovingly.

"Just of his pistol." He returned the wallet to

Simmons's coat. "He's going to be quite angry enough when he wakes up."

"So your honesty is a result of pragmatism rather than moral scruples?" She began pinning her hair up again.

"Exactly so. Moral scruples are an expensive luxury," he said blandly.

Her snort was an eloquent comment on his dubious logic.

He grinned. "Theft is a fairly benign response to attempted assault. You are the one who was ready to blow his brains out."

"Only if necessary." She tugged down her battered hat. "How was I to know you would come charging to the rescue?"

He gave her a narrow-eyed look as he got to his feet. "Did you really think I would abandon you to your fate?"

Their gazes caught and held for a moment before she turned to lift her knapsack. "There wasn't much time for thinking."

And Maxie was not the sort of female to sit and wait to be rescued. Robin retrieved the water pots he had set down before attacking Simmons. He offered his companion a drink, which she accepted gratefully; she still looked shaky.

He drank also, then dumped the rest of the water and packed the pots away. When they left the clearing, the only trace of their brief occupancy was Simmons lying peacefully on his back with his hands trussed up in front of him.

As they made their way back to the road, Maxie said, "Your so-called fidget stick is a weapon, isn't it?"

"Yes. After we met the highwaymen, I decided that some form of self-defense might be useful." He held back a branch so she could pass. "A fighting stick adds force to one's blows."

"You are a never-ending source of alarming skills," she remarked, though her sarcasm lacked its usual bite.

"Always used for the forces of good," he said piously.

His remark elicited a faint smile, but she still looked far more upset than he would have expected. He guessed that what distressed her was not so much the attack itself as what it represented. He was going to have to insist on some explanations about her background and her mysterious mission in London.

Near the edge of the road, a depressed-looking horse was tethered. Robin stopped and eyed it speculatively. "I suppose this belongs to your friend back there?"

"He's no friend of mine, but I believe this is his horse. I saw it at . . . I saw it once before."

"Good." He untied the reins and swung into the saddle.

"You're not going to steal it?" she exclaimed. "What happened to pragmatism?"

"I would have turned the horse loose anyhow to slow pursuit, so we might as well ride it and put a few miles between us and Simmons." He offered his hand to Maxie. "The poor beast isn't up to carrying two people very far, but it will give us a start."

"You are nothing if not practical, Lord Robert."

Her hand was icy cold when he pulled her up behind him, and her arms around his waist were tighter than the sedate pace of the horse required. He would wait until she had recovered some of her composure before questioning her.

Several miles later, as the last light was fading from the sky, Robin halted at a fork in the road. "Time to send our fiery steed back to its owner."

They dismounted and he turned the horse around, giving it a slap on the hindquarters to send it ambling back in the direction from which they had come. "Swinging west here, away from the direct route, might throw Simmons off the trail. I hope so. He doesn't seem the sort to give up easily." He put his hand out. "Give me the pistol."

She handed it over, then gave a cry of outrage when he unloaded the remaining ball and pitched the weapon into a heavy patch of shrubbery. "Damnation, Robin! Why did you do that? A pistol could be very useful."

"Guns are beastly things." He sent the ammunition pouch crashing after the pistol. "When they are present, people get killed unnecessarily."

"Maybe Simmons will need killing!"

"Have you ever killed anyone?"

"No," she admitted.

"I have. It isn't an experience one enjoys repeating."

She flushed at the coolness in his tone. Most of the stories he had told her were pure fairy tale, but she did not doubt that he spoke the truth about having killed. "I didn't really mean that. About killing him, I mean."

"I know you didn't." His voice softened and he put a comforting arm around her shoulders as they made their silent way into the night.

The Marquess of Wolverton was half asleep and thinking dourly that he should have stopped in Blyth when his carriage creaked to a halt. He looked out and saw his driver talking to a burly, disheveled fellow who had been trudging along in the dusk.

Giles climbed from the carriage. "More trouble?"

The burly man growled, "I was robbed and me 'orse was stolen." After a glance at the crest on the carriage door, he said with a fair attempt at humility, "Could yer lordship give me a ride to the next town?"

"Of course." Giles waved the man into the carriage, then climbed in himself, thinking that there was even more crime on the highways than he had expected. He lit two of the interior lamps, then pulled a flask of brandy from a compartment. "That's quite a black eye," he said conversationally as he poured a generous measure for his guest.

"Won't be the first."

Giles surveyed the other man's bulk. "I shouldn't think so. You're a boxer, aren't you?"

"Used to be. The name's Ned Simmons, but I fought as the Cockney Killer." Looking pleased, he swallowed the brandy with one gulp. "You ever see any of me matches?"

"Sorry, I don't follow boxing, but a friend of mine won a good sum on you once." Giles cast his mind back. "For defeating the Game Chicken in nineteen rounds, I believe."

"Twenty-one rounds. Aye, 'twas the best mill of me life."

"It must have taken several men to beat you tonight."

The comment was a mistake. Simmons erupted with oaths and excuses, the gist of which was that he had been defeated unfairly. Giles listened with only moderate interest until the words "yaller-headed fancy man" caught his attention.

Concealing his sudden interest, Giles said, "This blond man must have been a strapping fellow."

Simmons hesitated, visibly wondering whether to admit an unflattering truth. "Kind of a skinny cove, actually, and talked like a swell," he said grudgingly. "Wouldn't have thought 'e could fight the way 'e did. Even so, 'e couldn't 'ave taken me if 'e 'adn't jumped me from behind, and if 'is wench 'adn't been pointing a pistol at me."

Giles repressed a smile. Robin and the Sheltered Innocent must have been along this road very recently, and it sounded as if the latter bore some resemblance to her formidable aunt. "How did they come to attack you?"

Simmons's face went blank as an oyster. "Can't say more. Confidential business."

Giles was debating whether to offer a bribe for more information when a horse whickered outside.

Simmons peered out the window. "It's me 'orse! Bloody bastard probably couldn't ride. 'Ope 'e broke 'is neck when the nag threw 'im."

The marquess had never seen a horse that could throw his brother, much less a tired hack like this one. Robin must have turned the beast loose. Thank God he wasn't adding horse theft to his other crimes.

What the *devil* had Robin gotten himself mixed up in?

The horse was caught and tethered to the back of the carriage, and they proceeded to the next town, Worksop. Simmons fell silent, leaving Giles to his speculations. At a guess, the Londoner was the man Lord Collingwood had sent after his niece. Rather a rough sort to charge with escorting a gently bred female, though the more Giles heard about Maxima Collins, the more he doubted her gentility.

Obviously Lady Ross hadn't yet found the fugitives. With luck, Giles would reach them first. When he did, he was going to have a great many questions for his wayward younger brother.

At Simmons's request, Giles left him at an inn that was little better than a hedge tavern. He himself stayed at the best inn Worksop had to offer. It fell well short of the standards of Wolverhampton, but at least the sheets were clean.

When he fell asleep, his dreams were not of the runaways and potential scandals, but of Lady Ross. She really was a rather splendid Amazon.

Simmons had worked in this part of the country before, and within an hour of reaching Worksop he had purchased another pistol and recruited several men to aid him in his pursuit.

Later, as he held a piece of raw beef to his black eye and gulped pints of local ale, he thought about the blond swell who had jumped him from behind. Collingwood wouldn't like it if his precious niece was harmed, but there was nothing to prevent Simmons from breaking her fancy man in half.

As he drank his ale and brooded, he planned what he would do when he met the slick bastard in a fair fight.

Chapter 10

They walked for nearly an hour before finding a sufficiently isolated shed. If they had stayed in their original camp, Maxie would have stewed some vegetables and ham together, but under the circumstances, they settled for bread and cheese.

After they finished, Robin leaned back against the hay, his pale hair silvered by the moonlight that washed in through a high, narrow window. "I think it's time for you to explain what is going on. Is the road to London going to be filled with large gentlemen who want to abduct you?"

Though Maxie was not used to confiding in anyone, she owed Robin an explanation. He was far too skilled at lies and casual theft, she didn't know his real name, and he was almost certainly some kind of swindler, but he had helped when she needed it.

She reached up to release her hair for the second time that evening. "I'm not quite sure what is going on. I don't even know where to begin. What do you want to know?"

"Whatever you are willing to tell me," he said gently.

Suddenly she wanted to reveal everything, about her strange background and how she came to be an alien in England. "My father, Maximus Collins, was a younger son of what is called a 'good family.' His expectations were not great to begin with, and he quickly wasted them in gaming and dissipation."

She smiled wryly. "My grandfather decided that Max was a useless, expensive nuisance, which was probably true. He offered to settle the debts if Max would remove himself from England. Max had no choice but to agree. I expect that bailiffs were about to overtake him. He decided to go to America."

Rain was beginning to patter on the roof. She burrowed deeper in the hay and wrapped her cloak around her shoulders, wishing it were thicker. "My father wasn't a bad man, merely rather casual about things like money and propriety. He quite liked the New World, because it is less rigid in its ways. Max stayed in Virginia for a time, then wandered north.

"After a spell in New York, he made the mistake of trying a winter journey from Albany to Montreal. He almost died in a blizzard, but was rescued by an Indian, a Mohawk hunter. Max ended up spending the rest of the winter at the hunter's longhouse. That's where he met my mother."

She paused, wondering what Robin's reaction would be to the knowledge that she was a half-breed. Such an ugly word, half-breed, more American than English.

His voice revealing only interest, without a shred of distaste, Robin commented, "The Mohawks are one of the Six Nations of the Iroquois confederacy, aren't they?"

"Yes," she said, surprised and pleased at his knowledge. "The Mohawks were Keepers of the Eastern Door, defending the Nations from the Algonquian tribes of New England. Four of the six tribes live mostly in Canada now, because they were loyal to the British during the American Revolution. But at least my mother's people survive with their pride and traditions. Not like the Indians of New England, who were virtually destroyed by disease and war."

"It's not a pretty story," Robin said quietly. "From what I've read, the Indians were a strong, healthy, generous people when the Europeans first came. They gave us corn, medicines, and land. We gave them smallpox, typhus, measles, cholera, and God knows what else. Sometimes bullets." He hesitated, then asked, "Do you hate us too much?"

No one had ever asked her that, or guessed at the buried anger she felt on behalf of her mother's people. Oddly, Robin's perception eased some of that anger. "How could I, without hating myself? After all, I am half English. More than half, I suppose, since I spent less time with my Mohawk kin. They accepted me with more warmth than my English relations did."

She shivered with a chill that came from inside. Even among her mother's clan, she had not truly belonged.

Hearing the faint chatter of her teeth, Robin moved over and put his arms around her. She tensed, not wanting passion, then relaxed when she realized that he was only offering comfort.

With one hand stroking her back, he murmured, "Families can be the very devil."

"Can't they just?" Her head rested against his shoulder, and slowly his warmth and nearness dispelled her chill. She felt so much at home in Robin's arms.

Too much so. Reminding herself that the last thing she needed was a man as charming and heedless as her father, she straightened and took up the story again. "My mother was young and restless, interested in the world beyond the longhouse. In spite of the vast differences, she and my father fell in love."

"They were both rebelling against the lives they were born to," Robin observed. "That would be a strong bond."

"I think you're right. It didn't hurt that my mother was very beautiful, and my father quite dashing. When spring came, Max asked her to come away with him, and she did. I was born a year later. We lived most of the time in Massachusetts, but every summer we would visit the longhouse. My mother wanted me to know the language and ways of her people."

"Did your father go with you?"

"Yes, he got on famously with my mother's kin. Indians are a poetic people, and love stories and games and laughter. My father could quote poetry by the yard, in English and French and Greek. He spoke the Mohawk language well, too." She laughed a little. "Lord, that man could talk. I remember him holding the whole longhouse spellbound as he recited the *Odyssey*. Now that I've read it myself, I know that he translated it rather freely, but it was still a magnificent tale."

Her smile faded. "There were two other babies that died soon after birth. My mother died herself when I was ten. Her family offered to take me, but my father refused. He'd never found a steady job that suited him, so after Mama died he became a book peddler and took me with him on his journeys."

"So you grew up traveling. Did you enjoy the life?"

"Most of the time." Maxie turned around so that her back nested against Robin's chest. "Books and education are revered in America. Since many of the farms and villages are very isolated, we were always welcome wherever we went."

Her voice became dry. "Too welcome, sometimes. Indian social customs are very different from European ones, and unmarried women have a degree of freedom that is often considered wantonness by European standards. There were always men interested in testing the virtue of a half-breed like me."

His arms tightened protectively. "No wonder you learned to be so wary."

"It was necessary—if I'd told Max about such things, he might have killed someone. Or more likely been killed himself—he was a talker, not a fighter." Before today, she would have said the same about Robin, but no longer. "I'm not ashamed of the ways of my mother's people. Why shouldn't women have the same freedom before marriage that men do? But the choice had to be mine, not something forced on me by a drunken backwoodsman who assumed that I was a woman of easy virtue."

"Only a fool would believe that," Robin said softly.

Glad he understood, she went on, "We had a regular route through New England and northern New York. Besides a standard range of books, we would also bring special orders to people."

"Fascinating." Robin linked his arms around her waist. "What was your usual stock?"

"Mostly New Testaments, chapbooks of sermons and songs, pirated editions of English books. But there were other kinds as well. A farmer in Vermont ordered one book of philosophy every year. On our next visit, he and my father would discuss the previous year's book. We always stayed two days with Mr. Johnson. I think it was the high point of his year."

She smiled. "Peddlers like my father did a good business, enough so that publishers put out books just for the traveling bookseller trade. Things like *The Prodigal's Daughter,* which piously decried immoral behavior."

"In great detail, no doubt," Robin said with amusement.

"Exactly. How could people know how wicked the behavior was unless it was described?" She chuckled. "We sold a lot of copies of that one."

Her story made it clear to Robin why Maxie was such a remarkable mixture of maturity and innocence. What an unusual life she had led, being raised between two cultures, not quite belonging to either, and living an unrooted existence. Clearly her father had been well educated and charming, and she had adored him. Equally clear was that Max had been feckless to a fault. Robin would lay odds that Maxie had grown up managing their business and generally taking care of her casual parent.

And that strange background had produced this independent young woman who fit so perfectly in his embrace. Holding her had certainly dispersed the damp chill of the night, and Robin was warm in a way that had nothing to do with the temperature.

Reminding himself sharply that the last thing she needed right now was for him to become amorous, he remarked, "An interesting life, but an unsettled one."

"I used to think there was nothing I wanted more than a real home," she said a little wistfully. "We spent winters in Boston, staying with a widow whose children had grown. I was always glad to return there and know that we would be sleeping under the same roof for the next few months. But all in all, it was a good way to live. There was always enough to eat, plenty of books, and people to talk to. Being a peddler suited my father. He had restless feet."

Robin was not surprised to hear that. But at least Maximus Collins seemed an affectionate father, more so than the late, upright Marquess of Wolverton. Though the world would not agree, he thought that Maxie had been more fortunate in her parents than he had been in his. "What brought you to England?"

"Max wanted to see his family again. He wanted me to meet them, too."

Robin felt her tense. She had implied rather strongly that her father's relatives had been less than gracious. Knowing the English gentry, he was not surprised. "Your father died here in England?"

"In London, two months ago. His health hadn't been good. In fact, I think that is the main reason he came back—to see England once more before he died." Her voice broke for a moment. "Max was buried at the family estate in Durham. Then, right after I had decided that it was time to return to America, I overheard a conversation between my aunt and uncle."

Maxie recounted what she had heard, and how she had decided to go to London to investigate. She even included her fears that her father might have decided to try some genteel extortion, her flat voice refusing any possible sympathy.

"That brings us to the present," she finished. "I still have trouble believing there was foul play involved in Max's death. Yet the fact that my uncle sent someone like Simmons after me seems to confirm my worst suspicions. It may be solicitude, but it seems more likely that he is determined to prevent me from learning the truth. What do you think?"

"Obviously your uncle is concealing something," Robin agreed, considering the possibilities. There was at least one that did not involve criminal behavior on anyone's part, but he preferred not to speculate about it to Maxie. "I agree that your best chance of learning what happened lies in London. But it could be dangerous, and nothing you learn will bring your father back. Is it worth the risk?"

"I must know the truth," she said, her voice hard. "Don't try to persuade me otherwise."

"I wouldn't dream of it," Robin replied mildly. "In the meantime, it is late and we are both tired. Morning will be soon enough to decide how to avoid Simmons and reach London."

"You'll help me?" she asked uncertainly.

"Yes, whether you want me to or not. I have nothing better to do, and this seems a worthy task." Robin lay back in the hay, taking Maxie with him.

She tried to wriggle away. "It's been a long day, and I really don't want to end it by having to fight you off."

"You're still underestimating my intelligence," he said soothingly. "Not to mention my sense of self-preservation. I'm well aware that you will stick a knife into some cherished part of my anatomy if I become unruly. However, it's a cold night, and we'll both be warmer if we cuddle up together. Agreed?"

With a soft sigh, she stopped struggling. "Agreed. I'm sorry to be so suspicious, Robin."

"Now I understand why." He brushed a very light kiss on her temple, then tucked his blanket around both of them.

The hay made a soft, fragrant bed. She relaxed, her back curved against his front.

"Like Mrs. Harrison kept saying, you're just a little bit of a thing." He looped an arm around her waist and drew her closer, spoon-style. "I thought Indians were a tall people."

"Every race has exceptions. My mother was small, and I ended up the shortest person on either side of my family."

"But fierce to make up for it." There was a smile in

his voice. "Do you have a Mohawk name as well as your English one?"

After a moment's hesitation, she replied, "To my mother's kin, I am Kanawiosta."

"Kanawiosta." The name rippled from his tongue. Except for her father, Robin was the only white man ever to speak it. "Does it have a particular meaning?"

"Nothing that is easily defined. It implies flowing water, and also improvement, making something better."

"Flowing water," he said thoughtfully. "It suits you."

She laughed. "Don't romanticize my name. It could just as easily be translated as 'swamp beautifier.' How many English folk know the original meanings of their names?"

"Robert means 'of shining fame,' " he said promptly.

"But you prefer Robin, as in Robin Hood." Did the fact that he knew the meaning prove that Robert was his real name? Given his magpie assortment of knowledge, it probably meant nothing.

The chill was going from her bones, dissolved by the warmth of his embrace. He made a wonderful blanket. Sleepily she said, "This is rather like bundling."

"Bundling?"

"A frontier custom for courting couples," she explained. "Distances between homesteads mean that sometimes young men must stay the night at their sweethearts' houses. Guest rooms are rare, so they'll share a bed, both of them wearing clothing to keep matters from getting out of hand. Usually the bed will be divided by a board down the middle, with jagged teeth on top."

"Sounds like a custom the English could practice profitably. Over here, being caught in a garden kissing a girl can lead to a fast and unwelcome marriage." He smiled into the darkness. "I'm sure your countrymen realize that neither bundling board nor clothing will stop determined people."

"Jumping the board is not uncommon," she admitted. "There are a number of bundling ballads that say things like 'Bundlers' clothes are no defense,/ Unruly horses push the fence.' "

Robin laughed and she joined him. His laughter was as warming as his arms. "Sometimes the wedding takes place sooner than expected." She yawned again. "But farms need children, so most people don't think it any great sin."

Then, warm and secure for the first time in far too long, she drifted into sleep—listening to the wind, the rain, and the steady beat of Robin's heart.

Chapter 11

Maxie awoke in a haze of warm pleasure. The scent of hay filled her nostrils, and Robin's slumbering body protected her from the damp dawn air. One of his hands was resting on her breast. It felt nice—*very* nice—but it wouldn't do for him to wake and think a precedent had been set. Gently she moved his hand down to neutral territory.

Her movement roused him. Lazily he rolled onto his back and stretched, his body going taut alongside hers. She propped herself up on one elbow, admiring his tousled golden hair. He must have looked very like this when he was a little boy who had longed for a pirate patch and saber scars.

She smiled. "Good morning. I slept well. Did you?"

He smiled back, with such stunning effect that all she could think of was how wonderful it would be to see him like this every day for the rest of her life. "Very well indeed," he said in a husky morning voice.

He put a casual hand on her shoulder as he settled into the hay again. At least, it started as casual. Their gazes met, and there was a long, dangerous moment of intense mutual awareness.

Slowly, as if against his will, his hand began sliding down her sleeve. His warm palm brought the flesh under it to vibrant life. As her breath quickened, she thought of the bundling song, and of how clothing was no barrier to determined couples.

His eyes darkened and his hand paused so that his thumb could stroke the sensitive inside of her elbow.

She caught her breath, shocked at how much sensation was there.

He caressed her forearm until his hand came to rest clasping her wrist. The skin was bare, and her pulse throbbed against his fingertips.

The rip in Robin's shirt exposed the hollow at the base of his throat. She wanted to lick it. She wanted to tear the rest of the shirt off so she could see and touch the lean, muscular body that had cradled her all night. She wanted to be a woman of the Mohawk who could give herself without shame or doubt.

But one thing she had in abundance was doubts. Her face must have shown her thoughts, for he exhaled in a rush and abruptly rolled away. "A wonderful way to spend the night," he said breathlessly as he got to his feet, "except for the part about separating when we wake up."

She ran unsteady hands through her hair. "P-perhaps it was a mistake to sleep that way."

He looked offended. "I've never made a mistake in my life. At least, not any that I couldn't explain away afterward."

She laughed, and suddenly everything was all right. "Next time, I'll make a point of getting up as soon as I wake."

"I'm glad there will be a next time. We need practice."

Still chuckling, she got to her feet and prepared to face the day. It was gray and chilly, but the rain had stopped. Robin had brought kindling into the shed the night before, so there was enough dry wood to build a fire just outside the door.

Clear rainwater was available in a stone trough, so she made tea while Robin toasted bread on a pointed stick. With the last of Mrs. Harrison's sliced ham, it made a hearty breakfast.

As Maxie steeped her herbal tea, Robin asked, "Do you mind if I shave inside this morning? It's rather raw out there."

"Go right ahead." She eyed his ripped shirt, trying

not to notice the bare chest below. "We'll have to find you another shirt. I think this one is beyond repair."

He made a face. "I'm more than a little tired of it anyhow." He took out his folding razor and a piece of soap, then knelt by the pot containing the rest of the warm water.

Robin was as religious about shaving as she was about her herbal tea, but it was a task he had always performed out of her sight. She guessed that he would have done so this morning if not for the increased sense of domesticity between them.

"Have you considered not shaving?" she said. "I'm so nondescript that no one notices me, but you are much more distinctive looking. A beard would help disguise your appearance, which would make it harder for Simmons to track us."

He lathered the soap in his palm, then spread it over his cheeks and jaw. "My beard grows out red, which is even more conspicuous than my normal appearance. But you're right that we must make some changes. We've been set on by highwaymen and are being pursued by Simmons. It's time for a new strategy."

She studied him over the rim of her mug. There was something very intimate about watching a man shave. Though she had seen her father do it hundreds of times, she had never recognized how profoundly masculine whiskers were. "What do you have in mind? We still haven't enough money for coach fare. Unless you think you can earn enough by performing magic shows?"

"I have an idea. It wouldn't be the fastest route, but we would be very hard to follow. Are you familiar with the drovers?" He stropped his razor half a dozen times on a short leather strap, then stretched the skin of his cheek so that he could removed a swath of red-blond whiskers.

Those same whiskers had gently prickled the nape of her neck the night before. Her toes curled and she swallowed hard. "You mean the men who drive livestock to the cities?"

"Correct. All cities must have food brought in, and London is so large that it draws supplies from the whole of Britain." He wiped the blade clean of soap and whiskers with a tuft of hay, then began work on the other side of his face. "Most of the cattle eaten in the city are driven in from Wales and Scotland."

"All the way from Scotland?" She raised her brows. "It must be very tough beef by the time it arrives."

"The beasts are generally fattened in southern pastures before going to market," he explained. "And it isn't only cattle, though they are driven the farthest. Drovers herd sheep, geese, pigs, even turkeys, though not over such great distances."

Diverted, she asked, "How does one drive turkeys?"

"With great difficulty," he said, a twinkle in his eyes. "It's quite a sight. At the end of the day, the turkeys will roost in trees for the night, hundreds at a time."

She spent a delighted moment envisioning branches bowed with sleeping turkeys. It distracted her from thoughts of Robin's chiseled, soap-edged features. "What has this to do with us?"

"The droveways follow the high country when possible, and they avoid toll roads. Frugal travelers sometimes accompany the drovers, for companionship and safety. Or sometimes just for the adventure of it." Having finished his cheeks and jaw, he stretched his chin to shave his throat.

She watched in fascination while a glistening drop of water trickled into the hollow of his throat, then slid down the center of his chest, dampening the curling hair.

Noticing her fixed stare, he asked, "Is something wrong?"

"Mere female nerves," she said quickly. "Seeing a razor so close to a throat makes me nervous."

He grinned. "I haven't done any serious damage to myself yet." With three smooth strokes, he completed the job, then wiped the blade clean and snapped it back into its horn handle.

He may not have hurt himself, but he had certainly raised merry Hades with her peace of mind. Relieved that he had finished before she turned into a perspiring wreck, she said, "I see the advantages. Are there any droveways nearby?"

"One runs west of Nottingham, a couple of days walk from here. At this season, there's a good chance of finding drovers on it within a day or so."

"Have you traveled with drovers before?"

"Yes. That's why I know this particular route." He dipped his facecloth in the warm water, then wrung it out and wiped his face and throat clean. "Once I fell in with a group of drovers when I ran away from home."

Running away had the ring of truth. "You must have been a rare handful for your mother."

After a long pause, he said, "Not in the least. She took one look at me after my birth and promptly expired from shock."

No amount of insouciance could disguise the underlying pain of his statement. "I'm sorry," she said quietly.

"Nowhere near as sorry as my father was." Robin went to the open door of the shed and tossed his shaving water outside. "I look just like her, according to the pictures. He couldn't see me without flinching."

She wanted to weep for the child Robin had been. Instead, she asked softly, "Why are you telling me this?"

He was silent for the length of a dozen heartbeats, his profile as cool and remote as the gray sky. "I don't know, Kanawiosta. Perhaps because sometimes I weary of being obscure."

It made the back of her neck prickle to hear him use her private name. For the first time, he was voluntarily revealing something of what lay beneath his polished, impenetrable exterior. Perhaps it was because the night before, she had exposed so much of herself. Or perhaps sleeping in each other's arms had removed some of the barriers that had separated them.

She thought of the traits she had sensed when trying

to teach him to listen to the wind, and the woman he had wanted to marry who had refused him. Like a ball of yarn, he was made of tangled strands of humor and evasion, intelligence and guile, consideration and cool detachment. Now he was handing her a loose end of the skein, to unwind if she chose.

If she did, what would she find at the heart of his mystery, when all the complex strands had been raveled away?

As soon as she formed the question, she knew the answer. At the heart of all that wit and easy charm lay loneliness.

Desdemona had been relieved when Lord Wolverton sent word to her after hearing reports of the runaways on the Rotherham road. At least the two were safe. However, the marquess had given her no other clues, and she had not seen him again. She would have to locate her quarry the hard way.

Heaving a sigh of weary exasperation, she climbed out of her carriage in the dusty high street of still another village. It seemed as if she had been crisscrossing the north Midlands forever, seeking traces of her niece and the unprincipled rogue who was taking advantage of her. Her opinion of Lord Robert Andreville was not improved by the fact that the pair was still traveling by foot. One would think that any self-respecting rake would at least hire a post chaise. The fellow had no style.

She had become adept at asking questions. The tiny villages, where all strangers were noted, were the best places for hearing news, and the best people to ask were the elderly folk who clubbed together at the local public house. Shopkeepers were also good.

For the third time that day, Desdemona entered the only shop in a tiny village, Wingerford by name. As usual, the shop was a jumble of oddments such as needles and thread, bolts of plain fabric and cheap ribbons, pottery jugs, staple foods like salt and sugar, and jars of sweets for children. A ginger cat snored softly on a pile of used clothing, his nose covered by his tail.

At Desdemona's entrance, the stout proprietress hurried forward to greet her, eyes sharpening at the sight of the expensively dressed visitor. "How may I serve you, my lady?"

"I wonder if you might have seen my niece and her husband on this road within the few days," Desdemona replied. "She's dark and quite small, only about five feet tall, and dressed like a boy. He's about average height, very blond and good-looking."

"Aye, they were in this very shop yesterday." The woman's gaze held shrewd appraisal. "The gent had torn his shirt and needed a new one." She gave a modest cough. "He bought a hat and some undergarments as well. I didn't have anything as fine as what he was wearing, but he seemed satisfied."

Desdemona went into her prepared story. "It is the greatest nonsense. My niece's husband made a silly wager about walking to London, and my niece decided to accompany him. They haven't been married long and she considered such a journey a great lark. I didn't approve, of course, but it wasn't my place to forbid it."

She gave a doleful sigh. "There would have been no harm in it, except that the girl's father has taken seriously ill. We are trying to find them in hopes that she can reach her father before it is too late." Desdemona's voice had a slight quaver; if she told this story many more times, she would believe it herself. "Did my niece or her husband mention anything about the route they were taking from here?"

"Indeed?" The proprietress raised her brows, her expression delicately conveying that she had grave doubts about the story but wouldn't dream of calling her distinguished visitor a liar.

The next move was Desdemona's. A respectable woman like this one might be offended by an outright bribe; something subtler was called for. She glanced around the crowded shop until she found an appropriate object. "Oh, what wonderful ribbon. I have been

searching forever for just this shade of blue." She
pulled a spindle from a mound of fabric trimmings.
"Would you consider selling this to me for, oh, five
pounds?"

"Five guineas and it's yours." The ironic gleam in
the shopkeeper's eye left no doubt that she knew what
the real transaction was.

"Splendid," Desdemona said heartily, as if she didn't
know that the true value of the ribbon was less than a
pound.

The shopkeeper wrapped the spindle in a length of
creased paper. "Happen that when I was in the back of
the shop I heard the young couple talking. Something
about droving."

"Droving?" Desdemona said, perplexed.

"Aye, there's a big droveway west of here. Maybe
they intend to travel along with the drovers. Wouldn't
be the first time that gentry folk decided to travel that
way as an adventure."

Desdemona pursed her lips. It made sense, while
complicating her search still further. "Could you tell
me exactly how to find the droveway?"

The proprietress' eye drifted to her customer's hand.
Desdemona handed the money over, and received de-
tailed instructions.

Before leaving, she asked one more question. "Were
my niece and her husband getting on well?"

The shopkeeper shrugged. "Seemed to be on easy
terms. Leastwise, they laughed a lot."

Desdemona gave a false smile. "So pleased to hear
that. I was afraid the rigors of primitive travel might
put them at odds with each other. That would be a pity
when they are newly wed."

As Lady Ross's carriage rumbled off in a cloud of
dust, the shopkeeper permitted herself a wide, gap-
toothed grin of satisfaction. That pair of young rascals
were the most profitable customers she had ever had.

The big Cockney, who claimed he was looking for
two thieves, had been good for two pounds, but it was
the nobleman with the crest on his carriage who had

tipped her off that something strange was afoot. *He* was looking for two young cousins, off on a lark. That time the search was on behalf of a dying granny, not a father. His lordship been good for five quid. And now here was the lady, looking for her niece and nephew-in-law. Should have held out for ten pounds.

As she lifted her skirt to tuck the five guineas into a purse slung around her waist, she wondered if anyone else would be along. More than that, she wondered what would happen to the fugitives when their pursuers caught up with them.

She gave a cackle of laughter. She'd put her money on the blond gent. With a tongue as gilded as his hair, that young fellow could talk his way out of anything.

Chapter 12

They heard the lowing before they saw the small, windswept stone building. Aptly called the Drover Inn, it stood on the crest of a hill overlooking an expanse of rolling green hills. Soon they were close enough to see a vast herd of black cattle grazing in the meadow beyond the inn.

"We're in luck," Robin said. "A good thing it's Sunday."

She looked at him askance. "Why?"

"Those are Welsh Black cattle. Good Welsh Methodist drovers won't travel on Sunday, which is why they are here and not some miles down the track."

"I see." She gazed longingly at the inn. "Robin, do you think the treasury could stretch to getting a room for the night, and a hot bath with it?"

"Luckily we've been getting ripe at the same rate, but I know what you mean. I'd wrestle Simmons with one hand tied behind my back in return for a bath." He looked thoughtful. "Perhaps it's time for a magic show. After a quiet Sunday, people will be in the mood for a bit of entertainment."

He paused for a moment to place coins and a handkerchief in convenient spots. After he picked a pretty ox-eye daisy and made it disappear, they headed toward the inn.

Drovers and assorted other folk lounged about outside, chatting, smoking, and enjoying the late afternoon sun. No one gave the newcomers anything more than a casual glance.

Maxie followed Robin into the inn, where the landlord and his wife presided over the taproom. A subtle, quicksilver change passed through her companion. Though his features didn't change an iota, he took on a different personality.

He announced himself as the Remarkable Lord Robert and began making coins vanish, then reappear in improbable places. He was greeted by waves of laughter. A handy pack of cards was pressed into service, witty jokes were made, and empty tankards were juggled in the air.

Robin ended by producing the daisy from his handkerchief and handing it to the landlady with a bow. His performance was masterful, with a rippling flow of words that amused without becoming so glib as to make conservative country folk wary.

Maxie watched a little wistfully, thinking that Robin was almost a stranger again. The closeness of the night she had told her story and the next morning had vanished as soon as they began walking. The day that followed had been mercifully uneventful. They had laughed and joked. They had even spent the night sleeping like two friendly spoons, and awakened without any unruly passions on either side.

It had all been very pleasant and unthreatening. Yet she would like to have seen more of the deeper, more complicated man who was the real Robin. She would like to know more about the hard roads he had traveled before they had met.

Show over, her companion came to the corner where she was waiting. "Success," he announced. "There is a double room available under the eaves. The landlord and his wife will also throw in dinner, breakfast, hot baths, and washing water for the princely sum of fourpence."

"Splendid. What do you have to do in return?"

"Perform two shows in the taproom during the evening." His voice became reverent. "After which—a hot bath."

"Life is good," she said solemnly.

"So it is."

For a moment, she thought there was a flash of the deeper Robin in his gaze, but he said only, "Now we must find the head drover and ask for permission to travel with the group. It will be off by seven o'clock tomorrow morning."

She winced. "We'll scarcely have time to grow tired of civilized living."

He grinned. "A rolling stone may gather no moss, but it does acquire a certain polish."

Laughing, she followed him outside. Laughter was almost enough.

Maxie sank into the tin tub of steaming water with a shiver of ecstasy so intense that a Puritan minister would have sent her straight to hell. After days of hasty, partial wash-ups in cold streams, a real bath was bliss unbounded.

When her skin started to wrinkle, she rinsed the soap from her hair and reluctantly emerged. The tub was set behind a screen, but she still preferred to be dry and clothed before Robin returned from his second performance.

An image of him finding her in the bath flashed through her mind, followed by a highly erotic scenario of what might happen next. Cheeks flushed, she vigorously toweled herself dry. It wasn't Robin she needed to put a knife into, it was herself.

She had watched his first show, laughing with everyone else. Then she had slipped upstairs and washed all of their clothing that wasn't currently being worn. The garments were now draped on a chair in front of the fire. They had to pay two pence extra for the coal, but it was worth it to know there would be clean, dry clothing in the morning.

She used her one shift as a nightgown. It was heavenly to feel the whisper of soft muslin against her skin, to have her body unbound by tight clothing. For this one night, she was going to sleep like a proper female, even though in the morning it would be back to boots and breeches.

After roughly toweling her hair, she sat cross-legged in front of the fire and began the time-consuming business of combing and drying the thick tresses. It was quiet, except for an occasional rumble of distant laughter from the taproom or the lowing of a restless cow. This was the first time she had been really alone since she had met Robin, and the solitude was pleasant. Ruefully she admitted that it wouldn't be half so enjoyable if she hadn't known that soon he would return.

Her mind turned to London and speculations about what she would find there. The days had not diminished her determination to learn the truth about her father's death, and to see justice done if he had really been murdered. Yet part of her was afraid of learning what had happened. She had loved her father in spite of his failings, but she would not enjoy confronting new evidence of his weaknesses. And if Lord Collingwood was the villain, justice would be tempered with regret, though not enough to swerve her from her duty.

It was easier to live in the moment, in this journey, which had taken on an odd, suspended-in-time quality. In the past lay grief, in the future lay hard decisions, not only about her father's death, but about the rest of her life.

She stopped combing, her hands relaxing in her lap as her thoughts went to Robin. Though she had resented his presence at first, his help had proved invaluable. He had given her a great deal, and her sense of equity said that she must do something for him in return.

Giving him her body was an obvious solution. It would be highly pleasurable, and her herbal tea should prevent awkward consequences. Yet she feared that her complex mixture of feelings for Robin might become love if they became fully intimate. She didn't need that kind of pain to add to her grief for her father.

There was also a distinct possibility that such a gift would not be welcome. Robin was clearly attracted to her, but he seemed to share her doubts about the wisdom of becoming lovers.

She smiled wryly and resumed her combing, fluffing the straight black strands in the fire-warmed air. She was like the cat who was always on the wrong side of the door. She had never liked being an object of lust. Now she found that she wasn't entirely happy being an object of unlustful friendliness, either.

Climbing the steep staircase while balancing a heavy copper of steaming water would have been tricky at the best of times. The task was made more difficult by the amount of ale Robin had drunk. Exercising care, he managed to get up the steps without incident. He rapped on the bedchamber door to warn Maxie that he was coming, waited a few seconds, then entered.

She was sitting cross-legged in front of the fire, combing the hair that cascaded straight and glossy black almost to her waist. Smiling, she asked, "How did the second show go?"

He stopped, momentarily stunned. While she was always lovely, for the first time since they had met she was also perfectly and exquisitely feminine. The flickering flames of the fire limned her body in warm light and turned the thin fabric of her shift translucent.

He had known that her shapeless boy's apparel concealed a trim female figure, but the actuality far surpassed his imagination. She was beautifully proportioned, with curving hips, a slim waist, and breasts that would fit perfectly into his palms. His mouth went dry, and his self-control came perilously close to collapse when he saw the shadowy circles of her areolas dimly visible beneath the shift.

It was hard not to stare at the low neckline of her shift, where the glinting silver chain complemented the smooth dark ivory of her skin. It was harder yet not to cross the room, lift her in his arms, and discover if his passion might ignite hers.

Remembering that she had asked a question, he managed to say, "The show went well. Unfortunately, everyone wanted to buy me a drink afterward, and I couldn't avoid accepting several of them."

Her smile faded, and she studied his face with a hint of wariness. "You're three sheets to the wind?"

He pondered. "Only about one and a half. With luck I won't have a hangover, but I will certainly sleep like a hibernating bear and wake up with great reluctance. You're in charge of pouring cold water in my face to get me moving tomorrow morning."

She chuckled. "Sounds like fun. I suppose we'll have to rise about six if we're going to leave at seven."

"I'm afraid so." Released from his temporary paralysis, he went to the screened tub and poured in the hot water. This was not the sort of dandified establishment that believed perfectly good water should be thrown out merely because it had been used once. Warming it was good enough for guests at the Drover.

Standing behind the screen, he removed his brown coat and laid it over the top of the screen. "Expect a long day. Drovers move slowly, but they travel for twelve hours or so."

Maxie rose lithely to her feet and began plaiting her hair into a heavy ebony braid. "Then I had better go to bed now."

She seemed a little uneasy. Guessing why, he said casually, "Strange how different it is to be in a bedroom."

"You're right. We've slept together quite peacefully the last few nights, but for some reason sharing a bed in a real bedroom is different." She bit her lower lip— her lush, sensual, dusty rose-colored lip—as she considered. "Not quite proper, in a way that I didn't feel before."

If she had given him the least encouragement, any honorable doubts he had about the wisdom of lying with her would have been out the window. But obviously she was not trembling on the brink of uncontrollable passion. "A pity we don't have a bundling board." He unbuttoned his shirt and draped it across the top of the screen. "I'll sleep on the floor."

Her glance flickered to his bare shoulders and the portion of his chest visible above the screen, then quickly away. "Nonsense. We have this room because of your performing skills, and I would be a poor sort of person to condemn you to a hard floor because of missishness. You've behaved yourself so far, and I trust that you will continue to do so. Besides," she added practically, "it's a large bed."

She would be less trusting if she knew what he was thinking. It was an extremely mixed blessing that women did trust him, because that trust bound him as securely as fetters of steel. "I can't imagine you as missish."

She slid under the worn counterpane and closed her eyes. "I think missishness is a luxury for those females who have the money and leisure to indulge in it. A woman who has to make her own way in the world hasn't the time for such things."

He finished undressing, then lowered himself into the tin tub with a happy sigh. The older he got, the more he appreciated simple creature comforts. Amazing to remember some of the conditions he had endured in his adventuresome days. Youth had the damnedest ideas of what was amusing.

By the time he had finished, dried himself, and put on the other pair of drawers that Maxie had washed and dried for him, his companion was asleep, her breathing soft and even. She looked very young in the flickering firelight, her face unlined and innocent. Yet even asleep she had the quality of fierce independence that was so much a part of her.

He spent a few minutes washing the rest of his clothing and hanging it by the fire. Then he climbed into the bed, carefully keeping to his side. Hard to imagine how the Americans managed bundling. Even wearing as many layers as an Eskimo wouldn't have been enough to protect Maxie's virtue. What protected her was a fragile thing called trust. . . .

He would have liked to roll over and put his arms around her as he had the last two nights, but she was right: Being in a bed was different from sleeping in a hedgerow, and much more dangerous. Beds were for making love in a way that barns were not, not that a pile of hay couldn't be a delightful spot to dally on occasion.

He forced himself to relax, to ignore the knowledge that an alluring female body was just inches away.

On the whole, it would have been easier to sleep with a scorpion.

Chapter 13

Maxie was not surprised to wake and find herself snuggled up against Robin. The room had cooled as the fire died, and her companion's warmth had attracted her like a lodestone.

In her travels to isolated New England farmsteads, she had sometimes shared a bed with children or spinsters of the household. Nights contending with elbows, knees, and semiconscious struggles for the bedcovers had taught her that most people were not easy to sleep with.

Interestingly, she and Robin were natural bed partners in the strictest sense of the term. Through the night they easily shifted and adjusted to each other's movements, always close, always comfortable. More than that, she always woke happy and well rested, even on the night when they had slept on the hard cold earth. Robin seemed to sleep equally well.

It was first light, the sun still below the horizon. They would have to rise soon, but for a few minutes more she could drowse with her head on Robin's shoulder and her arm across his bare midriff. Under the blanket he was wearing drawers, which was the absolute minimum permissible for bundling. In fact, she thought sleepily, it was undoubtedly less than the minimum.

She pushed her braid back, then stroked an idle hand down his chest. The light, springy hair felt pleasant against her palm. Though Robin gave the impression of being slightly built, he was surprisingly well muscled. Or perhaps not surprising when she recalled how efficiently he had dealt with Simmons.

Low on his left side, below the blanket, her fingertips found the puckered ridge of an old scar. She considered it gravely; from the roughness and shape, it appeared to have been made by a bullet. What had Robin been doing to get himself shot? Something nefarious, she feared. He was lucky to have survived. Like a cat, he must have multiple lives. Thank God.

Under her palm, his heart beat with a strong steady rhythm. The room was now light enough to see his perfectly carved profile, relaxed and almost boyish in the pearly dawn. He made her think of angels, beings from another realm of existence who were bright and terrible in their beauty.

She wondered if the fellowship of angels contained a few rogues. Not the evil, arrogant entities like Lucifer who had rebelled against God and become demons, but ones that were simply different, too mercurial and unconventional to be content singing in heavenly choirs. Perhaps one such angel rogue had looked down and seen an earthly female who needed protection on a long journey, and come to aid her on her way.

She smiled, wondering what it was about Robin that inspired such whimsy. When they met in the glade with the fairy ring, she'd thought of Oberon. But he was quite human, which made him all the more appealing. Acting from pure affection, she raised her head and brushed his lips with hers.

Robin stirred at her light touch and turned toward her, finding her lips to return the caress. His prediction about drinking so much ale that he would have trouble waking must have come true, for he was even more asleep than she. The knowledge gave her a delicious sense of naughtiness. She could kiss him and pretend that it didn't count because he wouldn't remember.

When his tongue touched her lips, she opened them. The kiss deepened, developing the languorous richness of roses baking in the summer sun. His hand drifted down her back and hip, as deft at caressing as at conjuring. The thin muslin of her shift was an insubstantial barrier, and she felt the slow, sensual pressure of each individual finger. If she had known how, she would have purred like a pleased cat.

When her arm went around his neck, she knew it was time to stop. Her simple enjoyment of closeness was changing to a serious wish to continue what they had begun. He was bound to become fully conscious soon, and it would hardly be fair to turn suddenly prudish when she had been cooperating wholeheartedly.

She steeled herself to move away, but she had waited too long. Before she could summon the resolve, he lifted his hand to cup her breast. She gasped as liquid fire flowed through her limbs. She needed more breath, yet could not bring herself to break off the endless, drugging kiss.

She was growing dizzy when he lifted his head away and murmured, "You are so lovely."

He had called her beautiful before, but that meant nothing compared to the husky passion in his voice now. As she drew a shuddering breath, he pressed his lips to her throat. The light rasp of his chin was a piquant contrast to his velvet tongue and the intimate touch of his breath.

He found the hollow at the base of her throat, then moved below the angle of her collarbone, over the swell of her breast. He was like the sun, heated and powerful, bringing exuberant life to everything he touched.

Adrift in sensuality, she did not realize that he had nuzzled aside the shoulder of her shift until he drew her nipple into his mouth. She sucked in her breath, electrified. His tongue lapped the tip to aching hardness, moving in a rhythm that pounded in her blood. Arousing. Compelling. Intoxicating.

"Robin, Robin . . ." Her last, faint resistance crumbled, for she could no longer remember why she had any doubts. Her hands kneaded his bare back, moving restlessly over his ribs and under the edge of his drawers. He was lying half across her, and the hard heat of his arousal pressed the outside of her knee. She moved her leg, deliberately rubbing that throbbing maleness.

He made a choked, yearning sound. Catching the hem of her shift in his left hand, he raised it to her hips. His palm skimmed the tender flesh inside her thighs with long, smooth strokes. Then he touched her intimately with his magician's fingers, probing the slick, hot folds. Chaotic waves of sensation surged through her and she moaned, her whole being a scarlet blaze of need.

His breath rough and hot, he whispered in her ear. "Ah, God, Maggie, it's been so long, so dreadfully long. . . ."

Desire splintered. leaving Maxie stunned. Desperately she wondered if she might have heard wrong, but even in the tempest of passion, she couldn't lie to herself about something that mattered so much. "Not Maggie," she said with ice-edged precision. "Maxie."

Robin's eyes snapped open, so close that she could see shock and something that was almost horror in the azure depths.

After a paralyzed instant, he flung away from her, throwing off the blanket and sliding from the bed. He staggered when he tried to stand, almost falling. Uncharacteristically clumsy, he sagged onto the edge of the mattress, bracing his elbows on his knees and burying his head in his hands. "Christ, I'm sorry," he said hoarsely. "I never meant for that to happen."

He was shaking violently. Lord only knew what torment filled his mind, but she sensed that it went far beyond frustrated desire.

Cold and bereft, she sat up as she struggled to find composure in the chaotic midst of confusion and thwarted passion. Dear God, but she had been a fool.

When she had mastered her instinctive, irrational rage, she managed to say, "It wasn't your fault. Blame it on the bed." Hating herself for her jealousy, she added caustically, "You wish that I was this Maggie?"

The muscles of Robin's back went rigid with strain,

the hard planes sharply defined under his fair skin. After an excruciating silence, he said from behind his hands, "Some questions shouldn't be asked. And if they are, they shouldn't be answered."

Slow, humiliating heat rose in her face at the knowledge that she'd been a fool again. Yet she could not stop herself from asking, "Shouldn't be, or can't be?"

His hands dropped away from his face. All his dazzling, concealing frivolity had been stripped away, leaving the bare bones of anguish. "Can't be, I suppose."

He stood and walked to the window to stare out at the misty hills. Though he was leanly built, taut muscles flowed smoothly beneath his fair skin, like the languid power of an Adirondack mountain lion.

If he had been awake enough to know who she was—if it had been her whom he had really wanted—all of that male beauty would still be in her arms. They would be naked together, making love in the muted light of dawn.

Trying to bury her aching sense of loss, she asked quietly, "Is Maggie the woman you wanted to marry?"

"Yes." He exhaled wearily. "We were friends, lovers, partners in crime for many years."

Partners in crime? Maxie did not want to think of that now. "She died?"

He shook his head. "On the contrary. She is happily married to a man who can give her a great deal more than I."

Maxie felt a spasm of rage at the absent Maggie. A woman who could abandon a man like Robin for another of greater fortune was not worth such misery.

She would have said as much if words would have cured Robin of his grief, but logic held no sway in matters of the heart. Besides, Maggie's choice might have been made more for security than wealth. As a woman who longed for stability herself, Maxie could understand that. Life with Robin might be stimulating, but it would surely lack security.

The light was a little stronger, revealing faint parallel lines across his back. It took her a moment to realize that they were the result of a savage whipping. Her heart twisted as she wondered what untold story lay behind those wicked marks.

She couldn't do anything about long-healed scars, but she could stop the goose bumps produced by the chilly air. She rose and took Robin's shirt from the chair where it had dried.

As she draped it around his shoulders, she said succinctly, "Your Maggie is a damned fool."

Robin turned his head and looked down at her, a faint smile on his face. His blond hair was more silver than gold in the half-light. He pulled the shirt over his head, then wrapped his arm around her shoulders and tucked her close against his side. "She isn't, but I appreciate your partisanship."

Since Maxie's shift provided little protection against the cold, she slipped her arm around Robin's waist and leaned against him. Wherever they touched, there was warmth. The accidental passion of the bed had vanished, but there was still a spark of physical awareness between them. She supposed there always would be, even if they never acted on it.

There was also an odd kind of closeness. It must be rather like the feeling of soldiers who have survived a battle together. Thinking it might be good for him to talk, she asked, "What is Maggie like?"

He hesitated, weighing his answer. "Strong. Intelligent. Brave. Integrity to the bone. Rather like you, Kanawiosta, even though you look nothing alike." His arm tightened around her shoulders. "Except that you are both beautiful."

They fell silent, watching the sun inch above the horizon. She supposed that she should feel honored by his comparison, though it was not enough to eradicate the pain of knowing that he had been making love to her by accident, his drowsy mind filled with dreams of another woman. No wonder he had been ambivalent about the desire he felt for her.

She thought of the complicated mental landscape

that she had dimly sensed when trying to teach him to listen to the wind. Some of the black places in his soul must be the agony of loss felt by a man who would not give his love often, but would give it wholeheartedly when he did.

She remembered also his bedrock core of honor. Though he loved another woman, he was also genuinely fond of herself, at least enough that he would not want to hurt her. That explained his restraint; an affair where her heart was available and his wasn't would definitely cause harm.

Her own ambivalence had not been eased. She felt a sudden, debilitating wave of bitterness at the way she was caught between two very different cultures, understanding both but belonging to neither. Among her mother's people, an unmarried woman could lie with a man without censure. If she were a true daughter of the Six Nations, living in her own home among her kin, she would have been proud to take a lover.

But she was not her mother; she was a half-breed.

True, she was no sheltered English miss, raised to bestow her body only on a man who would pay the price of marriage for the privilege of bedding her. But she was enough a product of her father's culture that she feared to express desire freely. To lie with a man without marriage would make her a wanton in the eyes of white society.

Yet there was no prospect of marriage with Robin. Life with her father had taught her that it was impossible to coax a restless man to settle down, a mistake to even try.

Even if Robin's loneliness had led him to make another quixotic offer, as when he had suggested going to Gretna Green, their backgrounds were too different to allow a permanent union. She would be a fool to hope for promises of love eternal, and a fool to settle for less. That did not mean there could be nothing honest and true between them, but giving in to passion would damage her heart and her future, possibly beyond hope of repair.

Refusing to let herself weep, she turned her face into Robin's shoulder. His other arm came around her.

"You must be sorry that we met," he said soberly. "I seem to be causing more trouble than I'm preventing."

Voice muffled against his fresh-scented shirt, she replied, "I'm not sorry if you're not sorry."

He pressed his cheek against her hair. "No, Kanawiosta, I'm not sorry."

Her throat tightened. Yes, there was something very real between them. But it would never be love.

She resolved that from now until they parted in London, she would behave logically. She would accept and enjoy his wit and his friendship, and she would not allow herself to wish for greater intimacy.

Yet in the privacy of her mind, she acknowledged that logic would make for cold memories when Robin was gone.

Chapter 14

The carriage pitched and swayed in the rutted track. Desdemona Ross braced herself wearily, avoiding the long-suffering expression of her maid and hoping the vehicle wouldn't break an axle before they reached their destination, an isolated inn called the Drover. It was a regular stop for traveling herds, and more easily reached on hooves than wheels.

With a final lurch, the carriage halted. Desdemona let herself out without waiting for her coachman to open the door. For a moment she stood in the afternoon sunshine and savored the absence of rocking. The wind blew restlessly over the barren hilltop, rippling the grasses and twisting the clouds overhead. From the aroma, a herd had been through recently.

In spite of the directions she had received, it had taken time to find an accessible spot along the old ridgeway. She wondered if Maxima and Lord Robert had been here. Well, she should soon know. She set off toward the inn, which was made of wind-eroded stone and had served drovers for centuries.

When she circled her carriage, she saw another vehicle, one with a familiar crest on the door. She gave a smile of satisfaction. Apparently she had moved fast enough to overcome the lead that the Marquess of Wolverton had achieved after the incident with the highwaymen.

Speak of the devil ... The door of the inn swung open and the marquess himself emerged. The tall powerful figure paused in the doorway for a moment. Then he gave her such a pleasant smile that Desdemona was temporarily disconcerted.

Reminding herself that they were adversaries, not friends, she said, "Good day, Lord Wolverton. I gather that you have not found our mutual quarry."

"Not yet. Shall I share with you what I have learned?"

Desdemona hesitated, glancing at the inn, then back at the marquess. Reading her unspoken objection, he said helpfully, "You can always interrogate the inn-keeper later to discover if I have been withholding information, but I think it would not be a bad thing if we talked."

Good Lord, was she that transparent? Desdemona sighed; yes, she was. No one ever had any trouble knowing what she thought, which was a drawback for a woman with political interests. "Very well," she said, knowing she sounded ungracious.

The marquess offered his arm as if they were in St. James's Park, then led her away from the inn. Though she was a tall woman, he towered over her.

He said, "I trust that you've suffered no ill effects from the attempted robbery."

"None whatsoever." She glanced at him out of the corner of her eye. He really was a fine figure of a man. "I hope that you've suffered no effects from almost being shot by me."

His eyes twinkled. "On the contrary—my miraculous escape has made me appreciate life more than I have in years."

"If you wish me to take a wild shot at you sometime in the future, I shall be pleased to oblige."

He chuckled. "I'm not sure I'd trust you to miss a second time." When they were out of earshot of servants, he said more seriously, "A group of Welsh drovers came through two days ago. My brother and the Sheltered Innocent joined them here."

"Your brother and who?"

"Sorry, I've got in the habit of thinking of Miss Collins as the Sheltered Innocent," he said, not looking very repentant.

Her eyes narrowed at his impudence, but she held her tongue. She'd save any caustic comments until she'd heard what he had to say.

"They will be near Leicester by now," he continued. "I'm not positive about the identification of Miss Collins—she has a talent for remaining unnoticed—but someone entertained the drovers with juggling and sleight-of-hand in return for food and lodging. That had to be Robin. As a boy he was fascinated by legerdemain, and he practiced until he became quite adept."

It made the rogue sound rather likable. Fighting an inclination to soften, Desdemona asked, "Where was my niece while Lord Robert was playing the mountebank?"

"Upstairs taking a bath." The marquess gave her a measuring look. "Miss Collins has had ample opportunity to escape and hasn't taken it, which supports the conclusion that she is traveling with Robin of her own free will.

Desdemona made a growling noise deep in her throat.

After a startled moment, Wolverton's lips twitched, as if suppressing a smile. "I think it's likely that my brother has offered Miss Collins his escort to London. It's exactly the kind of eccentric, honorable thing he would do, and it would mean that she is in no danger. Quite the contrary. It also explains why the young lady has no wish to run away from him."

Though Desdemona admitted privately that the marquess might be right, she was unwilling to concede that aloud. "Your imagination does you credit, but I am not convinced."

They came to a boulder on the brink of the hilltop. Since it was too steep to continue walking, she sat down, making sure that her voluminous cloak was thoroughly wrapped around her. "For all you know, Maxima may have been imprisoned upstairs rather than bathing. It's also true that when a woman has been bullied enough, she can become too intimidated to try to escape. I will not be satisfied until I speak to her myself."

"Somehow, I am not surprised to hear that," her companion murmured, sitting next to her and crossing his booted legs.

She gave him a frigid glance. "What are your intentions if you find the pair of them before I do—to buy your family name free of scandal, whatever the cost?"

"That's one possibility." His slate eyes were steady. "I won't know until the time comes."

"If you are forced to choose between justice and your brother, what will you do?"

The marquess sighed and looked out over the rolling hills. "I sincerely hope it does not come to that. You know the girl, Lady Ross. Is she so virtuous that it is unthinkable she could behave with less than perfect propriety? Your niece is no green girl, and I've heard that Americans are less rigid in their ways than we are."

Fairly caught by the question, Desdemona felt color rising in her face. Wolverton watched her quizzically, and she could see the moment when he made an intuitive leap.

"Just how well do you know her?" he asked, his gaze sharpening. "Miss Collins has only been in this country a few months, and you said that you were going to Durham to visit her."

She looked down at her parasol, toying with the jade handle. "We've never met in person," she said in a suffocated voice. "However, we have corresponded extensively, and I feel that I know her quite well. She has an educated, thoughtful mind. I have never seen any signs of coarseness or immorality."

"Good God, you've never laid eyes on the girl?" Exercising heroic restraint, the marquess continued more mildly, "Perhaps your concern for her is excessive. My inquiries imply that she is a very independent and forceful young lady. If she is also a virtuous innocent, she is in no danger from my brother. Perhaps you

should wait for her in London. I'm sure she will arrive
there soon, and you would be spared this tedious
searching."

Lady Ross stood and glared down at him. "Perhaps
you are right and Maxima will reach London safely.
However, I lack your touching faith in your brother's
integrity, so I will continue to search until I have personally assured myself about her welfare."

Giles would have been disappointed if she had let
herself be dissuaded from her quest. He stood also, and
studied her face, which interested him more than the
fate of the Sheltered Innocent. The features shaded by
her deep-rimmed straw bonnet were stronger than was
fashionable, but well shaped and really quite attractive.
A stray shaft of sunshine also penetrated the shadows
and showed that the brows he had assumed were
brown were actually auburn. "What color hair are you
concealing under that very decorous bonnet?"

She stared a him, her gray eyes wide and disconcerted.

Though Giles was usually a model of propriety, he
gave in to an irresistible urge to misbehave. Moving
slowly enough so that she could stop him if she really
wanted to, he untied her bonnet and lifted it from her
head.

He caught his breath at the sight of the blazing red
hair that coiled around her head in thick braids. A few
bright tendrils had escaped and were curling down her
long neck. She no longer looked like a high-minded reformer. If she loosed that hair, she would be a pagan
goddess of the hills.

"You see why I cover it up." Lady Ross said, her expression vulnerable. "It is not decent hair. Men love it
or hate it, but they never respect it. My sister-in-law,
Lady Collingwood, was in despair when she brought
me out. She said that my appearance was better suited
to a courtesan than a lady."

Giles had never thought much about red hair one
way or the other, but he found that he had a nearly
overpowering urge to let hers down and bury his hands

in it. He wanted those glossy, light-struck curls to flow through his fingers and coil around his wrists. He wanted to bury his face in the silky mass so that he could see and taste nothing but shining strands.

Good God, what was he thinking of? He was approaching forty, a model of sober, responsible behavior. Certainly he was well past the age where raw, sexual heat should be scrambling his wits. After drawing a deep breath, he said lightly, "There is nothing inherently moral or immoral about hair."

He touched one of the lustrous braids, half surprised to find that it didn't sear his fingertips. "Yours is very lovely, and not the least bit indecent."

"I'm not so sure," she said wryly. "I've found that if I wish to be taken seriously, I must cover it up."

Wanting to confirm a growing suspicion, he said, "I've thought all along that your concern for your niece is greater than the situation warrants. Why do you mistrust men so?"

She looked away. Her skin had the milky translucence of the true redhead. "I don't mistrust all men. Fathers and brothers are well enough, and some others."

That explained a great deal. Giles said quietly, "I recall hearing that your late husband, Sir Gilbert, was an unsteady sort of man."

Her head whipped around, her expression hardening. "You are presumptuous, my lord. If a man with your reputation for rectitude can be so impertinent, it is hardly surprising that your brother is a thoroughgoing rogue."

She snatched her bonnet from his hands and yanked it onto her head, covering her flaming hair, and with it her moment of vulnerability. As she stalked away, her back was very erect within the concealing folds of her cloak.

It occurred to Giles that he had never seen her when she wasn't wrapped like an Eskimo. What would she look like in less enveloping clothing? Though she was rather stout, she seemed to have an abundance of pleasing womanly curves. He liked a woman who was a proper armful. A pity her ladyship was so prickly.

The speed of Lady Ross's retreat was inhibited by her light slippers and the necessity of picking her way carefully through the grass. He caught up with her easily. "In two days, the drovers will be going through the town of Market Harborough. You can get there in time to intercept them."

"Will you be there, Lord Wolverton?" Her voice was chilly, her face now safely hidden behind the rim of her bonnet.

"Of course. I think it the best possible place to find our fugitives." In spite of his optimistic words, Giles doubted whether Robin could be intercepted unless he wanted to be. Elusiveness was surely an important skill for a spy, and his brother would not have survived so many years on the Continent if he weren't expert at avoiding detection and pursuit.

The marquess chose not to reveal one important fact. If Robin continued on his present path, he would pass near his estate, Ruxton. It was quite possible that he and the Sheltered Innocent might decide to go to ground there for a time, particularly if they suspected they were being pursued.

If he did not find them before then, Giles would seek the pair at Ruxton. Given Lady Ross's suspicious nature, it would be a good deal better for all concerned if he was the one to locate the fugitives.

Chapter 15

Maxie took a bite of her sandwich, a slab of ham between two thick pieces of fresh bread, then leaned back against the sun-warmed stone wall in contentment. "Traveling with drovers has only two drawbacks."

Robin swallowed a mouthful of his own sandwich and washed it down with a draft of ale. "What are they?"

"The noise of several thousand cattle, plus assorted humans and dogs. And the aroma. *Especially* the aroma."

He chuckled. "Eventually you won't notice."

"I live in hope." She swallowed the last bit of ham. "But I like the drovers. They remind me of the farmers in New England. They have the solidity, the realness, of those who live close to the earth."

"Because they're entrusted with their neighbors' money, drovers have to be good steady fellows. I believe they must be at least thirty, married, and householders to be granted a license."

She wrinkled her nose. "Too many things in England seem to require licenses and regulations."

"The price of civilization." Robin's eyes twinkled mischievously. "An Englishman who finds it burdensome can always go to America to find life, liberty, and happiness."

"Individuals have more liberty in America," she said slowly, "but one can pursue happiness anywhere. Unfortunately, no law can assure that one finds it."

He gave her a wry glance of acknowledgment, then

turned to his sandwich. The herd was settling for the night and most of the drovers were having their evening meal inside the tiny inn. She and Robin had stayed outdoors, partly because of the fine weather, more because her masquerade depended on not being seen too closely. She was getting very tired of her infernal hat.

A flicker of movement caught her eye. She glanced up to see a maple seed spinning slowly to the ground. The sun struck the wing-shaped structure, turning it to translucent gold. Supported by a light breeze, it spun almost weightless for long, long seconds before it finally curved to the ground, landing only a foot or so from her hand. She released her pent-up breath and gave a smile of pure pleasure.

She did not realize that she had been observed until Robin said quietly, "When you watched that seed fall, your expression was that of a person having a religious experience."

She started to answer frivolously, then changed her mind. Perhaps Robin could not truly understand, but he would accept. "In a way, I was. Among my mother's people, all nature is seen as one great whole. A maple seed is as much an aspect of spirit as a cloud, the wind, or a human soul. If one takes some of a squirrel's hoarded nuts for food in winter, one must leave enough so that the squirrel and her family can survive, for they have as much right to the gifts of the earth as humans do."

His brows drew together with the total attention he gave to subjects that interested him. "That is utterly different from the European concept of nature as an enemy that must be mastered, or a servant to do man's bidding."

"Frankly, I think the Indian way is better and healthier." Her gaze became unfocused as she tried to define concepts that did not fit easily into English. "My mother had the ability to experience nature's oneness merely by looking at a flower or a cloud. To see her in that state was to understand joy."

"Was she practicing a kind of meditation?"

Maxie shrugged. "That's probably the best English word, though it hasn't quite the right nuances. I would say that she would become part of nature's flow, like a raindrop in a river."

"Can you do the same?"

"I could to some extent when I was a small child. I think most children can—that's what much of Wordsworth's poetry is about." She paused to search for words again. "Even now, sometimes when I am contemplating the natural world I feel as if . . . as if the energy of the earth is about to rise in me. If it did, I would become part of nature's flow."

She sighed. "It never quite happens, though. I suppose I've read too many books and spent too much time in the white man's culture to be fully harmonious with the earth. It's frustrating to have wholeness almost within my grasp, yet not quite achieve it. Perhaps someday."

"Wholeness—it's an appealing concept." He made a face. "Probably because I am naturally fragmented."

"Not really—you just think that because you live so much in your head. Watch this, and try to imagine what it is like to be this seed. Use your spirit, not your mind."

She almost took his hand, but refrained when she remembered what had happened before. Instead she picked up the fallen maple flier, then tossed it into the air. It caught the breeze and glided away, glowing like a butterfly.

Her spirit went with it, reveling in the freedom of being skyborn, the joy of sliding down a sunbeam. Beneath the bright energy was a yearning for a fertile spot where it would be possible to send roots deep into the earth, sprout branches toward the sky, grow into a mighty tree, give birth to new life.

After the flier drifted to earth again, she became objective enough to wonder if the desire for home and roots belonged to the maple seed or to her. Both, probably, or the spirit of the seed would not have resonated so deeply within her.

She was pulled from her reverie when Robin murmured, "I think I understand a little, Kanawiosta. Trying to be one with nature is not a religious act, but a manner of being."

"There's hope for you yet, Lord Robert." Though glad he understood, she did not want to say more about something so essentially private. She gestured toward a mysterious operation taking place a hundred yards away. "What is Dafydd Jones doing?"

Robin glanced toward the broad, ruddy-faced drover. "He's setting up a portable forge. You may not have noticed, but the cattle are shod so they won't go lame on the journey. Bringing a forge saves having to find a local blacksmith."

"How does one shoe a beast with cloven hooves?"

"Two separate pieces are used for each hoof. They're called cues, I believe," he explained. "Most likely the smith has brought along preformed cues and will use them rather than forging new ones. Very little hot iron work is needed that way."

Intrigued, she rose to her feet. "I think I'll go watch."

Dafydd Jones was one of the few drovers fluent in English, so she had talked with him occasionally as they followed the herd. His Welsh accent was so strong that she could not always understand what he said, but she loved listening to his mellifluous baritone.

As she approached, he said, "Care to help me, lad?"

She looked doubtfully at the dozen bullocks grazing placidly nearby. "I don't know if I'd be much use, sir. I've never worked a forge, nor cued an ox, and surely you would be needing someone larger than me."

"All ye need do is hand me the cues and the tools as I ask for them." Mr. Jones indicated the supplies, then lifted a coil of rope and tossed it over a beast that had been separated out by one of the short-legged herd dogs. When the loop had settled nearly to the ground, the Welshman pulled it tight around the bullock's legs and jerked. The heavy animal fell to the ground with a bellow, more surprised than angry.

Maxie handed a preformed metal piece to the drover. He swiftly hammered the cue in place, bending the ends of the nails over and pounding them into the edge of the hoof, all the while controlling the thrashing bullock. Only one cue needed replacement on this particular beast, so it was released to scramble up and make its way to quieter pasture, its tasseled black tail twitching indignantly.

The rest of the waiting cattle were shoed with equal ease. Behind them in the inn, male voices raised in Welsh song, a musical accompaniment to the setting sun. Maxie continued to pass cues and nails and hammer as needed, thinking how long the daylight lasted here. Strange to think how much farther north she was than in her native land, even though the English winters were so much milder.

His supper finished, Robin ambled over to watch. Even though he was behind her, she had a prickly awareness of his presence. She would miss him when they parted, she surely would.

The thirteenth and last animal proved as unlucky as its number. It was a nervous beast, with white rims showing around the dark eyes. Only the nipping teeth of the dogs kept it from bolting. Mr. Jones tossed the rope. After the bullock fell with an angry bellow, the drover moved in to begin the shoeing.

Suddenly, too swiftly for the eye to follow, the bullock broke free of its bonds and exploded to its feet, swinging its massive head and bellowing furiously. A sharp horn gored the Welshman in the ribs, ripping through his smock and knocking him to the ground beneath the raging iron-clad hooves.

Maxie froze, horrified and unsure what to do. The other drovers were in the inn and a scream would never be heard over their ale-fueled singing. If she tried to drag Mr. Jones away, the bullock would smash her to the ground like so much ragweed.

She had forgotten Robin. While she was still gaping,

he bolted past her and grabbed the beast's horns from
behind its head. Using all his wiry strength, he began
twisting the bullock's head sideways, trying to wrestle
it to the ground.

As the strain on its neck forced the animal off balance, he snapped, "Maxie, get Jones out of the way!"

A flailing hoof knocked her hat off and grazed her
shoulder as she stooped to grab the Welshman under
his shoulders. She was only half his size, but fear lent
power as she dragged him across the rough ground.
She didn't stop until the forge was between them and
the thrashing bullock.

She looked up to see a perilous tableau. Robin's
hands were locked around the bullock's straight horns
and his arms were rigid with effort as he kept the furious beast pinned to the ground. It bellowed continu-
ously and heaved against the human, but was unable to
use its brute strength effectively.

She was awed by the sheer power and mastery visible in Robin's straining body. Yet though he was temporarily in control, it was like having a tiger by the
tail. God only knew how he would be able to escape
without injury.

She was about to run to the inn for help when Robin
found enough breath to give a series of piercing whis-
tles. Several of the herd dogs raced over. Robin waited
until the dogs were close, then released the bullock.

Both man and beast scrambled to their feet, the enraged bullock trying furiously to impale the puny human who had caused such distress. Robin dodged
away barely in time, a horn missing his chest by
inches.

Before the beast could try again, the short-legged
herd dogs closed in, so low to the ground that they
skimmed below the bullock's kicks. Harrying the animal's fetlocks, they drove it back to the main herd.
With startling abruptness, it forgot its rage and began
grazing again.

Panting and disheveled, Robin crossed to where
Maxie knelt by the fallen drover. "How is Mr. Jones?"

Before she could answer, the Welshman pushed himself to a sitting position, muttering what sounded like Welsh oaths. Muddy hoofprints showed on his trousers where the bullock had trampled him. Switching to English, he said acerbically, "I'll not be sorry to see that beast turned into roast beef. Mayhap in the future I'll only shoe geese."

With Robin and Maxie's help, he managed to get to his feet. He winced, but after a gingerly exploration of his ribs, he said, "There's naught broken, thanks to you two."

Robin retrieved the rope that the drover had been using. After studying it, he held up a ragged end. "The rope was frayed and it broke when the bullock began kicking."

Mr. Jones examined the rope. "Aye. Easy to be careless, but one such mistake can kill a man. I owe you two a draft of ale and then some." His gaze fell on Maxie and his eyes widened. After a moment, he said with a smile, "You'd best put your hat back on, lass."

Maxie flushed, suddenly remembering, and recovered her hat. Her hand was trembling with the after-effects of danger as she pulled the brim down. "It seemed safer to travel as a boy."

"I'll not tell your secret," the drover assured her. "May I buy you some ale now?"

"Perhaps for Robin." She brushed grass from her knees. "I wouldn't mind a cup of tea."

"A pint would be pleasant," Robin said, "but I think both of us would prefer that no one else learn of this. It was a minor accident, after all."

"I wouldn't have thought it minor if the beast had killed me," Mr. Jones said dryly. "Nor would my wife and children. But if you don't wish to draw attention, I'll not mention it to the others." He dug into a pocket and handed two coins to Maxie.

When she tried to give the money back, the Welshman laughed. "That's not for saving me—such things can't be paid for, and if they could, I'd put a higher value on my life than two shillings. This is what I was going to give you for helping me with the cuing."

"Then thank you. It was . . . educational."

As Robin and Maxie made their way to the private spot by a hedgerow where they had spread their blankets, the drover disappeared into the noisy inn. A few minutes later a barmaid emerged with a tankard of ale and a steaming mug of tea. After delivering the drinks, she bid them a pleasant night and left.

Maxie settled on her blanket and sampled her tea. It had been liberally laced with milk and sugar. "Have you wrestled bullocks often?"

"No, but I've seen others do it," Robin replied. "I also learned at a tender age that I would never be large enough to overpower others by sheer size, so I would have to learn how to fight intelligently. The trick is not to let your opponent use his strength against you. Keep him off balance. If possible, turn his own strength against him."

"In other words, you used the same principles with the bullock that you did with Simmons."

"There was more than a passing resemblance between them."

Remembering Simmons's massive neck and shoulders, Maxie had to agree. Absently she rubbed at the bruise the bullock's hoof had left on her shoulder. "When Mr. Jones mentioned shoeing geese, did he mean that literally or metaphorically?"

Robin smiled. Though it was almost full dark now, there was enough moonlight to see the pale shine of his hair. "Believe it or not, that was literal. When geese are going to be herded long distances, they're driven through tar, then through a material like sawdust or crushed oyster shells. Pads form so that their webbed feet won't wear out before reaching their destination."

"It sounds safer than shoeing oxen." She took a swallow of tea. "Robin, you are an absolute gold mine of useless information. How do you keep it all straight?"

"But it's not useless," he protested. "One can never tell when one will need to shoe a goose."

"Or summon a herd dog." She set the mug on her knee, keeping her hand around it for balance. If Robin was engaged in a criminal life, constant observation must be what had kept him alive and free. "I gather that you learned the signals on the off chance you might need them someday."

" 'Someday' came rather quickly in this case." He sipped at his ale. "Do you ever drink anything with alcohol in it?"

"Never." That sounded too terse, so she added, "I decided when I was twelve that drinking was a habit I was better off without. My mother's people often have terrible trouble with alcohol. In fact, drunkenness helped inspire a new religious movement among the Iroquois."

"How did that come to pass?"

"Ganeodiyo of the Seneca—'Handsome Lake' to the English—was an old man, dying of drink, when he had a vision. In it, he was told that firewater was for the white man and that the Great Spirit forbade his people to drink it. Ganeodiyo foreswore alcohol and within a day he was healed of his illness. He began preaching his revelations—about faithfulness in marriage, love among families, children's obedience to their elders. There are Christian elements, but the essence is Indian."

She paused, hearing the remembered voices of her mother and her mother's kin. "Ganeodiyo said, 'Life is uncertain, therefore, while we live, let us love one another. Let us sympathize always with the suffering and the needy. Let us always rejoice with those who are glad.' He died only last year, at a great age."

Her throat tightened and she stopped. She had never spoken of such things to a white man, had never dreamed that she would. But then, she had never imagined a man like Robin.

Robin said quietly, "Clearly Ganeodiyo walked the same path as the world's other great spiritual teachers."

He pronounced the Seneca name exactly as she had. A faint question in his voice, he continued, "You said your cross came from your mother."

"She was a Christian, but she did not believe that invalidated the beliefs of her own people." Maxie touched the cross beneath her worn shirt. "She used to say that survival lay in blending the best of her own people's wisdom with the best of the white man's. She called it following the middle way."

"She must have been a remarkable woman."

"She was." Maxie's tone lightened. "Papa always said that he couldn't remarry because he would never find another woman who was such a good listener. He generally said that when I was winning a debate."

"At least he talked with you," Robin said dryly. "My father restricted himself to issuing edicts."

"All of which you disobeyed."

"I'm afraid so." He gave an elaborate sigh. "I have a constitutional inability to take orders."

Such rebelliousness might not have served Robin well in life, but it had certainly made him interesting. With a smile, she set down her empty mug and rolled up in her blanket. "A pity that you never met my father. You're the only man I've ever known who could have matched Max's magpie mind."

"Magpie?" Robin also lay down and wrapped himself in his blanket. "How insulting. I'll have to throw away the glittering stones I was collecting to give you."

She chuckled as she shaped her knapsack into a comfortable pillow. With other people scattered throughout the area, she and Robin had to keep a discreet distance between them. Yet she missed the comfort of sleeping in his arms.

As it was, he was both too near for safety and too far for comfort. Half asleep, she laid a tentative hand on the grass between them. She had no sense whatsoever where he was concerned.

To her great pleasure, he reached out to cover her

hand with his, his warm fingers interlacing with hers.
She relaxed, knowing she would sleep better because
they were touching.

Robin awoke to a cool, misty dawn. He was amused
and not surprised to find that he and Maxie had grav-
itated together during the night. She was now snuggled
against him, her exotically lovely face half hidden in
his shirt. He loved her dark skin, which had a sensual
warmth that made most other women look pallid and
only half alive.

Her trousered knee was tucked between his thighs,
and his hand was resting on the ripe curve of her bottom. Even though layers of clothing separated them, he
felt the unmistakable stirrings of desire.

But she aroused more than simple desire. She had a
special kind of innocent sensuality, a quality of being
totally comfortable with her body, that he had never
seen in a European woman. She also had intelligence,
humor and courage.

What she did not have was any obvious interest in
acquiring a mate. Her initial distrust of him had
turned to liking, even occasional approval, but he suspected that after she had investigated her father's
death, she would walk away like a cat, without looking back.

His arm tightened around her as he realized how
reluctant he would be to see her go. Maxie had revital-
ized him; he felt as if he had shed several decades of
weariness since they had met.

For the first time, he asked himself squarely what he
wanted of her. He was not interested in a flirtation, and
a platonic friendship was too limiting. And, though he
was entranced by her perfect little body, a casual affair
would not be enough. No, what he wanted was a companion with whom he could laugh and play and make
love. He had enjoyed that kind of relationship with
Maggie, until, because of some fatal lack in him, she
had retreated from intimacy.

It was more than unfair to compare Maggie and the

young woman in his arms; it was impossible. Yet both had generous and valiant spirits, and perhaps in time he might find the sort of closeness with Maxie that he had known with Maggie. It would take time for trust and openness to grow, for he and Maxie both concealed themselves behind practiced defenses.

But day by day, each was revealing more to the other. It was promising that Maxie had spoken of matters sacred to her mother's people. As for himself, more than once he had found himself saying things he had not meant to say, things that made him vulnerable in uncomfortable ways.

He smiled ruefully. He was willing to endure the discomfort in the hope that something lasting would come of it, but he feared that she had no interest in such an outcome. She wanted a real home and a man she could respect. Robin could provide the home, but he had done damn-all that was worthy of respect.

Nonetheless, he succumbed to temptation and lightly kissed her on the end of her elegant little nose.

Her long black lashes swept up and she regarded him with an unblinking brown gaze. "Which of us moved during the night?"

"We both did, I think."

She considered that thoughtfully. "People will be waking soon. We should get up, or at least retreat a few feet."

"Quite right." Yet he didn't release her, and she made no attempt to move away. Instead, her hand slid between his arm and his rib cage, drawing them even closer together. A good thing they were both clothed, or he would be forgetting how public this location was.

Luckily, it wasn't long until other voices began murmuring through the mist. He reluctantly removed his arm. "If anyone notices you're a female, it will do your reputation no good."

She smiled wickedly and sat up. "And if they think I am male, it will do both our reputations even less good."

He laughed as he stood and stretched the kinks from his muscles. He would worry about the future when they reached London. For now, he couldn't remember when the days had seemed so full of promise.

Chapter 16

Desdemona Ross had not realized there were as many cattle in England as she had seen in the streets of Market Harborough this morning. Without removing her gaze from the spectacle below, she finished her third cup of tea. This upper chamber at the front of the Three Swans had already been bespoken the night before, but she had used a combination of gold and bullying to secure it for herself.

When the Welsh Blacks first began flowing by, she had been tense with anticipation as she watched from her vantage spot. Now, an interminable length of time later, she was weary, bored, and fearful that her vigil was doomed to failure.

She had seen entirely too many blasted black oxen, a goodly number of Welsh drovers in smocks and trousers and long wool stockings, herd dogs with absurdly short legs, and a handful of country folk who were traveling with the drive. Occasionally she had glimpsed a couple of burly men in an alley on the other side of the high street. They seemed to be watching the drive as closely as she was. Perhaps one of them was the fellow Cletus had sent after Maxima.

What she had not seen was anyone who might be Maxima Collins. Neither had she seen the unreliable Lord Robert.

Setting her cup down, she wondered where the Marquess of Wolverton was. Surely he was near and watching as carefully as she. That is, unless he had already intercepted their mutual quarry, which would explain why Desdemona had had no success.

She had mixed feelings about Wolverton's absence. The man had a talent for getting under her skin, and whenever that happened, she acted like an idiot. Nevertheless, she had enjoyed their encounters.

The end of the cattle drive was finally in sight. Bringing up the rear were three dust-covered people and a pair of briskly trotting herd dogs. With a gasp, Desdemona leaned forward, squinting to confirm what she had glimpsed.

One of the three was a drover, one a light-footed man of middle height, and the third was a very small figure dressed like a boy and wearing a disreputable hat that had been described time and time again. As she watched, the man in the middle said something that set the other two to laughing.

Brimming with excitement, Desdemona raced for the stairs.

A cattle drive was not quiet in a country lane, but it was far noisier when the clattering hooves, aggrieved lowing, and yipping dogs were trapped between buildings. Maxie and Robin walked behind the unruly river of black oxen, along with Dafydd Jones and a cluster of beasts with missing shoes that slowed their pace. Mr. Jones was in charge of the laggards, with two dogs to prevent the oxen from wandering down side lanes. Most of the town's residents had prudently withdrawn behind doors to wait for the cattle to pass. The drive had taken much of the morning and was leaving the high street in dire need of cleaning.

Droveways usually avoided towns, but this route was essential in order to reach one of the important livestock markets. Being in a town gave Maxie a prickly feeling of danger after the openness of the ridgeways. Still, there had been no sign of Simmons since the encounter in the clearing. He must have given up the pursuit.

It was an unlucky thought. They were nearing the market square when a familiar voice bellowed, "There they are!"

Not fifty feet away, Simmons emerged from a doorway with a look of savage delight on his battered face. Beside him was another bruiser, just as large and even more brutal looking.

"Damnation!" Robin swore under his breath.

They both whirled, only to see two more ruffians coming purposefully from the opposite direction. They were trapped.

An ear-shattering whistle split the air as Dafydd Jones grasped the situation and acted with a speed that belied his slow-moving appearance. His whistled commands ordered the dogs to turn the last group of bullocks and bring them back along the street at high speed.

A well-trained herd dog does not question a command, no matter how contrary to custom. Within seconds, the street was blocked by churning, confused bullocks. Harried by the sharp nips of the dogs, some turned quickly and galloped full-speed along the cobblestones. Others milled and bellowed in confusion. It was a scene straight from Bedlam.

Robin grabbed Maxie's arm and called, "Many thanks!"

Mr. Jones waved and yelled, "Luck to you!"

Maxie caught a last glimpse of Simmons's furious face. He and his men were trying to fight their way through the clamorous, blaring oxen, but without success. They'd be lucky not to be trampled flat.

After that, she concentrated on escape, following Robin toward the next alley. The cattle kept a small distance away from the faces of the buildings, so it was possible to force a passage along the edge of the street. She felt small and horribly fragile as the massive bullocks jostled by, but as long as she and Robin stayed by the walls, they were safe.

After a chaotic interval of battling along the street, they reached the mouth of the alley and darted inside. Robin paused, touching her elbow lightly. "How are you faring?"

"Bruised but unbowed." She dragged a dusty hand

across her forehead. "Do you know your way around Market Harborough?"

"No, but we're about to learn," he said with a flashing smile.

She felt a burst of irrational exuberance. Robin might be a rogue, but under these circumstances, she couldn't imagine a better companion.

If the truth be known, she couldn't imagine a better companion for any circumstances.

Desdemona reached street level and flung the front door of the inn open just as the steady stream of oxen disintegrated into chaos. Aghast, she stared into the milling, bellowing mass. Bullocks were much larger close up than they appeared from above, and their horns a great deal sharper.

Angry shouts pierced the general clamor. She looked down the street to see two rough-looking men forcing their way through the cattle. Grimly she decided that if they could do it, so could she. She stepped out onto the street.

From behind her came a horrified cry from the landlord of the Three Swans. Ignoring his shout, she flattened herself against the front wall of the inn and began edging her way up the high street. She should have brought her coachman. No, her guard, he was bigger and stronger. He probably also had too much sense to do something this stupid.

Tenaciously she worked her way toward where she had seen Maxima. Ahead of her, the two ruffians disappeared down an alley. In the distance were two men of similar stamp, but not a sign of her elusive niece. Furious with exasperation, she rose on her toes and shaded her eyes, trying to see what was going on.

Her action was a disastrous mistake. A horn from one of the crowding bullocks caught the sleeve of her pelisse and dragged her sideways. When she tried to regain her balance, she became tangled in her skirts. The fabric of her pelisse ripped away entirely and she fell, sprawling across the filthy cobblestones.

She looked up to see the iron-shod hooves of a bullock descending on her, and knew that she was going to die.

Maxie and Robin followed the alley until it emptied into another street that paralleled the high. As they turned into it, a shout echoed behind them, proof that Simmons and his companions were too close behind.

The new thoroughfare was busy with traffic displaced from the high street, and they had to zigzag around incurious citizens. When the narrow road was blocked by a massive dray unloading goods at the rear of a shop, Maxie dropped to the ground to scramble under it, Robin right behind her.

They regained their feet on the other side of the wagon to find a draper's shop directly in front of them. After dusting his knees, Robin led the way inside and gave the woman behind the counter a smile of paralyzing charm. "Sorry to disturb you, madam, but we have urgent need of your back door."

As the dazzled female made confused sounds, he crossed the sales room and opened the only other door. Half expecting to have a bolt of fabric hurled at her, Maxie hastened after him.

A narrow corridor led to a kitchen at the back of the building. Robin gave the startled cook another disabling smile and they walked through into the garden. The iron gate at the bottom was unlocked and opened into another alley.

Like many old towns, Market Harborough had grown up on a twisted medieval street plan. Through pure bad luck, their route swung back and brought them into the view of one of Simmons's bruisers. The man shouted for his fellows. Even the background sounds of the cattle drive did not drown the sound of heavy pounding feet coming to join the pursuit.

Maxie and Robin pivoted and began racing through the tangle of alleys and lanes at top speed. If it had been dark, they would have been able to shake the hunters easily, but in daylight, the advantage was to Simmons, and the choice of routes was limited.

The next turn took them up a steeply angled lane where empty wooden casks were piled behind a tavern, redolent with the tang of hops. Struck by inspiration, Maxie panted, "Wait, Robin."

She tipped a cask on its side and waited for the pursuers to reach the mouth of the lane. Within seconds, the whole pack of them roared around the corner and started upward.

Gleefully she kicked the cask down the sloping ground, then reached for another. With a breathless gust of laughter, Robin joined her and they sent half a dozen casks crashing downward, booming and cracking as they collided with walls and one another. Filthy curses and abruptly curtailed squawks of protest followed the fugitives as they took off again.

Though the few seconds of rest had helped, Maxie's lungs still burned with strain. Nonetheless, she continued running, grateful for the active life that had given her stamina. Robin was paying her the compliment of assuming she was equal to what was necessary, and she would be damned if she would falter.

The next alley turned sharply to the right. When they swung around the corner, she gasped with dismay.

The alley ended in a brick wall, well over the height of a man's head, and there was no way out.

Desdemona was rolled onto her side by the grazing hooves of the first bullock, and her breath was knocked from her lungs. Even as she struggled to rise, she knew that her attempt would fail. In another few moments she would be past caring.

Then strong hands seized her and jerked her from the street to the relative safety of a shallow doorway. She came to rest with her face pressed into the shoulder of a wool coat.

Even without seeing her rescuer's face, she knew it was Wolverton. He swung her around so her back was to the door, his body shielding her from the buffeting of the oxen.

Fingers gripping his lapels, she went into a paroxysm of coughing from the dust she had inhaled. She realized with resigned self-mockery that a female could hardly appear at worse advantage than she did at the moment. It was the first time she had wanted a man to admire her since she was eighteen.

The thought was outrageous and unwelcome, but she did not push away. Wolverton's embrace was too welcome.

An amused baritone sounded in her ear. "Did anyone ever tell you that your courage greatly exceeds your common sense?"

A bubble of laughter escaped her. "Yes. Frequently."

Behind them the noise and turbulence of the cattle was diminishing. With regret, Desdemona stepped away from her rescuer. Her wobbly knees immediately betrayed her, but before she could fall, he caught her arm again.

Unsteadily she said, "I'm quaking like a blancmange."

"A perfectly normal reaction. You had a narrow escape."

She leaned back against the door, willing her body to behave. "Still, I'm very much in your debt, Wolverton. You might have been trampled yourself."

He gave a deprecating shrug. "I spend a fair amount of time with cattle, so I'm used to their ways."

Even though most of the British aristocracy derived their fortunes from the land, few of the men Desdemona knew in London would so casually confess to being farmers. Perhaps she spent too much time in London.

She pushed at her tumbled hair with a trembling hand. Her gown and pelisse were ruined, and her bonnet lay smashed in the street. "If I'd known that I was going to take part in a cattle riot, I would have dressed differently."

Behind them, the now-orderly oxen had settled

down and resumed their progress to market. The drover who had been at the end of the herd approached, concern on his weathered face. "I hope ye took no harm, ma'am," he said in a rolling Welsh accent. "I'd not forgive myself if you'd been injured."

"I'm fine." To prove it, she took a cautious step away from the door. This time her knees supported her. "It was foolish of me to come into the street when the drive was going through."

As the drover started to move away, Wolverton asked, "Why did you turn the cattle like that? It was dangerous."

The drover stopped, an opaque expression in his eyes. " 'Twas a mistake, sir. The dogs misunderstood the command."

Still pleasantly but with a hint of steel, the marquess said, "I've heard that when a drive is over, the herd dogs make their own way home all the way from southern England to Wales or Scotland while their masters return by coach. Hard to believe that dogs so intelligent would misunderstand a whistle."

"You've caught me out, sir." Though the Welshman's voice was properly abashed, there was a gleam of humor in his eyes. "The problem was not the dogs' lack of wit, but mine. I gave the wrong signal, and the dogs obeyed. Lucky no damage was done."

"I'm sure you will tell me that turning the cattle had nothing to do with the two people who were with you, and the four men who were after them," Wolverton said dryly.

"Nay, not a thing." The drover touched the brim of his hat with two fingers. "I must look to my beasts now. Good day to you and the lady."

Desdemona stared after the Welshman's broad back. "You mean he did that deliberately to help Maxima and Lord Robert escape?"

"Undoubtedly. That was definitely Robin, though I didn't see much of his companion under that dreadful hat." He smiled a little. "My brother has a talent for enlisting allies."

Desdemona frowned, perplexed. "Why would there be four men pursuing them?"

The marquess tucked her hand under his arm and headed toward the Three Swans. "We can discuss it over luncheon."

Desdemona opened her mouth to disagree on principle, then closed it again. She really didn't want to protest.

Chapter 17

U ndaunted by the sight of the brick wall ahead, Robin ordered, "Wait here."

He sprinted down the alley, his pace quickening. A stride from the wall, he hurled himself upward. His leap was just high enough for his outstretched fingers to catch the edge of the wall. Making it look easy, he swung lithely onto the wide brick top. Then he unslung his knapsack and lowered it strap first.

Maxie grabbed the strap. It stretched under her weight, but held. As Robin lifted, she walked up the wall. He grinned as he gave her a hand up beside him. "It's clear you didn't spend your childhood on useless things like embroidery."

She grinned back. "It was a point of pride for me to outrun, outswim, and outclimb all of my Mohawk cousins."

Their pursuers were almost to the foot of the brick wall. Robin gave a jaunty wave before the two of them swung down on the far side of the wall. He dropped to the ground first, then reached up and caught her hips to bring her safely to earth. She was acutely aware of the strength of his hands, and of the involuntary reaction of her body. A good thing they were running for their lives.

They found themselves in a well-tended garden behind a sizable town house. Directly in front of them was an archery target with bow and arrows lying beside it in the grass, as if someone had gone inside for a cup of tea and would be back soon.

As Robin started to cross the garden, she said, "Wait

a moment." She picked up the bow and flexed it a few times, getting the feel. Then she nocked an arrow and waited.

After angry muttering and scuffling sounds on the other side of the wall, a pursuer heaved gracelessly into view on the shoulders of one of his mates. Coolly Maxie took aim, then sent her arrow through the man's hat. He howled like a banshee and disappeared from view.

"Well done!" Robin said, his voice full of admiring laughter.

She laid the bow back on the grass, not without a certain smugness. Being a savage had its advantages.

"Gawd a'mighty, did you see what that little bitch did?" Simmons's associate retrieved his arrow-pierced hat, his face white under its habitual grime. "I coulda been killed!"

"If she wanted to kill you, she'd've done it," Simmons said brusquely. Even as he let loose a string of oaths that should have scorched the whitewash on the alley walls, the Londoner had to admit to himself that the two fugitives were worthy game.

Another of his men snarled, "I'm not goin' over that wall after 'em."

Simmons broke off. He knew Market Harborough, and he should be using that knowledge instead of wasting time. "We don't have to. There's a way around. If we hurry, we should be able to catch them. Now move your bloody backsides!"

As Maxie and Robin raced across the garden, an angry shout came from a window of the house.

"Try not to step on any flowers," Robin warned. "Hell hath no fury like an English gardener whose roses have been profaned."

They were rapidly approaching a wall covered with espaliered fruit trees. The branches were trained into stately lattices and tiny green peaches were visible among the leaves. Breathlessly she asked, "Are we allowed to profane fruit trees?"

"It's a grievous crime, but not so bad as injuring roses," he assured her as he swarmed up the espaliered branches.

The trees made an excellent ladder. Before anyone could emerge from the house and give chase, they were over the wall and down the other side on a quiet street.

As they paused to take stock, Robin said soberly, "The pursuit is amazingly tenacious. Your uncle obviously wants you back a great deal."

"So it seems," she agreed, her expression grim as she speculated about what Collingwood was trying to conceal. But when she looked at her companion her voice faltered. "I'm sorry to have involved you in this. It's more than you bargained for when you offered your escort."

He smiled, his blue eyes warm and intimate. "I didn't offer my escort, I forced it on you. And I'm not sorry at all." He gestured to the left. "A canal runs north from Market Harborough to Leicester. I think we should follow the towpath. It's less likely to be watched than one of the roads."

"Do you really think all of the roads are watched?" she said with alarm. "Simmons would need a small army for that."

Robin shrugged. "Perhaps the roads are safe, but when in doubt, assume the worst."

That made sense; she was sure that his experience of being chased greatly exceeded her own. She fell in beside him, trotting as quickly as her tired limbs could manage.

This section of the town was empty of traffic, but in the middle distance were several large buildings that looked like warehouses. Probably the canal was on the other side.

Before they could reach the warehouses, Simmons came pounding out of a lane in front of them, a smile of wicked satisfaction on his face and one of his cohorts at his heels. With sickening anxiety, Maxie

glanced behind and saw two more men emerging from
another alley. She and Robin were trapped, and this
time there was no helpful Dafydd Jones with a herd of
oxen.

They came to a halt facing Simmons. He waved a
hand at his men, who fell back into a silent circle as
the Londoner growled, "You're not getting away this
time. The wench is going back to her uncle, and you,
my pretty lad, are going to be taught a lesson for attacking me from behind."

"You should be glad I fought as I did—it gave you
an excuse for losing." Calmly Robin handed his knapsack to Maxie.

Appalled, she hissed, "For God's sake, Robin, surely
you're not going to fight him. He's twice your size."

He smiled and peeled off his coat. "One can refuse
a man's invitation to dine, or to play a game of cards,
but if he wants to fight, one must oblige him."

Overhearing, the Londoner said explosively, "You're
damned right you'll oblige. And I don't care how good
you are—a good big man will beat a good little man
every time."

"That depends on how good the little man is, doesn't
it?" Under cover of a sunny smile, Robin whispered to
Maxie, "Simmons's men will be absorbed in watching
the fight. Take advantage of that to escape." Seeing her
about to protest, he said sharply, "No arguments. Don't
worry, he's not going to kill me—it would get him into
more trouble than it's worth."

Before he could say more, Simmons came up and
began searching his opponent, his large hands patting
pockets and around the tops of Robin's boots. Robin
said pleasantly, "Are you looking for concealed weap-
ons, or is it just that you can't keep your hands off
me?"

Revolted, Simmons spat, "Filthy pervert!" and
swung a wild fist at the other man's jaw.

Robin sidestepped neatly and caught his opponent's
arm. Then he twisted it, at the same time rapidly piv-

oting. The larger man spun and crashed to the road with numbing force.

For a moment Simmons lay stunned. Then he rose to his feet, eyes narrowed and anger tempered by caution. "You didn't learn that in Jackson's salon."

"No, I didn't." Robin looked slight and elegant, a David to Simmons's Goliath. But his stance was that of a fighter as he balanced on the balls of his feet, knees bent, arms relaxed and ready. "I never claimed to be a student of Jackson's. I learned in a harder school, where the stakes were higher."

"So did I, laddie boy." The Londoner fell into the same stance. "If that's the way you want it, you've got it."

Maxie surreptitiously slid her hand into the pocket of Robin's coat and locked her hand around the striking stick. Then there was nothing to do but watch, half suffocated with tension. In spite of what Robin had said, she had no intention of abandoning him. Perhaps Simmons didn't intend murder, but there was a horrible chance that he might kill without meaning to. That was less likely if Maxie was a witness.

The two men slowly circled each other, their taut wariness sporadically interrupted by brief, violent clashes. Robin kept his distance as much as possible, moving in for a lightning hit, then darting out of range again. He had the edge in speed, but the other man had the lethal advantages of reach and weight.

To Maxie's disgust, she realized that Simmons was enjoying himself. After a particularly clever sally on his opponent's part, the big man said approvingly, "You're damned good, 'specially for a gentry cove."

He accompanied his words with a series of murderous punches to the head and shoulders. Robin skipped back, but was unable to block the barrage entirely. Several blows landed, leaving him gasping and off balance.

Simmons followed up his advantage with a fist in Robin's midriff that sent the smaller man to the

ground. Crowing with triumph, the Londoner moved in
to finish the fight.

A good deal less defeated than he looked, Robin
knocked Simmons from his feet with a scythelike
sweep of his leg. Even as the larger man was falling,
Robin exploded into a blur of movement too swift for
Maxie to follow. It ended with the Londoner face down
on the ground and Robin's knee in his back.

His hands applying a wrestling hold that could break
the neck of a man too foolish to surrender, Robin
snapped, "Yield!"

Even furious, Simmons was not a fool. He reluctantly raised one hand in submission.

Unfortunately, his cohorts were unwilling to accept
the result. With snarls and no thoughts for sportsman-
ship, two of them went after the man who had defeated
their employer.

Maxie screamed, "Robin!" She dropped his coat and
scooped a handful of dust and gravel from the road
with her empty hand, then flung it in the faces of the
bruisers. The men howled.

Robin used the moment's warning to leap to his feet.
A perfectly aimed kick knocked one man down. Without losing a second, he whirled and caught the second
man's arm, then flung him to the ground. Though his
lightning-quick moves had a dancer's grace, they left
both opponents sprawling, one with his arm bent at an
unnatural angle.

As Robin disposed of his two attackers, the third
man grabbed a rock and swung it at Robin's skull with
lethal force. Maxie dived at him and clutched his arm,
using her whole weight in an attempt to deflect the
blow. As he staggered, she smashed her fist and the
striking stick into his breast bone.

When her blow rammed home, he gave a strangled
squawk, but her assault was only partially successful.
The stone struck Robin just above the ear with a sickening thud. Though she had managed to reduce the
force, the impact was enough to send Robin crumpling
to the cobblestones.

Furious and terrified for Robin, she slashed at the third man's face with clawed fingers. As he tried to protect his eyes, she kneed him viciously in the groin. Then she jabbed him in the throat with the striking stick. He made an indescribable sound and folded over on himself like a suit of empty clothes.

The least damaged man present, Simmons lunged to his feet and grabbed Maxie in a bear hug, trapping her arms and legs. Thrash as she might, she couldn't free herself, though she managed a few good butts and bites.

"Stop that, you little hellion!" Simmons gasped, locking her hands behind her back in one meaty fist. With the other, he wrenched the stick from her hand and tossed it away. "My lads shouldn't've interfered in a fair fight, but by God, if you don't behave, you'll regret it."

Recognizing the need for a strategic truce, she stopped struggling. Her terrified gaze went to Robin. He lay senseless in the dust, his blond hair stained by the slow seep of blood.

Keeping a firm grip on her, Simmons scowled at the two men who were stumbling to their feet. "'You fought like a bunch of girls," he said contemptuously. "Worse—this little wench has more skill and spirit than the three of you put together."

His expression vicious, one of the bruisers drew back his foot to kick Robin.

Simmons snapped, "Touch 'im and I'll break your arm myself. You get over to the livery stable and bring the carriage 'round."

In a cloud of surly muttering, the two men left. The third bruiser still lay in the road, sublimely unaware.

Maxie wondered angrily where the citizens of Market Harborough were, but this was a drab backstreet, more warehouses than homes, and no one came. "Let me go so I can see to Robin," she said tightly. "He may be badly hurt."

"He'll survive, though it might 'a gone hard with 'im if you hadn't grabbed Wilby's arm." Simmons shook his head. "Wilby really shouldn't 'a done that. It's hard to get reliable help."

Maxie's sympathy was nil, but for the moment discretion was the better part of valor. Trying to sound resigned she asked, "What are you going to do with us?"

"You're going to Durham, trussed like a Christmas goose if necessary. Now, as for your friend, that's a question, and no mistake." Simmons frowned. "I could just leave 'im here, but 'e might come after me. 'E seems the stubborn sort. Mebbe I'll give 'im to the local constable, say 'e stole my horse."

After a moment's thought, he chuckled. "Aye, that's the ticket. By the time 'e's brought up to the magistrate, you'll be in Durham, and then you're Collingwood's problem." He rubbed his cheek, where a wide bruise was forming. "Better 'im than me."

As he talked, his grip on her hands loosened. Deciding that there was no time like the present, Maxie tried to wrench herself from his grasp. She managed to break away for a moment, but before she could get clear, he grabbed one of her wrists.

Another furious skirmish followed. Even knowing it was hopeless, she continued to struggle. She managed to get a good swipe at Simmons's face with her fingernails, scratching his bruised cheek until it bled.

"I warned you, you little vixen!" Simmons dragged Maxie over to the low brick wall that bounded the street and sat down. Then he turned her over his knee and began to spank her with a hard, massive hand.

For a moment, she was stunned with disbelief and the sheer indignity of what he was doing. The Iroquois did not believe in being violent with children. Her father had also preferred reason to force, so she had never been spanked in her life.

The fighting that had gone before had been fierce but without deadly intent. Now the last traces of her English restraint dissolved.

Maxie inhaled a deep lungful of air, then gave a Mohawk war whoop that vibrated the panes of glass in nearby windows. It was a savage explosion of sound unlike anything heard in England since the natives wore blue paint.

Simmons gasped, his hand suspended in midair. "Gawd a'mighty, what was that?"

And in the moment he was distracted, Maxie twisted, pulled the knife from her boot, and came up slashing.

Chapter 18

Robin never wholly lost consciousness, but for a time he was very disconnected from his surroundings. His body and mind became reacquainted in time for him to see Simmons put Maxie over his knee. Robin wanted to warn the Londoner that spanking her was not a wise idea, but his voice didn't seem to want to work. With dizziness and near blackout, he slowly pushed to his knees.

Maxie's war whoop gave an electrifying jolt to his system. He raised his head to see her swinging her knife at Simmons's jugular. Swearing, the Londoner dodged back. The glittering blade barely missed his throat, grazing his shoulder instead.

Before his bloodthirsty comrade could try again, Robin managed to croak, "Stop it, Maxie!"

Her wild brown eyes shifted to him. She hesitated, rage and reason warring in her expression.

In a moment before something worse could happen, Robin staggered over to Simmons, coming from an angle where the Londoner couldn't see him. Then he rendered the other man unconscious with the blood-stopping hold he had used before. It was dangerous, but Simmons's chances of survival were greater if he was knocked out this way than if Maxie was the one to end the fight.

Simmons made a choking noise, then keeled off the wall, almost taking Robin down with him. Maxie caught Robin swiftly, her hands supplying much-needed support. Her words, however, were tart. "You should have let me take care of him."

Robin clung to her as his eyesight darkened around the edges. For once, he scarcely noticed the delicious feel of her. "Sorry," he said unsteadily, "but I really don't like seeing people killed."

She made a sound that suggested both disdain and that the conversation would be continued at a more suitable time. But with an admirable focus on the immediate, she asked, "Can you walk? The others will be back soon."

He folded down on the wall and buried his face in his hands, trying to think his way through the shattering pain in his skull. "I'll need help."

She briskly resheathed her knife and helped him into his coat. Then she retrieved the striking stick, slung both knapsacks on her own back, tugged Robin to his feet, and pulled his arm over her shoulders.

As they wove their way down the street, he reflected with dizzy appreciation on how much strength was in her petite frame. Still, it was fortunate that the canal was only on the far side of the warehouses.

The question was, what would they do when they got there?

As soon as they entered the inn, Giles ordered a private parlor, with brandy immediately and food to follow. Lady Ross was still shaken by her narrow escape, and she let herself be escorted to the parlor with a docility that Giles did not expect to last long. Her face was gray beneath the flamboyant red hair.

After guiding her to a chair, he inspected her upper arm where the ox horn had gored. The pale skin visible through her slashed clothing was lacerated, but the wound was superficial, with little blood. "No serious damage done, though you'll have heavy bruising."

A maid brought the brandy. Giles poured a glass for his companion. She choked on the first mouthful, but color began to return to her face. "There will be bruising in a number of less mentionable places as well," she said with a crooked smile.

"You would know that better than I."

She pushed her loose hair off her brow with fingers that were almost steady again. "Give me a few minutes to go to my room and make myself presentable. Then I want to hear about the men who were after Maxima and Lord Robert."

Lady Ross restored herself to thunderous respectability very quickly. When she returned, her hair had been tamed and hidden under a cap, she had changed into another dress as drab as the previous one, and her full figure was swaddled in a shawl. Giles preferred her disheveled; nonetheless, her restrained appearance did nothing to slow the steady beat of sexual awareness.

The meal that had been ordered was brought as soon as she reached the parlor. By tacit consent, they ate before addressing the serious issues. When they had reached the stage of coffee, Desdemona cocked a brow at the marquess. "About those men?"

"One of them I recognized, and I suspect that he is the agent your brother sent after Miss Collins." Wolverton explained how he had aided the man called Simmons several days earlier. "So not only are you and I hot on the trail in our separate ways, but apparently Simmons and his helpers as well."

"There is an element of farce to this." Desdemona's mouth quirked in an unwilling smile. "But from what little I could see, I didn't like the looks of Simmons and his associates."

"Men who do such work aren't drawn from the most genteel ranks," the marquess said dryly. "If they had been hired to take Miss Collins back to Durham, I don't imagine they will hurt her, but they might not be so careful of my brother."

"From what you've told me, Lord Robert seems to have won every round so far." Desdemona took a deep swallow of scalding black coffee. "You said that he has been out of England for a number of years. Was he a diplomat or in the army?"

Wolverton sighed and toyed with his own cup, visibly weighing how to respond. "I'll tell you on the condition that you speak of it to no one."

"His behavior was that disgraceful?"

The marquess lifted his head, his slate eyes colder than she had ever seen them. "Quite the contrary. But what he did was highly confidential and there may be ramifications for years, even decades, to come. Nor is the story mine to tell."

"Your brother was a spy?" The deduction was not difficult. She added with heavy sarcasm, "One can see how he developed his notions of honorable behavior."

Wolverton's eyes narrowed at her tone. "Yes, he was a spy. A practitioner of the most dangerous and unrespected kind of warfare, utterly essential and utterly secret. Robin was hardly more than a boy, traveling on the Continent during the Peace of Amiens, when he stumbled over something he thought the Foreign Office should know. He was asked to stay on, and for the next dozen years he risked his life and sanity a thousand times over to protect his country and end the war sooner."

The marquess stopped, his silence gathering menacing weight, then finished in a soft, hard voice, "And so that people like you could sit safe and smug in England and judge him."

Blushing was the curse of the redhead, and Desdemona was true to her breed. Waves of hot, humiliated color spread from her hairline to her collar and below. "I'm sorry," she said painfully. "No matter how angry I am about what your brother has done to my niece, I should not have spoken as I did." She was more than ashamed; she also felt bereft at the withdrawal of Wolverton's usual warmth. To her relief, his expression eased.

"Your reaction is not unusual," he said. "Spying requires nerves of steel and a number of skills a gentleman shouldn't have. Robin was very, very good at it, or he would never have survived. He has been tested in ways that would break most men, and that very nearly broke him."

"Is that why you're so protective of him?" she asked quietly.

"I would be anyhow. He's the only family I have left, and even though I know he's ferociously competent, he's still my little brother." Wolverton sighed. "I know very little beyond what he has chosen to tell me since he returned to England, and I am devoutly grateful that I wasn't better informed during the years he was abroad. God knows it was bad enough wondering if I would ever see him again, or if he would simply disappear, one of the nameless unmourned dead, and I would never know how or when."

The marquess broke off abruptly, his face tight. Several heartbeats passed before he continued. "To give you an idea of the sort of thing he accomplished in his 'disgraceful' career, last year he helped frustrate a plot aimed at blowing up the British Embassy during the Paris peace conference."

Desdemona gasped, thinking who might have been killed in such an explosion. Likely the Foreign Minister, Castlereagh, perhaps even Wellington. The political ramifications were staggering, not only for Britain, but for the whole of Europe.

Wolverton smiled wryly. "You see why I said this must be confidential? That's only a sample of what Robin accomplished. I'm told the powers at Whitehall are considering making him a baron for services rendered, only they don't know what to say that could be made public knowledge."

"Being made a peer for espionage might be a first."

"Robin has been breaking new ground his whole life. As a boy there was no harm in him, but he could be mischievous in amazingly inventive ways." The marquess's expression lightened. "For example, I believe he was the only boy ever expelled from Eton on his very first day of school."

Desdemona chuckled. "A dubious honor. How did he do that?"

"He introduced six sheep into the headmaster's drawing room. I never did learn how he managed it. It was a calculated act, performed because he wanted to go to Winchester, not Eton." Wolverton smiled reminiscently. "Even if a title is offered, I'm not sure he would take it. Once when we were boys, we were swimming in the lake at Wolverhampton when I got a vicious cramp. I almost drowned. He dragged me out, an impressive feat considering that I was twice his size and thrashing like a reaper. When I recovered, I pointed out that he could have left me in the water and been the next Marquess of Wolverton."

"And?" Desdemona prompted.

His eyes twinkled. "Robin said that was the best possible argument for fishing me out of the lake."

Desdemona bit her lip. "The more I hear about your brother, the more dreadfully likable he sounds."

"Robin got all the charm and dash in the family. And despite what you think, he's honorable as well."

Desdemona surveyed the marquess's substantial frame, a faint smile on her face. "You seem to have inherited an adequate share of all three traits."

Wolverton stared for a moment, color rising in his face. Then he got to his feet and wandered to the window to avoid her eyes. It was the first time she had seen him disconcerted.

Served him right, she thought with satisfaction; he had been disconcerting her from the first moment they had met. Deciding that it was time to leave the personal, she asked, "Do you suppose Simmons and his men caught up with our fugitives?"

The marquess's glance outside had been idle, but his gaze sharpened. "Perhaps he did. There are two very battered-looking fellows walking down the high street. Since I saw one of them with Simmons earlier, my guess is that they tried and failed to take Robin and your niece."

She joined him at the window and incredulously surveyed the two mauled bruisers. "Your brother did that?"

"Probably. He was small and almost girlishly attractive as a boy. Such are the horrors of the English public schools that he had to choose between fighting or groveling. If he'd stayed at Eton, I could have looked out for him, but as it was . . ." Wolverton's voice trailed off.

"Obviously your brother had no taste for groveling." Suddenly aware of how close she was to the marquess's very large, very masculine frame, she unobtrusively edged away. "What now, my lord? I doubt they will return to the drovers."

His brow furrowed. "I agree. Now that our fugitives have been alerted, it will be almost impossible to find them on the road. There are too many routes, too many ways for them to disguise themselves. Perhaps the time has come for you to go to London and wait for your niece to call."

She eyed him suspiciously. The sense that they were allies was eroding rapidly. "You've something else in mind?"

"A possibility has occurred to me." He forestalled her question with one hand. "I promise that if I guess correctly, I will bring both of our runaways to you in London."

Avoiding the question of whether she would give up searching, she asked, "What if they don't wish to come?"

"I will use sweet reason to persuade them." He gave a half smile. "Using force on Robin would not be advisable."

Remembering the battered ruffians who had just passed, she had to agree.

Wolverton picked up his hat and prepared to leave, then paused. "Why were you named Desdemona?"

"It's a family tradition to give the boys Latin names and the girls Shakespearean ones," she explained.

"But your niece's name is Latin."

"There are occasional exceptions. My brother Maximus was named after Great-Aunt Maxima, and passed the name on to his daughter. Aunt Maxima died a few months back, ripe in years and wickedness. I'm going to miss her."

"Do you mean Lady Clendennon? She was the only Maxima I ever met." When Desdemona nodded, he said, "Forceful females are clearly another Collins family tradition. Less and less do I think your niece could have been persuaded to stay with Robin against her principles."

"That remains to be seen," Desdemona said dryly. Recalled to a sense of her mission, she tugged her shawl close, collected her reticule, and prepared to leave.

The marquess stood aside, but before opening the door, he halted and looked down at her, his gaze intense. As if mesmerized, he raised a hand to her face, tracing the lines of temple and ear, brushing across her cheek, caressing the curve of her throat. His touch was very delicate, as if he were trying to memorize the tones and texture of her skin with his fingertips.

She stood stock-still, fighting to maintain her composure. Everywhere he touched blazed with sensation. She had never known gentleness in her marriage, and it was shocking to realize how vulnerable she was to it.

She raised her eyes to Wolverton's and was immediately sorry. The warmth she saw there was far more dangerous than a blow. He was so large, powerful not only physically but in his air of authority. In another moment he would bend over to kiss her, and if that happened . . .

She jerked away and opened the door herself. "I shall hope to see you and our errant relations in London, Wolverton." Then she bolted.

Giles gazed at the door that had slammed in his face. Why would a strong-minded woman of the world become as skittish as a convent-bred virgin when he showed interest in her? The simple explanation was that she had taken him in aversion.

He had no doubt that in this case the simple explanation was wrong. It was not distaste he had seen in her eyes, but fear.

The Marquess of Wolverton had a well-deserved reputation as an easygoing man, but when he decided on something, he was immovable. As the sound of her swift footsteps faded away, he resolved that he was going to learn what lay at the root of Lady Ross's distress.

Then, perhaps, something could be done about it.

Chapter 19

Even though Robin did as much as he could, Maxie had to half carry him. The canal seemed endlessly distant. The back of her neck prickled in anticipation of Simmons waking or his men returning to come after the fugitives.

Given a choice, she would prefer Simmons himself. He had shown signs of a conscience, but she would trust his men no further than hungry wolves in a butcher shop.

She kept hoping that other people might appear, but the area seemed deserted. People must be eating their midday meals. As she and Robin entered the shadowed alley between two of the warehouses, she prayed for a miracle with what energy she could spare. They could not go much farther like this.

They emerged onto the sun-drenched wharf to find a loaded barge sitting at the mooring. A man and a boy were on deck preparing to cast off. The captain was a short fellow with a broad muscular figure and grizzled hair. He straightened and eyed the newcomers curiously, which wasn't surprising since Robin was draped over Maxie like a shawl.

A straightforward plea for aid seemed best. Letting her desperation sound in her voice, Maxie said, "Please, sir, can you help us? We were attacked and my husband has been injured."

The captain's startled face reminded her of how she was dressed. With her free hand, she yanked off her hat. The man blinked, his interest thoroughly engaged.

She had thought Robin beyond awareness, but he

murmured in her ear with irrepressible amusement, "Brought out the heavy guns, I see. Poor devil hasn't a chance."

"Hush!" she hissed, keeping an arm around his waist as the captain jumped to the wharf and walked over to the newcomers.

"You were attacked by thieves in town in broad daylight?" he asked, visible skepticism on his weathered face.

What story would be likely to appeal to a canal man?

When in doubt, tell some variation of the truth. "It wasn't thieves, but my cousin and his friends. They're trying to stop us from reaching London." She glanced back, having no trouble looking anxious. "Please, can we go with you for a little way? I can explain everything, but they will be here at any moment."

She turned a pleading gaze on the captain, trying to look like the sort of female a man would feel protective about. She should have paid more attention to her cousin Portia, who had spent years cultivating helplessness.

The freckled-faced boy ventured, "Mebee they're only lookin' for a free ride, Pa."

The captain studied Robin, who was wavering on his feet. "That blood looks real enough." Coming to a decision, he said, "All right, lass, I'll take you on faith for a few miles."

He stepped forward, stooped, then lifted Robin and slung him over a broad shoulder as if he were a schoolboy. "Come along."

Maxie followed, stepping across the narrow gap between wharf and boat. The barge was simply constructed with two blunt ends and a square cabin in the middle. Tarpaulin-covered mounds were secured to the deck, and the air was redolent with a strong, not unpleasant scent of wool. The cargo must be carpets, which Dafydd Jones had said were made in the area.

"I expect you would rather be out of sight if your

cousin comes," the captain said. "Take the aft hatch cover off, Jamie."

The boy scrambled to obey, excitement on his round face. The hatch cover was lifted to reveal a hold packed with more carpets. After Jamie climbed in and rearranged the rolls to create space, the captain deposited Robin's limp body. "Don't let 'im bleed on my cargo."

"I'll do my best," she promised. "Do you have some rags and water I can use to wash the blood away and bandage him?"

Jamie immediately bounced off to fulfill the request.

She climbed into the hold and knelt beside Robin, parting his golden hair to examine the damage. A lump was already forming, but she was glad to find that the gash was shallow and the bleeding almost stopped.

A minute later, Jamie returned with the supplies she had requested, as well as basilicum powder to put on the wound. As gently as possible, she washed away the blood and applied a bandage. Robin accepted it stoically, though she saw his hand opening and closing on the carpet beside him.

When Maxie finished her ministrations, the captain said, "Time we were on our way. Might be best to close the hold again."

"You're right," she agreed. "My cousin might follow if he guesses that we're trying to escape this way. It's . . . it's a complicated tale."

The weathered face looked satiric. "I don't doubt it."

After he lowered the heavy hatch cover, dragging noises sounded overhead and the slivers of light around the rectangular hatch disappeared. The captain must be putting carpets on top. She blessed him for his foresight. Even if Simmons followed the barge, he was unlikely to find their hiding place.

But the precaution made the darkness in the hold absolute. Their niche was about six feet long, four feet wide, and three feet deep, with yielding carpets beneath them. The effect was like a cozy coffin. She did her best to repress her distaste for the confinement. All that mattered was that they were heading away from Simmons, and the captain seemed to be a good ally.

Dimly she heard Jamie order the tow horse to get along. The barge began to move. Exhausted now that there was nothing more to be done, she stretched out alongside Robin. "Are you there?"

His voice a faint thread, he replied, "I have been more or less present through the last act, even though I had to be carted about like a wheel of cheese."

She smiled, relieved. "Sounds like your wits weren't scrambled by that rock."

"Of course not. My head is the most unbreakable part of me." Not quite able to conceal the strain in his voice, he said, "Is there any more water?"

She raised his head and shoulders so he could drink from the bottle. After corking what was left, she asked, "Did you sustain any damage apart from the head wound?"

There was a pause and more rustling sounds while he took inventory. Eventually he said, "Nothing to signify."

"Good. Then you can think up a convincing reason why my cousin Simmons and his merry men are after us."

"But you're doing such a good job of invention that it would be a pity to interfere," he protested.

"Next to you, I am the veriest amateur at tale-spinning."

"Perhaps at tale-spinning, but that was a splendid bit of acting. If I hadn't known better, I would have sworn that you were frightened and helpless."

"What makes you think I wasn't?" she asked, not sure whether to be flattered at his faith or offended by his lack of concern.

"Because, Kanawiosta," he said, amusement and approval in his voice, "a female who will attack a professional fighter three times her size is brave to the point of being suicidal." He rolled over and put one arm around her, drawing her close, then added in a drowsy whisper, "You make a wonderful bodyguard."

Smiling, she relaxed against him, her cheek resting on his chest. Though she knew it was irrational, she felt safe in his arms, as if the outside world could never harm her.

His breathing soon slowed and he slipped into a doze. It would have been easy for her to sleep as well, but she resisted the temptation. Instead she listened to the soft splash of water against the hull, and tried to think of a convincing story to tell the captain.

The barge *Penelope* was just entering the first of the Foxton locks when two men trotted into sight on the towpath, panting heavily. " 'Ey, you there!" the large one yelled in a cockney accent. " 'Old a minute; I want to ask you some questions."

John Blaine pulled his pipe from his mouth and surveyed the newcomer. The fellow looked like he'd been in a fight, and no mistake. "A canal boat doesn't stop when it's in a lock," he said tersely, then called to his son, "Open the ground paddle."

Jamie turned the windlass and water began flowing into the lower lock.

"Dammit, I'm speaking to you," the cockney barked.

Blaine did not find the stranger's attitude endearing. The little lady, on the other hand, had been quite charming. "And I've a job to do," he retorted. "Make yourself useful and help with the gates. I'll have time to talk at the bottom."

The water level between the first and second locks equalized and Jamie opened the gate between them. The horse pulled the barge forward, the gate closed behind, and the paddles on the next gate were opened so water could flow into the lower pound.

As he watched the *Penelope* drop rapidly below ground level, the cockney balanced uncertainly, as if debating whether to jump on the barge and put his questions forcefully. After a moment, he scowled and gestured to his henchman. The two added their considerable weight to working the gates and the paddles.

The Foxton locks consisted of two flights of five locks each, joined by a central pool where two boats could pass. Passage through ten locks is a slow business and Blaine could have found the time to answer a few polite questions on the way, but under the circumstances, he kept himself conspicuously busy.

Eventually the barge reached the bottom of the locks, seventy-five feet below where it had begun. With exaggerated courtesy, the cockney jumped on the vessel's deck and asked, "*Now* will you answer a few questions?"

Blaine tamped fresh tobacco into his clay pipe, struck a spark, and drew on the stem until it was burning cleanly. "What do you want to know?"

"I'm looking for two criminals, a blond man and a young lad. They're very dangerous."

"Aye?" Blaine's expression was bored.

The cockney began to stalk the length of the barge, his suspicious gaze searching for signs of his quarry as he began to describe the fugitives and enumerate their misdeeds.

It felt as if they had been trapped in the thick warm blackness for days, though it couldn't have been for more than an hour or two. Maxie snapped out of her drowsiness when she heard vibrations on the deck above. A rumble of voices cut through the softer sounds of lapping water.

Two men were talking, one in a harsh cockney accent. Though she strained to hear, maddeningly, she could not make out the actual words. Robin was still sleeping off the effects of the head injury, but she sat up, too tense to lie still.

She scarcely breathed as heavy footsteps approached, the planks creaking under the weight of a large man. Simmons must be near enough to push the shield of carpets from that cover, or to hear the hammering of her heart.

The footsteps halted within a yard of her head. This was infinitely worse than meeting an enemy in the open. Her nerves stretched to the point where she felt a hysterical desire to scream or pound the hatch with balled fists—anything to end the suspense.

In the silence, Robin stirred and drew in his breath, as if preparing to speak. Instantly she reached out, fumbling a little in the dark, and clamped one hand over his mouth.

In the charged silence, she clearly heard Simmons say, "Anyone who 'elps criminals is flouting the king's justice, and it will go 'ard with 'im."

She gasped at the pious way the scoundrel was invoking the law. The devil could cite scripture for his purposes, indeed!

Robin tensed when she first touched him, then relaxed and gave a nod of understanding. As the footsteps moved away, she started to lift her hand away. Before she could, he pressed his lips to her palm in a gossamer kiss.

She inhaled, shaken. Remarkable how different kinds of touch could produce such varied reactions. Why did that swift butterfly caress affect her when muting his speech had not?

The darkness around them was no longer charged with danger, but with intimacy. She reached out, her fingers drifting across his hair and the bandage. Finding his face, her hand curved to stroke his cheek. The faint masculine prickle of whiskers contrasted with smooth skin. It reminded her of the sensuality of watching him shave, and she blushed in the darkness.

Her fingertips delicately skimmed his lips, and he touched them with the tip of his tongue. She shivered involuntarily. When he curled his hand around her neck and drew her down on top of him, she was willing. More than willing. Her lips parted to meet his in an open-mouthed kiss.

She forgot her tension, her fear of the searchers above. Nothing existed but the man in her arms, the velvet roughness of his tongue, and the masculine power of his body. Wherever they touched, heat swirled through her veins to smolder deep within.

His hand slid down between their bodies until he reached the sensitive juncture of her thighs. When he rubbed her there, she gasped and rocked against him. The energy of passion and creation was flowing through her, sweeping her toward fulfillment in the eternal dance of mating and renewal. Her hand moved down his torso to rest on the taut, potent ridge of male flesh.

His whole frame went rigid. She caressed him, rejoicing in her power as much as she resented the clothing that separated them. He jerked up the back of her shirt and began stroking the small of her back, his palm warm against her spine. The skin-to-skin contact felt deliciously wanton.

Then the deck above creaked with heavy footsteps again. They both froze. The barge rocked in the water from the weight.

Closer, closer . . . stopping right next to their hiding place. Then Simmons's voice rumbled, appallingly close. His words were an unintelligible mumble, but the angry menace was unmistakable.

Jerked back to an awareness of their situation, Maxie felt like kicking herself. What had happened to her resolve to avoid deeper involvement with Robin? She had no more wit than a chipmunk. She eased herself away.

Robin clutched spasmodically at her wrist. She stiffened, and he released her instantly. His reluctance to let her go was evident in the slow, erotic slide of his palm over her wrist and the back of her hand. The feather touch added fuel to the flames that threatened to consume her.

When his fingers glided over hers, she felt the irregularity of the crooked, badly mended bones. Desire was joined by a dangerous tenderness. She could not have been more conscious of him if they had both been naked in a bed.

When their contact finally ended, she had to force herself not to renew it. If she touched him again when she was in this state, there would be no going back.

Wishing their hideaway was larger, she silently retreated as far as possible, flattening herself against a wall of bulging carpets. Her heart was hammering so hard that it almost drowned out Robin's harsh breathing.

Planks creaked as Simmons shifted his massive weight. There was a rasping noise, as if the carpets above were being pushed. Dear God, did he know there was another hatch below the pile?

A voice called from the front of the barge. With more squeaking of planks, Simmons moved toward whomever had spoken.

After that, there was a long silence while Maxie prayed he would not return to investigate further. When the barge began moving again, she expelled her breath, so relieved she was almost shaking. Even so, she kept her voice to a whisper when she said unevenly, "I'm sorry. It might not seem that way, but I wasn't really trying to drive you berserk."

"I know. What happened was my fault," Robin replied, his voice rueful. "Most parts of me are working, but my judgment appears to have been scrambled by that blow on the head."

She thought of the feel of his taut body against hers. Yes, all of his parts were working very well. Once again, the heat in her face made her grateful for the concealing darkness.

It wasn't like her to avoid a difficult situation. Deciding that it was time to grasp another bull by the horns, she said, "We seem to be cursed with a strong physical attraction and grave doubts about acting on it. A blazing nuisance, isn't it?"

He chuckled. "Attraction between male and female is what makes the world keep spinning. Since you and I are living in each other's pockets, the situation does get a bit awkward sometimes, but I wouldn't have it any other way. Would you?"

She thought about it—the restless aching in her body, the sheer, wicked pleasure she found in his embrace, the void that would be left in her heart after they said good-bye. Rather to her surprise, she replied, "No, I don't suppose I would."

"I'm glad to hear that," he said quietly.

The atmosphere between them changed, the sense of lambent passion dissipating. With unerring instinct, Robin reached through the darkness and found her hand. Then he pulled her into the sort of affectionate embrace that was normal between them. She relaxed against him, at peace again.

He murmured into her hair, "Are we ready for the captain's questions when he lets us out of here?"

She said "Yes," without elaboration.

His hand glided down her back. "Is there anything I should know in support of your story?"

"No. This will come as a shock to you, but I decided it will be best to tell him the truth."

"The truth," he said in a tone of wonder. "That would never have occurred to me."

She snorted. "That is one of the few things you've ever said that I believe unequivocally."

He chuckled. "Believe me, I tell the truth much more often than not. Keeping one's lies straight can be quite exhausting."

"I wouldn't know," she replied, trying to sound blighting.

She felt his chest shake with silent laughter. "Are we still married? Or are you going to retract what you said earlier about me being your husband?"

"I suppose we're still married," she said reluctantly. "I would rather not explain what we are. I don't think there is any good definition."

She felt his amusement again, but he didn't comment.

Now that Robin was awake and on guard, she felt free to relax and get some rest herself. She settled her head on his shoulder. Soon enough it would be time to face the world again.

Maxie didn't wake until the removal of the hatch cover let in the long rays of the setting sun. She looked up warily, but it was the barge captain's face above, not Simmons's.

"You two all right down there?"

"We are indeed, and very grateful to you," Robin replied. He got to his feet and swung up to the deck, then extended a hand to help Maxie out. "My name is Robert Anderson, by the way, and this is my wife Maxima."

She noted that he was now Anderson, not Andreville. Thank heaven he had the sense not to use a fraudulent title. The pair of them looked questionable enough without that.

She glanced around and found that the barge was moored at the bottom of a large lock. Nearby was a stone stable and a small lock-keeper's cottage surrounded by flower gardens. It looked peaceful and blessedly safe.

The captain took his pipe from his mouth. "I'm John Blaine. My boy Jamie is stabling the horse."

The two men shook hands. "I hope Simmons wasn't too rude to you," Robin said.

"Happen he was." A smile hovered behind the cloud of pipe smoke. " 'Fraid there was a bit of an accident. The fellow tripped on the tow rope and fell into the canal. Lost his taste for barges and went stomping off afterward."

Maxie smiled, wondering how Blaine had managed the accident.

He continued, "Care to join us for a bite of supper?"

His words reminded Maxie that they had not eaten since a very early breakfast with the drovers. Was it really only that morning that they had shared a pot of tea and a loaf of bread with Dafydd Jones? "Supper would be very welcome, Captain Blaine."

He gestured for them to follow him into the barge's simple cabin. The table was covered with cold food that had been prepared by Blaine's wife in Market Harborough. Fortunately, she had expansive ideas about what it took to keep her menfolk from starving, and there was more than enough mutton pie, bread, cheese, and pickled onions. The four of them ate in the cabin with the door open to admit the evening breeze.

Blaine waited until he had finished and stoked up another pipe before asking, "Now, Mrs. Anderson, you said you could explain everything? Your cousin"—there was a faint, sardonic emphasis on the word—"said that you and your husband were guilty of theft and assault."

Maxie said bluntly, "Simmons isn't really my cousin. I said that because it was simpler than the real explanation."

"I didn't see much family resemblance," he agreed. "So what is this real explanation?"

She sketched in the bare bones of the story: that her father had died in London, that she had reason to suspect foul play, and that her uncle was making every attempt to stop her from investigating. She told the truth, though with as few elaborations as possible, particularly where Robin was concerned.

She ended earnestly, "I swear, Captain Blaine, we are not criminals." At least, she wasn't; it was stretching a point to include Robin among the innocent. "I have stolen nothing except an old map of my uncle's, and we have committed no assault beyond self-defense to escape Simmons and his men."

The captain refilled his pipe, then used a taper to light the tobacco. "Was your uncle your guardian before you married?"

She shook her head. "Never. Even if I were unmarried, I've just turned twenty-five, so I'm well past the age of needing a legal protector. He has no right to interfere with me."

Not only Blaine, but Robin, looked at her, surprise in their faces. Because of her small size, people tended to assume she was younger than she actually was.

"Sounds like the truth, if not precisely the whole truth. I'd like to have seen that self-defense between you two and Simmons's gang." Blaine drew on the pipestem, and smoldering tobacco glowed in the dusk.

"I imagine that tomorrow you'll be on your way to London, but if you want to spend tonight in the hold, you're welcome to."

She leaned across the table and pressed a quick kiss to his leathery cheek. "Bless you, Captain Blaine. You and Jamie have been wonderful."

He almost dropped his pipe. Trying to suppress a pleased smile, he said to his son, "If you tell your mother about this, mind you mention that kiss wasn't my idea."

They all laughed. Then the evening turned social. Tea was brewed and they moved to the deck, where the rippling sounds of water life were a peaceful background to their conversation. It wasn't long before the lock-keeper and his family came out to join them, bringing warm spiced buns as a contribution.

After the lanterns were lit, Robin gave a juggling and magic performance. Then Maxie was coaxed into playing her harmonica. It was like an informal gathering of New England neighbors, and she felt a degree of contentment she would never have expected to find on this side of the Atlantic.

After the gathering broke up, she and Robin retired to the hold of the barge. As she relaxed within his familiar embrace she gave thanks for this strange journey. She was discovering a different England than that of her aristocratic relations, and it was a warmer, kinder country by far.

Most of all, she gave thanks for Robin.

Simmons cast about furiously for his quarry, but they had vanished without a trace. The thick-witted canal boat captain had offered a vague memory of seeing two people beg a ride on a wagon, and there had been several other possible sightings, but all came to naught.

Cursing himself for his failure, he reluctantly sent a message to Lord Collingwood saying that he had lost the trail and could not guarantee that the girl would not reach London. He finished by suggesting that his lordship might wish to make other arrangements to prevent his niece from learning the truth about her father's death.

As for himself, he would continue the hunt.

Chapter 20

Robin eyed the dark roiling sky without enthusiasm. They'd had blessedly good weather for most of the journey, but that was about to change. At the least, there would be heavy rain, and probably a thunderstorm of major proportions.

The oncoming storm helped him make up his mind. He asked Maxie, "Would you care to spend tonight in style?"

"If that means a bath, yes!"

She accompanied her remark with one of the vivid smiles that made his heart behave in odd ways, as if it couldn't remember how to beat. She was the gamest female he had ever met, cheerfully accepting everything that came their way. Sometimes she found him exasperating—and who could blame her?—but never once had she whined or sulked. Maggie had been the same way.

With a start, he realized he hadn't thought of Maggie in days. His companion's beguiling presence was making the past feel very distant. Which was as it should be, and about time.

They had made good speed since leaving the canal boat. Now they were on a southbound road near Northampton, only a few days from London. Their swing to the north on the canal, plus greater efforts to avoid notice, seemed to have shaken Simmons from the track. They had encountered no new adventures.

That was fine with Robin; being with Maxie and trying to keep his hands off her delightful little body was adventure enough. He managed to control his attraction by mentally considering her "unavailable," as if she were married, a very young virgin, or a blood relation. It had worked fairly well—that is, he had not had to apologize for his behavior again—but he still had a constant, simmering awareness of her.

He suspected that what really constrained him was the knowledge that if he got out of line again, she would retreat, perhaps even vanish. She might desire him, but she had made it clear that her mind ruled her body.

A flash of lightning, followed almost instantly by a horrendous thunderclap, interrupted his daydreaming. The rain began, not a gentle English shower but blasts of water that drenched them to the skin in seconds.

Pitching her voice above the torrent, Maxie called, "How far is it to this place you have in mind?"

"Not far." He increased their pace to a trot. "But this rain is nothing. For vile weather, you should have seen Napoleon's retreat from Moscow."

She laughed, as always amazed at his powers of invention. "Are you going to tell me you were with the Grande Armée then?"

Another thunderclap split the air. "For a while," he said airily, "but it wasn't very amusing, so I stole a horse and made my own way back to Prussia."

She asked teasing questions, which he answered with speed and improbability. He was still spinning tales when he suddenly announced, "This way. We're almost there."

He turned from the narrow road and pushed through a gap in a hedge. She followed, and found Robin waiting by a high stone wall that ran as far as she could see in both directions.

Puzzled, she said, "Perhaps my brain is getting a bit soggy. I can't see anything resembling shelter."

"We have to go over the wall." Robin jumped and caught the upper edge, then swung smoothly to the top. Then he lowered his knapsack for Maxie.

Aghast, she said, "Good Lord, Robin, what are you doing? Surely this wall surrounds a private estate."

"Yes, but the owner is away and the house is empty," he explained. When she still hesitated, he said, "I promise you, there will be no trouble."

She weighed his confidence against her doubts. As always, he looked limpidly sincere. She was reminded of what she had thought when they first met: the face of a man who could sell you a dozen things you didn't want. An angel rogue.

But his judgment had been reliable so far, although her wits might be deficient for trusting him. She grasped the knapsack and scrambled up the wall.

They dropped down on the other side into a stand of large trees, which blunted the force of the rain. Robin led the way along a faint trail, the earth sodden and spongelike beneath their feet. Eventually they emerged at the edge of the woods.

A flash of lightning illuminated the scene for a moment. She halted, startled by the sight of the stately dwelling outlined against the storm-darkened sky.

Some buildings would have seemed gothic and threatening under these conditions, but that was not the case here. The Jacobean manor house stood on a slight rise, surrounded by well-tended lawns and gardens. It was neither unusually large nor in any way ostentatious. What made it striking were the graceful proportions and the way it suited its setting like a gemstone. Even in the midst of nature's turbulence, it was serene.

"Robin, we shouldn't be here," she said with conviction.

"There are stewards and gatekeepers and such, but all have their own residences. The house itself is vacant," he said reassuringly. "We can stay with no one the wiser."

She still balked. "How can you be sure it's still empty?"

"I make it a point to know such things," he said vaguely. "Come along. I don't know about you, but I'm freezing."

After glancing about to be sure they were unobserved, she started forward. "What is the estate's name and who owns it?"

"Ruxton. For many years it has been a secondary property of one of the great aristocratic families. Perfectly maintained, but scarcely ever occupied," he explained as he led the way around the house toward the back door.

"What a pity." She studied the warm facade. "It should be lived in. Your English nobility are a criminally wasteful lot."

"I wouldn't disagree."

They stopped at a door leading into the kitchen. Robin turned the knob and found, not surprisingly, that it was locked. Without missing a beat, he pulled off his right boot.

To her amazement, he pried up a section of the heel and removed a pair of stiff wires with odd-shaped hooks on the ends. After donning his boot again, he inserted a wire in the keyhole.

"What the devil are you doing?" she exclaimed.

"Isn't it obvious?"

When she opened her mouth again, he said reproachfully, "Quiet, please. I'm out of practice, so I need to concentrate."

He couldn't have been very out of practice. After switching to the second wire, it took him only a minute to pick the lock.

As he opened the door, she gave him a glare that should have produced steam in the cold rain. "You have the most horrifying skills," she said through gritted teeth.

"But useful." He gave a beatific smile. "Wouldn't you rather be indoors by a fire instead of out in the rain?"

"It's a near-run thing," she muttered as she stepped inside.

The shuttered windows admitted enough light to show that the kitchen was neat and empty. Dully gleaming pans hung on the opposite wall, worktables stood scrubbed and ready, but of human occupation there was no sign. Apparently Robin's information was accurate. Nonetheless, she felt uneasy as she set her knapsack on the flagged floor and peeled off her soaking coat and hat.

As Robin headed for a door that opened to reveal a storeroom, he said, "I'll build a fire. In this storm, no one will notice a bit of smoke from a chimney."

Obviously he had been here before. Perhaps he had begged a meal from an indulgent cook in the days when the house was lived in? Or had he been a guest in his respectable youth?

Whatever the reason, it took him only a few minutes to locate and light a lantern, then build a coal fire and start water heating. Soaked to the skin and shivering, she was grateful to stand by the hearth and absorb the fire's warmth.

Robin disappeared again, then returned and draped a heavy shawl around her shoulders. "I found a cloakroom with a variety of old garments. While the bathwater is heating, shall we choose rooms for the night?"

She glanced around the kitchen. "To be honest, I'd rather stay here. It seems dreadfully intrusive to invade someone's home, even if it isn't regularly occupied."

"But this hasn't been anyone's home for many years." He lit a branch of candles, then smiled and beckoned with his hand. "Come see. We won't cause any harm."

She followed him from the kitchen, knowing that when he smiled like that, she would follow him to hell itself.

The flickering light showed a house that was handsome and appealing, with a human scale that Chanleigh lacked. Though most of the furniture was under holland covers, the shapes revealed timeless elegance. The satinwood tables needed only the brush of a hand to bring the waxed surfaces alive. Tall, shuttered windows waited to admit light, and rich oriental carpets muted the sound of their footsteps.

In the music room, she lifted the cover on the harpsichord to play a scale. The notes sang bright and true under her questing fingers. "Sad to think there is no one to appreciate all this."

"A manor house has a life span of centuries," he said pensively. "A decade or two of emptiness is a minor aberration. Ruxton has been a home in the past, and it will be again."

She hoped he was right. They went upstairs. At the top of the steps was a small, unshuttered round window, and she paused to admire the rolling hills. The landscape was less dramatic than Durhamshire's wild moors, but lovely and very welcoming.

Her mouth tightened. How could the owners not want to live here? Had they no impoverished relations who needed a home? Shaking her head, she went after her companion.

He opened a door and glanced in. It was large, with a wide four-poster bed and a rose-hued carpet underfoot. "Will this suit you for the night? I think it's the mistress's chamber. The master's room would be through that door."

She looked at him, remembering the Drover Inn. "In other words, a bed is more dangerous to share than a hedgerow or a haystack or a cargo of carpets?"

His blue eyes met hers, serious for once. "So it proved before. I think it best that I sleep in the next room."

Of course he was right. Damn him.

For the twentieth time, Maxie pushed up the flowing sleeves of her luxurious robe. It wouldn't do for the red velvet to trail in her dinner. Her mood had improved considerably in the last three hours. While Robin had bathed, she had stewed the ham and vegetables they had been carrying. Her principles about drinking alcohol didn't extend to cooking with wine, and a liberal addition of claret, along with dried herbs from the stillroom, had done wonders for the rather plebian ingredients.

During her turn in the tub—her rapturous, lavender-scented turn in the tub—Robin had pillaged the house's treasures to create a splendid setting for their meal. The formal dining room was too large for intimacy, so he had set the table in the breakfast room. Crystal goblets, silver utensils, and fine china gleamed in the candlelight, and delicate porcelain bowls held relishes and candied fruits from the stillroom.

With a blithe unconcern for property rights, he had also found two velvet robes for them to wear while their own clothing dried. Donning the sumptuous garment after her bath had made her feel like a princess.

She swallowed the last of her stew and leaned back with a contented sigh, pushing up her sleeves again. The robe was far too large and its hem dragged on the floor, but it was perfect for this lunatic occasion, when her freshly washed hair was loose as a child's and wool stockings warmed her feet.

She had decided to relax and enjoy the eccentric luxury. She had the odd feeling that the house welcomed them. Perhaps it was glad to have inhabitants, even transitory, illicit ones.

Surreptitiously she studied her companion. His robe fit him well and was a shade of blue that matched his eyes. The color set off his gilt hair and made him unreasonably, dangerously, attractive.

As he reached for his wineglass, the garment fell open at the throat. She was interested to note that there was a faint, reddish tint in the light matting of chest hair revealed. She supposed that went with a beard that grew out red.

As she poured herself more water from a silver ewer, she remarked, "Times like this, it would be nice to loll back in the chair with a glass of brandy in my hand."

"You can anyhow. Nothing in that picture says you actually have to drink the brandy." He raised his goblet, which contained the last of the claret he had appropriated to season the stew. "Shall we drink a toast to the future?"

She laughed and raised her cup. "Is a toast drunk in tea binding?"

"With symbolism, intent is everything, the details unimportant," he assured her.

She hesitated a moment, feeling a strange, deep longing. It was getting harder and harder to imagine parting from Robin, with his careless charm and quixotic humor and tranquil acceptance of her mongrel background. But a future with him came under the heading of dreams rather than of possible outcomes. Trying to hold him would be like trying to capture the wind in her hands.

Smiling wistfully, she raised her cup and emptied it in one quick swallow. She was an American, which meant that she should not accept that anything was impossible.

After pouring more tea, she selected a piece of candied ginger from a Chinese bowl. "Sometime in your checkered past you must have been a butler." She indicated the elegant table. "You do this so well."

"As a matter of fact, you're right. I have had a stint or two as a butler, as well as being a footman and groom on occasion."

She was taken aback, not having meant the comment seriously. "Is that true, or are you teasing again?"

"Quite true." He grinned. "Is it so hard to imagine me holding a real job?"

"It's not easy." She rested an elbow on the table, propping her chin on her palm as she studied his cool patrician countenance. She really shouldn't be surprised. Even wandering gentlemen with a rooted distaste for honest employment must sometimes have to work to keep food in their bellies.

"I'm sure you were a successful servant. You have the chameleon's ability to blend into any setting." She tried to define the impressions she had gathered in their travels. "Yet, though you talk easily with anyone of any station, you always seem apart, with the group but not of it."

His hand stilled around his wine goblet. "That, Maxima, is entirely too perceptive a comment." Before she could pursue the subject, he continued, "We'll be in London soon. Where do you plan to begin investigating your father's death?"

"The inn where he died. Surely there are servants who can tell me something. I also have the names of old friends he intended to visit."

"After you have learned what you can, and acted on it, what then?" His blue gaze was intense.

She shook her head and toyed with the silver tongs, trying unsuccessfully to decipher the intricate engraved initial. "Go back to America and find work in a bookshop, I suppose. I haven't really thought about it. The future seems too far away."

She used the tongs to drop a chunk of sugar into her tea. "No, that isn't quite right. Usually I have a vague idea of what the future holds. Nothing so grand as prophecy, just a sense that actions will be completed. For example, when my father and I traveled, I always knew when we would reach our destination, and when we would not. When we sailed for England, I didn't doubt that we would arrive safely, and I knew that I would meet my father's family. For that matter, when I left my uncle's house I was confident that I would reach London."

Intrigued, he asked, "Did you sense that you would have so many adventures along the way?"

"No, and I could never have imagined meeting someone like you." She gave him a fleeting smile. "But now when I look ahead, I can't project what will happen. It's like one summer when we planned to pass through Albany. There was no reason to suppose that it wouldn't happen, yet I couldn't see us there. As it turned out, my father fell ill. We spent several weeks in a village in Vermont and ended up missing Albany that year. It's rather like that now."

His brows drew together. "What do you feel?"

"A kind of blankness. Perhaps the future will take a turn I can't envision because it is too different from the past," she said slowly. "I've always known I wouldn't spend my whole life as a book peddler, though I didn't know how that part of my life would end. Yet as soon as my father said we were going to England, I knew I would never go back to the peddler's life."

"I've run across many different forms of intuition in my life, and I've learned not to discount them," Robin said, his expression intent. "If you consciously try, do you think you could get a better sense for what might happen in London? If there is danger, it will help if we are prepared."

"I don't know if that's possible, but I'll see what I can do," she said doubtfully.

Closing her eyes, she relaxed back in the chair and visualized a map of England. A silvery road coiled south from Durham, its brightness increasing in Yorkshire, where she had met Robin. What about London, the complex, pulsing heart of England? She let her mind drift.

Blackness, chaos, pain. The unthinkable . . .

With a cry, she jerked upright in the chair, a convulsive movement of her hand sweeping her teacup and saucer from the table to smash on the parquet floor. She stared at the scattered fragments, her heart hammering. "I broke it," she said stupidly.

"To hell with the china," Robin was already there, his arms circling her. As she hid her face against him, he said quietly, "Did you feel that something dreadful will happen there?"

She tried to look at the black, terrifying vortex that had almost consumed her, but her mind sheered away, as balky as a nervous pony. "It . . . it was literally beyond my imagination. Something too awful to understand."

His embrace tightened. "Could it have been your own death?" he asked quietly. "If so, I'm going to take you in the opposite direction tomorrow if I have to tie you to a horse."

She shook her head. "I've never feared death, so my own end would not be so upsetting." A horrifying thought struck to her. Could she have been dimly sensing danger for Robin?

As soon as the thought formed in her mind, she dismissed it. Her fear had nothing to do with Robin. "It wasn't your death, either. I . . . I think it had to do with what happened to my father." She swallowed hard. "Even though I've mentally accepted that my uncle might have arranged Max's death, in my heart, I haven't really believed it. But if my uncle was responsible, it would explain why thinking of the future is so upsetting. A murder trial would have hideous repercussions for the whole Collins family. Innocent people will be hurt."

"And you don't want that, even if your relatives haven't been particularly kind to you." He put his finger under her chin and raised her face so that she was looking at him. "I suppose it's foolish to ask if you want to leave well enough alone."

Her jaw hardened. "That's out of the question. I may fail to discover the truth, but if I don't try, I'll never forgive myself."

He nodded, unsurprised. "You're wise to proceed. The truth is seldom as bad as our fears." He smoothed her hair back from her temple, then moved away. "I'm going to make another pot of tea. Then I'll tell you every absurd story I can think of so that when you go to bed, you'll sleep well." He smiled. "And I know a *lot* of absurd stories."

After he headed off to the kitchen, teapot in hand, she whispered, "Thank you, Robin."

Their future together might be limited, but as long as he stayed by her side while she investigated her father's death, she could face whatever waited in London.

Chapter 21

The Marquess of Wolverton had estimated that if Robin and the Sheltered Innocent decided to stop at Ruxton, it would take them three or four days to get there from Market Harborough. Giles headed south, making routine inquiries, but with a signal lack of success. The pair had evaporated like summer mist.

He had intended to spend the third night at Ruxton, but a violent storm turned the roads to mire and slowed his carriage to the pace of a walking man. Irritated, he chided himself for spending too much time on futile searching. If he had given up a few hours earlier, he could have reached Ruxton. Now he must take his chances at the nearest inn. It was a gloomy prospect.

As his carriage lurched through the mud, he found himself thinking about Desdemona Ross, who had an alarming tendency to invade his mind, both waking and sleeping. He wasn't sure what to do about her, but he certainly wanted to do something.

His pleasant daydreams ended when a sharp crack sounded below his feet. The carriage jolted to a stop, the whole vehicle tilting precariously. He sighed as he stepped into the downpour; a carriage breakdown was a perfect end to the day. Outside, he called to his coachman, Wickes, "Shall we see how bad it is?"

Wickes handed the reins to Miller, a young servant who was acting as guard, groom, and part-time valet. After he clambered from the box, they slogged through the mud to survey the damage. "Axle's broken beyond repair, my lord," Wickes said glumly. "We'll have to send Miller to find a blacksmith."

Giles tugged his hat lower, trying to stop rain from running down the back of his neck. "We're within a mile or two of Daventry. There will be a smith there." He was about to dispatch Miller to town when he heard the jangling harness and rumbling wheels of another traveler behind them.

"Here's a bit of luck," Wickes said as he stepped into the road to flag down the approaching vehicle.

It wasn't a wagon, but another private coach—a carriage with distinctive yellow trim. A smile spread across Giles's face. Whoever had said that it was an ill wind that blew no good was right; this storm was definitely blowing well.

As he headed toward the coach, a tall female form stepped out into the deluge and started toward him. His step quickened, and as they drew together he exclaimed, "Get back inside, Lady Ross. There's no reason for you to get wet, too."

"Don't worry, Wolverton. I shan't melt." She gave him a wicked smile, her long lashes clumping from the rain and water dripping from the edge of her bonnet. "This is my chance to rescue you for a change. How could I pass up such an opportunity? I presume you have a broken wheel or axle."

He nodded. "I'd appreciate it if you would send someone from Daventry to help us."

"Why don't you come with me? Your men can look after the carriage perfectly well. I was planning to stop at the Wheatsheaf, which is quite a decent inn. You can get a room there also." She pulled her sopping cloak closer around her. "This is no weather for traveling."

The thought of spending time with her splendid ladyship was too appealing to refuse. Giles told his men to wait in the carriage until help arrived, retrieved a small bag that carried a change of clothes and a few other basic items, and followed Lady Ross to her carriage.

He climbed inside and settled squishily on the seat. Seeing that they were alone, he asked, "What happened to your maid?"

"The silly wench came down with a streaming cold so I sent her home." She cocked her head to one side. "Obviously I didn't take your advice about meekly going to wait in London. I came across one or two possible sightings of our fugitives, but I don't feel any closer to finding them. How was your luck?"

"About the same." Deciding there was no reason to keep Ruxton a secret any longer, Giles said, "Robin owns an estate near Daventry. I'm on my way to see if they might be staying there for a day or two. Care to go there with me tomorrow?"

"Definitely." She smiled wryly. "There are obvious advantages to being together when we find them."

Together. He liked the sound of that.

In Daventry, they found a blacksmith who was willing to go immediately to Giles's carriage in return for a payment that was only mildly extortionate. With that accomplished, they went on to the Wheatsheaf Inn.

Giles asked for a tea tray when they entered. The landlord gave the orders, then bowed them into a private parlor.

As Giles removed his cloak, his companion went to stand by the fire. "This seems very familiar," she remarked. "We always seem to be meeting at inns." She removed her dripping bonnet and shook her head. Her red hair tumbled in a vivid mass about her shoulders, curling wildly from the moisture.

Giles watched with pleasure as she absently combed her fingers through her fiery tresses in a vain attempt at straightening. He was definitely pro-redhead.

He started to make a light comment about the effect that meeting at inns could have on a reputation. Then rational thought fled as his companion removed her sodden cloak.

He had wondered what her appearance would be if she wasn't swaddled in layers of shapeless clothing. Now he learned the answer, and the knowledge was lightning in his veins.

He had thought her rather stout, in an attractively

feminine way. Stout, however, implied being large all over.

Desdemona was large only in certain places. Her saturated muslin dress clung more closely than a damped petticoat, revealing a spectacular figure in loving detail. Her legs were gloriously long and shapely, and the slimness of her waist made her dramatic curves look downright flamboyant. In particular, she had a remarkable pair of . . .

Giles hastily straightened his expression. A gentleman would say she had a lovely neck, since what she did have was not a subject for polite comment. Yes, indeed, Lady Ross had a very lovely neck . . . and the rest of her was very fine as well.

She glanced at him, and her face froze. "You are staring at me," she said accusingly.

So he was. Giles raised his bemused eyes to her face and said with regrettable candor, "Lady Collingwood was right."

Her face flared as red as her hair.

"That was not an insult," he said hastily. "You are a strikingly attractive woman. No man could fail to notice."

"You mean that you agree with my sister-in-law that I look like a light-skirt," she snapped. "You're both right, because that is exactly how too many men have tried to treat me." She reached for her wet cloak to cover herself.

Her bitter words gave the marquess an insight into why she was so uneasy about male attention. He stood and took off his wool coat, which had been protected from the rain by his cloak. "Put this on. Unlike your cloak, it's dry."

As she hesitated, he said in his gentlest tone, "I'm sorry for what I said. I meant no disrespect. It is only that I was surprised. You've done an excellent job of disguising yourself."

Warily she accepted the coat, as if expecting him to attack her. Wrapping it around herself, she withdrew again. The coat returned her to perfect decency, to Giles's regret.

The tea tray arrived, so he poured a cup and handed it to her along with the plate of cakes. At first she perched nervously on the edge of a chair, but she began to relax as the tea warmed her and Giles maintained his distance.

Deciding that it was time to learn why the lady was so skittish, he remarked. "You must have had a difficult first season. Innocence usually arouses protective instincts, but you have the kind of beauty that can make men forget themselves, especially young men with more passion than patience."

She stared at her plate and crumbled a cake. "The first time a young man caught me away from my chaperons, I felt horribly guilty, wondering what I had done to encourage him. Eventually I realized that the fault was not in my behavior." Her mouth twisted. "To defend myself, I took to wearing a long, sharp pin in my hair."

"I see why you have a low opinion of the male half of the race," he said thoughtfully. "And your come-out . . . that was just the beginning, wasn't it?"

"Why do you ask, Wolverton?" She raised her head, her gaze challenging. "If you are only expressing dishonorable intentions in a more than usually genteel fashion, I can't see that my past is any of your business."

He drew in a deep breath. "My intentions are not dishonorable, so"—the words came with difficulty—"that means they must be honorable."

Her jaw dropped, and she put her teacup down with a clink. Their gazes held in one of those kaleidoscopic moments when everything changes forever. For better or worse, there would be no going back.

When she spoke, her words seemed irrelevant, but he knew they were not. "I met your wife once when she was making her come-out. She was exquisite, like a porcelain figurine."

He set his own cup down, making sure to do so

soundlessly. Turnabout was fair play; if he was going to probe Desdemona, she had the right to do the same. "Yes, Dianthe was very beautiful."

"She and I could not be more unalike."

"I hope to God that is true," he said, unable to keep bitterness out of his voice. "If it isn't, this could prove to be the second great mistake of my life."

Desdemona had felt off-balance throughout this conversation, but the marquess's words steadied her. She was glad to know that he was as vulnerable as she was. "What went wrong?"

He got to his feet and began to pace restlessly. "It isn't much of a story. I was quite besotted when I married her. I couldn't believe that she had chosen me over so many others." He shrugged his broad shoulders. "Pure idiocy that I didn't recognize why: I was heir to the best title and fortune available on the marriage mart that year. But she was very skilled at pretending sweet, loving innocence. It was easy to be a fool."

"Yet surely she cared for you. No sane woman would accept a man she didn't like when she had so many other choices."

His expression became sardonic. "She didn't precisely dislike me, but during one of our charming discussions later, she revealed that she had been bored with me before the honeymoon was over. She had expected to be bored, but not quite so much, and so quickly."

Desdemona winced. The cruelty of it was far too reminiscent of her own marriage.

He continued, "Dianthe was quite the little philosopher, however. Boring I might be, but she was prepared to tolerate me in return for fortune and position. She had an amazing talent for spending money, and she wanted to be a marchioness."

"She died in childbirth, didn't she, along with the baby?" Desdemona had a vague memory of reading about the deaths. She had spared a moment of regret for the beauty's untimely end.

"Yes." He braced a hand on the mantel and stared

into the fire for a long time. "As she was dying, when it looked like the baby might survive, she told me that it was almost certainly not mine. She was rather apologetic. Women in her position usually try to provide a legitimate heir or two before going their own way. She had intended to do that as part of the bargain, but . . . mistakes do happen."

Desdemona ached for him. For the first time in her life she went to a man and made a physical gesture of comfort, not worrying whether he would react the wrong way. Laying a hand on his shirtsleeved arm, she said, "I'm very sorry. She didn't deserve you."

Though he managed to keep his voice steady, his arm was as tight as strung wire under her fingers. "I don't know about that, but it is certainly true that we had very different ideas about what we wanted of our marriage. My judgment was disastrously bad." His voice almost inaudible, he added, "The worst of it was not knowing how to mourn."

"I understand," she said quietly. "When my husband died, I felt relief, guilt, some impersonal sadness for such a pointless death. It was . . . complicated."

He raised his hand to rest it briefly on hers. "I never met Sir Gilbert Ross, but he had the reputation of a gamester."

"Among other things, most of them bad." It was Desdemona's turn to stare into the fire.

She had never spoken about her marriage to anyone, but the marquess's honesty deserved a like response. "He drowned in a ditch one night, drunk. Virtually the only considerate act of his life was to die when he was at high tide with his gaming, so there was enough to pay off his debts, with a bit left over. That, combined with a modest legacy from an aunt, enabled me to become independent. I found that widowhood suited me much better than marriage had."

He sighed. "A fashionable courtship is such an artificial thing. It's not surprising that you and I ended up choosing partners who were quite different than we thought."

"Very true, though in fact, I did not choose my husband."

"The match was arranged by your family?"

"No, my brother would surely have chosen better. During my London Season, Sir Gilbert was one of several serious suitors." She gave an acid smile. "My fortune was hardly on the order of yours, but I had a decent dowry, and men liked my looks, even if they didn't respect them.

"Gilbert courted me assiduously, but knew my brother would refuse permission if he made an offer. So he took me for a drive in the park one day and kept on going. He didn't bring me home until the next day."

The marquess frowned. "Did he . . . ?"

She looked into the fire again. "No, he was most respectful. He took me to an unoccupied house in the country, swearing undying love and saying that he couldn't live without me. I was furious, of course, but also rather flattered. He was very handsome, and I was young enough to think that it was romantic to have a dashing rake madly in love with me."

"I see," Wolverton said grimly. "He didn't have to lay a hand on you. The mere fact of having spent an unchaperoned night in his company meant that you were thoroughly compromised."

"Precisely. Everyone agreed that I had no choice but to marry him." Her full lips thinned. "I was too young to realize that there is always a choice, so I accepted my fate."

"And this is why you are so determined that your niece will have a choice, no matter what has happened?"

"Exactly. I will allow no one—*no one*—to coerce her into a miserable marriage." Desdemona lifted the poker and jabbed the glowing coals. "I should have resisted, but as I said, part of me was gratified that Gilbert wanted me so much that he was driven to desperate measures. I liked him well enough. He was very amusing, and I took the fact that he didn't ravish me as proof of genuine affection. Unfortunately, it was no more love than what your Dianthe felt."

"He was interested only in your dowry?"

"That was the main reason. But apart from the money . . ." She swallowed, not sure she could continue. The marquess put an unthreatening arm around her shoulders, and she relaxed a little.

"Gilbert told me once when he was drunk that he had made a list of girls who had decent fortunes, but who were not such great heiresses that he wouldn't be allowed near them. Then, after he had met us all, he chose me because of . . . because of my breasts." She spoke baldly, amazed that she could say aloud what had scarred her soul.

Wordlessly he pulled her closer to his side. She sensed that he could understand how humiliating she had found her husband's declaration; Wolverton's own experiences had been equally humiliating.

"The basic, underlying transaction in marriage is sex for money," he said reflectively. "The male supports and protects the female in return for sexual access. It's not very flattering for either party. Certainly I didn't enjoy learning that the hard way." His arm tightened. "You had the misfortune to be forced into marriage because of both lust and money. That seems particularly unfair."

"Lord, what fools these mortals be!" she said with a rueful laugh. "Is that what all the fine romantic phrases come down to: the man choosing the female who most arouses him, the woman accepting the man who can best provide for her?"

"That may be the basic transaction, but it is only a beginning. Humans are complicated creatures, and a good marriage must satisfy many needs and desires." He looked down, his slate-blue eyes glinting with amusement. "But in addition to affection, companionship, and trust, it is not inherently a bad thing to find one's partner physically attractive."

She looked away, shy again but content to stay

within the circle of his arm. "Are we back again to the fact that I look like a harlot?"

"Not really. I've never found such women very interesting—at least, not for more than an hour or two. You, on the contrary, are nothing if not interesting. I admire the idealism of your political work, and what you have done on behalf of a niece you have never met. I like your directness." He chuckled. "I also like the fact that your blushes make it easy to know what you are thinking."

The wave of color that went over Desdemona confirmed his last words. She found herself on the verge of scuffing her toe in the carpet like a child.

He finished his recitation of her virtues by saying, "The fact that I like and respect you as a person is the foundation. However, I am absolutely delighted that you also look like the most expensive kind of opera dancer."

She had to laugh at his absurd and marvelous chain of logic, and the way it dissolved her self-consciousness about her unladylike appearance. For perhaps the first time in her life, a man's admiration was pleasing rather than menacing.

Then she raised her eyes, and laughter ceased. Her breath caught at what she saw in his eyes. Certainly there was desire, but also affection and kindness. When he bent over, she did not try to avoid his kiss.

It began as a light, undemanding caress, quite unlike the slavering assaults of the young men who had sometimes cornered her when she was a girl. Her husband had seldom bothered to kiss her at all, instead going directly to his satisfaction.

Giles, however, preferred a leisurely exploration. His lips brushed hers with slow sensuality, finding pleasures she had never imagined. At first she simply accepted, but soon she began to want to respond. She slid her arms around his neck and relaxed against him. Their bodies fitted together as if designed for each other. With him, she didn't feel like a vulgar, oversized

Amazon; she felt like a woman who had met her match.

He began stroking her back underneath his coat, which was still draped over her shoulders. His hands warmed her through the damp muslin of her gown. She did not realize the effort his restraint was costing him until she shyly touched her tongue to his. He made a sound deep in his throat and crushed her to him so that she felt the full force of his male strength. She stiffened, hating the feeling of being overwhelmed.

Instantly he ended the kiss and stepped back. His breath unsteady, he stroked her tangled red curls. "I'm sorry. It's perilously easy to forget myself. I didn't mean to alarm you."

"You didn't. At least, not much." Desdemona was more than a little unsteady herself. "Where do we go from here, Wolverton?"

He gave her a slanted, hopeful smile. "Perhaps a courtship? Spend time together, learn to know each other better. Decide if we might suit."

"I'd like that." As soon as she spoke, she felt a shiver of nerves. "But it will take time. As I said, I've enjoyed my independence."

"Have you also enjoyed your loneliness?" he asked quietly.

She looked down at her ruined slippers and shook her head. "But if we are courting, let us do it honestly. If I decide that I can't bear to marry again, I shall say so. And if you decide that I am an impossible virago, you must tell me. None of this nonsense about feeling obligated to marry me because you raised my expectations. They say that's why Wellington married his wife, and a sad business that has proved to be."

"Agreed. That common sense is exactly what I like about you. As the next step in this courtship, perhaps you could call me Giles." His mouth twisted. "Dianthe always called me by my title, which was appropriate since it was the lord she married."

"Fool woman. Very well, Giles." She surveyed him

thoughtfully. "Do you think you can manage to call me Desdemona with a straight face?"

"Probably not." His eyes gleamed with humor. "When you came blazing into Wolverhampton, it occurred to me that Othello may have had a point when he strangled his Desdemona. The thought has returned once or twice since then."

"That is a ridiculous and unworthy comment." She tried to look severe but found herself succumbing to undignified hilarity. What a silly chit Dianthe must have been, to find Giles boring.

"True," he agreed cheerfully. "Is that why you're giggling?"

"I am a widow of mature years and serious pursuits," she stated. "I do not giggle." Then she hid her face against his shoulder in a vain attempt to muffle the sounds of her lie.

Chapter 22

Robin was right about the number of humorous stories he knew. By the time they were ready to retire, Maxie had laughed so much that she could scarcely remember the black anxiety she had felt when trying to look toward the future. Arm in arm, they climbed the stairs, Robin carrying a candle and Maxie holding up her red velvet skirts so she wouldn't trip and break her neck.

He accompanied her into her room and lit the bedside candle, then turned to go to the adjoining chamber. The candlelight cast strong shadows across his face, illuminating the chiseled planes. In his flowing blue velvet robe, he looked like a medieval lord who had stepped out of the past. He was the most desirable man she had ever seen, and she wanted to untie his sash and bare his beautiful body and pull him onto the bed.

Without conscious thought, she placed her open hand on the triangle of skin exposed by the loose folds of his robe. His heartbeat accelerated beneath her palm as raw sexual tension pulsed between them.

Mouth dry, she asked, "Whose turn is it to be sensible?"

"Mine, I think." He touched her hair, letting the shining strands spill over his wrists. Then he lifted her hand and kissed her fingers before releasing them. "Remember, I'm just next door. If you have a nightmare, call and I'll be right here."

"I know." Forcibly repressing the impulse to risk a

good-night kiss, she stepped back and began braiding her hair for bed. "Pleasant dreams."

After he closed the connecting door, she removed her robe and slid between the fresh sheets. Yet despite the comfort of the bed, sleep eluded her. The reason had nothing to do with her disturbing sense of a dark future. It was simply that the four-poster was too wide, too cold, too empty.

She rolled onto her stomach and pummeled the pillow irritably, using the excuse of making it more comfortable. Though it might be wise to avoid greater intimacy with Robin, wisdom made a poor companion for the night. The very difficulty of being without him reinforced the knowledge that she was following the right course. Damn, damn, *damn*.

An hour of tossing and turning brought her no closer to sleep. Scowling, she sat up and pondered. Perhaps if she opened the connecting door between the bedchambers, she would feel closer to Robin. Less alone.

She slipped off the high bed and padded over to the door, shivering a little in her light muslin shift. It was raining again, and the air had a raw chill that reminded her of a New England November. Quietly she opened the door and listened, hoping to hear the comforting sound of Robin's breathing over the steady drum of rain on the windowpanes.

She heard him, but the sound was not comforting. His breathing was choked and shallow, like that first night when they had slept on bracken pallets on a north country moor. He had claimed a nightmare then, but he had had none since.

The bed creaked as his weight shifted. Then he began to talk in a language that was not English, his flexible tenor laced with anguish. She frowned and entered his room. He was speaking a German dialect. Though she did not speak the language, she recognized the words *das Blut* and *der Mord*. Blood and murder.

With a harshness that would have woken her even through a closed door, he suddenly cried, *"Nein!*

Nein!" and lashed out frantically at some unseen
threat.

Alarmed, she scrambled onto the wide bed and laid
a hand on his shoulder to wake him from the nightmare.

He exploded under her touch, rolling over with
blinding speed. Before she could even speak his name,
he seized her shoulders and forced her down into the
mattress. His torso was bare and damp with perspira-
tion and his breath came in wrenching gasps as he
sprawled full length on top of her, his forearm pressed
across her throat so hard that she could scarcely
breathe.

She was terrifyingly aware of the trained strength in
his taut body. If she struggled, he might throttle her or
break her neck. Trying to lie absolutely still, she drew
as much air as she could through her constricted throat,
then said sharply, "Robin, wake up! You're dreaming."

For a dreadful moment the pressure on her throat increased, cutting off further speech. Then her words
penetrated through his nightmare. Blindly he whispered, "Maxie?"

She managed to say, "Yes, Robin, it's me."

He flung violently away from her to lie on his back,
his fair skin ghost-pale in the darkness. "Christ, I'm
sorry," he said hoarsely. "Are you all right?"

Gratefully she drew a deep breath into her lungs.
"No damage done." She sat up and leaned toward the
night table to light a candle, then turned back to Robin.

To her horror, she saw that he was shaking so hard
that the mattress vibrated. She wrapped her arms
around him in an instinctive gesture of comfort.

He responded with a desperation that threatened to
bruise her ribs. She drew his head against her breasts
as if he were a child. Thinking he might have fallen
victim to malaria on his travels, she asked, "Are you
having an attack of fever?"

"No." His voice trembled with the effort of trying to
sound composed. "It was only a nightmare."

She stroked his head. "There is no such thing as

'only a nightmare.' The Iroquois understand that and say that dreams and nightmares come from the soul. What was disturbing your rest?"

After a silence so long that she began to wonder if he would answer, he replied in a voice so thin it was nearly inaudible, "The usual—violence, betrayal, killing men who might have been my friends in other times."

His bleak tone was chilling. She thought of the farmer who had discovered them in his barn. Robin had conversed knowledgeably about the war in the Peninsula without ever actually saying that he was a soldier. Yet she now realized that he hadn't denied it, either. "You really were in the army?"

"I was never a soldier," he said with bitter humor. "Nothing so clean as that."

"If you weren't a soldier, what were you?"

"I was a spy." He lay back on the pillow and wiped his face with a shaking hand. "For a dozen years, from the time I was barely twenty. I lied, I stole, sometimes acted the assassin. I was very, very good at it."

She felt the shock of surprise that comes when a fact is utterly unexpected, yet so clearly right that it cannot be doubted. "That explains a great deal. I thought you were a common, garden-variety thief or swindler."

"It would have been better if I *had* been a common criminal. I would have caused less harm." Distorted faces began to crowd around him, images of those he knew, plus a blurred legion of unknown others who had died because of information he had passed on. His shaking worsened, and he wondered with despair if it was possible for a body to shatter into pieces.

It was the worst panic spell yet. He wished Maxie were not here to see his weakness, yet he could not stop himself from clinging to her as a lifeline in a sea of shattering emotional turbulence.

Before the images could overwhelm him, she spoke again, her low voice pulling him from the drowning pool of pain. "A thief works only for gain. I can't believe that you became a spy for simple greed."

"It's true that spying is no business for someone who wants to get rich. I took it up because I thought that defeating Napoleon was a good cause, and spying was a way to make myself useful. Yet as time passed, I became more and more aware of the blood on my hands ..."

When she tilted her head, her silky hair brushed his cheek with the bittersweet tang of lavender. "Tell me how you began. Surely you didn't study spying at Oxford."

"Cambridge, actually." He found a shadow of amusement in how aptly she had gauged him. "After my second year, there was a truce on the Continent for the first time in a decade. I decided to take a holiday in France. I soon realized that it was only a matter of time until the war resumed again.

"By chance, I learned something that would interest the Foreign Office, so I sent the information to a semidistant cousin of mine who had a position there. Lucien immediately came to Paris to talk to me. He was impressed with what I had discovered, and suggested I stay in France when the truce ended. Besides my natural deviousness, my mother was a Scot, which gave me an entrée to the Scottish community that had settled in Paris after the failure of the Jacobite rising of 1745. Since they despised Napoleon, they made excellent allies."

He had always admired his slightly older cousin; it had been gratifying to win Lucien's approval. Growing up, Robin had received damned little approval in other quarters. It had been seductively easy to convince himself that he would be doing something brave and valuable.

"At the beginning it was almost a game. I was too young and heedless to realize that ... that I was selling my soul, a piece at a time." The suffocating panic began to rise again. "By the time I understood what I was doing to myself, there was nothing left of it."

"An interesting metaphor," she said softly, "but

false. You may have forgotten how to find your soul, but you can't lose, sell, or give it away."

He gave a humorless smile. "Are you sure about that?"

"Quite." She took his hand in hers, and the panic retreated a little. "If you had no soul, you could not suffer the kind of guilt you feel now. In my experience, dedicated villains sleep peacefully at night."

"By that standard, I must be a saint," he said wearily.

"You said once that your friend Maggie was your partner in crime. I wondered then what you meant. She was also a spy?"

"Yes. Her father was killed by a French mob. I helped her escape. She had no reason to return to England, so we became partners. I spent much of my time traveling about the Continent, but home was wherever Maggie was. Most often, Paris."

"Comrades and lovers," Maxie murmured. "She was the linchpin. When she left you, things fell apart."

He nodded. "When we were together, I was able to keep the worst of the demons under control. I didn't start to unravel until later. How did you know?"

"Feminine intuition," Maxie said rather dryly. "I suppose that your stints as a servant were in pursuit of information."

"Exactly. People tend not to notice servants. A footman or groom can learn everything that goes on in a house."

She pulled the blanket over them. Its weight was welcome; he hadn't realized how cold he was. But the vital warmth came from Maxie. She was sweetness and sanity, her breasts soft beneath her thin shift, her gentle hands soothing.

"It has just occurred to me that many of your absurd tales might be true," she said. "Did you really share a jail cell in Constantinople with a Chinese sailor?"

He smiled faintly. "God's own truth. Li Kwan taught me some amazing fighting techniques that have saved my life several times over. Our combined talents got us out of that hellhole."

"What about Napoleon's retreat from Moscow?"

Robin made a choking sound and began shaking again, as if the chill of a Siberian wind were still in his bones.

She tightened her embrace. "It's obvious why such memories are horribly painful. But surely your work helped your country, perhaps contributed to saving lives by ending the war earlier."

"Perhaps, yet often what I did was downright trivial." His mouth twisted. "One of the triumphs of my dubious career was the not very difficult deduction that Bonaparte was planning to invade Russia because of the number of books on Russian geography he had on his library shelves."

She gave a soundless whistle. "The deduction might have been simple, but how the devil did you manage to get into the emperor's private library?"

"You don't want to know."

She smoothed his sweat-damped hair back from his brow. Shadowed lines showed at the corners of his eyes. For the first time, he looked every minute of his age, and then some. "It was war," she said with compassion. "Though killing someone to gain entrance must have been dreadful, it wasn't really different from shooting a soldier on a battlefield."

"It wasn't murder that time, but seduction," he said in a voice of self-loathing. "A chambermaid, plain and rather shy, but sweet. Jeanne was so grateful for the attention. I pretended to be a loyal French soldier who was recovering from wounds, and who wanted to see where his beloved emperor worked. It wasn't hard to persuade her to take me there." His fingers curled into her arm with bruising force. "I hated using women like that—taking what should be best and truest between men and women and perverting it. But I did it anyhow. God help me, I did it."

"There are men who ruin women for sport. At least

you had a reason," she said quietly. "Did Jeanne ever learn that you had been using her?"

"No. I told her that my regiment was being sent to Austria, and bid her a fond adieu. She . . . she wept and prayed for my safety. I still see her face . . ." His voice broke.

Maxie grieved for plain, sweet Jeanne, and for Robin, who had betrayed his own code of honor. Yet surely there had been a positive aspect to their affair. "Jeanne may have wept for losing you, but I guarantee that it did wonders for her confidence to know that a man like you had wanted her."

When Robin started to reply, she put a finger to his lips. "Don't tell me that it was a betrayal on your part—I concede the point. But you brought her some happiness, and you let her keep her pride and dignity, which you didn't have to do."

"The fact that I was never unnecessarily cruel doesn't make my actions right," he said flatly.

Her brow furrowed as she tried to put herself in his place. "Being amoral would be a great advantage for a spy. For someone like you, who is innately decent, it was obviously ghastly. How did you manage to keep going for so many years?"

He exhaled roughly. "By walling off my worst deeds, as if they had been done by someone else. That worked for a long time. But after the war ended and there were no more crises, the walls began crumbling."

"Hence, nightmares."

"Exactly."

Gently she stroked his taut spine, thinking of when she had tried to teach him to listen to the wind. Once again, she sensed the tangled threads of his character, and this time she understood why so many strands were spun from raw, black pain. His spirit seemed terrifyingly fragile. Though he may not have lost his soul, he was drawing ever closer to emotional breakdown. Strange to think that this darkness had always been beneath his laughter.

Empathy had left her drained. It would be easy to let

matters rest here. By morning, Robin would have re-built the walls that saved him from madness and would be as jaunty as ever. But the fragmentation that had enabled him to survive was now in danger of destroying him.

Her mother had taught her that dreams must be renewed, and nightmares must be released. For Robin to become whole, healing light must be brought into the knotted blackness at the center of his spirit.

She shivered, feeling helpless. He needed someone stronger and wiser, but for now, she was all he had. Delving deeper into his pain would hurt them both. Yet for the sake of Robin's sanity, she must try, even if he ended by despising her.

She let her spirit float freely with the wind and rain that were cleansing the night sky. Then, after some of their strength had entered her, she opened her eyes and began to speak.

Chapter 23

Softly Maxie said, "Tell me the rest of what haunts you, Robin."

He gave a ragged sigh. "I've said too much already."

"Do you think I am too fragile to hear the truth? I am not a sheltered English innocent from the schoolroom. I have seen enough of life to understand hard choices."

"But you are also as honest as sunshine. How can you not despise what I am?" he asked despairingly.

Because I love you. The words came from deep within her, so powerful that it was difficult to keep them from her lips. But she managed, because the last thing Robin needed was unwanted declarations of love.

Instead, she replied, "I've a fondness for rogues, especially honorable ones. In the time we've been together, you've done considerable good and no harm. You saved Dafydd Jones from being trampled. You stopped me from killing Simmons, for which I was grateful as soon as my temper cooled." She kissed his temple, feeling the hard beat of his pulse. "Tell me what you've done, Robin. Burdens are lighter for being shared."

"There were so many things," he whispered. "Endless lies. Informants I worked with who were captured and died most horribly. The French major I assassinated because he was a fine soldier who would have been able to hold a walled Spanish town against a siege indefinitely."

"Surely your informants knew the risks as well as you did. As for assassination—" she hesitated, to choose her words, "no decent person could rejoice at committing such a deed, but a siege is a dreadful thing that often ends in horrible slaughter. Did your action prevent one?"

"With their commander dead, his troops withdrew from the town without fighting. Lives were saved, which was good. But nothing can make it right to murder an honorable man who was doing his duty. I'd met him a couple of times. I liked him." Robin's misshapen hand opened and closed on the counterpane, his nails gouging the fabric. "I liked him, and I put a bullet in his back."

"Ah, Robin, Robin," she said, heart aching. "I see why you said that war would have been cleaner. For soldiers the issues are more clearly drawn, the responsibility left in higher hands. Your work was far more difficult. Often you must have had to choose between different evils, trapped in a world of grays without easy blacks and whites, never sure if you had made the right decision. A dozen years of that would be too much for anyone."

"Certainly it was too much for me."

In the distance thunder sounded, and cold rain beat harder on the glass. Feeling as if she were moving blindfolded through a marsh, where a misstep might lead to disaster, she asked, "Is that assassination the worst thing, the very worst, for which you hold yourself responsible?"

The shaking began again, but he didn't speak.

Her voice more insistent, she said, "Tell me, Robin. Perhaps the pain will fester less if you share it."

"No!" He twisted in her arms, trying to break free.

She held tight, refusing to let him escape. Again she said, "Tell me."

He choked out, "It was in Prussia. I had obtained a copy of a treaty with grave implications for Britain."

She thought back to what she knew of the wars. "The Treaty of Tilsit, where France and Russia made a secret alliance in hopes of bringing Britain to its knees?"

He tilted his head back and looked at her. "For an American, you're well informed about European affairs."

"The subject interested my father, so we followed the news together," she explained. "You actually managed to learn what was in the secret articles of the treaty?"

"Within hours of its being signed." He gave a bitter smile. "I told you I was good at my trade. But getting the information was the easy part compared to getting it back to England. The French soon discovered what had happened, then came in pursuit. I had to get to Copenhagen, so I rode west for days, using every trick I knew to elude them. Finally I was sure I had escaped. I needed to stop and rest. My horse was half dead, and I no better. I knew a family in the area, prosperous farmers. They hated the French, and had helped me in the past."

His voice cracked. "They greeted me like a long-lost son. I told them I had been pursued, but that I had escaped and there was no danger. I was so sure." A staccato pulse throbbed in his throat. "I was catastrophically wrong."

"The French found you?"

He nodded. "I slept for over twelve hours. Herr Werner woke me the next morning, when he learned that French troops were searching the neighborhood. I said I would leave immediately and went to the barn, but my horse was gone.

"Then I realized I hadn't seen Willi, their youngest son. He was sixteen, about my height and build, my coloring. He had conceived something of a hero worship for me. When I saw that my mount and saddle were gone, I had a horrible premonition that he was in danger. I ran into the forest toward the main road, trying to stop what was going to happen." His eyes spasmed shut. "I was too late."

Maxie felt his pain resonating deep within her, but knew she must force him to the end of the tale. "What happened?"

"Willi had decided to lead them away from the farm. I was on higher ground, and could see how he deliberately let a squad of French cavalry spot him. He had my horse, a coat the color of mine, and he was bareheaded, showing that damnable, indentifiable blond hair. As soon as they saw him, they gave chase. He tried to outrun them. My horse was very good, and Willi might have escaped, but another squad came galloping along the road from the other direction.

"When he realized he was trapped, he bolted into the forest, but he hadn't enough of a lead. The two squads caught him quickly. They gave him no chance to surrender, just shot him down. At least a dozen musket balls hit him." Robin shuddered, a film of sweat covering his body. "Willi was a bright lad, and he managed to outwit them. A small river ran through a deep gorge in the forest, and he survived long enough to reach it. The horse screamed as it plunged over the cliff into the water."

He buried his head against Maxie, shaking with the agony of a man at the limits of his endurance. She asked no more questions, only caressed him, whispering soft words in her mother's tongue, saying that everything would be all right, that he was a valiant and honorable warrior, and that she loved him no matter what he had done—all of the things she could not say in English.

She guessed that for Robin, the boy's death had come to symbolize everything that was innocent and courageous and doomed. The Treaty of Tilsit had been signed nine years earlier, and Robin would not have been much more than a boy himself. The wonder was not that he was close to breakdown, but that he had survived, and functioned, for so long while burdened with such terrible responsibilities and guilts.

For a long time there was no sound but rain and distant thunder and grief. Gradually the echoes of anguish faded, though he still held her as if she were his one hope of heaven.

Voice stark, he continued, "The French would have

liked to retrieve the documents, but the river was high.
They decided the water would destroy what the bullets
hadn't, and they left. I stayed and helped the Werners
search until we recovered Willi's body. His parents
never said one word of reproach. In some ways, that
was the hardest thing of all. They even apologized because Willi had destroyed my horse and insisted I take
their best mount as a replacement."

"It sounds as if Willi brought disaster on himself,"
Maxie said quietly. "If he hadn't intervened with his
misplaced gallantry, you might have escaped cleanly
with no one suffering."

"Perhaps, perhaps not." Robin drew an unsteady
breath. "But the fact remains that if I hadn't stopped at
the Werners' farm, Willi would not have died."

"Only God can know that, Robin. Perhaps it was
Willi's time to die, and he would have slipped on the
stairs and broken his neck at that same moment if you
had not come. Perhaps he would have gone for a soldier when he was a year older and died fighting the
French. Of course you feel grief and regret, but cruci-
fying yourself serves no good purpose." She stroked
his forehead, wishing she could soothe away the pain
inside.

"I always tried to do the right thing," he said
bleakly. "But too often, I didn't know what the right
thing was."

She sighed. "I think most of us do the best we know
how. There is really nothing more we can do."

"My best wasn't good enough."

His knotted pain proved that she had not done
enough, either. She looked into her own past, then said,
"After my mother's death, I attended a condolence ceremony held by members of her clan. It helped me a
great deal."

Praying that she could remember or improvise
enough of the ritual to help Robin, she lightly covered
his ears with her hands and recited, *"When a man
mourns, he cannot hear. Let these words remove the
obstruction so that you can hear again."*

After lifting her hands from his ears, she laid them over his eyes. *"During your grief, you have lost the sun and fallen into darkness. I now restore the sunlight."*

When she took her hands away, she saw that he was watching her gravely. Crossing her hands on the center of his chest, she intoned, *"You have allowed your mind to dwell on your great grief. You must release it lest you, too, wither and die."* She felt the rise and fall of his breathing beneath her palms until she lifted them away.

"In your sorrow, your bed has become uncomfortable and you cannot sleep at night. Let me remove the discomfort from your resting place." She smoothed her hands across his shoulders and down his arms, then said quietly, "Willi has gone to his rest, Robin. Can't you do the same?"

His eyes closed and he pulled her down against him. At first his heart was pounding as if trying to break free of his ribs, but gradually it slowed to a more normal speed. She held tightly, feeling that some of his inner darkness had been dissolved by the light. Though it was not complete healing, it was a beginning.

He slid his hand into her hair and rested his palm on her nape. "How did you become so wise, Kanawiosta?"

"The usual way," she said wryly. "By making mistakes." She settled her head on his shoulder, so tired from the emotional storms she could scarcely stay awake.

"Whatever the reason, you have wisdom," His hand skimmed down her back, coming to rest on her hip. "Too much to consider marrying me."

His statement acted on her fatigue like a spray of ice water, shocking her to full wakefulness. For a stunned moment she replayed his words to ensure that she had heard properly. Then she sat up and stared at her companion.

Robin lay on the pillows and watched her with the patient stillness of exhaustion. The candlelight played over the stark planes of his face and bare chest, but it was too dim to read the color or expression of his shadowed eyes.

Torn between shock, amusement, and desperate longing, she asked, "Is that an offer, or merely a product of your bizarre sense of humor?"

He sighed, turning his gaze from her to the ceiling. "It wasn't intended as humor. I guess I can't quite bring myself to make a direct offer. If we did marry, the advantages would all be to me. You would be a fool to accept, and you're too intelligent not to know that."

She didn't know whether to laugh, cry, or shriek. The scalding emotions of the night had forced her to admit that she loved Robin, though she wasn't sure that she understood or even wholly trusted him.

Which was not the same as saying that she distrusted him; she didn't doubt that he would be true to any commitment he made. And she understood him a good deal better now than she had an hour before. Still . . . "Marrying you is not without appeal, but I can't imagine what sort of life we would have. Our backgrounds are hopelessly different, and even though I've been a wanderer in the past, that isn't what I want for the future."

"No more do I. I promise you that I can keep a roof over your head." His mouth quirked satirically. "I am not quite as improvident as I look."

"Robin, look at me." When his gaze turned to her, she asked, "Why do you want to marry me? You have said nothing of love."

His eyes closed in a quick spasm of sorrow. "I can promise many things, Kanawiosta. Security, fidelity, my best efforts to make you happy. But love? I don't think I am very good at love. It is one thing I would be wiser not to promise."

Even when her father had died, Maxie had not ached like this. Robin's painful, despairing honesty made her want to weep. Instead she lifted his damaged left hand

and kissed it, then pressed it against her cheek. "Do you want me because I am here and Maggie is not?"

"No." His eyes opened and his fingers tightened around hers. "What I feel for you has nothing to do with Maggie. I did, and do, care for her deeply. I always will, but I don't want you as a substitute for her." Amusement flickered across his handsome, rogue angel face. "You are far too much yourself ever to be mistaken for anyone else."

She felt adrift, uncertain how to react. "Caring and loyalty are valuable, even vital. But is that enough?"

"Don't forget passion." He tugged her hand to bring her down next to him. "I haven't for one minute since I met you."

He rolled over and embraced her. Their lips met, and she thought she would dissolve in liquid fire. There had been kisses and caresses before, but always they had been shadowed by doubt. This time was utterly different. Robin's formidable skill and concentration were for her, and her alone.

She responded with all her wistful yearning. The drama of the night had scoured away normal defenses, and their emotions twined as intimately as their bodies. For a wild, sweet interval, there were no questions, only taste and touch and discovery. No matter how tortured Robin's past, despairing his present, and uncertain his future, she loved him.

He trailed kisses down her throat, then slid her shift off her shoulders to bare her breasts. Cupping them together, he murmured, "Lovely. So perfect and lovely."

As he rubbed his face in the shadowed cleft he created, she was struck by the contrast between her brown skin and his fairness. Then he lapped her nipple with his tongue and she forgot the contrast, forgot her doubts, forgot everything but the pure flame of desire.

Her hands skimmed over his back, tracing the faint ridges of scar tissue from that long-ago whipping. Someday she would have to ask him about that, and the bullet wound, and his misshapen hand—about every perilous incident that might have ended his life before they had a chance to meet. But not tonight. Ah, God, not tonight.

Abruptly he pulled away and buried his face in the pillow, his shoulders heaving. "Passion is too easy." His voice was ragged. "Neither of us, I think, is in a state to make decisions."

She was left gasping. Her hands clenched the counterpane as she stared at the ceiling and tried to collect her scattered wits. Why the devil couldn't she have gotten involved with a selfish man who was interested only in his own pleasure?

Because she could not have loved such a man. Speaking with great care, she said, "I gather this means you are undergoing another crisis of conscience."

He emerged from the pillow with a twisted, self-mocking smile. "Exactly so."

Gently he pulled her shift up over her shoulders again. His hand lingered for a moment on her breast. Then he moved his arm away, his fingers knotting into a fist. "You're remarkable. After all I've put you through tonight, you should be having shrieking hysterics."

"Believe me, I'm tempted." Limbs still trembling with reaction, she rolled over and propped her head on one hand so she could see his face. "How serious are you about marriage?"

"Completely," he said, his eyes lambent with passion.

She closed her eyes for a moment to marshal her thoughts before speaking. She wanted to say that she loved him, but didn't dare, not after his painful doubts about his ability to love. Neither did she want to give him a new source of guilt if the morning light made him change his mind about his proposal.

Was marriage to Robin why she had been unable to sense her future course? She thought about London, and immediately veered away, shaken by that horrible, black anxiety. But the fleeting contact reinforced her belief that her anxiety had nothing to do with Robin; it

was more like a wall of fire that she must pass through
in order to have a future.

Trying to suppress an involuntary shiver, she said,
"You are right that this is not the time to make decisions. I must learn what happened to my father, and
you have a great deal of sorting out to do."

He leaned forward and pressed a light kiss on her
forehead. "I'll sort as fast as I can. In the meantime, at
least you aren't saying no." He twined a lock of her
dark hair around his forefinger. "I may be acting like
the next thing to a lunatic, but I don't think I've ever
felt happier in my life than these last days with you.
I've been wishing this journey would never end. Now,
since there will be no final answers until it does, I want
to get to London as soon as possible. It's just that . . ."

She waited patiently for him to continue.

His eyes slid away and his hand stilled. "I don't
know if it is wise to marry a woman because I need her
so much. I think that might not be good for either of
us."

She studied his expression. The detachment that he
had worn like a cloak was gone, and she savored the
feeling of closeness. But it was difficult to think
clearly when her blood was drumming in her veins. On
a deeper level, she still felt the majestic, pulsing ener-
gies of passion and creation, the belief that together
they would find a measure of wholeness.

With sudden dismay, she realized that she had been
behaving like her demure Collins cousins. Since
meeting Robin, she had been defending her virtue,
worrying about the future instead of living in the present, protecting her heart from possible hurt.

But acting like a respectable Englishwoman would
not save her from pain; it would only deny her the
deepest desire of her heart. It was time to dispense
with European reason in favor of Iroquois wisdom. She
wanted Robin. She wanted to give and receive, to be
the kind of whole, wise, passionate woman her mother
had been, even if it was only for an hour. She wanted
to live in this moment as freely as the wind and the

rain. And in her bones, she knew that doing so was right.

She gave him a smile filled with love. "Your problem, Lord Robert, is that you think too much."

Then she leaned forward and kissed him.

Chapter 24

He could not resist her, yet for one crazed moment, as he thought of all of the people he had damaged, he tried. "Are you sure this is what you want?"

She smiled and raised herself above him, bracing herself with one arm. "Perfectly sure."

Waves of ebony hair framed the exotic features that had entranced him from the moment they had met. She was Kanawiosta, daughter of another land and another race. With her hair spilling over her shift-clad breasts, she looked like a pagan earth goddess, too mysterious for mortal man to know or possess, with a feminine power that could sear him to cinders.

But when she bent to him again, her lips were warm and real, her small, capable hands generous in their caresses. Surrendering, he opened his mouth to her drugging kiss.

He wanted to inhale her inside of himself so that she could mend the holes in his frayed spirit. He wanted to bury himself inside her and find shelter from the storm that had been raging in his head for a lifetime.

As the kiss intensified, she skimmed her hands over his shoulders and chest, the warmth of her touch glowing through his skin and reaching deep inside him to melt ancient aches. Finally she interrupted their embrace and pushed herself up with one arm, her eyes black with desire and her chest heaving under the translucent shift. "I'm glad you changed your mind."

"You changed it for me." He circled her breasts with his hands, using his thumbs to caress her nipples. They hardened, thrusting against the thin fabric. She closed her eyes and smiled, making a sound like a pleased cat.

He pushed her shift from her shoulders and down to her waist so that he could admire the sweet curve of her breasts. They were exactly right—not too large, not too small, deliciously crowned with circles the texture of sheared velvet. Huskily he said, "You belong in the Garden of Eden, where clothing was unknown."

"Eden was in a warmer climate than England," she said practically. Her smile turned wicked as she looked at his drawers. Even through the loose linen, his response to her was blindingly obvious.

"If we're going to pretend this is Eden, these must go." She tugged at the drawstring, then caught hold of his drawers and began pulling them off. It would have only taken a moment to remove them if she hadn't helped. Instead, her wandering, teasing hands made the process take much longer, and almost reduced him to incoherence.

When they were both as bare as Adam and Eve, he drew her forward so that she was lying on top of him. Her breasts crushed against his chest, the nipples a distinct, teasing pressure.

He could not get enough of the heated depths of her mouth. His hands glided down her back to linger on the ripe curves of her buttocks. Lost in yearning, he kneaded the firm muscles that lay beneath her satiny skin.

She sucked in her breath, and her lower body rocked against his. Her legs parted a little and his heated shaft slid between her thighs, rubbing against her with an intimacy just short of intercourse. She made a tiny mewling sound and her teeth nipped his collarbone when his hips thrust upward once, then again.

He wanted this to be slow and perfect, as she deserved, but she was making a shambles of his control. Struggling against the white heat that threatened to consume him, he caught her in his arms and rolled so that their positions reversed and he was above.

"Not so swiftly, Kanawiosta." He caught her wrists

and pinned them to the mattress on both sides of her head. "In interests of justice, I deserve a chance to drive you mad."

"I'm a great believer in justice," she said with a ravishingly feminine smile.

Taking his time, he grazed her breasts with his chin, the hidden whiskers delicately abrading the silky, lavender-scented skin until her body thrummed with desire. He bent his head and took the tawny tip of one nipple into his mouth, sucking and tugging until it was so rigid it grooved his tongue. Then he turned to her other breast.

When she exhaled feverishly and twisted against him, he trailed his mouth downward, over the arc of her ribs and the taper of her narrow waist. He paused to swirl his tongue around her navel, then nibbled the flat arc of her belly.

She strained against his pinioning hands, panting, "You've gotten your wish. In another five seconds, I'll be raving."

"Excellent." He straightened up and claimed her mouth again in a lushly sensual kiss. Abandoning all pretense of being in control, he released her wrists and wrapped one arm around her. His other hand glided downward, following the path of his earlier kisses until his fingers became tangled in feathery black curls.

She quivered when he first touched the hidden folds of female flesh. They were slick and swollen with moist heat.

He probed deeper until he found the exquisitely sensitive nub he sought. The gentle friction of his finger caused her to writhe frantically.

He broke their kiss so she could drag great gulps of air into her lungs. Then he closed his eyes, blocking out the beguiling sight of her so he could concentrate on the subtle messages of her body. Harder *here*. Back and forth again and again *there,* as her breath roughened and her hips bucked.

As the heady scent of passion filled his nostrils, her pliant nakedness became his whole world. It had been unutterably long since he had held a woman like this, and never had he felt such deep yearning.

The wildness built higher and higher, filling her mind with crimson fire. When she could bear no more, she cried out, her thighs clamping on his hand as a vortex of sensations swirled through her. The enfolding strength of his embrace held her safe as her spirit spiraled skyward, soaring falcon free.

As she returned to earth, she sagged against Robin, dazed and trembling. He lay on his side, holding her close against him while one hand caressed her from shoulder to hip in long, easy strokes. She tilted her head back, and the satisfaction she saw in his eyes assuaged her sense of selfishness.

But underneath his composed surface, his body was tense and unfulfilled. She lay back on the pillows, then caught his hand and pulled him across her. "Your turn, Robin."

It took only a single slow, wanton roll of her hips to splinter his calm. His face stark with urgency, he parted her legs with one knee, then probed her intimately, separating the delicate folds. Nothing more was needed, for her body was still wetly welcoming.

He braced himself over her and positioned the velvety head of his shaft. Then he thrust forward, sheathing himself in her willing flesh with one swift stroke.

The pain was brief but intense, a shock wave that swept through her whole body in an instant. Then it was gone, leaving a not unpleasant sense of internal stretching, and the deep satisfaction of knowing that they were mated in the dance of life.

The effect on Robin was far worse. He stiffened, his expression stunned. "Good God, Maxie! Why didn't you say something?"

She smiled and slid her arms around him, clasping his hard buttocks to hold him tight against her. "Because I knew you would get one of those maddening attacks of gentlemanliness. You can't help it, you're an Englishman." She rolled her hips upward, drawing him deeper. "You're thinking too much again, Robin. Don't."

Unable to resist, he drove into her again and again, his breath fractured and irregular. Though she had never experienced such sensations, she knew in her marrow how to respond, how to match his rhythm and resonate to his passion. She welcomed the flagrant maleness of his assault as much as she rejoiced in the female power that could inflame and absorb such desire.

His body arched and went rigid. "Ah, God . . ." he groaned, his voice a low, shuddering prayer. Though she did not reach the same fiery pinnacle as before, she felt an echoing sense of release and fulfillment.

As his body softened, she smoothed her hands over his sweat-slicked body, feeling the slow relaxation of his muscles. She touched her tongue to his shoulder, liking the saltiness, and the pounding of his heart, so close it seemed like her own.

He rubbed his cheek against hers, then rolled away and slid from the bed. Too exhausted even to be curious, she simply watched him cross the room. Garden of Eden indeed. Robin must be used to the casualness of naked lovers, but it was new to her, and an unanticipated pleasure. He was like a mountain lion, sleek and lithe and utterly masculine. The memory of what it had been like to have him inside her made her exhale roughly.

He went to the washstand and opened the drawer. After removing something, he returned to the bed and handed her a neatly folded towel. She used it to cleanse herself, and was pleased to see there were only a few spots of blood. It would have seemed gauche to stain a stranger's bed.

When she was done, he stretched out alongside her and drew her into his arms again. "Was I such a pathetic case that you felt compelled to do your utmost to patch me up?" he asked with rueful amusement.

She smiled. "I suppose there is a grain of truth in that, but it hardly does justice to either of us. I've wanted you from the time we met, Robin. Tonight I decided to stop acting like a demure English miss and behave like a woman of the Mohawk." She made an exaggerated face and nipped his shoulder. "We are famed for our ferocity. We take what we want, white man."

Tenderly, he massaged the back of her neck, his thumb exactly fitting a hollow he found there. "You had me thoroughly baffled. Given your age, your contraceptive tea, and general lack of maidenly vapors, I had assumed you were not a virgin."

"Among the Iroquois, many families share a longhouse. Children learn early what is natural between men and women."

"You also said once that women of your mother's people have a freer acceptance of their desires. Certainly you are comfortable with yourself like few women I've ever known." He gave her a quizzical glance. "But that makes it even harder for me to understand why I was the first for you. Are American men such fools?"

She grimaced. "As I said once before, there were plenty of men who thought a half-breed was fair game, but I decided early on that I would not be used so casually. Yet because we traveled so much, there was little opportunity to develop the kind of relationship where I could be sure I was desired for myself." Which was true as far as it went. What she did not say was that resisting advances had been easy, because she had never met a man who attracted her half as much as Robin.

He kissed her on the forehead. "Whatever the reason, I am greatly honored to be your choice."

She eyed him sternly. "You're not going to make some silly remark to the effect that since you ruined me, it's your duty to give me your name in holy matrimony, are you?"

"I might if I thought I had any chance of success, but I know you well enough to realize that such an argument would never work." He ran his hand down her body under the blanket. "Besides, you don't seem ruined to me. You seem quite enchantingly flawless."

She gave a low chuckle. It might not do to talk of love, but it seemed fair to say, "You're rather wonderful yourself. It was worth waiting."

He kissed the edge of her ear. "Good night, Kanawiosta," he murmured. "No more bad dreams for either of us tonight."

She rolled over and nestled her back against his front. Her body was so relaxed that she could have knotted herself up like a pretzel and still fallen asleep.

With such physical and emotional closeness between them, she could easily sense Robin's mood. The combination of confession and passion seemed to have greatly eased his inner darkness. Even if they had no future beyond the next few days or weeks, his innate strength and resilience should enable him to continue the healing process.

It was gratifying to have been able to help, though she suspected that her principal virtue had been her foreignness. It was often easier to reveal one's secret torments to someone with no connection to one's normal life.

She suppressed a little sigh. In spite of his proposal, she still couldn't see them as having a future together. He could tell her anything and it wouldn't matter, because she would not be there as a reminder of when he had succumbed to weakness.

Now she was the one thinking too much. All that mattered was that Robin had healing, and that she had tasted a sweetness and pleasure she would never regret.

Chapter 25

Washed clean by the storm, the dawn sky was pale and clear when Maxie woke. It was nearing the summer solstice and the sun rose very early, so she couldn't have had more than two or three hours sleep, yet she felt amazingly refreshed.

Robin still slept, his spun-gold head resting by hers and his arm across her waist. His face was peaceful and very young. Hard to remember his despair of the night before, or to believe that he had done the things he had; this morning he looked scarcely more than a schoolboy.

That image was belied by the scar on his side. She studied the location. It was a miracle that the bullet hadn't destroyed some vital bit of anatomy.

Her arm tightened around him. She really ought to wake him, but couldn't bring herself to do so. The previous night had been very special. Since they might never again be so close, she was reluctant to end the lingering magic.

She brushed a kiss against his hair. His absurdly long lashes swept up and he smiled at her. At close range, his azure eyes had the impact of a cannonball. If she weren't already in love with him, she would be after that lazy, intimate smile.

He murmured, "I always sleep well when I'm with you."

"The effect is entirely mutual." Touching the old bullet wound, she continued, "I suppose that this and your various other scars were received in the line of duty."

He nodded. "I got that one in Spain."

"What about the whip marks on your back?"

His expression became ironic. "I was innocent of the crime I was flogged for, but since my real actions would have hanged me, it seemed better not to defend myself."

"And your hand?"

He raised it so that the irregular outline was clearly discernible. "A determined gentleman wanted me to write a letter that would endanger a friend of mine. I was reluctant. After the fellow had broken several of the bones, I mentioned that I was left-handed and couldn't possibly write anything."

She shuddered at the sheer cold-bloodedness of the torture. "That must have been excruciating."

He made a vague sound of agreement. "It was several days before the bones could be set, which is why they aren't all straight. I was very fortunate that infection didn't set in and that the hand still works properly."

"You've lived altogether too exciting a life." She leaned forward and tenderly pressed her lips to the scar left by the bullet. The ridged flesh was rough against her tongue.

His nipple was only a few inches away. Curious whether it was as sensitive as hers, she nibbled her way over. The soft nub of flesh hardened deliciously against her tongue. No wonder Robin enjoyed kissing her breasts so much.

When she transferred her attention to his other nipple, he sucked in his breath. "Be careful, Maxima, or you might get more than you bargained for."

She glanced up, making her eyes wide and innocent. "How much more?" Her hand crept down his torso and curled around warm male flesh. He was already half erect, and he instantly firmed to full hardness.

His fingers dug into the sheets. Voice uneven, he said, "Aren't you sore after last night?"

She considered. "Not especially. All of those years of riding and walking, I expect." She began caressing him, her thumb stroking the rim of the velvety head. "I'm not sure I've got the knack of making love. More practice wouldn't go amiss."

He gave a gusty sigh of laughter. "You win, witch."

He made one of his lightning-quick movements, as he had the night before when she had tried to waken him from his nightmare. Before she could blink, she was lying under him, but this time he was fully awake, his eyes alight with laughter and his hands and mouth spinning a web of intoxicating pleasure. He remembered precisely what she had liked the night before, and found a dozen new ways to please her as well.

When she was whimpering with desire, he entered her. He was very gentle at first. When it became clear that she felt no discomfort, he intensified his lovemaking, filling her with swift, hot pleasure.

As she hovered on the verge of shattering, he reversed their positions again so that she was above. She clung to him, feeling as if she were spiraling into the sky, higher and higher until she fell into the sun. As he poured himself into her, she splintered into fire, glorious and terrifying.

Then she collapsed, shaking, on his chest, her legs lying outside his. He had been right that she was getting more than she had bargained for. A woman might sell her soul in the hope of finding a lifetime of such delight. A good thing she'd been telling the truth when she said that a soul couldn't be sold, lost, or given away; otherwise she would be damned for eternity.

Robin lazily stroked her back, his affection as warming as his passion had been. When they had both recovered some semblance of sanity, he said, "Enough of letting chance control our journey. Today we go to London."

She raised her head and looked at him. "How? We haven't the money for coach fare, even from this distance."

He gave her a bright smile, the one she had always distrusted. "I'll explain later. But now we must rise so we can leave before the estate workers are up and about."

Working together, they removed all signs of occupancy within the hour. After a quick breakfast, they collected their knapsacks and left. It was still early enough that there was no one about to see the trespassers.

Their path took them by the stables behind the house. Instead of walking by, Robin swerved and went in a side door. Alarmed, Maxie followed into the dimly lit stable, where horses whickered drowsily at their entrance.

Mindful that grooms might be sleeping on the upper level, she kept her voice low, but still managed a full measure of outrage when she asked, "What are we doing here?"

"Finding transport." Calmly Robin walked down the aisle, studying the box stalls on each side. Most of the horses were for field work, but there were several riding hacks as well.

When he led a gelding from its stall, Maxie planted herself in front of him, fire in her eye. "Blast it, Robin, I don't want to be a party to horse theft. Or do you intend to turn these loose a few miles down the road, like you did with Simmons's nag?"

He circled around her and tethered the horse, then went for another. "Not this time. We're going to need the beasts for the rest of the journey."

"*Robin!*"

"Don't worry. I've written a note to explain what has happened to the horses." He pulled a folded piece of paper from his pocket and spiked it on a nail that protruded from a post.

Not pausing to read it, Maxie followed Robin into the tack room. "You say you're not a thief or a swindler," she said tightly. "But you're not a spy anymore, either. The war is *over*. What the devil do you think you're doing?"

"We won't get into trouble." He lifted a saddle from a stand. "I know the owner of the estate."

She stared at him, her hands clenched. The feelings of trust and closeness were gone, leaving her baffled and uneasy. "Why the blue blazes should I trust your word, Lord Robert?"

The skin whitened over his cheekbones. "I'm sorry you feel you must ask that."

She took a deep breath, knowing that she was on the edge of saying something irrevocable. When she had mastered some of her anger, she said quietly, "I believe that there was honesty between us last night. But today is another day, and there is still far too much that I don't know about you."

"I'll answer any question you ask," he said gravely. "But . . . I would prefer to defer it until later."

Maxie wanted to weep with frustration. It was certainly possible that Robin knew the estate's owner, but it was equally plausible that he was indulging in a bit of casual larceny. When one has killed, seduced, and betrayed, taking two valuable horses might seem like a mere prank.

He balanced the saddle against his hip and lightly touched her cheek with his free hand. "Trust me just a little while longer, Kanawiosta?"

When he spoke like that, she had no choice. She exhaled wearily. "In for a penny, in for a pound. But you can't postpone the day of reckoning much longer."

He sighed. "I know. But this journey has been a special time. It isn't only you I've discovered, but in a real sense, myself. I'm not quite ready to face reality."

She gave him a smile, a little crooked but genuine. "Are you proud of the fact that you can reduce me to a mound of quivering aspic, or is it unnoteworthy because you have that effect on all females?"

"You overrate my charm." He leaned over the saddle and gave her a quick kiss. "But I'm glad you're susceptible. It keeps the balance of power a little more equal."

As he headed back to the main stable area, she sputtered, "What is that supposed to mean? You've been winding me around your finger ever since we met!"

He saddled the first gelding, then turned to her. "Surely you know that if you asked me to crawl on my hands and knees through a bed of hot coals, I would do it."

She blinked. "Wouldn't you at least want to know if I had a good reason for making such a request?"

He smiled. "Yes, and I'd wear my asbestos drawers as well. But I'd still do it if you asked."

An odd, breathless sensation fluttered in her chest as she gazed at him. He was either completely serious or the best liar on the face of the earth. Or perhaps insane; she mustn't forget that possibility. Wearily she found another saddle—the oldest, shabbiest one in the tack room—and saddled the other horse.

Robin led the way outside and they walked the horses quietly to a small gate in the estate wall. Maxie stared at the toes of her boots while he picked the lock. When they went outside, he relocked the gate, then they mounted and headed south.

When they were far enough from Ruxton for Maxie to feel safe, she asked, "Can we reach London today?"

"Yes, though it will be evening when we arrive."

She frowned, trying to calculate the state of the treasury. "Can we afford a night's lodging when we get there?"

"Not really. We have enough for tolls and food for the day, but that's about it. However, I have friends who can put us up."

"Won't they ask awkward questions?"

"Not these friends." He sighed. "Our casual habits will have to change, which is one reason why I haven't wanted the trip to end. Respectable folk would already consider you horrendously compromised, but it doesn't count since nobody knows. In London, however, we will rejoin the real world. Besides investigating your father's death, I assume you will want to visit your aunt. We're going to have to behave with a semblance of propriety, and make sure that our lies about the journey match."

She made a face. "I suppose that means separate beds."

"I'm afraid so. If any of your relations—or mine, for that matter—discover that we have been traveling together, there will be a loud outcry demanding that we marry immediately."

"Why should you be concerned about that?" she said dryly. "I thought marriage was what you wanted."

He chuckled. "I can think of nothing that would make you fly off more quickly than being told that you *had* to marry me."

"I am quite capable of resisting social pressure, particularly from people I don't know," she retorted.

"So am I, but I learned a long time ago that superficial conformity simplifies one's life enormously."

"When in Rome, do as the Romans do?"

"Exactly. And that goes double for London." He glanced over at her. "Luckily I can obtain funds tomorrow, so we'll have no problems in that area."

"Dare I ask where you intend to get the money, Lord Robert?"

"From a banker, very boring and legitimate." His eyes danced. "Did you know that you always call me Lord Robert when you are disapproving?"

She thought for a moment, then gave a reluctant smile. "I suppose that silly fraudulent title symbolizes everything I don't know and don't trust about you."

"Do you truly distrust me?" he asked quietly.

She was not surprised that the question had resurfaced; it was at the core of their relationship. Luckily, they were entering a small village, which gave her time to think about her answer. After they threaded their way through the narrow high street and returned to the open road, she said, "It's no credit to my good sense, but I do trust you, at least to a point."

"What is that point?" He didn't look at her as he asked, and his expression was cool and unforthcoming.

"I am sure you would not knowingly cause me harm, and I believe you will always try to honor your word." She gave an exasperated sigh. "But perhaps I'm wrong. A wise woman once told me that being in love reduces one's intelligence by half, and eliminates good judgment altogether." She stopped in sudden consternation, realizing what she had just revealed.

Robin turned his head swiftly, his blue eyes intense. Catching her horse's bridle, he brought them both to a halt. Then he backed his horse next to hers, so close their legs touched, and bent over for a long, fiercely emotional kiss.

As she responded, her arms sliding up to circle his neck, she was startled by the depth of feeling her oblique declaration had unleashed. Robin might feel incapable of declaring love himself, but it seemed that her love was not an unwelcome gift.

As they resumed riding, the tension of the early morning was gone, and they were friends again.

One of the Wheatsheaf's chambermaids had been assigned to help the distinguished lady guest dress. Unfortunately, Desdemona's fresh gown was as dreary as the one she had worn the day before. She really must do something about her wardrobe.

As the maid fixed her hair, Desdemona thought about the previous evening. After their mutual baring of souls, both she and the marquess had retreated emotionally, and the dinner conversation had been general rather than personal. Yet even though Giles was the sort of rich landowner whom Desdemona had often opposed politically, she had to admit that his mind was both humane and tolerant. Probably more tolerant than her own, if she were going to be absolutely honest.

She had become wary as bedtime approached, wondering if he would try to persuade her to join him. But he had treated her with unexceptionable propriety. Except for one thorough good-night kiss, the memory of which made her lips curve into a daft, cat-in-the-creampot smile. . . .

Hastily Desdemona rearranged her expression, gave the maid a half-crown, and went down to the parlor to break her fast. She was prepared for some constraint when she met the marquess again, and was perversely disappointed that he was not down before her.

With the unspoken hope that he would appear, she ordered enough food for two. The meal arrived shortly before Giles did. He tapped on the open door, then hesitated, his expression uncertain. "May I join you?"

The fact that he was equally shy dissolved Desdemona's nerves. "Please do," she said cordially. "I can't speak for the deviled kidneys, but the coddled eggs and sausage are excellent."

He took a chair opposite her. "I've been to the smith. My coach won't be ready before tomorrow at the earliest."

"No matter." As domestic as a wife, she poured him a cup of tea, adding milk as she had seen him do the night before. "We can go to your brother's estate in my carriage. Afterward, I can either return you to Daventry or take you on to London if you don't feel like waiting for your repairs to be completed."

"That's very good of you." He served himself eggs and sausage. "I'm in no mood to cool my heels here for another day."

"Do you think we'll find our fugitives at Ruxton?"

"I doubt it—I'm beginning to think of them as will-o'-the-wisps, eternally flitting away just out of reach," he said dryly. "Will your niece call on you when she arrives in London?"

She shrugged. "I hope so, though I wouldn't wager major money on it. Will your brother go to Wolverton House?"

The marquess shook his head. "The place is closed with only a caretaker at the moment. I'd been thinking of selling it, actually, but I'm reconsidering." He gave her a level look. "Perhaps I'll be spending more time in town in the future."

Desdemona liked the sound of that. She found herself smiling again. Lord, she was behaving like a schoolgirl suffering her first case of calf love.

No, that wasn't true. As she looked down and meticulously spread marmalade over her toast, she realized

that she had never felt this way before. She had been
a shy and bookish girl, slow to develop interest in the
opposite sex. In her salad days she had been tormented
by unwanted advances, and she had married young and
without love. Surely she was permitted a little folly
now. Glancing up, she asked, "How will you find Lord
Robert?"

"Money must be high on his list of priorities, so I'll
leave word with his bankers," Giles replied. "I'll also
let some of Robin's friends know that I'm looking for
him."

The conversation brought Desdemona's fancies to
earth. While she had come to trust the marquess, Lord
Robert was still a doubtful quantity. If he had harmed
Maxima, the repercussions would certainly affect the
fragile feelings growing between herself and Giles.

Resolutely she reached for another piece of toast.
Let the future take care of itself. Today she would enjoy the hours spent with the most attractive man she
had ever known.

The roads were muddy, so they didn't reach Ruxton
until almost noon. The gatekeeper was happy to admit
the marquess, but when questioned, said that Lord
Robert had not visited.

Unconvinced, they entered and went to the estate office. The steward, Haslip, was frowning over his books
when Giles and Desdemona entered. The frown disappeared when he glanced up to see the man who had
hired and supervised him for years.

"Lord Wolverton!" He got quickly to his feet. "This
is an unexpected pleasure, my lord. Will you be staying for a time?"

Giles shook his head. "I only stopped by to see if
my brother was here."

Haslip hesitated. "Perhaps he was, but I'm not sure."

When Giles raised his brows, Haslip said, "No one
saw him, but this morning two horses were missing
and this note was in the stable." He handed a piece of
paper to the marquess. "I don't know if this is his lord-

ship's handwriting. If it is, well enough, but maybe it was forged by a clever thief. Whoever the fellow was, he took the two best mounts in the stables."

Giles scanned the note. It said only, "I need the horses," and was signed "Lord Robert Andreville." The writing was his brother's distinctive back-slanting script.

"That's his hand." Giles passed the note to Desdemona. "So he was here last night. At what time was it noticed that the horses were missing?"

"About nine o'clock."

"I'll look in the house and see if he spent the night. If he arrived late, he probably didn't wish to waken anyone," Giles said smoothly. Better not to mention the Sheltered Innocent; where she was concerned, the less said, the better.

Haslip obviously had questions, such as how his new employer had entered a walled estate, why he had left without notifying anyone of his presence, and why he needed two horses. But the steward said only, "Very good, my lord. I'll fetch the keys."

After being let into the manor house, Giles dismissed Haslip. Then he and Desdemona spent some time searching the house, finishing in the kitchen.

"They were here, all right," Desdemona said after prowling through the stillroom, the china closets, and a tin bathing tub with a few drops of water inside. She held a newly washed and polished crystal goblet up to the light. "It appears they dined in some style."

"Robin has always had style," Giles remarked. "I looked through the linen closet. Judging by the number of sheets that had been used once, then carefully refolded, they slept in separate beds. Perhaps all our worries were for naught."

"We shall see," Desdemona said tersely. Still, she was willing to accept the possibility that a couple could travel together without the man ravishing the woman. A day earlier she might have disagreed, but association with Giles was teaching her that a mature man did not invariably act like a lust-crazed youth.

Perhaps Lord Robert really had offered his escort to Maxima from pure altruism.

But even if there had been no misconduct, the questions of propriety and reputation remained. "Since they're on horseback, they could be in London tonight."

"Yes." The marquess gave her an encouraging smile. "In another day or two, this whole imbroglio should be cleared up."

As she led the way from the house, Desdemona thought wryly that the problem of Maxima might be on the verge of solution, but the problem of the marquess was a good deal more challenging. Still, it was the sort of challenge she could relish.

Chapter 26

A fter a long day in the saddle, London assaulted Maxie's senses so fiercely that it made Boston seem like a market town. Wearily she followed Robin's mount through the dusky streets, her only interest in their destination being when they would arrive.

It was a rude shock when Robin reined to a halt in front of the grandest mansion in a section of the city full of grand mansions. "We're stopping here?" she asked, dismayed.

He gave her a reassuring smile as he dismounted. "This is it. The knocker is up, so my friends are in residence."

"Looking as we do, they won't feed us at the kitchen door, much less allow us into the parlor," she muttered as she swung her tired body from her horse.

He chuckled. "Don't worry, they've seen me in worse case."

Her feet planted on the cobblestones, she scrutinized the massive facade, feeling like a mud-stained provincial. Pride came to her aid; she would be damned if she would turn coward now. What did it matter what a parcel of overbred English aristocrats thought of her? If Robin thought it fitting to bring her here, she'd not skulk in like a craven hound.

She held the horses while Robin wielded the knocker. The door was quickly opened by a liveried and bewigged footman. The servant made a slow, insulting scan of the visitor, looking as if he had found a barrel of long-dead fish on the steps.

Before the footman could speak, Robin said imperiously, "Call someone to take our horses." He had made one of his instant transitions, this time into pure aristocratic hauteur.

The footman sputtered, then subsided under his visitor's disdainful eye. Within another minute, the butler appeared and the footman found himself leading the horses back to the mews.

In spite of her resolutions, Maxie was hard-pressed not to cringe when she set foot in a marble-floored foyer so vast that a cavalry company could have mustered in it. The vaulted ceiling soared two stories above, statues that must have been stolen from Greek temples stood on pedestals around the edges, and a sweeping double staircase dominated the center of the room.

She was not familiar with grand houses, but this one might have been a royal palace. Lord, for all she knew, the building was Carlton House with the Prince Regent carousing upstairs.

Robin, however, was as nonchalant as if he owned the house. He asked the butler, "Is the duchess in?"

Less easily intimidated than his minion, the servant said loftily, "Her grace is not receiving."

"That is not what I asked," Robin said with soft, lethal precision. "The duchess will see me. Tell her Lord Robert is here."

The butler's face showed rapid mental calculations that weighed the visitor's accent and manner against his unsavory appearance. Then he bowed slightly and went off.

Duchess? Maxie wondered if the august lady would prove to be Robin's grandmother, and he the adored family black sheep or something equally appalling. She had decided early in their acquaintance that Robin was well-bred, but was he really from the highest levels of English society? With a sick feeling in her stomach, she admitted that it was quite possible, even probable.

Rigid with discomfort, she avoided Robin's eye, pulling in on herself in this strange and possibly hostile territory. Every muscle in her body tense, she prowled about the foyer like a cat investigating a new home. Even her companion's air of command hadn't gotten them invited into a drawing room.

She had reached the farthest corner of the foyer when she heard the sound of swift footsteps. Turning, she saw a glorious golden creature racing down the sweeping staircase. The woman didn't see Maxie; instead, she hurled herself at her visitor, ignoring his filthy clothing. "Robin, you wretch! Why didn't you let me know you were coming?"

Robin reached out, laughing, to catch her up in his arms. "Show a little care, Maggie! Think of the future Marquess of Wilton, if not of yourself."

"You're as bad as Rafe," the duchess said fondly. "It could be a girl, you know."

"Nonsense. You're far too efficient not to provide the requisite heir on your first attempt."

For a moment the two stayed loosely linked in each other's arms with the casualness of long intimacy. The duchess was almost as tall as Robin, with the same blazing blond looks.

In her quiet corner, Maxie felt a shock so profound that for a moment her vision darkened. She had thought herself prepared for whatever this house had to offer, but not this. God in heaven, not this! How could he have brought her to his mistress's home? *How could he?*

In all the long journey from the north, Robin had never seemed further away. His gilt hair shone in the lamplight, and even in his shabby, travel-worn clothing he was unmistakably an aristocrat. Not since her early childhood, when she had been taunted by white children, had Maxie felt so much a half-breed and an outcast, so irredeemably small, dark, and alien.

Releasing the duchess, Robin said, "I want you to meet someone very special."

As he led Maggie across the foyer, Maxie was near paralysis from a volatile blend of fury and social confusion. What did one do in the presence of a duchess? In particular, what did a female dressed as a male do?

The answer floated up from a grande dame she had known in Boston: a citizen of the American republic bowed to no mortal, only to God, and only then if so inclined. That being so, the mistress of Maxie's lover certainly did not rate a curtsy.

On the other hand, since Maxie was dressed as a boy, removing her hat was appropriate. She did so, but nothing could be done about her expression, which must have been ferociously hostile.

The duchess's halted, her eyes widening in surprise. They were changeable gray-green, not blue like Robin's.

"Maggie, this is Miss Maxima Collins. Maxie, the Duchess of Candover." Robin laid a light hand on Maxie's arm. "I am trying to persuade Maxie to marry me."

The gray-green eyes reflected shock, swiftly followed by brimming amusement. The duchess's features lacked the symmetry of perfect beauty, but her radiant charm was far more potent than mere beauty could ever be. No wonder she haunted Robin's dreams.

At the sight of the duchess's amusement, Maxie teetered toward explosion. Obviously Maggie thought Robin's declared interest in a grubby undersized tomboy was some kind of joke.

Maxie's fury was allayed when the duchess said with genuine warmth, "My dear, how marvelous to meet you!" She gave a conspiratorial smile. "I do hope you can bring yourself to accept Robin. He has a number of redeeming qualities, though I expect you want to murder him just now, don't you?"

The comment was so accurate that Maxie was thrown off balance. "I am considering the best method, as a matter of fact." Though her teeth were gritted, she was determined to match the duchess' aplomb. "Boiling oil seems too quick."

Maggie chuckled. "I gather he simply brought you here, without a word of explanation?"

"Exactly so, your grace." Maxie glanced at Robin, who didn't even look ashamed of himself. His hand still rested on her elbow, and she drew comfort from his touch even as she wanted to wring his neck. "Robin made a vague reference to calling on friends, no more."

"The result of too many years spying, where the less one says, the better." Maggie waved her hand around her. "I was shocked myself when I first saw this mausoleum." She cocked her head to one side consideringly. "You're an American?"

Clearly she shared Robin's ear for accents, as she had shared so much else with him. The thought did not improve Maxie's temper. "Yes, I am. My father was English, however. A younger son of the sixth Viscount Collingwood." She was immediately ashamed of herself for feeling the need to mention her noble relations, but it was too late to recall the words.

The other woman's brows drew together thoughtfully. "Collingwood. The seat is in the north, isn't it? Durham?"

"Yes." That sounded too curt, so Maxie added, "I was visiting with my uncle and his family through the spring."

Robin gave her a quizzical glance when she mentioned the Collingwood connection, but said only, "Having arrived in London with pockets to let, we were hoping Candover House might have room for us for a night or two."

"I'm sure we can find space." The duchess turned to Maxie. "Let me show you your room so you can rest and refresh yourself."

"If you don't mind, your grace, I'd like to have a word alone with Robin first." Maxie's voice was even, but there was a dangerous glitter in her eyes.

"Of course." The duchess waved toward a door. "You can be private in the small salon."

As Robin followed his companion into the room, he studied her expression uneasily. He had known she would be startled to find herself in Maggie's house, but her barely suppressed rage was far greater than he had expected.

As soon as he closed the door behind them, Maxie whirled around, every inch of her small body quivering with fury. "How dare you bring me to your mistress's house!"

"Maggie hasn't been my mistress in some years," he said mildly. "She is still, however, my friend, and she and I have been in the habit of relying on each other. Since you and I needed a place to stay, it seemed natural to come here."

He crossed the salon to the fireplace and leaned against the marble mantel. "I knew I could trust her and Candover to accept two shabby travelers without questions, outrage, or dangerous gossip. Here you can make the transition back to respectable young lady with no one the wiser."

Maxie's hands knotted into fists, but she maintained a tenuous control. "You identified yourself to the butler as Lord Robert, and your duchess referred to you the same way. I thought you said it wasn't a real title."

"You are the one who said it wasn't real. I merely didn't correct your misapprehension," he pointed out. "Apparently your father didn't explain all the odd quirks of the title system. For example, the use of 'Lord' with one's Christian name is the exclusive prerogative of the younger sons of dukes and marquesses, so I am correctly styled Lord Robert Andreville."

Her wide brown eyes narrowed as she assimilated his statement. She looked more exotic, and more dangerous, than ever. "You said you weren't a nobleman."

"I'm not. Lord Robert is a courtesy title. I'm a commoner, like you. If my brother should die, which God forbid, I would be instantly ennobled." He shrugged. "It doesn't make much sense."

"Your father was a duke?"

He shook his head. "The Marquess of Wolverton. One step lower on the ladder."

"So you were on your family estate when we met." She stared at him as if he were a complete stranger.

"What kind of man are you? From beginning to end you've deliberately misled me, letting me think you were a homeless wanderer, a thief, or worse. How many other lies have you told me?"

"I've always told you the truth." Robin shifted his weight from one foot to the other, his gaze not meeting hers. He was falling into the exaggerated coolness that was his reaction to nerves or guilt. Yet even knowing it was a mistake, he could not remove the calm detachment from his voice. "Though I'll admit to a few falsehoods spoken to others in your presence."

Maxie's anger exploded into pure, coruscating rage. In one smooth motion, she seized the porcelain figurine standing on an elegant end table and hurled it at Robin.

The statuette shattered on the marble fireplace inches from his outstretched hand. He didn't move, even when splinters of china struck him, but the fingers of his left hand whitened where they clenched the edge of the mantel.

"I don't care if every word you spoke was approved for accuracy by God Himself! You must have been educated by lawyers or Jesuits," she said contemptuously. "Your intent was deception, even if you appeased your delicate conscience by manipulating the truth rather than saying outright lies." Her voice broke. "What a fool I've been to believe you."

Her raw pain sliced through Robin's defensiveness with razor swiftness. Shaken, he took a deep, steadying breath. "You are right—I was using the truth to create a false impression. But I swear it wasn't my intention to make a fool of you."

"Why, then?"

She stared at him, the fine planes of her face tight, her vulnerability making him ache for having unintentionally hurt her. Distractingly, the present was overlaid with images of making love to her. Her sweetness, her generosity, her sensuality and passion.

As their gazes locked, he wanted her with crippling intensity, physical and emotional need so closely interwoven that he could not separate one from the other. He had wanted her from the first instant he had opened his eyes and found that an enchanting, forceful wood nymph had tripped over him.

That being the case, why had he acted so stupidly? How could a man noted for subtlety and perception have been such a bloody bedamned fool? As he delved into the deeper recesses of his mind, the answer became obvious. "I'm not very fond of Lord Robert Andreville," he said painfully. "If I didn't like the fellow, I could hardly expect you to. And from the moment I met you, I wanted—very much—for you to like me."

Difficult though it was, he should have tried honesty sooner. Maxie's tense body eased as her fury dissipated. Their locked gazes held for another endless moment.

"I see," she said. But if anger had gone, there was still bleakness. She crossed the room to lean her shoulder against the opposite end of the mantel, her arms folded across her chest. In a tone that echoed Robin at his most detached, she asked, "Did you bring me here to get Maggie's approval? Or did you simply want to shock her by demonstrating the depths to which you have fallen since she left you? It would be impossible to find another female as beautiful and aristocratic as she is, so I assume that you decided to go in the opposite direction. Producing a disreputable savage will certainly show her a thing or two."

"Good God, you can't possibly believe that I brought you here for any such reason!" Understanding her anger made Robin feel a little sick. "You are a woman of wisdom and character and would be a credit to any man lucky enough to win your regard. And even covered with mud and looking like you have been dragged through a bush backward, you are beautiful."

Her lips thinned. "Like a good peddler, you always know the right words. But sometimes, Lord Robert, words aren't enough."

He deserved that, but he still felt as if she had

rammed her fist into his solar plexus. "I plead guilty to being an insensitive dolt. To say that I brought you here for Maggie's approval has the wrong connotation, but it's true that I wanted you to meet her. You are the two most important women in my life, and I think you might become friends."

Maxie stretched one arm along the mantel and rubbed the carving, as if it were the most interesting thing in the world. "If she disapproves of me, as she surely does, what then?"

"She won't disapprove of you." He covered her hand where it rested on the marble. Her fingers jerked at his touch, but she did not pull away.

"I think what you are really asking is if I would choose you over her." He tightened his clasp. "The answer is yes. Even if Maggie were wrongheaded enough to try to interfere, she would fail. You are the only one with the power to divide us."

Maxie's eyes closed and a spasm of emotion crossed her face. Unable to keep his distance any longer, Robin stepped forward and enfolded her in his arms.

Unresisting, she buried her face against his shoulder as if exhausted. No matter what their verbal conflicts, on the level of physical touch there was always harmony between them. He held her close, hoping that the embrace was soothing her as much as it was helping him.

Because of Maxie's forceful character, he tended to forget how small she was. He felt a surge of protective tenderness; her head barely reached his chin, and he was not a tall man. "Your head is heart high." With one hand he pulled the pins from her hair so that it fell down her back in a shimmering ebony mantle. "I'm a complete idiot, Kanawiosta. When we were traveling together, I wanted to block out the past and the future, because for the first time in years I was happy."

He caressed her taut spine, sliding his fingers through her silky tresses. "I knew that sooner or later I must explain myself, but I was a lazy coward and preferred to delay as long as possible. I didn't consider how unfair I was being to you. You seemed like the earth—wise, nurturing, infinitely strong. I overlooked the fact that you have scars and fears of your own."

Head still bent, she asked, "What other surprises have you in store for me?"

He thought a moment. "Well, I'm fairly affluent. Among other things, I'm the owner of Ruxton."

That caused her to look up, a flash of exasperated amusement in her eyes. "You mean you were stealing your own horses?" When he nodded, she said, "To think of the anxiety I felt!"

"I said you needn't worry."

"The duchess is right." Her voice was severe, but her lips twitched with suppressed humor. "You are a wretch."

"Guilty." He sighed, no longer amused. "That's why it seemed such a good idea to be someone else."

Maxie looked directly at him, her expression grave. "We must talk more about that, but not, I think, tonight."

"Good—I wouldn't be up to it right now. Any more than you are probably up to deciding whether or not to marry me." The words were said lightly, but he held his breath, needing to know if the events of the evening had angered her so much that marriage was out of the question.

She shook her head, her face troubled. "I don't know, Robin. We are even further apart than I thought." Raising her hands, she fidgeted with his shabby lapels. "I don't know whether I can fit into your English world, or if I even want to try."

"We are closer than you realize, and this English world is not the only possibility." He brushed a kiss on her hair. "But now is not the time for talking about that, either. The important thing is that you are not saying no." He smiled a little. "Thank you for not hitting me with that china figurine. Perhaps you should have. I was being incredibly obtuse."

"I wanted to make a point, not damage you, but I should have held on to my temper." She winced. "I hope that statuette wasn't a cherished family heir-loom." Her gaze went to his wilted shirt. "If I call you Lord Robert when I'm exasperated, what does it mean when you call me Kanawiosta?"

He said slowly, "I suppose it means that I am speaking from the heart, and hope you will listen the same way."

"That's not a bad reason." After a long silence, she glanced up with a trace of mischief. "If I married you, would I have a title? And if so, what would it be?"

"You would be called Lady Robert Andreville. Lady Robert for short, or perhaps Lady Robin."

Her eyes widened. "Seriously? That isn't another one of your jests?"

"God's own truth."

Maxie threw her head back and laughed. "What an absurd system! No wonder the American founding fathers discarded it."

The door opened and the Duchess of Candover entered. Seeing her guests in each other's arms, she began a hasty retreat. "Sorry. I guess you didn't hear my knock."

"No need to run off." Robin released Maxie without haste. "We've negotiated a truce."

Too wise to comment, the duchess said, "Rafe just sent a message that he will be leaving Westminster earlier than he had expected. Would you two care to join us for dinner in an hour or so? I would love to have you, but if you're too tired, you may prefer trays in your rooms."

After glancing at Robin, Maxie said, "I accept with pleasure, your grace, though I warn you, I have only one dress with me, and it will be considerably the worse for travel."

"My maid can brush and press it for you." The duchess's gaze fell on the fragments of broken china, and her face lit up. "How splendid! You broke that ghastly replica of the Laocoön."

Maxie's face flamed. "I'm sorry. It was entirely my fault. I will replace it as soon as I can."

"Don't you dare!" The duchess smiled impishly. "It was a wedding present from one of the Whitbourne cousins who disapproved of Rafe marrying me. Three people being eaten by snakes is hardly an amiable gift, don't you agree? I've been leaving it on the edge of the table, hoping one of the maids would accidentally knock it off, but with no success."

Maxie chuckled. It took a real lady to make a guilty guest believe she was doing her hostess a favor. "If you have anything else you wish broken, I shall be happy to oblige."

"Done!" The duchess turned. "Shall I take you to your room now? There is time for a bath or a nap if you wish."

Expression set, Maxie followed the duchess upstairs. It had been hard enough to imagine that she and Robin could resolve the personal issues that separated them. Now she had been plunged into an alien world where few would welcome her. The sooner she learned whether she could live in it, the better.

Chapter 27

After Maxie emerged from a luxurious bath, the duchess sent her own French maid to assist. The well-trained maid, Lavalle, did not betray disapproval of such an irregular guest by so much as a single twitch, though there was a pained expression on her face as she handed over the newly pressed gown. However, Maxie's fluent, if Canadian-accented, French soon won Lavalle over.

Maxie donned her plain white muslin gown, then sat patiently while the maid twisted her dark hair into an elegant chignon. The result was presentable. Nonetheless, Maxie took a nervous glance at the mirror when a footman came to summon her. Then, head high, she followed him downstairs to the small salon.

Robin and the duchess were talking casually, their golden heads close together. His clothing had also been refurbished in the last hour, and a fresh shirt and cravat had been conjured up from somewhere, probably the duke's own wardrobe. He looked so perfectly at ease that Maxie's qualms returned. He might belong in a duke's house, but what the devil was she doing here?

Robin glanced up and stared, his azure eyes glowing. As he rose and came forward, he said softly, "You look absolutely delectable."

Maxie colored, but his admiring gaze warmed her right down to her toes. "It's good of you to say so, but this dress would not be fashionable even in Boston, much less London."

"Believe me, men are much less interested in fashion than in the total effect, which in your case is ravishing." He took her arm and guided her to a seat between himself and the duchess. "Mind you, I may be prejudiced because that is the first real dress I've seen you wear."

Robin's appreciation and nonsense relaxed her to the point where she could join the conversation without self-consciousness. The duchess was wearing a dress as simple as Maxie's own, another example of the other woman's exquisite tact. Robin had also given warning of Maxie's drinking habits, because she was offered lemonade, even though her two companions were drinking sherry.

The duchess was frowning at the mantel clock when the door opened. Maxie knew instantly that it was the Duke of Candover who entered. While Robin was a chameleon, capable of playing a thousand roles, the duke was unmistakably an aristocrat, incapable of ever being anything else. He was also quite staggeringly handsome, a fit mate for the glorious Maggie.

"Sorry to be late, my dear," the newcomer said, "but Castlereagh waylaid me just as I was leaving." Seeing the visitors, he paused, a broad smile spreading across his face. "Robin, you rogue. What brings you to London?"

The two men shook hands warmly. Then Robin introduced the duke to Maxie. As Candover bowed over Maxie's hand, she saw that his hair and complexion were as dark as her own, but his eyes were a cool northern gray, with humor and friendly speculation lurking in the depths.

"Collins," the duke said as he straightened. "Are you related to the Collins of Chanleigh?"

"The present Lord Collingwood is my uncle, your grace."

"Then we're some sort of cousins, the second or third degree." Candover gave her a smile that for pure, paralyzing impact almost equaled Robin's. "It's always a pleasure to meet a new cousin, especially an attractive one." Offering his arm, he added, "Since I'm unfashionably famished, perhaps we can go right into dinner. I'm a great deal more amiable when I've been fed."

She smiled and accepted his arm, thinking that on the contrary, the duke could hardly have been more congenial. Perhaps Robin had been right to bring them here.

As the duchess had promised, it was a simple family dinner by British standards, though there was ample food, all of it superbly cooked. Maxie was grateful not to have to deal with the endless courses considered essential at Chanleigh. She had feared there might be some beastly London dining customs that would show her for an ignorant provincial, but her concern was unfounded. She had seen more forks and spoons in Boston.

Conversation was also easy as the three Britons unobtrusively made sure that the American would not feel excluded. Maxie was touched at the consideration, and a bit amused as well. Had she been so obviously overpowered by Candover House when she had first arrived? Apparently so, though not necessarily for the reasons that the duchess thought.

The men passed up the pleasures of port to join the women for coffee in the drawing room. Maxie was glad; even though the duchess had been everything amiable, Maxie was not quite ready for a tête-à-tête with Robin's mistress. *Former* mistress.

When the Candovers became involved in a discussion of an impending trip to the country, the guests drifted over to the French doors with their coffee cups. Behind the house was a garden so lush that it was hard to believe they were in the heart of one of the greatest cities in the world.

Maxie studied their hosts. There was a bond between the duke and duchess so powerful that it was nearly tangible. "Even if she married him for his money," she murmured, "there is a good deal more than that between them now."

Robin gave her a quizzical glance. "Where on earth

did you get the idea that Maggie married Rafe for his
fortune?"

"From you, that morning at the Drover Inn. You said
that your Maggie had gone to a man who could give
her more than you could." She gestured expressively at
their surroundings. "All this, and a ducal title as well.
It is rather a lot. Still, it doesn't ring quite true. The
duchess doesn't seem especially mercenary, and by
your own admission you are also a wealthy man."

"Another case of me accidentally misleading you.
Your instincts are quite correct. Maggie is not a woman
who can be bought, only won." He turned and looked
out the glass doors. "When I said that she went to
someone who could give her more, I meant emotionally, not financially. Money and position were never
the issues."

"Is it still so painful, Robin?" she asked quietly.
"Now that I've met her, I understand why she is so
hard to forget."

"The pain is in the past." He gave Maxie an oblique
glance. "Now I'm thinking about the future."

It was Maxie's turn to stare outside. They seemed to
be moving in a complex emotional minuet. One of
them would find and share an insight, then they would
swing apart and absorb what had been said before
coming together again. Then there would be another
moment of revelation, and another stepping back. But
each time they moved together, they came a little
closer.

Perhaps it was necessary that they learn about themselves and each other in small steps. Certainly she
wasn't ready to comment on Robin's latest remark. Too
much had happened.

She shifted her gaze so that she saw her own reflection in the glass rather than the darkened garden beyond. In her simple dress and restrained coiffure, she
could almost have been an elegant Boston lady. Her
lips quirked upward. "Covered with mud and looking
as if I had been dragged through a bush backward?"

"Not the most poetic compliment, but true. The

first—" Robin chuckled, "or rather, the second, thing I noticed after you jumped on me at Wolverhampton was how beautiful you are."

"I did not jump on you," she said indignantly. "I tripped. If you hadn't been lurking there like the serpent in Eden . . . !"

He grinned, then drained the last of his coffee and set the cup and saucer on a table by the French doors. "For someone who had misgivings about London society, you seem quite at ease."

She arched her brows. "Surely you don't expect me to believe that everyone in the beau monde is like the Candovers."

"They would be exceptional anywhere," he agreed. "But society is merely a collection of individuals, and London has great diversity. One can find a congenial circle and ignore the rest. For that matter, one needn't even spend time in London."

"My experience of society has not always been so fortunate." Maxie heard the brittleness in her tone. She considered stopping there, but on impulse she continued. It was time for another step in the minuet. "Though America is a republic, there are those who are fascinated by the aristocracy. As the son of a lord, with considerable wit and education, my father was welcome in the homes of many of what are called the 'better families.'

"Max was considered eccentric, of course, because of being a book peddler, and he had no money. But even so, during the winters when we lived in Boston, we were invited out to dinner two or three times a week. Clergymen, professors, wealthy merchants— they all welcomed the Honorable Maximus Collins."

She finished her coffee and set it aside, then stared into the garden again. "It was one such evening when I was about twenty that I overheard Mrs. Lodge, my hostess, talking with some crony of hers. That's when I learned that Max wouldn't accept an invitation unless I was invited also. Mrs. Lodge was willing to tolerate that in order to enjoy dear Mr. Collins's charm and

breeding, but if the little half-breed cast any lures out
to the menfolk, Mrs. Lodge was fully prepared to cut
the connection. Standards must be maintained, you
know. Hard to believe that a gentleman like Mr. Collins had married a savage, but men were helpless vic-
tims of their lusts."

She gave Robin a sidelong glance. "And of course,
everyone knew what those sluttish heathen women
were like."

He muttered a blistering oath. "No wonder you think
poorly of society, if that has been your experience." He
laid a light hand on her shoulder. The comforting
warmth of his touch made it easier for Maxie to shrug
dismissively.

"Not everyone was like that. In some houses I was
welcome rather than being an inconvenient necessity. I
never told my father what I had heard. Max enjoyed
those evenings so much. It would have been a pity to
take some of them away from him."

Robin's hand tightened. "Mrs. Lodge was surely a
bigot, but she may also have been speaking from the
cattiness that some aging women feel toward young,
attractive females."

Her mouth twisted. "You really think so?"

"I doubt if Boston beldams are very different from
London ones. Take away the race prejudice and what is
left is exactly what any jealous matron might say about
a lovely young girl."

"Perhaps you're right. Mrs. Lodge had three muffin-
faced daughters with not a waistline among them."
Maxie gave a wicked smile, suddenly amused by an incident that had been a secret pain for years. "Why is it
so much easier for us to be clear-sighted about another
person's problems than about our own?"

"It's a law of nature, like the sun rising in the east,
and apples falling down from a tree rather than up."
Seeing that she had recovered her humor, he dropped
his hand. "I suppose that tomorrow we will go to the
inn where your father died?"

She was going to nod, then stopped as she was

gripped by sudden panic. She had come the length of England to find answers, yet now she was afraid of them.

Did she fear what she would learn, or the fact that when the mystery of her father's death was resolved, she would be faced with a decision about Robin? She loved him, he wanted to marry her. . . . It should be simple, but it wasn't.

"Rather than go there directly, perhaps I should call first on Aunt Desdemona. She saw my father several times before he died. She might be able to tell me about his activities."

Robin nodded. "Shall I accompany you, or would you rather ask Maggie for the company of a maid?"

She made a face. "Respectability is so tedious. Since a frail flower like me can't cross town in a carriage without a companion, I would rather have you. Besides, if Aunt Desdemona proves villainous, you would be far more useful."

"For which vote of confidence I am duly grateful," Robin remarked. "If you don't mind waiting until the end of the morning, I'd like to visit my banker and my tailor first. I was having some new clothing made up. With luck, it won't have been sent to Yorkshire yet." He cast a jaundiced eye on his frayed sleeve. "I shan't miss this coat."

"May I have it? I've some very fond memories of that coat."

"Take it with my blessings." Robin hesitated. "Would you allow me to have another gown or two made up for you? Having only one will prove a nuisance here in London."

"I suppose you're right," she said without enthusiasm. "But I don't want to waste time on fittings."

"No need. Maggie's maid can take the measurements from this dress." His gaze moved appreciatively over her figure. "It looks simple, but the cut and fit are excellent."

"Thank you. I made it myself. Lack of funds makes one wonderfully versatile." She raised a hand to cover her yawn. "I'm ready to retire. It has been a very long day."

Under her breath, Robin said, "I'm going to feel very alone in that bed tonight."

Their gazes caught. Lord, it was only last night that they had become lovers. This very morning, they greeted the dawn like pagan fertility gods, naked and unashamed. At the memory, heat coiled through her, molten and urgent.

Robin felt it, too. A rapid pulse beating in his throat, he murmured, "I'd give you a good-night kiss, except that I'd end by carrying you upstairs and not letting you go until morning."

She tried to smile. "We might not make it that far, which would be a real breach of hospitality."

"No one stands watch in the corridors here." He reached out and touched the center of her palm. "We could spend the night together and no one would be the wiser."

Her heartbeat accelerated as he drew slow, sensual circles in her palm with a fingertip. She looked at their hands. Even the highest stickler would not be shocked to see that light touch, yet she felt . . . wanton. As depraved as if she had publicly stripped off her gown.

His fingers glided to the fragile skin on the inside of her wrist. Back and forth, caressing the pulse point, raising her blood to fever heat. She swallowed, ready to agree to anything.

He said huskily, "Shall I come to you later?"

His heated gaze drifted over her. They were lovers, they knew each other's bodies intimately, and with the deftness of a thief, he was picking the lock of her willpower. . . .

The image made her want to giggle, which broke the spell he had cast. She pulled away. "I'm sorry. It doesn't make much sense, but it doesn't seem right to lie with you in this house."

She meant Maggie's house, of course. Robin closed his eyes and his face changed, the planes seeming to shift and harden. When he looked at her again, reason had returned. "I understand why you feel that way, though I wish it were otherwise."

She paused on the verge of leaving. "You won't have nightmares if you're alone, will you?"

"If I do, they won't be as bad as the ones in the past." He smiled with a warmth as intimate as a kiss. "You were right—burdens are lighter for being shared."

As she went to say good night to her hosts, she realized how easy it would have been for Robin to use her concern to talk his way into her bed. Underneath all his dangerous charm and wicked skills there really was an honest man.

It was a warming thought to take to her solitary rest.

The Duke of Candover was brushing his wife's long wheat-gold hair. Margot leaned back, face contented and eyes half closed. "What do you think of Robin's friend Maxie?"

He smiled. "I like her. Did Robin tell you how they came to turn up on our doorstep?"

"Not in any detail." After a moment she added, "He wants to marry her."

"Really!" Rafe's hand stilled. "He can't have known her long."

"What does that matter? I wanted to marry you the first night I met you."

"You never told me that before." He felt absurdly pleased as he resumed brushing.

"You are quite conceited enough," his wife said, then jumped with a squeak when he tickled her ribs.

"She's not at all in the common style," Rafe observed. "Intelligent unconventional, versatile. Rather like Robin, in fact. And very lovely, in a very individual way."

"I knew you would notice that," the duchess said tartly.

Rafe grinned. "I prefer blondes myself." Setting down the brush, he began to massage her neck and shoulders. "Does it bother you to see him with another woman? I find it a little surprising that he brought her here."

"On the contrary, I would be surprised, and hurt, if Robin didn't feel he could come to me." She gave a self-mocking smile. "I suppose every woman, in some selfish corner of her mind, would like her former lovers to remember her with a heartbroken sigh and the words, 'What a woman she was. If only things had been different . . .' "

"Like I thought about you for a dozen years?"

"*Exactly* like that," she said with a gurgle of laughter. "But I truly want to see Robin happy, not pining for the past or marrying some vapid girl because he is lonely and there is no one better to be found."

"I can't imagine him doing anything so foolish."

"I'm not so sure," Margot said, a line appearing between her eyes. "I've been concerned about Robin ever since we left Paris. Even though his letters were always amusing, they felt brittle, as if he was hiding his real state of mind. But tonight when I saw him, he was like his old self again." After a moment, she added, "No, better than that."

"Do you approve of the inappropriately named Maxima?"

"Very much so." Margot chuckled. "The poor girl was bristling like an angry cat when we were introduced because Robin hadn't bothered to explain where he was taking her, but on the whole, she behaved with great restraint. In a world full of nobodies, she is very much *somebody*."

"I suggest you go slowly with your overtures of friendship," Rafe said dryly. "Miss Collins may not be enthusiastic about Robin's close friendship with another female."

Hearing between the lines, Margot tilted her head back to look up at him. "Surely you know that you needn't be jealous of Robin? I had thought that you and he had become friends."

Rafe ran a caressing hand down her slim arching throat. Though he had learned to accept his wife's relationship with Robin, it had not been easy for a passionate and possessive man. "Not jealous. Envious, perhaps, for all the years he had you and I didn't."

She shook her head, her solemn gray-green eyes fixed on his. "He had Maggie, the spy. But the circumstances that created her are done, and so is she."

"I know that. You are Margot now." Rafe leaned over and gave his wife a slow, possessive kiss. "And Margot is *mine*."

Then he swept her up in his arms and carried her to their bed and proved it, in the most profound and satisfying of ways.

It was very late when Lord Collingwood reached the Clarendon Hotel, but in spite of his fatigue, he had trouble getting to sleep. After a half hour of tossing, he sat up and reached for the flask of spirits he had left on the bedside table.

In the dark, he drank directly from the flask while he contemplated his mission. Maxima might be in London already. Perhaps, God forbid, she had already discovered the truth about her father. The thought made Collingwood queasy.

He took another swig of brandy. As if the situation wasn't sufficiently fraught with potential scandal, there was also the question of the blond mountebank his niece had taken up with. If he was still with her, the fellow would be another source of trouble. He'd have to be removed from the picture.

It was a damned bad business any way one looked at it. What made it worse was that he was rather fond of Maxima, in spite of her irregular upbringing and ancestry. That was why he was going to all this effort. If he failed, Althea would say that it was his fault for not being more ruthless.

Stifling a groan, he buried his head under the pillow again. Family was the very devil.

Chapter 28

Desdemona entered her sunny parlor, reveling in the pleasure of being in her own home again. Everything seemed so normal that she could almost believe the last mad weeks had been imagination, the result of too much lobster or too many political dinners.

At the sound of a carriage stopping outside, she peered out the window, then smiled. There was nothing imaginary about the broad athletic figure of the Marquess of Wolverton, who was now mounting the steps. He had said he would call this morning at the unfashionable hour of eleven, and the clock was chiming as he knocked. Desdemona liked a man who could be relied upon. As she waited for him to be shown in, she rang for coffee.

After greetings had been exchanged and coffee poured, Giles said, "My brother is in London. In fact, I missed him this morning at the bank by only a few minutes."

"Splendid! Did they have any notion where he was staying?"

"Unfortunately not, but at least we know now that he has arrived in London and that he's not trying to avoid detection. I should locate him in the next day or two, and surely he will know where your niece is."

She was about to reply when her parlor maid entered and bobbed a curtsy. "Excuse me, my lady, but Miss Maxima Collins and Lord Robert Andreville are here to see you." She sniffed disapprovingly. "Neither of 'em have proper calling cards."

Desdemona's jaw dropped. Rallying, she said, "Show them in anyhow, Alice."

A minute later, the object of her long pursuit walked calmly into the parlor.

Desdemona had been told that her niece was small, dark, and attractive, but that description did not do justice to the reality. The ebony-haired young lady who entered was petite and self-possessed, with a face as striking as her perfectly proportioned figure. Though her muslin dress was demure, nothing would make Maxima Collins seem like a butter-wouldn't-melt-in-her-mouth miss. She did not look like someone who would be easily victimized by life.

Maxima studied her tall and titian-haired aunt, apparently equally surprised. Desdemona thought with amusement that they must look like two cats touching inquiring noses.

Maxima said, "I hope you'll forgive this unannounced intrusion, Aunt Desdemona." She indicated her companion. "This is my friend Lord Robert Andreville. Robin, Lady Ross."

Desdemona spared a glance for her niece's escort, then another which bordered on a rude stare. The golden Lord Robert looked like a gentleman, not a rogue, and he was handsome enough to turn any female's head. No wonder the girl had run off with him.

He bowed gracefully to his hostess. "Your servant, Lady Ross." Then he straightened with a smile that would have given palpitations to a more susceptible female.

Not being susceptible, at least not at the moment, Desdemona favored him with a darkling look and a brief nod of acknowledgment. To her niece, she said, "My dear girl, I'm so glad to finally meet you. I've been concerned for your safety."

"Whatever for?" Maxima asked, her eyes wide and innocent.

Desdemona heard the marquess chuckling. From the corner of her eye, she saw that he was enjoying the situation hugely.

Lord Robert hadn't noticed his brother's presence, but at the sound of laughter he glanced across the room. "Giles! This is a coincidence. I didn't know you were planning to visit London this spring, or that you knew Lady Ross."

"I didn't know the lady, and I wasn't planning a trip," Wolverton replied. "You're responsible for both conditions."

"Indeed?"

"Lady Ross and I have been haring across England for the last fortnight, separately and together, trying to find you two," the marquess explained. "And now you walk in, bland as butter, as if paying morning calls on an elderly aunt."

"Aunt Desdemona is not elderly," Maxima pointed out.

"Thank you," the unelderly aunt muttered, feeling that the situation was rapidly getting out of control. Though to be fair, it had never been under control in the first place.

"I was speaking metaphorically." Giles glanced at Desdemona with a fond smile. "I have, in fact, noticed that she is not elderly. Miss Collins, since confusion seems the order of the day, let me introduce myself. I'm Wolverton, elder brother of your scapegrace escort."

"Ah, yes," she said thoughtfully, "the one whom, if he died, which God forbid, would cause Robin to be instantly ennobled."

Wolverton blinked as he sorted that out, then nodded. "Exactly so."

"I think we should all sit down and have some coffee," Desdemona said in a voice of heroic restraint, ringing the bell for more cups and another pot.

Maxima sat opposite her aunt. "Why were you worried about me, Aunt Desdemona? Did Uncle Cletus write you?"

"I arrived at Chanleigh shortly after you decamped. Under questioning, Cletus and Althea admitted that you had left unexpectedly and probably had little money. I deduced that if you were coming to London, it must be the hard way."

Another tray arrived, and Desdemona poured coffee for the new arrivals. She continued, "A lone young female, attempting to walk hundreds of miles across a strange country filled with rogues and robbers and Lord knows what—of course I was worried. So I decided to come after you."

"That was very good of you, but you needn't have been concerned." Maxima's wide brown eyes showed mild surprise that anyone could have been anxious. "It was a pleasant, interesting journey, and nothing of note happened."

A choking sound came from Lord Robert. Maxima abandoned mildness to direct a dagger look at him. Her escort assumed a look of unreliable innocence, then glanced at his older brother. "How did you become involved, Giles?"

"Lady Ross was told that her niece had been forceably abducted by my womanizing brother," was the succinct reply.

Lord Robert's brows arched. "Really, Giles, womanizing? What did I do in my blameless months in Yorkshire to deserve that?"

"It's what the villagers told me," Desdemona said stiffly. "So I went to Wolverhampton to make inquiries."

"Lady Ross fails to do the occasion justice," the marquess said cheerfully. "In fact, she swept into my library like an avenging fury, slammed her parasol across my desk, accused and convicted you in absentia of all manner of crimes and moral turpitude, threatened you with the full might and majesty of the law, then swept out again."

Turning a fiery red under the interested gazes of her niece and Lord Robert, Desdemona scowled at the marquess. She had been rather intemperate that day, and it was most ungentlemanly of him to mention it.

"Womanizing *and* moral turpitude?" Lord Robert gave his hostess a sympathetic look. "Having heard that, of course you had no choice but to try to rescue your hapless niece from me."

His statement elicited an eloquent sniff from Maxima. "Your fears were understandable, but quite misplaced, Aunt. In fact, Lord Robert insisted on accompanying me solely out of concern for my safety." A note of exasperation entered her soft, well-bred voice. "Like you, he assumed that I was a helpless incompetent who would never survive the trip."

Lord Robert gave her a smile of obvious affection. "That misapprehension didn't last long, Maxie."

"Maxie?" Desdemona repeated. "What a vulgar nickname."

Her niece bristled. "It is what my father called me, Aunt Desdemona, and it is what I prefer."

"Your father called me Dizzy, and I didn't much like that, either," Desdemona said dryly.

"Dizzy?" Wolverton said with interest.

Ignoring him, Desdemona went on, "But if you prefer to be called Maxie, I shall try to become accustomed." She surveyed her niece's small, composed figure. "Perhaps you should stop calling me aunt. There are only a few years between us, and I don't seem to have done a very good job of aunting. Perhaps it is better if we simply try to become friends."

Maxie gave a shy smile. "I would like that very much."

Desdemona sipped more coffee, then sighed. "This is an awkward topic, and probably an auntly one, but I cannot help but be concerned for your reputation." She glanced at Lord Robert. "Doubtless things are somewhat different in America, but surely you are aware of the English proprieties?" The lift at the end of her sentence was accompanied by a pious hope that she would not have to become more specific.

"If you mean what I think you mean," Maxie said in a tone whose frostiness would have done credit to a patroness of Almack's, "I assure you that Lord Robert has behaved as a perfect gentleman." The effect was spoiled when she added something under her breath that sounded like, "I was the one who didn't."

Desdemona stared at her niece, sure that she had misheard. Giles, who was closer to the girl, suddenly had a fit of coughing that sounded like a doomed attempt to stifle hilarity.

Deciding that abandoning the topic was the better part of wisdom, Desdemona asked, "Where are you staying? I would be delighted to have you here."

"That is very kind of you, but we are staying at Candover House. The duke and duchess have been most hospitable."

The marquess straightened, startled. "You're staying with Candover and his wife?"

"Yes." It was Lord Robert who answered, a hint of challenge in his voice. "And why not?"

"Why not indeed?" Giles murmured.

Desdemona wondered what that was about. She would make Giles explain later when they were private Turning back to her niece, she asked, "Did you leave Chanleigh so suddenly because Althea was plaguing you? She never could abide anyone disagreeing with her."

Her niece hesitated, weighing her answer. "That was part of the reason," she said finally. "I also wanted to meet you before returning to America."

"You're leaving England?" It was a possibility that had never occurred to Desdemona, though it should have.

An opaque look came into the girl's rich brown eyes. "My plans are somewhat uncertain."

In a way, the news that Maxie might go back to America was welcome. Any indiscretions that had occurred would not have scandalous repercussions. Then again, Desdemona thought with a return to gloom, nature being what it was, perhaps there would be other kinds of repercussions.

Maxie set her coffee aside and leaned forward, her hands clasped tensely in her lap. "Please, Desdemona, if you don't mind, could . . . could you tell me about the times you saw Max before he died?"

Looking at her niece's earnest face, Desdemona guessed the true reason the girl had come to London. Max had been devoted to his daughter, and obviously the feeling had been mutual. It must be very hard to know that her father had died alone and far away.

"Of course I don't mind talking about him," she said, settling back in the sofa with a nostalgic smile. "It was so good to see Max again. I was just a child when he left for America, but he wrote the most wonderful letters." She grinned. "Incidentally, I have his gold watch for you. It was taken from the body of a dead highwayman."

Her statement caused a lively set of explanations on both sides. After the incident had been discussed, the marquess got to his feet. "You ladies will have a great deal to say to each other. If you like, Robin, you can leave your carriage for Miss Collins, and I'll give you a ride to wherever you want to go."

Robin exchanged a glance with Maxie, who nodded. After a flurry of farewells, the two men left the house and climbed into the Wolverton town carriage.

Giles asked, "Where do you want to go?"

"Whitehall, please. Since I have the afternoon free, I might as well pay a visit to some of my old colleagues." Robin settled in the backward-facing seat opposite his brother. "It sounds as if Lady Ross led you a merry dance."

"No more so than her niece did you. Since her ladyship was threatening all and sundry Andrevilles, I decided that it behooved me to find you first, in the hopes of heading off scandal or your incarceration." Giles set his hat on the seat beside him. "Did Simmons ever catch up with you?"

Robin's brows rose. "Yes, in Market Harborough. How do you know about him?"

"I gave the fellow a ride near Blyth. He was nursing his injuries and plotting revenge on the 'yaller-headed fancy man' who had jumped him from behind."

"Of course I jumped him from behind. The fellow is twice my size," Robin said with irrefutable logic. "If there is one thing I've learned over the years, it's that 'fighting fairly' is a dangerous luxury."

"I assume he's the fellow Lord Collingwood sent after Miss Collins?"

"Exactly." Robin shrugged. "She didn't want to go."

"Apparently not. Simmons said she held a pistol on him."

"Life in the forests of the New World is rather different from a London drawing room, so she is in the habit of solving problems with a certain directness. In Market Harborough, for example, she had to be restrained from sliding a knife between Simmons's ribs," Robin explained. "When we first met, I had difficulty persuading her to accept my escort because she thought I looked useless."

"She's hardly the first to make that mistake." The marquess smiled reminiscently. "Miss Collins is not at all what I expected. On the overwrought occasion when I met Lady Ross, I countered her charge that you were a vile seducer with the suggestion that she and her niece were deliberately plotting to entrap you."

Robin laughed. "No one who knows Maxie could think such a thing. There isn't a duplicitous bone in her delightful body. Full frontal assault in broad daylight is her style, not sneak attack." He gave his brother a slanting glance. "I've asked Maxie to marry me. Will you have any objections if she agrees?"

Giles raised his brows. "Would it matter if I did? You're both of age."

"If you mean would your disapproval stop me, the answer is no. But I would very much prefer that you welcome her into the family. She has not always been accepted as she deserves." Robin glanced down and made a minute adjustment to his elegantly tailored sleeve. "I thought it was time I settled down."

Giles laughed. "I'm not sure that marriage to a pocket-sized hoyden with the courage to cross England on foot, attack a professional bruiser, and dine with a duchess is what I would call 'settling down,' but for what's it's worth, you have my blessing. The two of you should suit very well. Is the lady reluctant?"

"She has her doubts." Robin chuckled. "But I'm using every bit of my fabled charm to persuade her."

As Giles set Robin down outside Whitehall, he uttered a fervent mental prayer that the girl would accept his brother's proposal. It had been obvious as soon as the pair of them had entered Lady Ross's drawing room that Robin had recovered from the blackness of soul that had afflicted him. If it took a dark-eyed dazzler with a temper to make Robin laugh again, Giles was more than willing to welcome her as a sister-in-law.

Chapter 29

When Maxie returned to Candover House, she was relieved to find that Robin had not yet returned. That meant their visit to the inn where her father died must be postponed until the next day.

More and more she was concerned about what they would find. According to Desdemona, Max had seemed tense during his stay in London. As Maxie had listened, she had felt the hovering shadow of anxiety. It seemed all too probable that he had been involved in some nefarious project that had brought disaster on his head.

But Desdemona had been a delight. Finally Maxie had found an English relation that she actually felt related to. Her father had said several times that his daughter reminded him of his little sister. Now Maxie understood why: Under their superficial differences, the two women were very similar. Her aunt might be a strong-willed eccentric by the narrow standards of English society, but Maxie didn't doubt that Desdemona would manage splendidly in the American backwoods.

Robin's brother had also been a pleasant surprise. Though there was little family resemblance, the marquess had a lurking smile and tolerant attitude much like Robin's. He had also been amiable to her, in spite of her irregular background. Perhaps he might not object to her joining the aristocratic Andrevilles.

When she reached her bedroom, Maxie went to hang up her cloak. She swung open the wardrobe doors, then gasped with surprise. In the brief hours since Robin had suggested augmenting her supply of clothing, four

gowns had appeared, with matching slippers neatly
lined up below. In addition, accessories such as gloves,
stockings, and shawls were folded on the shelves that
ran down one side of the wardrobe.

She hung up the bonnet, then pulled out the most
elaborate garment. It was a lovely silk evening gown in
a shade of crimson that would suit her coloring admi-
rably. She didn't bother trying on any of the dresses.
Given the combined talents of Robin and Maggie, everything was bound to fit perfectly. They must have
been a formidable team in their spying days.

As she closed the doors of the wardrobe, she smiled
wryly. Robin didn't even have to be present to distract
her from brooding about her father. Now she could
brood about *him*.

It was incredibly tempting to grab his offer of marriage with both hands, before he changed his mind. But
she could not escape the belief that her principal virtue
was that she was available while the woman who was
Robin's first choice was not. If Maxie weren't in love
with Robin, they might have been able to make a comfortable marriage, enjoying each other's company and
bodies without major conflicts. Though they might not
reach the highs of a love match, they would also avoid
the lows.

But since she did love him, the imbalance of emotion would be disastrous. It would be slow poison to
live with Robin, always knowing that he had chosen
her largely because she had been there when he had
been having a bad night.

Wearily she rubbed her temples. Unless Robin really
and truly wanted to marry *her,* Maxima Collins, half-
breed American and not at all a lady, she would be a
fool to accept him. Once she went back to America, he
would forget her soon enough.

With a growl, she decided to find a distraction before she started chewing on the furniture. She was willing to be wise and noble about turning Robin down,
but being gracious as well was too blasted much to ask
of herself.

Unclenching her jaw, she went down to the library. When she had seen it the night before, Candover had noticed the naked lust on her face and invited her to browse to her heart's content.

The enormous chamber was unoccupied except for a fuzzy black ball on one chair. Maxie studied it a moment before deciding that it was either a misplaced fur muff or a sleeping cat.

She began to prowl, randomly pulling volumes from the shelves. Candover had books she had always wanted to read but had never been able to obtain. There were volumes of poetry, history, philosophy, art, and everything else that might challenge or delight a mind.

Deciding to be methodical, she pushed the rolling library ladder to the far corner of the long room and climbed to the platform at the top. With a complete disregard for propriety, she hitched up her dress, crossed her legs under her, and pulled a volume from the top shelf. With diligence, she calculated happily, she might finish working her way through the library somewhere about the year 1850.

Lost in an epistolary novel by Montesquieu, she had almost forgotten where she was when the sound of someone entering the room caught her attention. She glanced up from her book to see the duchess enter, then close the door and lean against it.

Since the other woman didn't look above eye level, she must have thought she was alone. Maxie frowned, wondering if she should announce her own presence. Before she could, the duchess swayed, then stumbled over to sit on a long sofa.

Alarmed, Maxie hastily descended the ladder. "Are you unwell, your grace? Shall I call someone?"

The duchess' lovely face was an interesting shade of gray-green that did not complement her eyes. Attempting to smile, she said, "Don't do that. The reason I slipped in here was to avoid alarming anyone. Rafe has every servant in the house hovering over me, and he's the worst of all."

She leaned back and closed her eyes. "There's nothing wrong with me, except that I haven't yet acquired the knack of breeding properly. Most women are ill in the morning, but for me it seems to be the afternoon."

"I see," Maxie said sympathetically. From the slimness of the duchess' waist, it was obviously quite early in her pregnancy. "Lie back and put your feet up on the sofa."

While the other woman meekly obeyed, Maxie found a soft, warm blanket on another sofa and spread it over her. "Perhaps you should have a little something to eat."

The duchess shuddered.

Maxie said soothingly, "Many pregnant women find that it helps to eat several times during the day. Nothing elaborate, perhaps something like tea and biscuits."

The duchess considered. "It's worth a try."

A quarter hour later, after the expectant mother had warily consumed two warm scones and a cup of tea, her normal color returned. Curling up in the corner of the sofa, she said, "Thank you for your advice. I feel amazingly better." She made a face. "At least, until the next time."

"Don't worry, your grace, the nausea disappears magically sometime after the third month."

Unable to keep curiosity from her voice, the duchess said, "You sound like a midwife."

"I'm not that, but I've had a colorful past." Maxie swallowed the last bite of a scone. "Did Robin tell you about my background?"

"Of course not." Her hostess gave her a stern look. "He is the last man on earth to talk about another person's private business. Sometimes it is impossible to get him to say anything useful about *anything*. And I wish you would call me Margot."

"Not Maggie?"

"My real name is Margot and that is what I use now. Maggie is a nickname Robin gave me, and it lasted through my spying days. I'm sure that to him I'll always be Maggie, just as I'll never really think of him as Lord Robert." She tilted her golden head to one side as if weighing whether to say more. Making up her mind, she said, "I know you're uncomfortable with me, but I'm no threat to you. On the contrary, I would like to be friends."

Maxie had to give the duchess full marks for confronting an awkward situation head-on. "I haven't meant to return your hospitality with churlishness. But I must admit that I have trouble understanding the relationship between you and Robin."

"You haven't been churlish. I think you have dealt very well with a situation that would send most women into strong hysterics." Margot sipped reflectively on her tea. "I met Robin when he saved me, at considerable risk to himself, from a French mob that had killed my father. I had a passionate desire to fight Napoleon any way I could, so we decided to work together.

"We were young and had only each other to trust, and there was a great deal of caring between us. It was easy—and very rewarding—to become lovers. Nonetheless, I had been acquainted with Robin for a dozen years before I was really sure of his name, station in life, or nationality."

She set her teacup down and began to turn her wedding ring absently. "It may be hard to understand this outside of the context of war. Robin would go off for months at a time, risking his life in ways I tried not to think about. Then he would show up, blithe and good-natured, as if he had been strolling around the corner. I think there is a great deal that he never told me, to spare me from worrying even more.

"In some ways we were very close. Yet there were other parts of our lives that never touched at all. Eventually, it seemed wrong to be lovers, and that ceased. But the friendship and trust remained, and always will." Her gray-green eyes drifted out of focus. "Perhaps the outcome would have been different if I hadn't been in love with Rafe before I ever met Robin—it's impossible to say. But I suspect that Robin and I are too much alike ever to have made ideal mates."

Her manner changed, becoming brisk. "Perhaps now you can better understand why I genuinely want to see Robin happy."

Maxie's throat tightened. It couldn't be easy for the duchess to bare her soul to another woman who was very nearly a stranger. "I appreciate your openness, Margot."

"It's in my own interest to make peace with you. If you take me in dislike, it would affect my friendship with Robin, and I would hate that." She smiled with a hint of mischief. "Perhaps you could try thinking of Robin and me as brother and sister. Rafe found that helped."

To mask her thoughts, Maxie leaned forward to pour more tea for herself. It couldn't have been easy for Robin and Candover to become friends when they loved the same woman, but they seemed to have done it. She must do her best to match their maturity. Besides, it was very easy to like Margot. Glancing up, she said, "What you are doing is more than generous, to both Robin and me. It's easy to understand why Robin is in love with you."

"Robin was never in love with me. Not then, not now," Margot said firmly. She started to continue, then stopped. "I won't say any more. Perhaps I've already said too much."

Margot had convinced Maxie that she was not in love with Robin, but there was nothing in her words that proved that the opposite was not the case. Still, the duchess was offering a wise and tolerant female ear, and Maxie wanted to take advantage of that. She said hesitantly, "Robin has asked me to marry him, but it's hard to imagine someone with my mongrel past being accepted in his world."

"Nonsense. You have manners, education, and looks. With that and a dash of arrogance, you'll be acceptable at the royal court itself. The trick is never to apologize for what you are."

Maxie smiled. "It sounds like something you learned

the hard way. But surely you had no trouble taking your place in society."

"You'd be surprised," the duchess said darkly. "When I married Rafe, my situation was not unlike yours. You and I are both the daughters of younger sons from noble families—respectable birth, but not absolutely top drawer. You have what you call your mongrel ancestry, while I have a distinctly shady past. There was plenty of fodder for gossips, and I was not at all what the Whitbournes wanted for the head of the family."

Maxie frowned. "Everyone knows about you and Robin?"

"That is one of the bits that few people know, and all of them are discreet. But it was impossible to conceal my spying career—too many people met me when I was playing the role of a scandalous Hungarian countess."

Fascinated, Maxie said, "Yet society accepted you."

The duchess smiled wickedly. "Luckily Rafe numbers Medusa among his ancestors. When someone displeases him, he can turn them to stone with a glance. From the beginning, he made it clear that anyone who was rude to me was doomed."

Maxie laughed. "Did he petrify the Whitbourne relation who gave you the statuette of the Laocoön?"

"Not quite, but their paths crossed at a ball soon after, and the female in question has been amazingly polite ever since."

"You make a life here seem possible," Maxie said soberly.

"If you want it, it is within your grasp." The duchess regarded her shrewdly. "Are you ready to try your social wings? I'm having a small dinner party tonight. It won't be one of Rafe's political entertainments, merely a few couples who are close friends and genuinely nice people. You don't have to attend, but if you're willing to try, I can also invite your aunt and Robin's brother so there will be a few familiar faces."

So soon? Quelling her first reaction of panic, Maxie said, "Tonight is as good a time as any."

"Well done! Truly, I think you'll enjoy yourself."

Perhaps she would, but even that would not be enough to dispel the black fog that still clouded her future. The mere thought was enough to dim Maxie's enjoyment of the afternoon.

Refusing to give in to anxiety, she gestured toward the fur ball on the adjacent chair. "Is that a cat or a muff?"

"A cat, Rex by name."

Maxie scrutinized the featureless black fur. "Is he ill? He hasn't moved since I got here an hour and a half ago."

"Don't worry, he isn't dead, just tired." Margot chuckled. "Very, very tired."

Knowing he was the center of attention, Rex stretched luxuriously, revealing a portly feline body. Then he rolled onto his back, four tufted feet aloft as he returned to his nap.

Any lingering tension in the room dissolved as the two women laughed together. Maxie decided that no matter what the future held, she was very glad to have made Margot's acquaintance.

Maxima's departure left Desdemona in a happy state of mental and verbal satisfaction. It had been duty that originally sent her after an unknown niece. Now it was a pleasure to discover the real Maxie, who was far more interesting than the insipid imaginary maiden whom Desdemona had thought needed rescuing.

As they had talked, Desdemona had come to recognize that her brother had found contentment in the eccentric life he had chosen. The knowledge pleased her. Perhaps it was being in London that had made him seem distracted when he had visited.

Desdemona had also discovered a resemblance, both mental and physical, between Max and his daughter. It was in her niece's face when she laughed, and in her eclectic education and lively mind. There were those who would think that Maximus Collins had wasted his life, but the daughter he had raised was not a bad memorial to his mortal span.

Lord Robert had also been a pleasant surprise. He was obviously more than willing to do the gentlemanly thing by Maxima, and the girl herself was not indifferent to him.

It would be an excellent match. Desdemona lay back on the sofa and beamed at the ceiling, chastising herself for having such an unprogressive thought. She was a modern, independent woman and had been fully prepared to support her niece if the girl didn't want to marry the man who had compromised her.

But obviously such support would be unnecessary, and not only because Maxima was quite capable of managing her own affairs. In the last few day Desdemona had begun to think that marriage was not necessarily a bad thing, at least not when it was founded on mutual respect and affection.

Her smile broadened as she had another unworthy thought. Lord Robert was wealthy, intelligent, handsome, his character was—unconventional but honorable— and he was from the very highest rank of society. Althea would be absolutely *apoplectic* if her despised half-breed niece married such a supremely eligible man. It was a delightful prospect.

Desdemona allowed herself a few more minutes of beatific contemplation before going to her study and applying herself to the correspondence that had accumulated in her absence. As she worked her way through the pile, she noted how much of it was related to her work. When had she stopped having time for her friends? She must enlarge the boundaries of her life.

Toward the end of the afternoon, the parlor maid came with a note. "This has just been delivered, my lady. The footman is waiting. Will you be sending a response?"

Desdemona scanned the note. It was from the Duchess of Candover, inviting her to a small dinner party that evening. Since Miss Collins might feel shy among so many strangers, the duchess hoped that Lady Ross would honor them with her presence. Almost as an afterthought, she mentioned that Lord Wolverton had also been invited.

It was charmingly written. Though Desdemona knew the duke from her political work, she had not yet met his new wife. It was good of the duchess to be so considerate of her houseguest's situation. Desdemona scribbled out an acceptance and handed it to her maid to take to the waiting footman.

Then panic set in. Merciful heaven, what would she wear? She rang for her personal maid.

Recovered from the cold she had contracted in the Midlands, Sally Griffin responded with bright-eyed interest. After bobbing a curtsy, she said, "Is there a problem, my lady?"

"Tonight I will be dining at Candover House, Sally. My niece is staying there, and the duchess was kind enough to invite me, so I could satisfy myself that Miss Collins is in good hands." Desdemona hesitated, then continued self-consciously, "We have only a few hours. Do you think any of my gowns could be altered to be more . . . more . . . fashionable?"

Sally's eyes lit up. "Do you mean you're finally willing to flaunt what the good Lord gave you? I've always said there's not a lady in London with a figure to match yours."

As Desdemona blushed, the abigail continued, "I've always thought that with a bit of altering the Devonshire brown silk would be smashing. But there's no time to waste."

Before her mistress could have second thoughts, the abigail seized her hand and tugged her to the stairs. "When I was turned off without a reference, I would have starved or had to go on the streets if you hadn't been willing to take me on. I've wanted a chance to do something special for you ever since. Tonight you'll be as fine as five pence, or my name isn't Sally Griffin."

Half-protesting, Desdemona let herself be swept along. Giving Sally free rein might prove to be a disaster, but it was a good guess that the result would not be boring.

And the one thing she did not want was for Giles to be bored.

Chapter 30

Lavalle, the French maid, had dressed and coiffed Maxie, then left to see to the duchess' toilette. The unfortunate result of having only one lady's maid for two ladies was that the lady who was done first was left with the time to work up a good set of nerves.

Maxie knew it was foolish to worry so much about a dinner party. Whether or not she got through it without disgracing herself and Robin was a minor issue in the great scheme of things. Her father's death and the unresolved relationship between her and Robin were far more important. Nonetheless, she paced, occasionally muttering to herself the duchess' advice: *Never apologize for what you are.*

It was a relief to hear a knock at the door. Thinking it was Lavalle returning to correct some oversight, she called, "Come in."

In walked Robin, as nonchalant as if they were in a Midlands barn instead of a duke's mansion. Dressed in formal evening wear, he looked good enough to eat.

He raised his brows in mock surprise. "Sorry, miss. I was looking for someone who had been dragged through a bush backward, but I appear to have come to the wrong room."

Laughing, she crossed the room and hugged him. "It feels like days since I've seen you rather than hours."

With true gentlemanly skill, he managed to return her hug without crushing her gown or her hair. "Excellent. My goal is for you to reach the point where you can't bear to let me out of your sight for more than ten minutes."

The devil of it was, she already felt that way, though she didn't want to admit it. She stepped back and pivoted, the crimson silk swirling above her ankles. "I've never worn anything so fashionable in my life. Do I really look all right?"

"You look ravishing." His slow gaze went over her, taking in every detail of her appearance from her upswept ebony hair to the graceful high-waisted gown that showed her figure to perfection. "Exotic. Ripe and lusciously sensual. Dangerously kissable." He took a deep breath. "I'd better stop before I rip that very fetching gown off. But I would be remiss not to mention that you also look intelligent, elegant, and confident."

"That's a wonderful list." She made a face. "But if I seem confident, some of your duplicity must have rubbed off on me."

"It would be my pleasure to rub anything I own on you," he said earnestly.

She had to laugh again. Obviously Robin had come to jolly her out of any nervousness, and he was succeeding beautifully. As she picked up her long gloves, she asked, "Are there any beastly English social rituals I should know because failure would doom me to be an outcast forever?"

He shook his head. "The good manners you learned from your parents and at those Boston dinner parties will be fine."

"Speaking of manners, since I'm nominally an innocent maiden, you really shouldn't be in my bedroom."

"True." He gave her a wickedly intimate smile. "But we both know how nominal the innocent maiden label is."

Trying without success to look severe, she took his arm and guided him toward the door. "Nonetheless, we should await the other guests in some sober place like the library."

"Before we do, I have something for you." With a sleight-of-hand flourish, he produced a slim, velvet-covered jewelry box. "You said that I'm a magpie, and

we're a breed known for collecting glittering objects to
present to the objects of our adoration. Here's the
proof."

Dismayed, she said, "It's quite definite that nominally innocent females do not accept valuable gifts
from gentlemen."

"How fortunate that I am not a gentleman." His expression turned serious. "I don't know what the future
will bring, Kanawiosta. I hope to God that we will find
out together. But even if you choose to take a separate
path, I'd like you to have something that came from
me."

She gave him a level look. "You also want to make
sure that I will have something valuable as insurance
against possible financial problems."

One corner of his mouth turned up wryly. "I could
have used you in my spying days. You have the most
unsettling ability to read minds."

"Not all minds." She opened the box, then caught
her breath. Nestled in the white silk lining were a
necklace and matching earrings. Magnificent rubies
and tiny, starry diamonds were set in delicate gold fil-
igreed medallions. "Oh, Robin, how exquisite. You
don't do things by half, do you?"

"Actually, I did in this case," he replied. "If I'd
thought you would accept them, I would have bought
a whole parure, everything from combs to diadem and
belt."

Her eyes widened. "You're not joking, are you?"

"Not this time."

Her gaze fell away from the intensity in his eyes.
There was no question that he wanted her. She wished
that she could be sure it was for the right reasons.

"These will be perfect with this gown." She stepped
over to the mirror and removed her plain gold studs.
Then she slipped on the dangling ruby earrings.

As she turned her head, light splintered brilliantly
through the swinging gems. Robin fastened the necklace for her, then stood at her back, his magician's
hands gliding over her upper arms before coming to

rest on her waist. She marveled at how easily he could arouse her, with only the lightest of touches.

After taking a slow breath, she studied herself in the mirror. She had never looked better in her life. The rubies were splendid with her dark coloring. She did not look like a hoydenish colonial book peddler; she looked like a lady. And if she felt like a fraud inside, it didn't show in her face.

Her gaze went from her own image to Robin's. He was the quintessential English aristocrat, a creature of refined features, cool detachment, and exquisite tailoring. Yet his hands held her as if she were the most precious being on earth, and there was honesty in his eyes.

Quietly he said, "You've spoken as if you think that the only possible future for us is in England, but that's not true. If you prefer, we could live in America."

She looked up in surprise. "You would do that for me?"

He kissed her below the ear, his lips warm and firm. "In an instant. The one great blessing of wealth is the freedom it brings. Together we can create the life we want. Even if you'd be willing to stay in England, I would want to visit America, meet your mother's people, see the land that shaped you."

When she shivered a little, it was as much because his offer moved her as in reaction to his kiss. "But you would prefer to live here, wouldn't you?"

He hesitated, then nodded. "It's strange. I've spent almost my entire adult life in foreign lands. I can speak a dozen languages with varying degrees of skill, and find a good meal or a cheap bed in any city on the Continent. Yet when I returned to England last winter, I felt more at home than when I actually lived here."

She put a hand over his where it rested on her waist. "You left a boy and returned a man. Surely that made a difference."

"You're right—I no longer have a youthful need to rebel against everything familiar." He kissed her again, this time on the exquisitely sensitive angle between throat and collarbone.

Her breath quickened. She was acutely aware of his nearness and compelling masculinity. The mirror revealed that awareness in the brightness of her eyes and the sultry fullness of her lips.

Robin saw it, too. His hands tightened. "A good thing most of the men coming tonight are happily married, or I'd worry about someone carrying you off. You are irresistible, Kanawiosta."

At that instant, she made a promise to herself: No matter what happened in the future, she must make love with him at least one more time. If she didn't have that to look forward to, she would be unable to leave this room without ravishing him on the spot. Voice uneven, she said, "We'd better go down now."

He exhaled. "Or we won't make it out of this room for the next two hours." He stepped back, then offered his arm formally. "Ready for the den of lions, my lady?"

He might be willing to leave his country for her sake, but he would lose more by going than she would by staying. She must do her best to see if she could find a place for herself among these alarming aristocrats.

Tucking her hand under his arm, she said, "The lions can't have sharper claws than the good ladies of Boston, Lord Robert."

With Robin beside her, she could face anything.

Wolverton had sent a note suggesting that he escort Desdemona to the dinner party. She had agreed with alacrity, but now that it was too late for her to back out, Desdemona was staring at her reflection with blind panic. "Sally, I can't possibly go out looking like this! When you said you would alter the gown, I didn't know you intended to cut it to the navel."

"Now, now, my lady, you're exaggerating," the abigail said soothingly. "The décolletage is stylish and not at all extreme."

"The gown might not be extreme, but my figure certainly is!" She swung an accusing gaze on her maid. "You kept me away from the mirror until it was too late to change either the gown or the hair, didn't you?"

"Yes, ma'am," Sally said, unrepentant. "Please trust me on this—you look fine and fashionable, and that handsome marquess will be groveling at your feet."

Desdemona's face blazed with heat. "Have I no secrets?"

"Of course you do," Sally said, soothing again. "But only a fool wouldn't see what's right in front of her nose."

In other words, she had been gazing at Giles like a mooncalf, Desdemona thought gloomily. She might as well have hung a sign around her neck. Her very, very bare neck.

Obviously reading her mind, Sally said, "You should wear your pearls instead of the cameo. They'll make you feel a mite less exposed."

The triple strand of pearls did fill the vast expanse of bare skin better, though Desdemona still felt as if she were in one of those beastly nightmares where one is caught in public in one's shift. Again she studied herself with horrified fascination. A shift would not have been half so revealing. "I look like a harlot."

"But the very most expensive kind, my lady," Sally said with a naughty smile.

Desdemona began to laugh. "I'm being absurd, aren't I?" She turned to the mirror and tried to see herself objectively. Devonshire brown was a dark shade with reddish tones that did not suit many women, but Desdemona had to admit that it was perfect with her vivid titian hair and fair complexion.

Sally had also scorned her mistress' usual severe hairstyle in favor of a tumble of waves and curls threaded with a thin gold chain. She had even talked her mistress into accepting a subtle application of cosmetics. Desdemona acknowledged to herself that if the image in the mirror belonged to a stranger, she would have thought the woman a dashing and not unattractive female. In an Amazonian sort of way.

The rap of the door knocker sounded through the house; the marquess had arrived, and it was too late to change now. Desdemona put her shoulders back and straightened to her full height. Unfortunately, the action emphasized a portion of her anatomy that was quite prominent enough already, but the only way she could survive the evening was by pretending that she was comfortable with her own appearance.

Giles was waiting at the foot of the steps. As Desdemona descended, he simply stared at her, his expression stunned.

Anxious again, she stopped and clutched the railing. She was a tough old fowl dressed up as a game pullet, and she was making an absolute fool of herself. She raised her shawl around her shoulders and started to draw it close.

The marquess mounted the two last steps and caught one of her hands in his, effectively preventing her from hiding in her shawl. "Forgive my stupefaction, Desdemona. I knew you were lovely, but tonight you positively take my breath away." He lifted her hand to his lips and kissed it.

Her fingers tingling, Desdemona exhaled the breath of air she hadn't known she was holding. There was absolutely no doubt about the sincerity of Giles's admiration. Best of all, the warmth in his eyes didn't make her feel hunted. It made her feel ... quite pleased with herself.

She smiled up at the marquess and took his arm. "Shall we be off?" It was going to be a good evening.

Maxie and Robin had spent so long talking that by the time they went downstairs, guests had begun to arrive. Margot came to greet them at the entrance of the small salon. Inside, six or eight people were talking with the ease of established friends.

After a smile for Robin, the duchess said approvingly, "Maxie, you look marvelous. Thank heaven that

Rafe prefers blondes. Let me introduce you to the other guests." More quietly, she said, "Courage! Most of the people in this room have backgrounds every bit as unusual as yours."

Before they could move forward, a tall blond man and a slim, quietly lovely woman with brown hair came up to them. With a broad smile and an outstretched hand, the man said, "Robin, I'm sorry I missed you at Whitehall this afternoon." As they shook hands, he studied Robin shrewdly. "You're looking much better than when I saw you last in Paris."

"There was considerable room for improvement." Robin drew Maxie forward. "Miss Maxima Collins, meet Lucien Fairchild, the Earl of Strathmore. The lady, I suspect, is his wife, whom I have never met."

The tall young woman smiled. "Correct. I'm Kit Fairchild. It's a pleasure to meet you, Miss Collins."

The name Lucien rang a bell. After responding to the countess' greeting, Maxie said, "You're Robin's semidistant cousin in the Foreign Office?"

Lord Strathmore chuckled. "Second cousin, once removed."

"Luce was always better at details than I," Robin remarked.

So this was the man who had coaxed Robin into a life of espionage. He didn't look dangerous, but then, neither did Robin. Maxie said thoughtfully, "You may be semidistant cousins, but you resemble each other more than Robin and his brother do."

"If they were horses, their traits would be worth breeding for, don't you agree?" Kit said, face straight but eyes dancing.

Maxie decided she was going to like Lucien's wife. They were on a first-name basis within minutes. No longer concerned about her American guest, Margot went off to greet others.

A pair of new arrivals approached their group. Robin broke off what he was saying and stared. Maxie had never seen him so thoroughly startled. Rallying, he extended his hand to the newcomer, a darkly handsome man with an easy smile. "The last time we met, you were calling yourself Nikki and cheating an Austrian lieutenant at a horse fair outside Vienna."

"He deserved to be cheated," the man said as they shook hands. "That piebald you got from me was all right, wasn't it?"

"First class. Excellent stamina, which was useful for a shady character like me." Robin shook his head. "In all the times we passed messages back and forth, it never occurred to me that you weren't a genuine Gypsy horse trader. But since you're here, I assume you're Lord Aberdare, the infamous Gypsy Earl."

Aberdare grinned. "Don't blame yourself for not guessing that I was more than I seemed. Not everyone in Lucien's far-flung network was an old school friend."

"It wasn't for lack of trying," Strathmore said dryly.

Everyone laughed. Then the group split by gender as the men started exchanging news. Taking over the introductions, Kit said, "Maxie, this is Clare Davies, the Countess of Aberdare."

Lady Aberdare was scarcely taller than Maxie, with dark hair and vivid blue eyes. "I'm delighted to meet you." She studied Maxie, then gave a smile of satisfaction. "That gown looks better on you than it ever would have on me."

It took Maxie a moment to understand. Then she exclaimed, "Good heavens, did Robin and Margot plunder your wardrobe on my behalf?"

"Not quite. I was having several gowns made up. Since you and I are about the same size, Margot asked if there were any garments that I was having second thoughts on." Clare smiled. "I was regretting the crimson one. The fabric was lovely, but no Methodist minister's daughter could comfortably wear that color in public. You, however, look quite splendid."

A little helplessly, Maxie said, "I was expecting to be shredded. Instead, everyone is being so *nice*."

The others laughed. "London society has more than its share of cats and worse, but you won't meet any tonight." Kit gestured around the room. "I must say that the men here have turned out rather well for a group of overprivileged Old Etonians."

"Rabble-rouser," Clare said without rancor. "Kit is our residential radical."

The conversation turned to politics, with all of them agreeing that the recent war between Britain and the United States had been a piece of utter nonsense that never would have happened if women ran the government. As they spoke, a footman came around with sherry for the two countesses, and lemonade for Maxie. She felt delightfully pampered, and had never enjoyed a party more in her life.

Desdemona and Giles arrived together, acting as if they belonged that way. Her aunt looked positively spectacular; Giles was having trouble taking his eyes off her.

After greeting her aunt and Giles, Maxie looked around for Robin but didn't see him. Lady Strathmore was nearby and not engaged in conversation, so she asked, "Kit, have you seen . . ."

Then her voice trailed off as the woman turned toward her. Eerily, she was Kit, yet at the same time not Kit. Marie blurted, "You're not Lady Strathmore, are you?"

The other woman chuckled. "You're correct, I'm not Kit, I'm here sister, Kira Travers. You're very observant to deduce that so quickly. Some people never do grasp that there are two of us. And no, my sister and I did not plan to wear gowns the same shade of blue—we simply do things like that. Last year our darling daughters were even born within twenty-four hours of each other."

Maxie grinned. "I'm glad to know I wasn't imagining things."

"You're Miss Collins, the American, aren't you? My husband is also from your side of the Atlantic." Kira scanned the room, then gestured him over.

Maxie stiffened as a rangy, brown-haired man approached. He would surely recognize her as a half-breed, and he would be more likely to have prejudices on the subject than a Briton would.

Kira said, "Miss Collins, my husband Jason Travers, the Earl of Markland."

He bowed politely. For a moment Maxie thought that his pained expression was for her. He quickly dispelled that by saying, "My wife loves using my title, knowing that it hurts my Yankee heart to hear it." He gave Kira a deeply affectionate smile. Looking back to Maxie, he said, "You have Indian blood?"

She straightened to her full height. "My mother was a Mohawk," she said warily. He could insult her if he liked, but if he said a word, one single word to disparage her mother, she would go upstairs for her knife.

He must have guessed what was in her mind, because there was a distinct twinkle in his eye when he said, "I hope you don't hold to the old feuds. Since my great-grandfather was a Huron, that would make us blood enemies."

She had to laugh. So much for anti-Indian bigotry. Making a connection on the name, she said, "Are you the Jason Travers who owns the Travers Shipping Company in Boston?"

His face lit up. "You're from Boston?"

It took them only a few minutes to establish that they had several mutual acquaintances. The two of them could have spent the rest of the night talking.

When the dinner gong sounded, Robin appeared at her elbow. Amused, she asked, "How do you do that? You're like a cat, with the ability to materialize in a spot that was empty two seconds earlier."

"Some of my best spying lessons came from cats. Move quietly, sleep with one eye open, and always be prepared to bolt if the situation takes a turn for the worse." Robin gave her a smile of warm approval. "You're taking to the murky and shark-infested waters of London society like a racing swan."

"I'm having a wonderful time. Margot was right about these being genuinely nice people."

It increased her own enjoyment to see how pleased Robin was. London might have its share of sharks, but if she had a handful of friends like the people she had met tonight, the sharks wouldn't matter.

Chapter 31

Before the evening was half over, Giles had decided that he should spend more time in London. Much as he liked his Yorkshire neighbors, the dinner conversation there was never this good.

After a short spell over the port, the gentlemen went to find their ladies. Giles's gaze immediately went to Desdemona. His stern, worldly reformer was glowing like a schoolgirl. There was nothing girlish about her appearance, though; sitting next to her at dinner had made him feel like a lust-crazed youth. It had been all he could do to keep himself from staring at her lovely ... neck. Every time she laughed, or lifted her wineglass, he had wanted to drag her from the room to a place of greater privacy. And she knew it, too, the red-headed vixen.

It would have been amusing, except that he found himself feeling twinges of uncharacteristic jealousy every time one of the other men looked at her. Candover and Desdemona had been political acquaintances for years, but Giles was willing to wager that the duke had never looked at her as admiringly as he did this evening. If Candover hadn't been a friend for several decades and famously besotted with his wife, Giles would have been tempted to suggest pistols at dawn.

He smiled at the absurd thought and deliberately turned to other guests. It was an easy, unstructured gathering, with people drifting from one conversation to another. Maxima Collins was fitting in effortlessly, with the wit and presence to equal any other woman in the room. She'd make Robin an admirable wife.

After a lively discussion of free schools with Lady Aberdare, he decided it was time to find Desdemona again. He looked around, and saw her talking with Robin in front of the French doors. This time, it was harder to laugh off his stab of jealousy. Why did she have to look so captivated? A stupid question; Robin had that effect on everyone.

Hating himself for resenting his own brother, he started toward the pair. As he did, Robin snapped his fingers and conjured up a lily of the valley that he must have stolen from one of the flower arrangements. Desdemona accepted the blossom with delighted laughter.

Giles's irritation soared to dangerous heights and his pleasure in the evening vanished. Damn Robin's effortless charm, his gilded tongue, and the impervious marble heart that enabled him to use his gifts so ruthlessly.

Not seeing Giles approach, Desdemona moved away to speak with her niece. Instead of following her, Giles said brusquely to his brother, "Join me for some fresh air."

Robin looked puzzled, but said amiably, "If you wish."

Robin was always amiable; it was another irritating trait. Fighting a losing battle with his temper, Giles stalked out to the spacious stone patio. He had no idea what he wanted to say to his brother, but he was damned well going to say something.

The two men walked to the wall that edged the patio. The famous Candover House gardens were lovely, but Giles showed no interest in the moonlit greenery. Robin studied his brother's grim expression uneasily, wondering what had happened. It was fortunate that Giles's bad moods were very rare, because Robin had always found them deeply disquieting.

Wanting to lighten the atmosphere, Robin remarked, "Lady Ross is splendidly formidable. I wish I'd been there when she swooped into your study with her parasol."

Giles braced his hands on the wall and stared into the night. "If you had been there, a great deal of trouble would have been avoided. I wondered what had become of you."

"Surely you weren't worried?" Robin replied. "Only that morning I'd said I might wander off if something—or someone—interesting came along. Perhaps it was a premonition."

"I reminded myself of that," Giles said with unmistakable dryness. "But I would have felt better if you had sent a note or left a message in the village."

"Sorry. I honestly didn't think of it."

"I'm sure you didn't." Giles's hands tightened on the wall, the knuckles going white. "You never did think of anyone but yourself."

Robin stiffened. "What is that supposed to mean?"

Giles glanced over, every trace of blue leached from his eyes, leaving them as flat as slate. "In all of those years of being a hero, did you ever spare a single damned thought for the people who cared about you? Did you ever wonder what it was like to wait for months on end, wondering if your only brother was dead, and if so, how he had died?" Hard lines appeared around his eyes. "I'm sure you didn't. After all, you had so much more interesting, important things to occupy your mind."

Robin stared at his brother, feeling as if a vast crevasse were opening under them. The crack had always been there, a fatal weakness in the foundation of their relationship, but both of them had preferred to ignore it. They had managed to be friends by never discussing what lay beneath the surface.

Now, for whatever reason, Giles wanted to break the silence and drag them both into the abyss. And if that happened, the bonds between them might fracture beyond any hope of repair.

Praying that Giles would be willing to return to safe ground, Robin said mildly, "Much of what I did was tedious beyond belief, with not a trace of heroism in sight. Of course there was always the risk that I would run out of luck, but I did my best to ensure that if anything happened to me, word would be sent to Wolverhampton as soon as possible."

"How thoughtful," Giles said with heavy sarcasm. "I'm sure that if I'd known that, it would have made a great difference."

Robin felt a familiar prickle of rebellion. "Is this about the fact that I was insufficiently deferential to the head of the family? I barely tolerated that from Father, and I will certainly not tolerate it from you."

"I'm talking about simple courtesy," Giles retorted. "You were constantly sending information to England, yet a letter a year seemed to be the best you could manage for your family."

Robin's eyes narrowed. "What was there to say? 'I've been lying, stealing, and occasionally killing. When I'm not busy with villainy, I live with a woman who has too much sense to marry me. I'm not dead yet. I hope you are well and the crops are prospering this year. Respectfully yours, Robert.' "

The effect of his words was explosive. Giles swung around, his rage showing in every line of his body. "Are you implying that I'm a coward? God knows that it wasn't my choice to stay safely at Wolverhampton. I would have given everything I owned to go into the army after I left Oxford."

The irrational intensity of his reaction was shocking. Realizing that he had inadvertently triggered a profound and painful regret in his brother, Robin replied, "I know perfectly well you're no coward. Frankly, staying under the same roof with Father took more courage than I've ever had."

Unmollified, Giles growled, "Someone had to take the family responsibilities seriously, and it certainly wasn't going to be you. You were too busy seeing the world and risking your life."

Beginning to feel anger of his own, Robin said sharply, "I *had* no family responsibilities—I barely had a place at the table. I wasn't the favored son, and my existence or lack of it never made a damned bit of difference at Wolverhampton. I always assumed that staying the hell out of England was the best thing I could do for the noble name of Andreville."

"Don't be childish," Giles snapped. "I was the heir, so of course Father spent more time with me, but he treated you fairly. He was downright generous, considering that your behavior was enough to try the patience of a saint."

"Ah, yes, our generous, fair-minded father," Robin said bitterly. "You were never around when he grabbed me and stared at my face as if he couldn't believe he had been so unlucky as to have me for a son. Only once did he actually say it was my fault she died—that he wished to God it had been her who survived, not me—but the thought was always in his eyes. Always."

There it finally was, almost palpable with pain: the memory of the woman whose death had ripped the heart out of a family.

Incredulous, Giles said, "Father actually said that to you?"

"Yes." Robin glared at his brother, so angry that he spat out what he had tried never to think. "You never said it aloud, but I always knew you felt the same way."

For the space of three heartbeats, there was silence. Then Giles asked, "Whatever gave you that idea?"

"Do I have to spell it out?" Robin said tightly. "She was your mother, his wife. You were five years old and adored her, a feeling that was entirely mutual. Every day she came to the nursery to read stories and sing songs to you. I understand that she even taught you to read."

Face ashen, Giles whispered, "How could you know that?"

"I learned it from the servants. Never having had a mother, naturally I was curious about what I was missing. It was my first exercise in information gathering. She was a legend in the servants' hall, you know, because her behavior was so unlike what they expected of a marchioness." Robin closed his eyes, fighting back a fresh wave of the desolation that had permeated his childhood. "God, how I envied you for having her, even if it was only for five years. In your place, I would have arranged a lethal accident for the brat who had killed my mother."

"Bloody hell, Robin, I never felt like that," Giles exclaimed. "Of course I mourned—losing her was the single worst event of my life. But I never blamed you for the fact that she died and you didn't."

"Father did. And he never let me forget it."

Giles turned back to the garden, his broad shoulders rigid. "When a woman dies in childbirth, most surviving family members accept it as the will of God. A few, like Father, blame the child. Others are like me. They ... they cherish the baby who survived because it is all they have left of the woman who died."

Robin's voice softened. "You did that well. It made the guilt worse. I was responsible for your mother's death, yet you were always so patient with me."

Giles made an impatient gesture. "Stop talking as if you committed murder. Mama loved babies—I know that she miscarried at least twice between my birth and yours, possibly more than that. She was delighted when her pregnancy was advanced enough to make it likely to be successful. She used to tell me about the new brother or sister I would have, and how I must watch out for you." His voice caught. "I've wondered if she suspected that she would not survive. Her health had always been delicate, and she had to have known that continued pregnancies were dangerous. Yet I'm willing to swear that she was facing the risk willingly. Did your informants tell you that?"

"I never asked about the events surrounding her death. I ... I didn't want to know more."

Giles sighed and ran a hand through his hair. "You were several weeks early and not expected to live. After she died, Father locked himself away and wouldn't speak to anyone. The household was in chaos. I heard one of the maids say that you would die without a wet nurse, so I rode my pony into the village. The miller's wife had just lost a baby a few days after birth, so I went to her house and practically dragged her back to Wolverhampton. I insisted that your crib be put in my room, so I could listen during the night and be sure you were still breathing."

Robin stared at him, his chest constricted. "I never knew that."

"It's hardly to be expected that you would—you weren't much bigger than a loaf of bread at the time." Giles made an obvious effort to master his emotions. "You were so like Mama—not just your appearance, but your quick tongue and your charm. Your precocity delighted everyone who met you even when you were behaving like a limb of Satan. I resented the way you got away with tricks that I would have been whipped for."

"Since Father despised me whatever I did, I decided to give him good cause," Robin said dryly. "I was a damned sight better at being outrageous than I ever was at obedience."

Giles shrugged. "Obedience is overrated. Father found my abilities useful, but no matter how hard I tried, I never seemed to be quite good enough."

Beginning to understand what this conversation was really about, Robin asked quietly, "Why are we talking about this after so many years? What do you want of me?"

Giles stared at his large capable hands, looking oddly vulnerable. Beyond the garden walls, a carriage rumbled along the Mayfair cobblestones.

After a very long silence, he said in a voice that was almost inaudible, "It sounds so childish. I suppose what I really want to know is that . . . that I matter to you. You're the only close family I have. I tried to be a good brother, but because you always went your own way, no matter what the cost, I wasn't usually in a position to help you. Not with Father, not at school, and certainly not when you decided at a ridiculously young age to enter one of the most dangerous trades on earth."

Robin frowned. "Of course you matter to me. How could you not know that? Surely you remember how I followed you constantly whenever you came home from school. You were incredibly patient. I wanted desperately to be like you. It was frustrating when I realized that was impossible. We were simply too different."

"Were and are," Giles said, still looking at his hands.

"Being unlike doesn't mean that caring is impossible," Robin said haltingly. "You were far more my father than our esteemed parent. Whatever I know of honor, discipline, and loyalty I learned from you." He sighed. "I suppose that one reason I became a spy was because I wanted you to be proud of me, and espionage was something I knew I could do well. Granted, it's a low, dishonorable pursuit, but against a monster like Bonaparte, the work was important. It hurt that you disapproved of what I was doing, but once I began, I couldn't draw back."

Giles glanced up, his gaze intent. "I never condemned your activities. Actually, I was enormously proud of your courage and cleverness."

Robin raised his brows. "You were? Every argument we ever had was over my work. It simmered between the lines of your exceedingly rare letters, and came to a boil that last time we met in London, four years ago."

His brother looked away. "I'm sorry I lost my temper that night, but I was concerned. You looked ready to break. I thought it was time to let Britain struggle on without you."

"I was not at my best then," Robin admitted. "But retiring to a quiet life in Yorkshire would have driven me mad. For me, it was better to keep working and take my chances."

"As you said, we're very unlike. For me, Wolverhampton has always been my retreat and my redemption."

There was another long silence before Robin said

wearily, "After our mother died, there was never enough love at Wolverhampton, not with Father's grief and anger poisoning us all. I didn't dare ask you for too much, for fear that your patience would run out. I couldn't bear the thought of that."

Giles smiled humorlessly. "I felt much the same way—that if I did anything that might strain our relationship, you would flit off like a dragonfly and never return."

Robin swallowed against the dryness in his throat, feeling more vulnerable than when he had searched Napoleon's library. "You were the salvation of my childhood, Giles. Now, you're one of two—no, three— people I would give my life for. I wish I had known how to say that sooner. I'm sorry you ever spent a single moment thinking that I didn't care."

Giles rubbed his forehead, his broad hand obscuring his face. When he lowered his arm, there was a gleam of moisture in his eyes. "Brothers are supposed to love each other, but I thought that with us, most of the feelings were on my side."

One of the knots tied around Robin's heart dissolved. Giles was right; brothers were supposed to love each other, and the two of them did. After almost thirty-three years of complicated living, he had discovered a bedrock simplicity that had always been there. Without speaking, he reached out a hand to his brother. Giles gripped it hard.

More than when he had returned to Wolverhampton, Robin felt that he had come home.

As he released his brother's hand, Robin said, "We should have talked like this years ago. Still, why tonight, in the middle of a first-rate dinner party?"

Giles gave an embarrassed laugh. "When I saw Desdemona being charmed by you, every brotherly resentment I ever felt came boiling to the surface. I don't mind you fascinating all the other females, but I very much minded about her."

"Believe me, you have nothing to fear. Our whole conversation was about you—the woman thinks you walk on water. I did not disabuse her of the notion. I gather that you have hopes in that direction?"

"I do." Giles smiled. "I think I'll go find her. I'm happier when she's nearby."

Robin understood perfectly. The discussion with his brother had been valuable and long overdue, but he felt as if he had been through an emotional threshing machine. Which meant that more than anything on earth, he wanted Maxie.

Chapter 32

Robin found Maxie talking to Lord Michael Kenyon, a tall man with chestnut hair and the whipcord toughness of a trained warrior. She glanced up mischievously. "Lord Michael tells me that he met you in Spain. When coaxed, he said something about you being disguised as an Irish priest at the time?"

Robin rolled his eyes. "I'm afraid so. During the Peninsular war, a whole network of priest-spies operated from the Irish College of Salamanca University. I occasionally masqueraded as one when I was on the Peninsula." He made a face. "I also managed to get shot. I'm sure that Lord Michael didn't mention that he found me bleeding all over my stolen dispatches, and had the sense to haul me into Wellington's headquarters."

So that was how Robin had acquired that dreadful bullet scar. Not caring whether she shocked the other guests, Maxie rose onto her toes and pressed a light, swift kiss on Lord Michael's cheek. "Thank you. It must have taken a whole regiment of guardian angels to keep Robin intact."

Lord Michael gazed down at her, startled but not at all displeased. He had remarkable green eyes. "I'd heard that American women were enchantingly direct, but never been so lucky as to see a demonstration. Are there more like you in Boston?"

Robin said fondly, "Maxima is unique anywhere."

"I was afraid of that." After exchanging a few more words, Lord Michael moved away.

Maxie gazed after him. "Is there a Lady Michael that didn't come tonight?"

"He's unmarried. Are you interested in applying for the position of wife?" Robin said dryly.

She gave him a look. "That's an absurd comment even for you. I was merely curious—even though he flirts very nicely, his heart is not the least bit available."

"Interesting. According to Margot, he's spending the Season with Lucien and Kit with the idea of taking a wife if he finds a lady to his taste. Perhaps he's found one." Losing interest in the subject, Robin continued, "I came to see if you were interested in some fresh air. The Candover gardens by moonlight are quite a sight."

As much as Maxie was enjoying the other guests, she was ready for some time alone with Robin. They walked together to the French doors.

Before going out, he glanced around. "It's a bit cool this evening. If I know Maggie, she will have put some shawls here for female guests who might want to go outside."

Sure enough, a pile of softly folded fabric waited on a small table to the left. As Robin took the top shawl, Maxie said admiringly, "Margot thinks of everything."

He shook out the dark paisley shawl, then draped it around her shoulders, his hands caressing. They stepped out into the flagstone patio. After Robin closed the door, they strolled across the stones and down the steps into the garden itself. A scattering of low lanterns marked the paths for guests, but weren't so bright as to interfere with the magic of the night. The voluminous shawl hung all the way to Maxie's knees, protecting her from the cool evening air.

Even warmer was the arm that Robin laid over her shoulders when they were out of sight of the house. They were walking much closer than was proper. Not that she minded; quite the contrary. They had already been so close that it was an effort to remember society's strictures.

She looked up to make a comment, then frowned. Robin's light expression was gone, and in the moonlight he looked deeply weary. "Is something wrong?"

He gave her a slanting glance. "I should have known you'd notice. Giles and I just had the worst argument of our lives. Very fatiguing."

She stopped and stared at him. "That's dreadful. No wonder you're looking a bit gray. I thought you two got on very well."

"We always did, to a point, but there's a lot that never got said." Robin sighed. "Tonight we both aired a lifetime of resentments."

"From what I've seen, it's easier for sisters to be friends than brothers," she said gravely. "Brothers often compete with each other, which can interfere with warmer feelings. It must be even harder when the elder is heir to a great title and fortune."

"You're right—I've seen that with other brothers. It's probably a blessing that Giles and I are so different." Robin hugged her shoulders and started them walking again. "We decided that the underlying cause of tonight's argument goes all the way back to my mother's death. My father blamed me for it, which warped the whole family. Giles became serious and responsible and tried to take care of everyone, which no child should have to do, and I grew up rebellious. As a result, Giles and I were incapable of showing how much we meant to each other. When I returned from France last fall, I wasn't sure if Giles would want me at Wolverhampton. I didn't realize that he was hurt by the fact that I had gone so far and stayed away so long."

"Did you and he manage to resolve your differences?"

Robin smiled. "Yes, thank God. We're closer now than we ever have been in the past."

"I'm so glad." Unable to keep the vehemence from her voice, she added, "But your father deserved to be whipped. Taking all of his guilt about his wife's death and piling it onto a defenseless infant was despicable."

"Guilt—my father? What for?"

"Your mother didn't get pregnant without help," Maxie pointed out tartly. "Do you know if she had a history of problems with childbearing?"

"As a matter of fact, Giles said that she was never strong, and she'd had several miscarriages."

Maxie nodded, unsurprised. "If your father had shown more restraint, her health might not have broken down."

After a long silence, Robin said in a wondering voice, "I never thought of that."

"Any woman would."

He smiled ruefully. "A pity we didn't have a sensible female like you at Wolverhampton to sort us all out."

Their wanderings had brought them to the folly, a tiny, circular Greek temple. The columns and proportions were so perfect that Maxie suspected that some earlier duke had bought the temple in Greece and had it shipped home in pieces.

Side by side, they climbed the steps. The folly was a pleasant, airy place, with curved benches built against the half-walls. A rectangular stone altar stood toward the rear, waiting for picnics rather than sacrificial goats. In the moonlight, the effect was quite enchanting.

Robin looked down at his companion. The moonlight made her features a symphony of elegant planes and shadowed contours. No longer able to wait, he raised her chin and kissed her.

He had meant it to be light and affectionate, but as soon as their lips touched, his emotional control disintegrated. In the last few days, he had been battered by the memories of every bad experience of his life. He would not have survived if not for the woman in his arms, and he yearned for her as a man dying in the desert thirsts for water.

They had been doing a slow dance of desire, begin-

ning when he had gone to her room and building
through the evening with lingering glances and private
smiles. But what he felt now went beyond passion to a
raw need for her blessed warmth and the bewitching
mysteries of her body.

He slid his hands under the wool shawl so he could
knead her soft curves. When she made a little purring
sound of response, he teased her nipple between his
thumb and forefinger. It hardened immediately under
the layered silk.

He wanted more, much more. Catching her by the
waist, he perched her on the stone altar. She inhaled
with surprise, then relaxed, her hands curling over the
edge of the altar.

Raising her made it easier to reach various delicious
bits of her anatomy. He put his hands over hers, trapping them against the stone. Her fingers fluttered for
an instant under his, then became still.

He leaned forward and rubbed his cheek against
hers. Her skin was petal smooth, cool on the surface
with radiant life pulsing below. He blew lightly in her
ear, then traced the delicate whorls with his tongue.
She hummed with pleasure, stretching her neck like a
cat.

The shawl was so large that she was sitting on it, yet
still had enough fabric to cover her shoulders and
chest. He nudged the shawl aside with his chin. The
dark wool slithered down and pooled on the back of
his hands where they held hers to the stone. Her position thrust her breasts forward alluringly.

He tasted the sensual arc of her throat. She was sane
and whole and he wanted to devour her, to make that
sanity and wholeness part of himself.

When his trailing lips reached her necklace, he
quickly skipped lower. He'd paid a small fortune for
the thing, but rubies and diamonds were cold and life-
less compared to the satiny swells above her
décolletage. He kissed them with ardent tenderness, in-
haling the haunting womanly scent from the cleft between her breasts.

Trying to mask his urgency, he released her hands so he could shape the ripe curves of her buttocks with his open palms. Then his hands slid forward, gliding over the gentle curve of her abdomen toward the sensitive mound between her thighs.

She said breathlessly, "Time to stop, I think."

"Not yet." Under the shimmering skirt, her knees were several inches apart. He spread them farther and stepped between so that she could not close them again. He was so close he could feel her sultry female heat.

He sought and found her mouth, wanting her to be so beguiled that she would not question what he was doing. He lifted her skirt and petticoat with both hands and rested his palms on her stocking-clad knees while he deepened the kiss. Then he massaged upward, over her garters, seeking her hidden female essence.

She responded with openmouthed generosity, but she was too clever to be distracted. When he caressed her inner thighs, she turned her head away and instinctively tried to close her legs. She couldn't, and the pressure of her knees against his hips inflamed him still further.

Trapped by his body, she became still. "Robin," she said unevenly. "Robin, we should go back inside now. This is not the right time or place."

She was not afraid—not yet. To frighten her would be unforgivable, but he was incapable of moving away.

His breath ragged with effort, he straightened and wrapped his arms around her. A hard pulse beat in his temples, a harder one in his loins, where his straining sex was pressed against her intimate heat, trying to tear through his tight garments to meld with her. She was so small, so easily enfolded, yet supple with female strength. "I'm sorry," he whispered. "You're right, but—Christ, I have the most absurd feeling that if I don't have you, I will die."

He tried to sound amusing, to make a joke that

would obliterate the foolish melodrama of his words, but for once frivolity failed him. The hammering of his blood repeated, *If I don't have you, I will die. If I don't have you, I will die.*

That stark need was not only for tonight, or for the physical act of union that his body demanded. He wanted her for always, his mistress, his match, his mate. But he also, rather frantically, wanted to make love to her right now.

Unable to repress a forlorn hope, he said, "You didn't want to lie with me in Maggie's house . . . but we're not in the house now."

"Oh, Robin, Robin, you're a wicked, silver-tongued devil, half angel and half rogue." She gave a soft sigh that held both gentle reproach and laughter. "What am I to do with you?"

He shut his eyes, embarrassed that she knew him so well, yet grateful that she could still speak with affection.

Her hand brushed his hair, then fell away to skim his face. Her fingers were cool against his heated forehead and cheek.

She stroked her thumb across his parted lips, then put her hands on both sides of his head and pulled him down for a kiss. As their mouths joined, her hand slid downward, gliding over his chest and hips. When it reached the fall of his breeches, her palm curved, clasping the hard ridge beneath the taut fabric.

He went rigid as fire coursed through his veins.

She murmured, "I hope no one else decides to come outside for a walk." Her fingers went to the top button of his breeches.

After a stunned moment, he unfastened the buttons himself, his fingers tangling clumsily with hers. When he had freed himself, he touched her, trailing his fingers through the soft curls to the sweet female secrets below. The silky, pliant folds were fever-warm and swollen with moisture.

She gave a longing sigh that maddened him. He raised her right leg and wrapped it around his hips, then did the same with her left. She was so open, so yielding.

As he prepared her for his entry, she whimpered and her calves locked around him. Further restraint was impossible. He buried himself inside her with one fierce thrust.

She gasped, on the edge between pleasure and pain. Panting, he forced himself to hold still so she could adjust. Just being within her was almost enough to bring him to culmination. Every part of his body was throbbing. He felt as if he had entered a safe harbor, yet at the same time a tempest raged in his blood.

The musky scent of sex surrounded them, as intimate as their bodies. Using his right arm to support her back, he slid his left hand between them until he was touching her just above where they were joined. He found the sensitive, hidden nub, then gently rubbed with his knuckle.

She moaned. As her hips began grinding against him, a long, slow shudder convulsed her and she buried her face against his shoulder. A series of swifter contractions triggered his own release without his moving. Violent pleasure suffused him, yet in the center of his scouring, chaotic climax was peace.

Gasping, he pressed his forehead against hers. "Oh, Lord. Maxie. I wish . . . I wish there was something I could do to give you the kind of comfort you give me."

Comfort. She sighed, glad he couldn't see her expression in the dark. When she had recognized the depth of his despairing need, she had given solace freely. In return, she had received mind-drugging rapture. It was not a bad exchange. Yet she could not help wanting to be a something more than a source of emotional comfort and sexual release.

That wasn't fair; Robin was giving everything he could. It was not his fault that he did not love her.

Hoping that her muscles were working and she wouldn't collapse back onto the stone altar, she eased away from him. "I think I've ruined your cravat."

"If so, I'll keep the remnants pressed in a book of poetry for the rest of my life." He followed the gallantry with a kiss.

A his lips caressed hers with gentle affection, she gave a superstitious shiver. She had promised herself that they would make love at least once more. Had that swift, heedless encounter been it? She tried to look forward, to believe that there was a lifetime of lovemaking ahead of them, but she could sense nothing except the black fog of despair.

When she shivered again, Robin said with concern, "You're cold. Time to render ourselves respectable enough to walk back into house" He disengaged their bodies, caught her around the waist again, and gently set her on the marble floor. As he produced a handkerchief for her to dry herself, he added, "Semirespectable will do. If we looked immaculate, no one would believe it."

"Immaculate is not a possibility." She smoothed down her crimson skirt. Luckily the shawl had protected her gown from the coarse stone. "I hope everyone will give us the benefit of the doubt and assume that all we've done is steal a few kisses."

"Naturally that's all that happened," he said in his best peddler's voice, saturated with unreliable sincerity. "After all, you're an innocent maiden and I'm a gentleman."

"Strictly nominal in both cases." Her hair was falling down. She located the hairpins and secured it again, hoping the result wasn't too wild, then draped the shawl over her shoulders.

Robin put his arm around her and they began strolling back toward the house. "One reason I took you to Ruxton was to see if you liked it," he said hesitantly. "I've always been fond of the place, even though I've only stayed there half a dozen times in my life. Do you think you could be happy living at Ruxton?"

She thought of the warm stone, the rolling green hills, and the house's gracious, welcoming air. Ruxton wanted to be a home, and she was a woman who had wanted a stable home all her life.

Her voice almost inaudible, she said, "Yes. If ... if things work out between us, I could be happy there."

Such a very big if.

Chapter 33

On the carriage ride home, Desdemona and Giles had talked casually, in words anyone could have overheard, but his large strong hand enfolded hers and she felt quite absurdly happy. She had not felt such a sense of bubbling anticipation since she was a child.

When they reached her home, Giles escorted her up the steps, then rested his hands briefly on her upper arms, his expression intent. His grasp tightened for a moment. She wondered if he was going to kiss her, right there in Mount Street.

Then her parlor maid opened the door. He dropped his hands, saying simply, "Good night, Desdemona. It was a lovely evening."

Yes, and it was too early for it to end. She said, "It isn't really late. Would you like to come in for a few minutes? Perhaps have some brandy?"

The marquess hesitated, clearly on the brink of refusing.

Amazed at her own temerity, she smiled up at him. "Please?"

"For a few minutes, then," he said after an unflatteringly long pause.

She sent the servants off to bed, then led Giles into the drawing room and poured them each a brandy. Sitting in facing chairs, they talked idly for a while, but the earlier ease was gone. The marquess watched her with a dark, brooding expression that made her uneasy. Though she had thought his regard was flattering earlier in the evening, now she was not so sure. Perhaps, she thought with profound depression, his interest in her had been a momentary aberration and now he was wondering how to disengage gracefully.

He finished his brandy and stood. "I think it's best that I leave now."

Desdemona stared at him, sure she had done something wrong.

Humor lurking in his eyes, he said, "Don't look at me like that, as if I've just cast my vote against your apprentice protection law."

She glanced away, struggling to control her expression. A proper female would have learned not to wear her heart on her sleeve by the age of seventeen. Yet here she was, on the shady side of thirty, acting like a naive fool.

Giles swore under his breath. "The problem isn't you, Desdemona, but me," he said bluntly. "If I stay, I am going to have a great deal of trouble keeping my hands off you, which you will probably find upsetting. It will certainly raise havoc with the slow, genteel courtship I have been planning."

Courtship? Hearing that filled Desdemona with relief. "I don't think you're likely to turn into a lust-crazed beast. And if you do"—she gave him a shy smile—"it's a risk I'm willing to take."

Giles smiled but shook his head. "Perhaps I'll manage to behave as a gentleman, but I can't guarantee it."

"Good!" she said recklessly.

He laughed, lines crinkling the tanned skin around his eyes. "Do you realize how much you've changed in the last fortnight?"

"I hope it's for the better."

"I certainly think so." He leaned against the fireplace mantel, his arms folded across his chest, his expression serious. "This may be too early for a formal offer of marriage, but I'd like you to consider the possibility."

Desdemona stared at him, her relief ebbing away. She had been drifting, delighted by his company and his admiration, but now that he had actually spoken, painful reality closed in.

He raised his brows at her expression. "Surely you aren't surprised. The prospect was first raised in Daventry."

"I guess I thought that after you had a chance to consider, you wouldn't really make an offer," she said in a small voice.

He gave the wry half smile she loved. "I'm not sure whether that shows lack of faith in me or in yourself." His smile faded. "You are living proof that a woman doesn't need a husband to have a worthwhile life. Even if you do wish to remarry, I can understand that you might prefer more promising material. Just . . . just tell me now, and I won't mention the subject again."

His statement reminded her that she was not the only one to feel uncertain. "I have no doubt that you would make a marvelous husband. The problem is—" she swallowed hard, "I don't know if I would make an adequate wife."

He caught her gaze with his own. "You are honest, beautiful, have a kind heart, and do not suffer fools gladly. To me, those seem like excellent qualifications for a wife."

She smiled at what he considered important, but her eyes slid away. "I don't know if I can give you an heir. It's true that my husband and I did not share a bed for very long, so perhaps I am not barren, but I am past thirty now—"

He cut her off sharply. "That doesn't matter. I'm offering for you because I want you to be my wife, not a brood mare. It doesn't bother me to think that Robin or a son of his will have Wolverhampton after me." Painful bleakness showed in his eyes. "My mother and my first wife both died in childbirth. I would not want to see that happen to you."

Desdemona looked down to where her hands were frantically twined in her lap. The trouble with half-truths is that they were not much protection after they were demolished. She should have known that the real truth could not be avoided.

She forced herself to look at him. "There is another,

more basic reason why I fear I would not be the wife for you. You are a warm, passionate man. Surely you want a wife who is the same. But I don't know if I am capable of being that kind of woman."

She hoped he would understand what she was trying to say, but no such luck. After a long pause, he said quietly, "Could you explain what you mean a little more clearly?"

Her shoulders bowed and her voice broke. "My husband ... he used to say that lying with me was like bedding an icicle. That any trollop on the streets was warmer than I."

Giles crossed the room and sat on the arm of her chair, then put his arms around her. "Hush, love," he said, rocking her gently, his cheek against her hair. "Few women are passionate in a miserable marriage. Don't condemn yourself because of the words of a selfish brute."

She clung to him, shaking, but his words eased some of the tight knot inside her.

He smoothed back her hair with a gentle hand. "You are so incredibly fair-minded. There is probably not another woman in London who would so conscientiously spell out her presumed failings when a marquess offered for her."

She leaned back in his embrace to look him squarely in the eye. "I'm not interested in marrying a marquess. I'm interested in Giles Andreville, who is the kindest, most amusing, most attractive man in England."

A slow smile spread over Giles's face. "It seems that we both think marriage is a good idea, so when shall we do it?"

Before she could answer, he bent his head and pressed his lips to hers. The desire that had ebbed while she was revealing her fears began to return. She kissed him back, wishing that she were more experienced.

He lifted his head and smiled into her eyes. "You don't kiss like a cold woman." He stood, then pulled her to her feet for another, longer embrace.

She loved the feel of his broad, muscular body. He was the only man who had ever made her feel delicate and feminine. She pressed against him, losing herself in his kiss.

He broke away, his breath coming quick and hard. "I think we can work matters out to our mutual satisfaction, don't you?"

Perhaps he was right, but she did not want to risk the unknown. Her gaze dropped to his cravat as she said haltingly, "Marriage is forever, Giles. It might be better if we don't do anything so irrevocable until we are sure. Or rather," she qualified, "until I am sure that . . . that I can fulfill my part of the bargain."

"There will never be any guarantees, Desdemona," he said gravely. "I think it is enough to trust that love will carry us through." He touched her cheek in a gossamer caress. "And I do love you, very much."

"I love you, too," she whispered. "But I don't have as much faith as you. I think it would be better if we . . . tried first."

He stared at her. "Desdemona, are you propositioning me?"

She nodded, blushing, and ducked her head again.

He wrapped his arms around her and began to laugh. Humiliated, she tried to jerk free.

He held tight, not letting her escape. "Do you have any idea how alarming it is for a man to be told that his whole future depends on one night's performance? The thought is paralyzing."

When she realized that he was laughing not at her, but at himself and the splendid absurdity of human nature, she was able to laugh with him. "It doesn't have to be only one night. We can take as long as necessary." She smiled mischievously and wriggled closer. "And while it's been a very long time since I've been this close to a man, if my memory serves, the indications are that you don't seem the least bit paralyzed."

Giles gasped, his arms tightening. "Shall we see if I can convince you that you will make the best of all possible wives?" He bent over for another kiss that left them both breathless.

Wordlessly she guided them upstairs to her room, her head resting on Giles's shoulder, more happy than she could ever remember being in her life. Somewhere during that last kiss, she had realized that he was right, that the powerful attraction she felt for him meant that she really was capable of being a warm and willing wife. But it would be a pity to skip the proof.

After closing the bedroom door behind them, Giles said softly, "Let me look at you."

Her maid had left a single lamp burning on the bed-side table. It gave enough light to show the intentness of his expression. Shyly she stood still while he circled around her. He unfastened her pearls, pressing a kiss on her nape when he was done. Then he used his fingers to roughly comb her hair down over her shoulders. He buried his face in it, murmuring, "I've wanted to do this for so long. Your hair is all fire and silk, just like the rest of you."

His breath warmed her throat; his admiration warmed her heart. With dawning confidence, she said, "I want to see you, too, Giles."

She untied his cravat, then unfastened his collar buttons so she could lay her hand on the warm expanse of his chest. Brown hair tickled her palm and she felt the acceleration of his heart.

Garment by garment, they took turns undressing each other. They moved with deliberate slowness, feeding the fire between them with soft words and gentle touches.

When her shift whispered to the floor, leaving her naked except for her stockings, he said huskily, "You are beautiful, so splendidly beautiful. Boadicea, the ancient British warrior queen, must have been like you, all red-gold hair and blazing womanly strength." He smiled. "Ever since Daventry, I've been thinking what a magnificent neck you have."

She blushed. "Is that what you were staring at all evening?"

"Of course it was your neck. Am I not a gentleman?" He slid his hands under her lush breasts, lifting and molding them. Breath rough, he said, "I've wanted to do this as well." He rubbed his face in the deep, warm cleft, then began licking and kissing her nipples, worshiping her with his touch.

She gasped and arched her head back. For the first time in her life, she loved her harlot's body, for it gave him such pleasure. More than anything on earth, she wanted to please him, to return the joy that was blossoming in her.

When they lay down together, it was as partners. When they joined, it was at her frantic urging, her need to have him become part of her. And when they cried out, it was together.

It was a night of shyness and discovery, passion and laughter, too precious to waste on sleep. She discovered that she was not a cold woman, not at all, and in the process she convinced Giles that only a complete ninny could have found him boring.

When not making love, they lay in each other's arms and talked, sharing their thoughts as intimately as they had shared their bodies. It was with the greatest of reluctance that Giles acknowledged the lightening sky outside. "Dawn comes too early at this season." His breath stirred her tangled hair. "I don't want to leave, but it's time."

She rolled over so that she lay half across him, her chin on his chest. There was no trace of the angry, defensive woman who had first exploded into his sedate life. Now she was all soft welcome. "Why leave? The servants will already have deduced what is going on."

"Except for my coachman, not necessarily." He smiled. "I admit that for persons of our advanced years, propriety is not of first importance, but I prefer there be no gossip around your name."

Smiling impishly, she wiggled her lush curves to such good effect that he drew her down for another kiss. When it was necessary for survival's sake to stop for air, he panted, "You're a shameless woman. And I'm a lucky man."

Her pale redhead's skin colored rosily again.

He said with interest, "Your enchanting blushes go much farther than I realized."

That made her blush even more. By the time Giles had finished investigating exactly how far the blushes went, another half hour had passed. After, as they lay twined together, she said softly, "I didn't know it could be like this."

"Neither did I."

She raised her head and regarded him with surprise. "Truly?"

"Truly." He stroked her bare shoulder. "I suppose I've had the normal amount of experience, but I've never before made love with my beloved. Nothing in the past has ever equaled this." He kissed her again, lingeringly. "Are you ready to make a decision about marriage, or do you need more time?"

She laughed and linked her arms around his neck. "Do you think I'm such a fool as to let you go?"

Chapter 34

The Abingdon Inn was on a street called Long Acre near Covent Garden. As the hackney carriage halted in front, Maxie's face tightened. Ever since she'd awakened, the black anxiety had been suffocatingly close. She could not shake the feeling that she was on a course that would shatter forever the life she had known. Yet she had no choice but to go forward.

She and Robin had agreed that it was best to simply visit the inn and make inquiries. Surely the death of a guest would be remembered. And if they did not receive straightforward answers to their questions, well, that would give her another kind of information.

Robin helped her out of the carriage. She took a moment to study the building. It was small and respectable, but only just. Her father had not had money for grander establishments.

Taking Robin's arm, she lifted her chin and walked to the door.

As the well-dressed young couple disappeared into the inn, the owner of the tobacco shop next door peered through the grimy glass of his front window, squinting to confirm that the pair matched the description he had been given: a blond fellow as cool as a lord, and a dusky little pocket Venus. The old man nodded. Aye, these must be the ones.

Turning to the lad who assisted him, the tobacconist said, "Go 'round the corner and tell Simmons that the folk he asked me to watch for are in the Abingdon now. Mind you hurry, and if he ain't there, go after 'im. There'll be a half-crown for you if 'e gets here in time."

And there'd be three quid, less the half-crown, for himself. Vastly pleased, the tobacconist treated himself to one of his own most expensive cigars.

They had agreed in advance that Robin would speak, since men were usually taken more seriously. When they found a spotty young clerk, Robin asked, "May we speak with the landlord, please?"

The clerk looked up from the newspaper he was reading. After in insulting glance at Maxie, he said, "I can rent you a room, but you'll have to pay for a whole day even if you only want it for an hour."

"We do not need a room," Robin said in a voice edged with steel. "We want to speak to the landlord. *Now.*"

The clerk considered making a surly reply, then thought better of it. "I'll see if Watson'll speak to you."

Maxie clenched and unclenched her hands as they waited. If it hadn't been for Robin's calming presence, she would be ricocheting from the walls. She was grateful that he didn't attempt conversation; in her present mood, she might bite his head off. She had fought off wolves in a winter blizzard with more composure than she was showing today.

Closing her eyes, she forced herself to breathe more slowly. The truth would have to be better than living with such anxiety.

The clerk returned and jerked his thumb over his shoulder. "He'll see you. Down the hall, last door on the left."

Watson was thin and balding, with an expression of chronic irritation. Not bothering to rise from his desk, he barked, "State your business and be quick about it. I'm a busy man."

"My name is Lord Robert Andreville," Robin said crisply. "About three months ago, one of your guests, a Mr. Collins, died unexpectedly."

"The American bloke." Watson's face went blank. "Aye, he turned up his toes here."

"Could you tell us something of the circumstances of his death?" When the manager didn't reply, Robin prompted, "Who found him, and what time of day was it? Was Mr. Collins still alive when he was found? Was a physician called?"

The manager scowled. "What business is it of yours?"

Unable to keep silent, Maxie said, "He was my father. Surely I have a right to know what his last hours were like."

Watson swung around to study her, his expression unreadable. "Sorry, miss." Glancing away, he said, "A maid found him in the morning. He was already gone. The physician said it must have been his heart. He went sudden-like."

"What was the physician's name?" Robin asked.

Watson stood, his expression surly. "You've taken enough of my time. There's nothin' more to know. Collins died and that's it. If it hadn't happened here, it would have been somewhere else, and I wish it had been. Now get out. I've work to do."

Maxie opened her mouth to protest, but Robin took her arm firmly. "Thank you for your time, Mr. Watson."

After her companion steered her out of the office and closed the door, she hissed, "I want to ask him more, Robin. He was hiding something."

"Yes, but he wasn't going to say more, not without physical violence, and it's premature to try that. There may be a better way to learn what we want." Instead of following the hall to the front of the building, Robin turned the other way. "Servants always know what's going on, and perhaps no one has ordered them to hold their tongues."

The door at the end of the passage led to a cobbled yard with stables built around three sides. Maxie followed Robin across the court to a set of open doors.

Inside, an elderly hostler was oiling a piece of harness and whistling tunelessly between crooked front teeth.

"Good day, sir," Robin said cheerily.

The hostler looked up, startled but not displeased to be interrupted. "Good day to you, too, sir. What can I do for you?"

"My name's Bob Andreville." Robin offered his hand. His accent had become distinctly American, far more so than Maxie's. "I was wondering, have you been working here long?"

"Nigh on to ten years." After wiping one oily hand down his trousers, the hostler returned Robin's handshake. "Name's Will Jenkins. You an American?"

"That I am, but my father was born in Yorkshire. This is my first trip to England. Would have come sooner, but for the war." He shook his head. "Damned fool things, wars. Americans and Britons should be friends."

"Ain't that the truth," the hostler agreed. "I've a cousin in Virginia. You from that part of the colonies?"

The two men continued in that vein while Maxie fidgeted, restless but realizing that Robin was right. They would learn far more from the friendly hostler than the hostile landlord.

Eventually Robin said, "A friend of mine, Max Collins, came here for a visit a few months back. Right before I sailed over myself, I heard he'd died, but no one knew exactly what had happened. I remembered he was staying at the Abingdon Inn, so I thought since I was in town I'd stop by to see what I could learn to tell his family." He pursed his lips. "We hear stories about how dangerous London is. Did thieves set on him?"

"'Twas no such thing. Mr. Collins died right here in his bed." Jenkins shook his grizzled head. "A sorry thing, that. He was a fine gent, very pleasant to everyone, even that mawworm Watson. It was a real shock when he killed himself."

The words hit Maxie like a cannonball, the impact so shattering that it was beyond pain. *He killed himself.*

He killed himself. As Robin inhaled sharply, she gasped, "No. Max wouldn't do that."

Jenkins said compassionately, "Sorry to be the one to tell you if he was a friend of yours, miss, but there ain't much doubt. The gent tried to arrange it so's no one would know, but he wasn't careful enough. Musta been upset about somethin' and decided he couldn't take it no more. Most everyone feels that way sometimes. Mr. Collins was one who did somethin' about it."

As a child, Maxie had once ventured onto a frozen pond during a January thaw. Even twenty years later she had not forgotten her terror when ice she had believed solid began breaking up beneath her. Desperately she had tried to retreat to the shore, but there had been no hope or safety anywhere as the ice splintered in all directions. She had plunged into the frigid water and nearly drowned before her father heard her screams and rescued her.

Her feelings now were similar to when the ice broke under her, but a thousand times worse. What Jenkins said was impossible, unbearable, and it was not water engulfing her but unbearable anguish.

"No," she repeated, burying her face in her hands. "Papa would never kill himself. *He wouldn't!*" Yet the pieces fit together with horrible precision. This explained everything that she had been unable to understand.

Mindlessly she whirled away, up the alley to Long Acre. She heard Robin call her name, but his voice was distant, of no importance.

When she bolted out of the alley, she collided with a man who smelled of onions. She lost her bonnet and almost fell, but managed to regain her balance. Blindly she raced into the street, heedless of the heavy traffic.

A hoarse shout sounded in her ear. Someone grabbed her arm, jerking her from the path of a horse that reared into the air, its pawing iron-clad hooves barely missing her skull.

Ignoring her rescuer, she broke away and resumed

running, as if somewhere there were a place where the past was different, where she would not have to believe that her father could have killed himself. She tripped and fell full-length on the filthy pavement. The breath was knocked out of her, yet she felt nothing when her knees and palms smashed into the cobblestones.

Scrambling to her feet, she was about to resume her flight when strong hands seized her. Robin's familiar voice said urgently, "Stop, Maxie! For God's sake, stop before you get yourself killed."

She tried to escape, but he wouldn't release her. As he hauled her out of the street, she clenched her hands into fists and struck him. "My father would never have killed himself and left me!" she cried, wild tears pouring down her face. "He loved life and he loved me. He would never have done that!"

Robin guessed that it was herself that she was trying to convince. He tried to immobilize her flailing fists by pinning her arms to her sides with an iron embrace. She continued to struggle frantically.

He gasped when one of her elbows smashed him in the stomach, knocking him breathless. She was a dangerous woman to hold against her will, but he dared not use more force. Desperate to calm her before she injured herself, he said sharply, "We don't know for sure what happened, Kanawiosta. Perhaps Jenkins was wrong. We need to know more."

She gave an agonized gasp and became still, her small body trembling in his arms. Somehow he knew that his words had produced the opposite effect of what he had intended: Rather than convincing her that the hostler might have been wrong, they had made it impossible for her to deny the truth.

He ached for her misery, knowing she was in some private hell that he could not share, not unless she would let him. Ignoring the curious onlookers, he continued speaking to her in a low voice, his lips near her ear, hoping the sound would soothe her even though she was beyond absorbing the words.

Then the instinct developed in his dangerous years on the Continent made Robin look up. Half a block away, on the far side of the stream of traffic, stood Simmons, his expression black.

Christ, why did the bastard have to show up now, of all times? Robin hailed a passing hackney. When it stopped, he swept Maxie up in his arms and pushed ruthlessly past a merchant who was trying to claim the same vehicle. To the driver, he snapped, "Mayfair as fast as you can. There will be an extra five quid if you can halve the usual time."

As the hackney lurched wildly into traffic, Robin settled on the seat and enfolded Maxie in his arms. Then he prayed for the wisdom to help her as she had helped him.

Simmons watched with a scowl as the hired carriage departed. Obviously the girl had learned the truth, and taken it even more badly than her uncle had feared. He beckoned to a scrawny urchin who worked for him regularly. "Find out where they go."

The lad darted after the hackney. When he reached it, he leaped up and grabbed a bracket on the back, then squirmed into a comfortable position for the rest of the ride.

When the lad returned, Simmons thought, at least he would be able to tell Collingwood where his niece was staying. It wasn't much, but it was all he could salvage from a job that had otherwise been a disaster from beginning to end.

Though Maxie was conscious, she was deep in shock, her body chilled and shaking. She seemed oblivious to Robin's presence. He cradled her on his lap through the ride back to Candover House, trying without success to infuse her with his own warmth.

When she first mentioned her father's death, Robin had considered the possibility of suicide, because it provided a plausible explanation for Collingwood's secrecy. What had Maxie said at Ruxton when talking about how she could not project her future? Something about a possibility that was literally unthinkable. Knowing her father better than anyone else did, it had never occurred to her that he was capable of taking his own life. Yet he had, and the knowledge had devastated her.

Back at Candover House, Robin carried Maxie inside past the startled butler, throwing orders over his shoulder for hot water, towels, bandages, and salve to be sent to her bedchamber. Then he carried her upstairs, laid her on her bed, and removed her ruined muslin dress and stockings. At the moment he didn't give a bloody damn about propriety.

When the supplies arrived, he dismissed the maid, then gently washed the blood and grit from the abrasions on Maxie's knees and palms. None of the injuries was deep enough to warrant bandaging, though the lacerations must have stung like the very devil when he spread salve on her raw flesh.

She didn't resist, cooperate, or show any discomfort during Robin's ministrations. She simply lay passively, eyes never meeting his. When he was done, she rolled away and buried her head in the pillows.

He wondered if her total withdrawal was an aspect of her Mohawk heritage. Not that the reason was important; what mattered was that she was shutting him out. He would never have guessed how much that would hurt.

When he finished, he pulled a blanket over her, then covered her knotted fist with his hand. "Is there anything I can do?"

She gave her head an infinitesimal shake.

"Kanawiosta, when I was drowning in grief, you told me that a burden shared is lighter," he said softly. "Is there nothing you will accept from me?"

"Not now." Her muffled voice was almost inaudible. "I'm sorry."

"Do you want me to leave?"

She nodded.

Heavy of heart, Robin stood. In spite of her petite

size, she had never looked fragile, but now the slight form under the blanket looked diminished and vulnerable. He did not try to define his feelings; he only knew that he would have willingly given everything he possessed to alleviate her misery.

Needing to express some of his tenderness, he touched her raven hair in a caress too light for her to feel. Then he forced himself to leave.

Having heard from her servants that there was trouble, the duchess waited outside in a chair, her hands patiently folded in her lap. When he emerged, she asked quietly, "What happened?"

He sighed, running his hand through his hair in frustration. "Apparently Maxie's father committed suicide."

"Oh, dear Lord." Margot's face whitened. Having lost her own beloved father under tragic circumstances, she would understand Maxie's distress all too well.

"I wish to God that I could do something." Robin's mouth twisted. "But all she wants is to be left alone."

"Give her time to absorb the shock," Margot advised. "Grief is a solitary affair. Sometimes one must go inward and come to terms with it before comfort from others can be accepted."

"I'm sure you're right, Duchess." He tried to smile. "But it's very hard to see her like this."

"Love hurts, Robin." Attempting to lighten the atmosphere, she continued, "So does hunger, and I find myself hungry very often now. Come and have tea with me." Taking his arm, she marched him off to the morning room.

Tea wasn't much, but it was better than nothing.

Chapter 35

They had finished a silent tea when the butler entered with a calling card. Margot's brows rose. "Lord Collingwood is here."

Suddenly alert, Robin said, "Shall we receive him together? I have a vested interest in anything he might have to say."

"Of course."

The butler left, then ushered the visitor in a few moments later. Lord Collingwood was a tall man with a thin, tired face. After bowing to Margot, he said, "Please forgive the intrusion, Duchess, but I have reason to believe that my niece, Miss Maxima Collins, is visiting you. I would like to see her."

"She's here," Margot admitted, "but unwell and not receiving visitors. Would you like to leave a message for her?"

Collingwood hesitated. While he considered, his gaze fell on Robin, who had withdrawn to an unobtrusive position at one side of the room. The viscount's eyes narrowed. "My niece was traveling with a man of your description."

Robin inclined his head. "I am Lord Robert Andreville."

That rocked the visitor. "Wolverton's brother?"

"The same."

Collingwood shook his head in disbelief. "And here I'd been worrying that the girl had been taken in by some rogue."

"Noble birth is hardly proof against villainy," Robin said dryly. "However, my intentions regarding Miss

Collins have been honorable. We met by chance. Knowing the dangers she risked, I offered my escort to ensure that she reached London safely." As he spoke, he studied Collingwood. If one looked closely, there was a faint resemblance to his sister, though he was a staider, more conventional creature than Lady Ross. Nonetheless, he seemed very much the English gentleman; not the sort to have an inconvenient brother murdered. No wonder Maxie had had trouble believing that her uncle could be so ruthless.

With a trace of humor, Collingwood said, "You certainly protected my niece from the Bow Street Runner I sent after her."

"Good Lord, Simmons is a Runner?" After a stunned moment, Robin had to laugh at himself. "I should have guessed. Maxie and I thought he was some kind of villain."

"Runners and the criminals they pursue often resemble each other," Collingwood agreed. "But Ned Simmons is one of Bow Street's best. I commissioned him to investigate my brother's death and do what he could to keep the matter from becoming public knowledge. Quite apart from the potential for scandal, I didn't want there to be any question about burying Max in holy ground. By chance, Simmons was in the north when my niece ran away, so I asked him to bring her back."

After Margot waved him to a chair, Collingwood said uneasily, "From what Simmons said, my niece was very upset after visiting the Abingdon Inn."

Robin nodded. "She learned that her father killed himself. The manager didn't talk—I assume that you or Simmons paid him to hold his tongue—but one of the servants told us. Maxie is taking the news very badly."

Collingwood exhaled wearily. "I was afraid of that—she was devoted to Max. I envied my brother his daughter. My own girls . . ." He broke off a moment, then continued, "I wanted to spare Maxima such a dreadful shock. That's why I tried to prevent her from reaching London."

"It was your attempt to conceal the truth that sent her off to investigate," Robin said acerbically. "Maxie overheard a discussion between you and your wife that implied there was some kind of foul play involved in her father's death."

"So that's what happened. At first I thought she had decided on impulse to visit my sister, Lady Ross. It wasn't until my sister appeared in Durham that I realized something was amiss. With every report Simmons sent, I became more alarmed. I'm grateful the girl didn't meet disaster." He grimaced. "Now that I don't have to worry about her life, I can begin to worry about her reputation."

"No one need know how she reached London, so her reputation is intact," the duchess pointed out. "The real problem is her reaction to the news of her father's death."

"I have some happier news for her." Collingwood studied Robin. "I gather you have constituted yourself her protector."

"You gather rightly."

"Then I suppose I can tell you Maxima is something of an heiress. It's a mere independence of five hundred pounds a year, but enough to keep her comfortably here or in America."

Robin's brows rose. In spite of Collingwood's disclaimer, it was a very considerable legacy. "From whom is she inheriting? She said her father left nothing."

"Our Aunt Maxima, Lady Clendennon, was Max's godmother. She was always fond of him. Though she complained about what a wastrel he was, she said it with a smile. She loved getting his letters." Collingwood sighed. "If Max's prudence had equaled his charm, he could have been prime minister.

"Aunt Maxima knew it would be absurd to leave Max any money, so she decided to make Max's daughter one of her heirs instead. After she died last winter, her solicitor wrote my brother in Boston, which is why he returned to England when he did. Since the lawyer was being uncooperative about executing the will, Max decided to go to London to talk to him personally."

"Why didn't your brother tell Maxie about this? I've gotten the impression that she handled their financial affairs."

"Max forbade me to tell her until the matter was resolved because he didn't want her to be disappointed if it didn't work out," Collingwood explained. "As it turned out, my aunt specified that Maxima could not inherit before her twenty-fifth birthday at the earliest. After that, the money was to be held in trust as long as Max was alive. Apparently my aunt was determined not to allow my brother to waste his daughter's inheritance.

"After Max died, that was no longer an issue, but the present Lord Clendennon was urging the solicitor to find a way to disqualify Maxima. I'm afraid that my cousin is a greedy devil, and the legacy will revert to him if she doesn't inherit. When Clendennon recently learned that Maxima's mother was a Red Indian, he suggested that she might be illegitimate, the product of a casual liaison, or perhaps not even Max's daughter."

Robin whistled softly. "I don't blame you for not wanting to tell Maxie that. She would have been enraged."

"And justly so. When Clendennon raised the issue, I had my solicitor write to a colleague in Boston. Last week I received a copy of my brother's marriage lines. Max and his wife were married by an Anglican priest, so Maxima is entirely legitimate." Collingwood gave a faint, satisfied smile. "Even if there hadn't been a Christian ceremony, I was prepared to argue that her parents were legally married under the laws of her mother's people. For that matter, illegitimacy would not necessarily have invalidated the bequest, but Clendennon might have used it as an excuse to cause legal trouble that would take time and money to resolve. This is much simpler."

"You've gone to considerable effort on your niece's behalf."

"Of course—she's family. Besides, I'm fond of the girl. I wish my own daughters had some of her spirit." For the first time Collingwood smiled. "But only some of it. Maxima would have been a rare handful to raise. An eccentric like Max was a better father for her." He rose to his feet. "I'll be staying at the Clarendon for several days. I'd like to see Maxima before I return to Durham. Will you tell her I called?"

"Of course," Robin said. "Do you want to explain about her inheritance yourself?"

The viscount shrugged. "Use your judgment. If she will see you and not me, tell her if you think it might cheer her up. I've made a muddle of the whole business, I'm afraid."

"Maxie is fortunate to have such a conscientious uncle," Robin said. "Given the constraints you had, there may have been no solution that wasn't muddled."

"Thank you." Collingwood's expression lightened a little as he took his leave. "Lord Robert, your grace."

When they were alone, Robin said, "I'm sure you noticed what I did in Collingwood's story."

Margot nodded thoughtfully. Drawing conclusions from sketchy data was the essence of the spy's art, and they were both very, very good at it. "But is there any way to prove it?"

"Not definitely, but with more information I can make a convincing case. Absolute proof isn't necessary." Profoundly glad that there was something he could do for Maxie, Robin headed for the door. "I'll start now. Heaven knows when I'll be back."

"I'll get you a key to the house. More dignified than having you pick the lock if you return late," Margot said. "I'll keep an eye on Maxie's room and try to ensure that she doesn't do anything foolish. Let me know if I can do anything else."

"Thank you." He smiled a little. "Actually, I know where I can get exactly the kind of assistance I need."

* * *

The door was open, so Robin rapped it with his knuckles as he walked through. Lord Strathmore looked up from his desk, his expression distracted until he saw who had arrived. With a smile, he got to his feet. "I'm glad you came back to Whitehall, Robin. Last night was enjoyable, but we really didn't have much chance to talk."

"Today won't be any better." After shaking hands, Robin took the chair his cousin indicated. "This is only a quick visit to ask for your help."

"Anything," Lucien said simply. "What's the problem?"

"I want to investigate a suicide that took place in an inn near Covent Garden two—no, closer to three— months ago."

Lucien frowned. "Your friend Maxie's father?"

Robin nodded; his cousin was also a master at putting fragmentary facts together. "I'm afraid so. She's distraught—they were very close. I want to learn as much I can about any extenuating circumstances that might make his death easier for her to accept. I want to talk to the maid who found his body, the physician who certified his death, and everyone he visited in London. And I want to do it all today."

Lucien's brows rose. "Shall I come with you? Two of us may be able to cover more ground."

Robin glanced at the files on the desk. "Aren't you busy?"

"Not anything that can't wait."

"Good. Since London isn't my turf, I'll need all the help I can get." Robin frowned. "I should have thought of this earlier, but being personally involved plays havoc with the judgment. There's a Bow Street Runner, Ned Simmons, who was hired by the Collins family to hush the business up. If I can find him, he might already know much of what I want to learn."

Lucien nodded. "I know Simmons, and he's very thorough. He frequents a tavern near Covent Garden. With luck, we'll find him there now."

Robin got to his feet, thinking that this was going to be easier than he expected.

Lucien also rose and collected a cane from the corner of the room, but he hesitated before coming around the desk. "Robin, there's something I want to say."

"Yes?"

His cousin fiddled with the polished brass head of the cane. "Strange," he said humorlessly. "My tattered conscience has been nagging me on and off about you for years. Yet I don't know quite how to put this into words." He glanced up, his green-gold eyes somber. "I guess I want to know how much you resent me for talking you into a career in espionage."

Surprised, Robin said, "You didn't hold a knife to my throat, Luce. I made the decision myself."

"Yes, but I didn't realize what I was asking." Lucien sighed. "It seemed like almost a lark at the time. You were clever and had a genius for languages. Of course you could stay on the Continent and coordinate the British spying network for half of Europe. Between us, we would break Bonaparte. Who would have guessed the wars would continue for another dozen years?"

"Don't blame yourself for encouraging me in my folly," Robin said mildly. "You're only two years older than I—of course you couldn't know what was involved. My life was my own to risk as I chose."

"Giles didn't think so," Lucien said dryly. "I don't think he's ever forgiven me for my part in your career. But risking one's life is relatively straightforward. The worst part of being a spy is the high spiritual price of fighting a shadow war."

Lucien slid the polished shaft of the cane back and forth between his hands restlessly. "I've learned quite a bit about that myself, but at least I spent most of my time in the relatively civilized confines of England. My wicked deeds were usually done at long range and involved faceless people. What you did had to be far more difficult. As time passed, you began to look as drawn as blown glass, and as likely to shatter."

Touched by his cousin's concern, Robin asked, "Are

you sorry that you asked me to work for the Foreign Office, or that I agreed?"

"That's the hell of it." Lucien smiled self-mockingly. "Ruthless spymaster that I am, I can't regret what you did—your contributions were truly vital. I guess my real wish is that I didn't feel so damned guilty about what the work did to you."

Robin laughed. Guilt he understood very well. "If it's absolution you want, Luce, you've got it. I'll admit that I came too close to the breaking point for comfort, but in the last few weeks, I've come to terms with my reprehensible past. I'll never be proud of some of the things I've done, but I'm not going to crucify myself any longer." As he spoke, he heard Maxie's words echoing in his own voice.

Lucien studied Robin's face shrewdly. "I've found that the right woman can do wonders for one's peace of mind."

"Indeed. And now it's time for me to repay a debt to this particular right woman. Shall we be off?"

With Lucien's help, it shouldn't be difficult to learn about the last days of Max Collins. Robin hoped to God that the information would make a difference.

Chapter 36

Maxie felt as if she were wandering in a shadow land of evil dreams, but knew that there would be no awakening. Her father had taken his own life, and the knowledge was a pain more devastating than she could have imagined.

Burrowed into her pillows like a woodland creature seeking refuge, she lost track of the hours. The pattern of sunlight slowly shifted across the floor, then disappeared as clouds obscured the sky. Someone entered and left a tray of food, then left without speaking. The room darkened, and eventually the sounds of the household faded as night deepened.

When a distant clock struck midnight, Maxie forced herself to sit up and take stock. She couldn't spend the rest of her life hiding in a bedchamber. How much time would have to pass before her hosts would feel compelled to coax her out—twenty-four hours? Three days? A week? Or would Margot's superb hospitality allow Maxie to stay here forever, a mad mourner served by silent maids?

Even if the duchess would allow that, Robin wouldn't. Maxie buried her head in her hands, wondering dully what would happen next. Finally it was clear why she had been unable to sense her path beyond London. The unthinkable had happened, and now she felt suspended, unable to go forward, unable to retreat, too numb to imagine anything resembling normal life.

Wearily she slid from the bed and found her dressing gown, one of the garments that had magically appeared in her wardrobe the day before. She stopped and thought. Had she really been in London only two days? It seemed a century since she had arrived, met Margot and her aunt, and seriously misbehaved in the garden.

Even that last memory was not enough to warm her.

She belted the robe around her narrow waist, then lit a candle and used it to light her way down to the library. Books had never failed to make her feel better. Perhaps being surrounded by them would help clear her dazed mind.

There was a desk at the far end of the library. She settled into the leather-upholstered chair behind it. The room was cool, and occasional raindrops spatted against the windows. Myriad volumes lined the room in friendly ranks, their titles reflecting dull gold in the candlelight. As she inhaled the pleasant scents of leather bindings and furniture polish, mingled with a faded tang of smoke, the knot in her chest eased a little.

A walnut box of pipe tobacco stood on one side of the desk. Moved by dim memory, she opened the box and put a large pinch of tobacco in a shallow china bowl intended for ashes. Then she used the candle to set the shredded leaf afire.

The pungent scent carried her back to ceremonies she had attended in her childhood. Among her mother's people, tobacco was considered sacred, and it was burned to carry prayers to the spirit world.

But as she watched the smoke twist and dissolve into blackness, Maxie was not even sure what to pray for.

It had been a long day, and Candover House was completely dark when Robin returned. Still, with the considerable help of Lucien and a startled but cooperative Simmons, he had found the information he wanted. Perhaps tomorrow Maxie would be willing to listen.

He let himself in with the key Maggie had given him. He had just relocked the massive front door when his instincts sounded a warning note. After a moment of intense stillness, reaching out with his senses, he recognized what was amiss. Though the household slept, there was a fresh scent of burning tobacco here on a floor that had no bedchambers.

Probably it meant no more than that a servant had smoked while checking that the doors were locked, or that Rafe was working late. Nonetheless, Robin followed the scent to the library, where a sliver of light showed beneath the door.

He entered quietly. Maxie was sitting at the far end of the room, her straight ebony hair cascading over her shoulders and her gaze fixed absently on a spiral of fragrant smoke. Though he was glad she had risen from her bed, her expression was bleak and infinitely distant. It hurt to see the dimming of her spirit. Perhaps what he had learned might rekindle her essential flame.

She looked up without surprise. "Good evening. Have you been skulking about London?"

"Exactly." He walked the length of the room and took a chair near her. Since she was barefoot and wore only a light robe over her shift, he took off his coat, removed several folded sheets of paper from an inside pocket, then offered it to her. "You must be freezing. Put this on."

She accepted the garment mechanically and draped it over her shoulders. She looked very small in the folds of dark fabric.

"I've learned some things I think you'll find interesting," Robin said. "Can you bear to listen now, or should I wait?"

She made a vague gesture with her hand. "It doesn't matter. Now will do if that's what you wish."

Wondering what it would take to break through her lethargy, he said, "Lord Collingwood called here today. His judgment might have been doubtful, but his intentions were good when he hired Simmons to prevent you from reaching London and investigating your father's death. Simmons is a Bow Street Runner."

She dropped another pinch of tobacco on the smoldering pile. "What is a Bow Street Runner?"

"A thieftaker. Mostly they work for the chief magistrate of Westminister, whose office is in Bow Street, hence the name," Robin explained. "However, Runners can be hired by private citizens for special tasks, which is what your uncle did."

Maxie nodded without interest.

"Collingwood also said that your Great-Aunt Maxima left you five hundred pounds a year, but specified that you couldn't receive it until you were over twenty-five and your father had died. Apparently your great-aunt had doubts about your father's financial capabilities."

The faintest of smiles touched Maxie's lips. "Justifiably so. Max was hopeless about money. It didn't interest him."

After a slow breath, Robin went to the crux of his story. "Though he may have concealed it from you, your father's health had apparently been deteriorating for some time. When he came to London, he not only called on your aunt's executor to learn the details of your legacy, he also visited two physicians. Both said that your father's heart was failing. However, it was possible that he might survive a long time as an invalid, in pain and unable to live the life he was accustomed to."

Maxie's head came up at that, her brown eyes finally meeting his, but she didn't speak. She scarcely seemed to breathe.

"I talked to several other people whom your father saw in the days before he died." Robin raised the papers he had removed from his coat, then set them on the desk. "Based on the details in here, I'd be willing to take an oath in court that your father decided to end his life so that you could inherit right away, and to spare you the grief of nursing him through a slow death. It's also a fair guess that he didn't want to die that way, helplessly waiting for the end. He knew your uncle would look out for you, so he wasn't leaving you alone."

Maxie was trembling, and her tongue licked out to moisten her dry lips. "How . . . how did he do it?"

"With a massive dose of digitalis, a heart medication that is a poison in large quantities. Both physicians had given him some, warning him to be careful how much he used because it can be fatal. It seems likely that your father thought he would have time to dispose of the bottles, but the medicine overcame him very quickly. If he'd had a little more time, no one would have realized that he hadn't died naturally."

Robin paused to let her absorb that before he finished, "Your father didn't abandon you carelessly, but because he cared so much. I think he wanted to give you, with his death, the security he was unable to give you in life. He was wrong not to know that you would rather have had him for whatever months or years were left, but his action sprang from love."

Maxie's brown eyes came alive then. She buried her face in her hands and whispered, "I don't know why, but that makes all the difference in the world."

"You and your father were everything to each other," Robin said quietly., "No matter how insulting strangers were, no matter how much you were taunted for your Mohawk blood, you always knew that your father loved you. To believe that he had killed himself, with no word or thought for you, was like being told that your whole life had been built on a lie."

She raised her head and wiped her eyes with the back of her hand. "How did you know that when I didn't?"

"By delving into the shadowy corners of my mind, you also opened yourself to me." He stepped over to her and covered her ears. *"When a woman mourns, she cannot hear,"* he quoted. *"Let these words remove the obstruction so you can hear again."*

He laid his hands lightly over her eyes. *"In your grief, you have lost the sun and fallen into darkness. I now restore the sunlight."*

He knelt before her so that their eyes were at the same level, then crossed his hands on the center of her chest. Her heart beat steadily against his palms. *"You have allowed your mind to dwell on your great grief. You must release it lest you, too, wither and die."*

He took her hands in his. *"In your sorrow your bed has become uncomfortable and you cannot sleep at night. Let me remove the discomfort from your resting place."* He raised her hands and kissed first one, then the other. "More than anything else in his life, your father wanted you to be happy. For his sake, you must find your way out of the darkness."

She closed her eyes, tears running down her cheeks. "How did you remember all that, Robin?" she whispered.

"The words are graven on my heart, Kanawiosta."

Opening her eyes, she said, "My father and I never discussed his health. He hated being weak. To take his own life, knowing that I would benefit and he would be spared suffering—it is exactly the sort of thing he would do, but I was too selfishly wrapped up in my grief to see that for myself." She gave a damp-sounding laugh. "Leave it to Max to be inefficient about ending his life. Without me, he was hopelessly disorganized."

"The most important things are always the hardest to see." Profoundly glad that she could laugh again, Robin released her hands and got to his feet, then leaned against the desk. Now that she had passed the crisis, he was acutely aware of her nearness, and her utter, unselfconscious desirability. Looking for distraction, his gaze fell on the burning tobacco. "Is there a special meaning to this?"

"Tobacco is sacred to my mother's people. It's burned to carry prayers and wishes to the spirits."

As Robin had said before, he believed in making sacrifices to the gods of fortune. He took a pinch of dried leaf and dropped it on the smoldering mound.

"What did you wish for?" she asked.

"If I tell you, will it prevent the wish from coming true?"

She smiled. "I don't think it makes a difference."

A moment ago, he had told himself that it was not the time to speak, but when he saw her irresistible smile he threw caution to the winds. "I was wishing you would marry me."

Her levity faded and she leaned back in the chair, tugging the coat around her. It had a faint, friendly scent of Robin. She had wanted the garment because in the future, when she was alone, it would remind her of what it was like to be in his arms. "That's a dangerous habit you have, offering marriage. If you aren't careful, I might accept."

"I would like nothing better," he said gravely.

She sighed and glanced down at her linked hands. While the question of her father's death was unresolved, she had been able to avoid this discussion, but she no longer had an excuse.

She raised her head and studied him. Robin was only an arm's length away physically, yet his blondness, casual confidence, and bone-deep aristocratic elegance represented a chasm too wide to bridge. "I think we are too different, Robin. I'm the child of a wastrel book peddler and a woman considered a savage by your countrymen. You are born of centuries of wealth, breeding, and privilege." She tried to speak evenly, as if her conclusion were easy and obvious. "The idea of marriage appeals to you now, but I think in time you would come to regret it."

"Would you have regrets?" he asked softly.

"Certainly I would if you did," she replied, knowing that her simple words contained the essence of the dilemma. Loving him, she would be unable to endure his regrets. No matter how carefully he hid them under politeness and charm, she would know.

"You're wrong, you know. The differences between us are superficial, but the similarities are profound," he said intensely. "We were both born outsiders, Maxie. In your case, it was because of your mixed blood, never wholly belonging with either your father's or your mother's people. I know something of what you endured because in spite of wealth, privilege, and endless noble ancestors, I was a natural misfit, no more at home in my world than you were in yours.

"Perhaps it would have been different if I'd had a mother, or if my father had been able to bear the sight of me." His expression became ironic. "But I probably would have been a misfit even if my mother had survived. Every generation or two the Andrevilles throw up a black sheep, and my keepers were convinced that I was one before I was out of leading strings. Something had only to be forbidden to attract me. Everything I did was wrong, proof of my natural wickedness. I questioned things that shouldn't be questioned, disobeyed orders I disagreed with, made up stories that were seen as malicious lies."

He held up his misshapen left hand. "The Latin word for left is *sinister,* which says a great deal about how left-handers are perceived. The tutor I had before I went away to school thought I used my left hand just to spite him. Sometimes he tied it behind my back so I must use the right, other times he beat my left palm with a brass ruler until it bled." He smiled without humor. "I was probably one of the few boys in England who thought that public school was an improvement over life at home."

For the first time, she fully understood the desolation of his childhood. No wonder he thought he wasn't very good at love. How had he survived with his humor and sanity and kindness intact? Her heart ached for him and Giles, two lonely boys who deserved so much better than what they had received. Thank God they had at least had each other.

Still . . . "Granted that both of us grew up feeling like outsiders," she said slowly. "Is that enough of a bond to hold us together? Are we defined by our weaknesses?"

"Not by our weaknesses, but by our trust." In his white shirtsleeves he looked lean and strong and overpoweringly attractive as he lounged against the desk, his hands curved around the edge. "We dare show our weaknesses only to those we hope will understand and accept us in spite of them. Even when I scarcely knew you, I found myself speaking of things I have told no one else, had barely even admitted to myself."

"That is part of what worries me, Robin," she said, matching honesty with honesty. "I wonder if you want to marry me because I was there when you were hurting. Have you come to think I am special because you needed to talk and I listened? Would any woman have done as well?"

"Do you think so little of my judgment?" He smiled with a sweetness and intimacy that melted her heart. "No other woman could ever be the same. With you, I am whole."

Seeing that she still hesitated, he said softly, "You taught me many things, but most of all, about love." He took a deep breath. "And I do love you, Kanawiosta."

Maxie sucked in her breath as she heard the words she had never thought to hear. "You said you were not very good at love."

"I didn't think I was, but between you and Giles, I've recently received an intensive education in the subject," he said wryly. "I believed that I loved Maggie as much as I was capable of, and that she left me because it wasn't enough, because there was some vital deficiency in me. Now I know it was not that I was incapable of loving more, but that I had not met the woman I could truly fall in love with. Maggie tried to explain that to me once, but it was beyond my understanding."

He was silent as he searched for words. "With Maggie, there were always emotional limits. With you, Kanawiosta, there are none." His knuckles whitened as he gripped the edge of the desk. "The morning we left Ruxton, you implied rather strongly that you loved me. Was that wishful thinking on my part?"

His words were a shining joy that filled her like the sun's radiance. "Lord, Robin, of course I love you," she whispered. "All my talk of our differences, my doubts about England—they were only smoke. My true fear was that I cared too much to be your wife if you didn't love me."

His coat fell from her shoulders as she stood and opened her arms. Robin walked straight into them.

From the beginning, their bodies had known that it was utterly right to be together. This time there was no doubt, only fierce, compelling desire.

They were lying on the Persian carpet, most of their clothing off, when Robin pulled back. "Damnation, I'm doing it again." He rested his forehead on her bare breast, his chest heaving. "I have trouble remembering that you don't want to make love in this house. I'm sorry." He smiled ruefully. "A pity it's too cold and wet for the garden tonight."

He was starting to move away when she slid her arms around his neck. "No need to go all noble, Robin. Now that I know that you love me, being here doesn't bother me at all."

His face became vivid with laughter. "I'm very, very glad to hear that."

He bent to her breasts again. She arched against him in wordless response to his mouth and hands and intoxicating nearness. Even more than fire, there was tenderness and understanding and mirth, all woven together into an emotion far greater than the sum of its parts.

This time passion was not a gift of solace, but a sharing of their innermost selves. She felt as if she were soaring through the tangled skeins of his spirit. Though the dark strands were still there, they no longer shivered with anguish, while the bright, sun-spun threads of his being flowed around her with joy and laughter. Together, they were whole.

Afterward she lay trembling on top of him, her hair spilling over his chest and face. Tenderly he smoothed it back so that he could see her face. "Really, love, we're going to have to get back into the habit of doing this in a bed. Stone altars and library floors definitely have their place now and then, but they aren't especially comfortable."

She stretched her body along his, loving his lean strength. "It's very comfortable where I am."

He smiled. "You do make a superlative blanket."

She crossed her arms on his chest and rested her chin on them. "Feeling like a hopeless outsider is wretched when one is growing up," she said thoughtfully, "but from what I can see, many interesting people start out that way."

"I've noticed that." He stroked her naked back lovingly. "I've also found that one needn't stay a misfit forever."

She grinned. "The two of us fit together perfectly."

After a spell of peaceful silence, Robin murmured, "You're sure it didn't bother you to make love here?"

"Quite sure," she said lazily.

He linked his arms around her and rolled swiftly over so that he was above. Her raven hair wove ebony patterns across the burgundy patterns of the Persian rug, framing her exotically beautiful face.

"In that case, my love," he said softly, "let's do it again."

Epilogue

It was a perfect day for a wedding, and the gardens at Ruxton were ideal for the ceremony and the wedding breakfast. The guest list was small, and many had been at Maxie's first London dinner party. The people she had met that night were becoming the closest friends she'd ever had.

Giles and Desdemona had stood up with the bride and groom. In a fortnight, Maxie and Robin would return the favor when the older couple became man and wife.

After the serious eating was done and the toasts had been drunk, Robin bent to her and said quietly, "Shall we take a walk? Our guests can manage without us for a few minutes."

"I'd like that."

Hand in hand, they strolled through the gardens, which were magnificent with early summer scents and blooms. In a few short weeks, Ruxton had become the home of her heart.

As they wandered into the woods, Robin said, "Did I mention how much I like your gown? I've never seen anything like it, but it suits you perfectly."

She glanced down at the exquisitely beaded and fringed dress with pleasure. It had been a wedding gift from Margot. "It's a loose interpretation of a Mohawk wedding costume. I sketched out the design and Margot found a dressmaker who was willing to make it even though she didn't have any dyed porcupine quills."

Sunlight shafted through the leaves and small birds

fluttered on all sides, filling the air with music. She nodded toward them. "Look at all the songbirds around us, Robin. It's as if they've come to help us celebrate."

He grinned.

Suddenly suspicious, Maxie looked more closely at the grass beside the path. "Lord Robert, did you tell the gardener to sprinkle grain along this path to bring the birds for us?"

He laughed, unrepentant. "What's wrong with creating a little magic? When I first saw you at the Wolverhampton fairy ring, I thought of Titania, the fairy queen."

She joined his laughter. "And I thought of Oberon. Our imaginations work in similar ways."

"Among many other things." He hesitated, then said, "I probably shouldn't ask, but these days, when you think about the future, do you have a sense of its course?"

She nodded. "Many, many happy years with you."

He raised their hands and kissed her fingertips. "That's what I was hoping."

The path led to a clearing that Maxie had not seen before. In the center was a fairy ring like the one at Wolverhampton. She stopped and gazed at it, feeling absurdly happy.

Robin drew her into his arms and gave her a kiss of aching sweetness. Then he whispered, "Now, Kanawiosta, show me again how to listen to the wind."